Isabeau Fallon, the Fallen Star is one of the finest thieves on Dyson's Ring station — until she's caught by the Skeldhi hunter, Sobehk. Trapped and altered into a Skeldhi-human hybrid sex-pet known as a *rehkyt*, her past is a closed door — until it literally comes back to haunt her in the form of E'sey Khan. Khan is a Skeldhi Lord-Officer intent on taking Fallon, who is actually the Moribund Company's prize code-cracker, away from Sobehk, the one man he ever loved, and making her his very own.

Seemingly random accidents and hidden programs converge to prove that there is more going on than the capture of a not-so-simple thief. There is a conspiracy afoot . . . and the small thief from Dyson's Ring station is in it up to her collared throat.

Publisher's Note: This book contains explicit sexual content, graphic language, and situations that some readers may find objectionable: Anal play/intercourse, substantial BDSM elements (including/not limited to bondage, domination/submission, whipping), menage (m/m/f), and homoerotic sexual situations (m/m, f/f).

Fallen Star
Copyright © 2019 Morgan Hawke
ISBN: 978-1-4874-2638-5
Cover art by Martine Jardin

Published by eXtasy Books Inc or
Devine Destinies, an imprint of eXtasy Books Inc

Look for us online at:
www.eXtasybooks.com or www.devinedestinies.com

Fallen Star
Interstellar Service and Discipline Book 3

A Tale from the Imperial Stars

By

Morgan Hawke

DEDICATION

For AK – who saw a Hero where I saw a villain and demanded that he be given his due.

And Jaynie – for her spectacular and thorough advice.

AK's SPs – I count myself lucky to know and have the support of such fine ladies.

CHAPTER ONE

Dyson's Ring Outpost Station
Under-City, in a back alley
Evening cycle

Fallon stared up at the deeply shadowed towering steel walls of the alley's dead end and ground her teeth. The door that was supposed to be at the end of this alley was nowhere to be found. "Damn it all, this isn't where I'm supposed to be!"

Most of the lights in the station's industrial deeps had gone out or been shot out, so it was hard to see as a rule, even with her night-sight eye augmentations. The worst part was that everything down in this steel maze of pipes and installations looked pretty damned uniform, right down to the corrosion stains. There was no telling how far off course she actually was.

She needed directions and fast.

In three steps, she reached the steel wall of the alley and a long pipe with a faded and peeling telecommunications logo. She lifted her knee and selected a slender tap from the array of small, delicate tools tucked into the battered leather of her tall boots. A swift punch with another one of her tools broke the pipe's casing and then it was just a matter of uncoiling her hotwire, jacking the tap into the communications wires, and shoving her wire into the data port at the base of her skull.

Her internal communications program spat code into

1

the wire.

She looked down at the grimy steel floor, sweeping a gloved hand down her black skin suit. She cringed in disgust. The suit was smeared with filth and the seams were torn in a number of places. All the pipes she had crawled through and the roofs she had nearly fallen from to avoid her pursuer had really taken a toll on the once-sleek leather. It was going to cost a fortune to replace the damned thing, but she didn't have much of a choice. She needed it for work.

"Station Master, spit it out and make it quick." The voice was electronic and annoyed.

She grinned. "Hey, Peter, this is the Fallen Star."

"Izzie! Where in fury have you been, wench?"

She rolled her eyes and shook her head. "I miss you, too, but right now, I'm in a jam. I need directions and quick."

"Stand by for subliminal download."

"Standing by." A trickle of white noise was introduced over the line. Fallon nodded. "Receiving download; thanks, Peter."

"Hey, no problem. You still playing pixie for the bad guys?"

Fallon sighed. "Got to make a living somehow." She stomped her feet to break the mud off her tall boots. They were crusted with muck to the knees. She didn't even want to think about what was snarled in her cropped shoulder-length black hair. *Bloody Fate, I need a bath . . .*

"You could always come down to Never-land and play pixie for me . . ." The pout carried crystal clear over the connection.

Fallon shrugged. "I love you, Peter, but I can't live hard-wired to a couch like you do. I've got a fully functional body. I'd like to use it."

"Fine, be that way, but you could visit. In fact, you

should visit. You're way overdue for a bug hunt. God only knows what's been dropped into your head between pirate ships."

Fallon winced. He had a point. She probably needed a thorough cleaning. "That's not a bad idea. Are any of the other lostlings down there?"

There was a heavy electronic sigh. "They're all outside. Come down and play with me, Izzie."

"Tell you what, as soon as I lose the guy currently on my tail, I'll drop by for a long visit."

"Who's tailing you?" The electronic voice was threaded with anger. "I told you not to play with the bad guys!"

"It's not the boss." Fallon sighed. "It's some white-haired foreign guy in pointy black armor."

"Fangs, pointy ears, weird eyes and perverted as all get out?"

Fallon frowned. That was exactly what was tailing her. "Yeah . . ."

"Come home now!"

Fallon's frown deepened. "Now?"

"Now, Izzie, I'm serious. The Imperium pays those guys to take criminals, and the Fallen Star is high on the criminal collection list!"

Fallon winced. "Yeah, well, being a *good* professional thief has its disadvantages . . ."

"Izzie, if they get you, you are not coming back!"

Fallon snorted. "Relax, Peter, there isn't any place I can't break out of —"

"Izzie! I'm not playing here! If they get you, you won't come back, because you won't *want* to come back, you'll want to stay with them!"

Fallon rolled her eyes. "Peter, you know nothing can hold me."

"Izzie, I mean it, get down here! Don't make me use the

codes to *get* you down here."

She gasped. He was actually threatening her with the command codes? "Peter!"

"Come home now, Izzie!"

"Okay, okay, Peter, I'll come home, but I don't want him following me down, so let me lose him first."

"Don't bother, let him follow, I'll take care of him. Follow the map and get your little ass down here right now."

She sighed. *Damned nanny.* You'd think she was still a skinny ten-year-old with scraped knees running through drainpipes from the bigger kids. "Okay, Peter, I'm on my way."

"Good. Go!" The line died.

Fallon rolled up her wire and tucked the tap back into her boot while scanning the information she'd just downloaded. She wasn't anywhere near where she was supposed to be. She groaned. *Piss . . .* She hadn't thought she had drifted that far off course. She was going to have to backtrack.

A low masculine chuckle echoed in the alley. "Dead end, thief."

Her heart slammed in her throat. *Blood and Fate, not again?* She turned sharply to look behind her. Her pursuer was little more than a silhouette of broad-shouldered moving blackness, yet he filled the alley with his intimidating presence.

Damnit! She'd known he was close, but she hadn't thought he was that close! How by burning fury was he finding her so fast? *The stupid, stubborn brute . . .* She turned her back on him and set her gloved hands on the steel wall, but it was too slippery with night condensation to climb. *Shit, shit, shit . . .*

"You are out of options, thief." His chuckle echoed at her back. "Yield and save yourself some grief."

She backed up against the steel wall and dropped into a

fighter's crouch with her fists raised. "I'm not down yet!"

"But you will be." He stepped across a small beam of light that cut through the misty darkness to caress his sculpted, overlapping black body armor. It shimmered with oily iridescence, as though made of midnight rainbows. Silver gleamed in the frost-white of his hair. Shadows deepened the pale and brutally handsome lines of his high cheekbones and strong jaw. Pairs of silver rings glittered in the lobes of his pointed ears, accentuating the decorative cuts along the lower arches. The long tail of his severe braid fell well past his broad shoulders and swung at his narrow waist as he approached. "You will go down, and you will yield."

Fallon felt her pulse beat in her throat. He was fully armored, and all she had was a thin layer of battered leather. Fate and damnation, she didn't want to fight him again, but she didn't have a whole lot of choice. "You haven't caught me yet."

"Oh, no?" His white brows rose over bright and amused sapphire blue eyes. Feline green-gold reflected in their depths. His full lips curved into a cruel smile. "Have it your way." The points of his canines gleamed. "But there's only one way out . . ." He opened his arms with his hands pointedly empty of the weapons she knew he carried, daring her to get past him.

She took the dare in a flurry of fists and feet.

The exchange of fists, kicks, and curses was vicious and short. He trapped her arm and grappled her into a chokehold with both of her wrists wedged up to the center of her back, wrapped in one large paw.

She was just too damned tired.

"This hunt is over, thief." His breath was harsh and hot against her ear. "You lose."

Fallon sucked a breath past the armored arm jammed

across her windpipe. *Bloody Fate, he has a tight grip.* Smart move on his part; she was very limber. If he gave her the smallest increment, she would wiggle free. She arched her spine, coming up on her toes to relieve the ache. Not that it did much good. He was more than a head and a half taller, and his shoulders were twice hers in width. *He didn't look nearly this big when he introduced himself in the bar.* But then, he hadn't been wearing pointy black armor, either.

She sucked air past his chokehold. "Sobehk, you are cutting off the circulation in my arms."

"Oh, really?" Sobehk's chuckle made the hair on her arms rise. "That's too bad, Fallon, or should I say, Isabeau Torne Fallon?"

Fallon froze. He knew her whole name? Where, by fury, had he heard that? Not even her boss knew more than her handle!

"Do you yield?" His voice was a sinister purr in her ear. "Or do I need to break something?"

Damnit, she couldn't afford the time off to heal a broken arm. "All right, fine, I yield, so now what?"

"Now, you go down." His foot hooked hers and she fell to her knees. He dropped down on one knee with her, keeping her wrists jammed tight up against her spine, with his arm snug around her throat. "And you stay down."

Fallon hissed to keep from yelping and arched back sharply. The uneven pavement dug into her knees, and both shoulders were painfully close to dislocation. "Take it easy on the arms, you big brute, I'm not a marine cyborg!" She was robotically augmented for agility, not power.

"No, but you are one slippery thief." His hand tightened on her wrists. "I'm not taking any chances with losing you again."

She bit back an escaping whimper. "Yeah, I'm a thief. What did you expect? This is a smuggling outpost.

Everybody's a thief." She wriggled her fingers, but all she could feel was his damned body armor. It had to be some kind of titanium alloy; he moved like it didn't weigh more than paper, but there wasn't a drop of give to it. She hadn't been able to land a single effective blow. Her foot was still bruised from that last kick she'd aimed at his kidneys. *This really sucks . . .*

Damn it! She didn't have time for this shit. She set her teeth. "Look, whatever you intend to do to me, beat me, fuck me, or whatever . . . Can you hurry up and get it over with? I have shit to get done."

His arm tightened on her throat. "What? Do you have a quota or something, thief?"

She turned her head slightly and sucked in a small breath past his chokehold. "Or something . . ." Blood and Fate, yeah, she had a quota; everyone on this blasted outpost had some kind of quota to fill. She was lucky that she was damned good at filling hers because this stupid game of hide-and-seek had taken far too much of her productive time. "Just do it, all right?"

"I'll get to it when I'm damned good and ready," Sobehk's voice rumbled in a deep growl. "If you wanted a quick end to this, you should have yielded two days ago when I caught you the first time."

Fallon snorted. "You could have given up two days ago when I got away the first time."

"Too bad for you." Sobehk actually chuckled. "Once I start a hunt, I finish it." His long teeth caught the lobe of her ear in a tender bite. "You shouldn't have picked me for a target."

Fallon tilted her head away from his mouth. "You shouldn't have pissed me off!"

He nipped at her exposed throat. "What? Don't you like sex?" He made a sound that might have been a growl, but it sounded a lot closer to an actual feline purr.

7

Fallon shivered in spite of herself. "Sure, I like sex — with guys that aren't assholes!" She tried to twist, even a little, but his grip on her arms was far too tight. "Look, grabbing people and kissing them within seconds of stating your name is not the way to pick up women."

"Is that so?" He purred right into the curve of her ear. "Then why did you kiss me back?"

Fallon felt her face heat. She *had* kissed him back; Sobehk was a damned good kisser. "So I kissed you, big fat hairy deal. That didn't mean I wanted to have sex in the middle of a crowded bar."

"Are you sure?" His deep chuckle curled straight down into her gut. "I didn't hear any complaints until after I had your bare tit in one hand, and you were ready to cum on my other."

"Of course not!" Fallon scowled as her cheeks flushed with more heat. "I was flat down on the table with your tongue shoved down my throat. I had to bite you to get your mouth off mine so I could *tell* you to stop."

"I thought you were just being affectionate." His voice practically purred then the sound drifted into a growl. "Until you took off on me."

Fallon pitched her voice as sweet as sugar. "And I thought you were just being a perverted ass-hole, which is *why* I took off on you."

Sobehk stiffened and his voice rumbled deep in his chest. "Is that why you took my turbo-glider?"

"Well, yeah." She winced under the increased pressure. If he gripped her any tighter, he was going to break her arm. "You pissed me off!"

Sobehk relaxed slightly and barked out a laugh. "You were pissed because I almost made you cum right there in front of everybody."

Fallon ground her teeth. She remembered only too well

exactly how close—and how fast—he had brought her to the trembling edge of orgasm. He was damned attractive, in a big, scary kind of way, and he was really good with his hands and his mouth. She had spent over an hour with her fingers in her wet flesh, trying to ease the burning hunger he had stirred in her before she had fled. *The smug bastard . . .*"And you're pissed now because it took you three days to catch me."

"Fuck, yeah, I'm pissed! Because of you, I'm way behind schedule, but I've got you now, and you're gonna pay for holding me up—with your ass." The brute was grinning, she could tell by his voice.

She scowled. "What, do *you* have a quota to fill?"

"Not anymore." Sobehk's voice purred with innuendo. "Your nipples are hard. I think you like being caught."

Her nipples *were* hard, and it pissed her off even more. "I think you like being a bastard."

"Oh I do, I love being a bastard to slippery little thieves that really need to have their asses smacked for taking things that don't belong to them."

"I don't know why you bothered chasing me; you got your glider back the next day!" Damnit, she couldn't reach anything with her fingers . . .

"I'm bothering because I've been rock-hard since that night in the bar—and I fully intend to do something about it." He dropped his arm, releasing her throat, and slammed a hand between her shoulder blades, shoving her face down onto the pavement. "And your tight little ass is gonna feel really sweet around my dick as I empty my balls in it."

Fallon had to turn her head or breathe concrete. *What? Does he plan to ass-fuck me? Bloody Fate, I hope not!* When he'd had her lying flat down on the bar's table, she had felt one monster of an erection pressing against her stomach. She honestly didn't think she could fit something that big up her butt. "Hey, I have a perfectly good pussy!"

"Don't worry, I'll get that, too." His grip shifted on her wrists as he reached for something she couldn't see. "Hold still."

"What are you doing?" Metal closed around her wrists. He was cuffing her? A shimmer went through her internal technology. *Force-cuffs? Where, by burning fury, did he get a set of those?* They were tightly regulated by the Imperium; not even the local cops had them. She ground her teeth. The cuffs were tuned to her augmentations. As long as those things were on her wrists, her arms were his to command.

She licked her dry lips. But her feet were still free, and her tools were in her boots. If she could get to her tools, she could tap into her own augmentations and release herself. It would be difficult as bleeding fury with her hands pinned behind her, but she'd done it once before; she could do it again. Her gaze flicked to the male practically on top of her. *Gimme one deep breath of space and I'm gone, you big bastard.* "Look, if you're taking me to enforcement for the theft of your glider, I'll be out in a matter of minutes. I'm on the payroll."

"I figured as much; you have some expensive body augmentation." His hands shifted on her arms. "Keep your wrists together."

She wriggled, but her wrists remained pinned together at her back, imprisoned by his order and her own augmentations. *Bloody Fate, I hate these things . . .* At least her arms weren't being jerked out of their sockets.

"Much better." He grabbed her by the short hair at the back of her neck and sat back, pulling her upright with him.

Fallon winced as she came up on her knees. "Must you rip my hair out by the roots?"

He pulled her head back and glared down at her. "If I were you, I'd be more worried about my ass than my hair, thief. Do you have any idea who you robbed?"

Fallon leveled a glare the big brute. "Yeah, a big-mouthed, white-haired pervert with pointy ears and pointy teeth that likes to have sex with total strangers in public places." *Wearing decorative and obviously expensive black body armor and carrying regulation force-cuffs* . . . She eyed him with suspicion. "Are you some kind of Imperial agent?"

"I'm not an Imperial anything." Sobehk's eyes narrowed. "I'm a *Mahf'dhyt*, you idiot."

She blinked. Was that supposed to mean something? She arched a brow at him. "Am I supposed to be impressed?"

"As a matter of fact . . . Yes." He bared his teeth in a triumphant smile and the heart of his blue eyes reflected feline green-gold. "I'm a Skeldhi enforcer, also known as a hunter, and you've just joined the ranks of Skeldhi *rehkyt*."

He was a *cop*? Her neck hairs rose in alarm. "I . . . what?"

He looked back at her and his smile broadened to show his pointed teeth. "Your people call us slave-hunters."

Fallon couldn't draw breath. *He's a slave-hunter?* But they were just an urban legend. A race that changed people into willing sex-slaves was just too fantastic to believe. They couldn't be really *real*. Could they?

But then, Peter had just said, these guys were paid by the Imperium to take people—and the people they took didn't *want* to come back.

CHAPTER TWO

Fallon winced as Sobehk's hand tightened in her hair. Caught, cuffed, and kneeling on the filthy deck plates in a disused alley in the bowels of the station—the whole situation sucked. Calling for help was a total waste of breath. Anyone that came would be more likely to slit both their throats just to steal her boots and his pretty armor.

"Considering that you're a criminal, I guarantee you're better off serving one of us than ending up in a penitentiary mining pit somewhere on the wrong side of space." Sobehk pulled a long, viciously back-curved dagger from his tall over-the-knee boot.

Fallon saw the blade and didn't think; she simply twisted as hard and as fast as her panicked body would move. Her hair came out in his hand and she didn't care. She threw herself forward, tucking her head to roll over her shoulder, and right out of his reach. The idiot only had the one hand on her. Fuck the cuffs on her wrists; her feet were perfectly functional. In one smooth motion, she was up on her feet and running for the open end of the alley.

"Oh, no you fucking don't!" His heavy boots pounded the pavement behind her. "Not this time!" He was gaining on her.

She sucked air and pushed her legs as fast as they would move but running with her arms pinned at her back was not going to get her far. She had to get the damn cuffs off and fast. She spotted the yawning mouth of an open pipe right at the edge of the alley and dove in, headfirst.

She landed hard on her shoulder and grunted with the jarring impact. She rolled up onto her knees. The interior of the pipe was utter blackness. She closed her eyes and opened them to trigger her night vision augmentation. The pipe's interior bloomed in a haze of green. It was filthy and just big enough to clear her head as long as she stayed on her knees.

She grimaced and started forward on her knees. She was already grimy, what was a little more dirt? But, if the pipe narrowed too much, she'd be in big trouble fast without the use of her hands to get her through.

"How far do you think you're going to get with force-cuffs on, you little idiot?" Sobehk's voice echoed from the end of the pipe. Scrapes and thumps announced his entry into the pipe. "Damned feral human . . ."

Fallon sucked in a sharp breath. He'd never followed her into a pipe before; why was he doing it now? She shoved deeper, her knees bruising on the trash clogging the bottom of the pipe. She had to find a place to get the damned cuffs off right now.

She turned at the first cross juncture and shoved forward, hoping like bloody fury that whatever used to be in this pipe wasn't corrosive; she couldn't afford a skin graft. She turned a few more corners and found herself staring at a sharp upward bend in the pipe. It might as well have been a dead end. Without her hands, she'd never be able to get up into it.

She was out of options.

Fallon looked back at the open pipe. She could hear the stubborn brute still cursing up a storm only two turns back.

"Don't you dare fall down a hole and get yourself killed! I want to kick your skinny ass first!" Crashes and hollow bangs accompanied his passage as his armor struck against the pipe's narrow confines.

If she was lucky, he'd take a wrong turn and get him, and that armor of his, stuck in a pipe. But her luck had sucked all damned day.

She looked around for someplace to sit. The pipe-bend was just big enough for maybe three people to fit, and the opening over her head looked like an easy climb if she had her hands. But, if he found her in this corner before she got the cuffs off, she might as well be in a steel cage.

The cuffs had to come off right now.

She moved to the curving wall right under the pipe's mouth and dropped down on her knees. Using the wall for leverage, she twisted. She had to get at the outside of her boot with her fingers, and they were at her back. Her legs shivered as she held them impossibly tight against her body while her fingers scrabbled along the outside of her boot. Her fingers found the correct pocket on her right calf and the tiny stylus-prod that she needed. She twisted around sharply to get the prod balanced on her thigh. Carefully, she bent down to get it in her mouth without knocking it off and into the filth on the bottom of the pipe. She sat back up with a sigh of relief, the stylus safe in the grip of her strong teeth.

She turned her head and angled the point very carefully past the rip in her shoulder seam and over the right place. She didn't want to lose her grip on the small instrument. She closed her eyes and focused her attention. She had to stab the correct nerve bundle to short-circuit the signal in her arm's augmentation, releasing the cuff on her wrist. It was deep in the ball joint of her shoulder, and it was not going to be easy to find. It was also going to hurt like screaming fury while she did it.

She jabbed the stylus in and pushed it deep into her shoulder. Agony screamed up and down her arm as blood slithered past the puncture. A moan slipped past her lips.

Gripping the tool tightly in her teeth, she began to dig. Small whimpers escaped her throat. She felt a tiny buzz of current against her lips, and her arm dropped. Her right arm was free!

With a gasp of pain and relief, Fallon released the stylus, leaving it in her shoulder. She twisted sharply, flapping her dead arm. The nasty thing flew off her wrist. The metal cuff hit the metal pipe with a loud bang.

She flinched. *Of all the stupid things to do!* If Sobehk was anywhere nearby, that sound just gave away her location. She leaned over and pulled the stylus from her arm with her teeth. She had to get that other cuff off. A small charge ran up her dead arm and her augmentation came back online. She lifted her arm and wiggled her fingers, allowing herself a fleeting smile. Her arm was weak, but she could use it. *Thank the Maker for nano-technology – self-healing robotics.*

She grabbed the stylus with her free hand and stabbed it into her other shoulder. Pain seared through her. She moaned before she could stop herself.

"What the fuck are you doing?"

Fallon looked over and stared straight into Sobehk's ice blue eyes. Her blood froze. *Caught . . .*

His face fell slack with astonishment. "How in bloody Chaos did you get that cuff off?"

"Shit!" She grabbed the instrument with her free hand and ripped it from her shoulder while scrambling to her feet. Clamping the stylus in her teeth, she jumped up to grab the lip of the pipe above her with her one good arm.

He came lunging into the bend. "Not this time, you little beast!" He grabbed her around the waist and hauled her back down.

She dropped, hitting the bottom of the pipe face down on her elbow with a hollow bang. She gasped with the vicious ache and the instrument fell from her teeth. She reached for the fallen stylus and his fingers closed tight on her shoulders. Searing pain ripped through her. She screamed and writhed in agony under him.

Sobehk pulled his hands from her shoulders. "Blood? You're bleeding? What in Chaos did you do to yourself?" He set his palm between her shoulders to hold her down and ripped open the shoulder seam of her suit. "Fuck, that's a lot of blood. Were you *trying* to kill yourself, you stupid little feral?"

Fallon twisted under him and slammed the heel of her hand into his jaw.

He grunted and fell back onto his knees.

Lightning-quick, she was back on her feet and jumping for the pipe.

"Oh, no, you don't!" He lunged up and hauled her back down.

She screamed obscenities and lashed out with her foot.

He grabbed her foot and pulled, dropping her hard onto her back then followed her down. "Stubborn little pain in my ass . . ." He straddled her, pinning her struggling body with his weight. "Hold still. I need to stop the bleeding." He grabbed the shoulders of her suit and ripped it further open.

She bucked and howled under him, insane with pain and fear.

"Hold still!" He had to use both hands to keep her down. "Stop fighting me, you idiot! You're bleeding out!"

Fallon couldn't see anything beyond his bulk holding her down. She twisted and fought, with everything in her desperate for escape.

"Damnit, you are not bleeding to death on me!" He pressed one hand on her chest, raised his fist. "Stop right now, or I'll knock you cold!"

Terrified beyond reason and in too much pain to care,

she shrieked and clawed for his eyes.

His fist came down hard.

And the world went very far away.

Fallon awoke lying on her stomach, bent over something relatively soft, with her arms pulled over her head. There was an ache in her jaw that simply would not go away and a bruise over her heart, too, but other than that, she felt pretty okay. She shifted to sit up and discovered that she couldn't. In fact, she couldn't move at all. *Huh?*

She opened her eyes and brilliance speared her. She winced and closed them to switch over from her night vision. She opened her eyes again and discovered that she was looking at a familiar cross alley.

She couldn't move because she was tied across the forward saddle of a two-man turbo-glider parked on its cycle tires. Both cuffs were on her wrists and bound together with fine cable lashed to a ring by the footboard. There was not one bit of give anywhere. Her ankles felt like they were similarly tied on the far side, but with her legs spread wide.

She was positioned as though waiting to be mounted.

What in fury . . . Memory slammed through her. The force-cuffs, the pipe, Sobehk's punch . . .

She was strapped across Sobehk's glider.

Fallon dropped her head. *Damnit, damnit, damnit . . .* She was well and truly caught, only this time she was also set for travel. The question was, where did he plan to take her?

Fallon shifted on the glider's saddle and felt a soft breeze on her naked back. Her suit had been split all the way down the back and spread open. She could feel the edges digging into the outside of her thighs, leaving her butt completely exposed all the way down and around almost to her navel.

The hair rose at the back of her neck. She really was waiting to be mounted.

"Awake?" His voice came from somewhere behind her.

That brutish bastard . . . Fallon twisted her wrists and glared at the cable that bound her. She utterly loathed being helpless.

"I stopped the bleeding and bandaged both your shoulders from whatever it was you jammed into yourself." Pavement crunched under his boots as he paced somewhere behind her. She felt the breeze of him moving between her spread thighs. "What in Chaos were you trying to accomplish?"

She blinked. He bandaged her? Why by fury would he do that?

"Answer me, you feral idiot!"

The sound of a sharp smack arrived only a bare moment before a scalding burn erupted across her ass. Fallon flinched in surprise. *He hit me?* She ground her teeth. What was a smack on the ass, when he'd punched her before? "Fuck you."

"That's better." Sobehk snorted. "Now, spit it out—what the fuck did you think you were doing?"

"I was trying to get the cuffs off."

"Is that so? It looked a lot more like a suicide attempt to me."

Fallon stared at the cuffs on both wrists. "It worked, I got one off." Not that it did any good. It was back on.

"It could have killed you! The way you were bleeding back there, I was convinced you'd nicked an artery with that stunt."

"So? What do you care?"

"Great Mother, you are so damned thick-headed! Do you *want* to die?"

Fallon dropped her head and scowled.

"Answer me, damn you!"

A sharp crack echoed in the alley.

Fallon's left butt-cheek erupted with stinging heat. She sucked in a sharp breath and flinched. "No, I don't want to die, you bastard!"

"Good! Because if you *ever* do something that stupid again, I'm going to make your ass regret it for a week straight!" He was shouting

Fallon hunched her shoulders. "If you hadn't put the cuffs on me, I wouldn't have had to do it!"

"You would have preferred death to me?"

Fallon nibbled on her bottom lip. "I knew what I was doing . . ."

"Right. Which is why you were bleeding all over the place?" His warm palms cupped the curves of her bare ass, rubbing the sting from his strike.

She cringed and shivered slightly, feeling utterly exposed and completely helpless under his hands. "So, now what?"

"I'm waiting for my thank you for saving your life."

Her mouth popped open. A thank you, when he caused it in the first place? Bloody Fate, the ego!

His fingers dug into her ass-cheeks in clear warning.

She closed her eyes tight. "Okay, all right . . . Thank you."

"Good. Don't do it again." His fingers released her ass, and he stroked her backside in a gentle caress. "I want you in one piece."

She suddenly focused on his palm moving across her skin. Seditious warmth coiled in low, moist places. An image of what she must look like seared across her inner eye. Her body bent over the glider with her suit sliced open and peeled back, the rolled edges framing her butt with her muscular legs splayed wide. There was nothing to block his view of her most intimate flesh.

Her nipples rose to tight points against the leather of the saddle.

A second image entered her thoughts. His brutally handsome body as it had looked in the bar, all raw muscle and arrogance. She could practically feel him towering behind her, staring at her, focused on her naked and exposed backside . . . Anything he wanted, he could take, and there was no way she could stop him.

Another memory, this one of her short skirt up around her hips as she lay back on the top of the bar table with him above her. The full, heavy, hot length of his cock had pressed against the juncture of her spread thighs. Only his slick leather pants and the thin silk of her panties had come between them as she moaned under his mouth. His fingers under the silk working her trembling wet flesh toward the flashpoint of climax . . .

For a brief instant she acknowledged that some dark and twisted part of her wanted him to take her. Take her hard and relieve the ache that had started three days ago and never really left.

Fallon shook the images from her mind and sucked in a breath in an attempt to control her runaway libido. "Fine, whatever. Are you going to beat me now or what?"

"Beat you?" Sobehk laughed, and it was not a pretty sound. He set his elbow beside her on the saddle of the glider and leaned over her to peer down at her. "I'm going to do something far worse." Dark innuendo purred in his husky voice.

Hard muscle pressed against her bare back. He wasn't wearing his armor. He didn't seem to be wearing his pants, either. She could feel the hot length of his cock pressed against her exposed butt. Her body jolted with interested heat. *Blood and Fate, what is wrong with me?*

"Worse?" She turned her head and looked up, utterly terrified, painfully excited and seriously pissed off, all at the same time. "Like . . . what?" What could be worse than a beating?

His blue eyes burned with heat and his smile was pure masculine hunger. "I'm going to get you good and hot, and then . . ." His thumb stroked the seam that divided her cheeks. "I'm gonna split your ass with my dick. And make damn sure you like it." His palm closed on her ass and squeezed.

Fallon's breath left in a rush. *Okay, that's worse.* In spite of the skittering of fear that danced up her spine, a flash of heat speared through her and her body clenched wetly. "I really don't see how I'm going to like having your cock crammed in my ass."

"Oh, you will." He smiled, baring long teeth. "I'm very good." He swept a hand down her bare back and turned to watch the progress of his fingers. His finger slid deep into the seam of her butt then circled the tight rose of her anus with intent. "And then I'll spend the next whole cycle jammed up your ass or down your throat."

A whole cycle of thirty days . . . Fallon clenched her hands into fists and shook with a rage that boiled from out of nowhere. "You can't just *keep* me, you bastard! That's kidnapping!"

"It's not kidnapping —" Sobehk's voice held both humor and a hard edge, " — if the person in question is legal property."

Fallon felt every thought in her head grind to a complete halt. "What?"

CHAPTER THREE

"Property . . ." Fallon shook her head, trembling in the tight bindings that held her over the saddle of the glider. That didn't make sense. Ice water rushed through her veins, dowsing the heat of her temper. She couldn't be indentured; her debts weren't that high. "But how . . ."

"I'm a Skeldhi *Mahf'dhyt*, an enforcer, remember?" Leaning over her, his broad chest against her sweating back and his elbows pressing into the saddle on either side of her body, Sobehk held her gaze steadily. "This station is one of the places your Imperium gave us free rein to pick up strays. I filed an inquiry of intent on you three days ago. No one challenged the claim. You, my ferocious little feral, were an unwanted stray open for collection." He tossed a derisive glance around the rusting steel alley. "Considering the conditions of this vermin-run station, and your likelihood of ending up in a mining pit, you could definitely use the rescue."

Fallon couldn't process what he was saying. It sounded too much like fantasy to be believable. "All this for taking your glider?"

"Actually, no." Sobehk chuckled. "I originally planned to spank a harsh lesson into your ass and then fuck you senseless. But when you slipped out of my hands the third time in a row, I realized that you'd make a damned fine *upuaht rehkyt*." He pushed up from her back to stand behind her.

Fallon snorted. He was staring at her ass again. "I got

away from you a lot more than three times."

"And every escape made me determined to catch your sweet ass that much more." His hands dropped heavily onto her hips. "After the last stunt you pulled to get the cuff off, I'm betting you go Prime." He cupped her ass in both hands and squeezed.

Prime? What the fuck was he babbling about now? Fallon writhed under his hands and clenched her teeth, fighting the overwhelming desire to press down and rub her aching clit against the saddle.

His finger slid down the seam of her ass, over the tight rose of her anus and then brushed against the plump outer lips of her cunt.

Her entire body went rigid with eager hunger. She bit her lips to keep from moaning. "Mother of Fate . . ."

"Feeling sensitive?" His fingers swept down the inside of her spread thighs.

She shivered and fought to think straight. "Sobehk, I have no interest in being anyone's slave!"

"You'll change your mind." He slid two fingers into her cunt.

She gasped and pulled against the cables that held her. A chill sweat broke out all over her body, making the seat she was strapped across slick under her belly.

"Oh yeah, you're nice and wet." He pulled his fingers back out and chuckled. "I think you're just about ready for your fuck."

She bit back a moan. She was dying for a fuck, but she wasn't about to tell him that.

He swept his other hand down her damp spine. "Ah, you've begun to sweat. Looks like the first dose has finally taken effect . . . About time too, I'm hard enough to pierce metal."

"Dose?" Fallon stilled. Had the bastard drugged her?

"Dose of what?"

"You've been injected with the first of four courses to genetically alter you into a Skeldhi-human hybrid, also known as a *rehkyt*. The lust you're feeling is part of the process. You'll get the second course as soon as I get you back."

Fallon's mouth fell open. "You're *altering* me?"

"That's right."

"You fucking bastard!"

"It's your own damned fault. I was planning to wait, but because of that stunt in the tunnel, there's a real possibility of you being in danger of infection. *Rehkyt* are designed to be resistant to most diseases and recover very quickly from physical damage. Once I get my load of cum in you, my DNA will boost your immune system."

"You can't!" Fallon twisted on the saddle, but there was no possible escape. "You can't alter me!"

"Really? Who's gonna stop me?" He pressed an oily slick finger against the tight rose of her anus. "Push out."

Her mind focused on the immediate threat of his finger. "What are you doing?"

"I'm greasing your ass for my dick. Push out or this is going to hurt a lot more than it needs to."

She cringed. She couldn't stop him; he was really going to fuck her up the ass. She pushed out. His finger slid past the ring of her anus. The invasion felt impossibly large . . . and darkly exciting. A small whimper of mortification escaped her.

"Mmm, you're awfully tight." He pushed deep. "No getting around it, it's gonna hurt when I shove my dick in this tight hole." He pulled back then pushed deep again, wriggling his finger around the interior of her ass. "I'm guessing that this'll be your first ass-reaming. Am I right?"

Fallon pulled on the cables that bound her as heat curled

in her bowels and pulsed in her clit. There was nothing she could do to escape. She was his to take any way he chose. "I fucking hate you!"

"I'll take that as a 'yes.' Not that it will stop you from cumming." He swept his thumb against her clit.

Ferocious heat gripped her core in a tight fist of need. The breath exploded from her lungs.

His chuckle made her skin crawl. "Oh yeah, you're just about there." He knelt, rocking the gilder. A warm puff of air caressed her most private flesh.

She pulled away instinctively, but she was too securely tied. *What now?* Something warm and wet stroked the intimate folds of her core. She choked.

"Mmm, nice flavor." His hands dug into her butt, parting the cheeks to give him better access to her vulnerable flesh. He pressed his entire heated mouth to her and sucked noisily.

Vicious delight speared straight through her. She exhaled with a helpless moan and her hands opened wide in shock.

He licked and lapped, stroking and nibbling the tender flesh with slow, drugging skill and obvious delight.

Ferocious tremors of raw pleasure scorched her with each touch of his tongue, drawing her into a tight knot of mindless lust. He was really, really good . . . Despite the fact that she couldn't stand him, the bastard's talented mouth was driving her to the explosion point fast. He was going to make her cum, and cum screaming.

And there wasn't a damned thing she could do about it.

Fire burned up her spine and seared the back of her skull then centered in her jaw. Pressure built. Suddenly her mouth filled. She spat and blood spattered on the pavement. A small white something lay in the pool. It looked like a tooth. She shouted in surprise.

Sobehk's mouth stopped. He rose up from behind her and leaned over her back. "What?" He looked down at the blood on the pavement and chuckled. "Hot damn, you're losing your teeth."

What? Fear raised every hair on her body. "My teeth?" Abruptly pain slammed through her skull and her mouth filled. She was forced to spit again. Another tooth hit the pavement and gleamed in its small pool of blood. "Blood and Hell!" Her voice was tight with shock.

"Relax." Sobehk swept a hand down her hip. "It's just your fangs."

She sucked in a sharp breath. "Fangs?"

"Just keep spitting; if we're real lucky, you'll get uppers *and* lowers."

"Lucky?" He was out of his mind! "I'm losing my teeth!"

"You're not losing them. You're getting new ones. It's part of the change." He stroked her back. "You'll be fine."

Fallon shook her head in frustration and fear. "Sobehk! What the fuck have you done to me?"

"Will you relax?" Sobehk straightened and dropped back down to his knees behind her. "This is nothing. Wait till you see what happens once you have an ass full of cum." His mouth covered her slick intimate flesh and his tongue began its torturous licking.

She shuddered under the insistent onslaught of burning delight. Another wave of heat, lust and painful pleasure ripped through her. She screamed. Another tooth hit the pavement in a spatter of blood. "Oh, Maker," she moaned.

"Did you just lose another one?"

She shuddered. "Yes."

"Good, one more to go."

"You ass-hole!"

"Be nice!" His hand cracked hard on her sweat-slick ass.

The strike blazed across her butt-cheek. She yelped and

choked on a mouthful of blood. One more tooth hit the pavement. "Fuck . . ."

"That makes four, right?"

She closed her eyes and moaned. "Yes."

"Good, then you should be done." His hands explored her butt with possessive delight. "I knew you'd get fangs. You were too aggressive not to, but all four? Oh yeah, you're gonna go Prime on me, I can feel it."

Fallon panted on the glider's saddle. She had no clue what he was talking about and she didn't care. She stared at the four teeth on the pavement and knew for a fact that she didn't want to play this game anymore. "Sobehk, let me go."

"What?" He laughed. "It's far too late for that." He leaned forward and attacked her vulnerable flesh with renewed dedication.

She writhed on the glider's saddle, unable to escape his mouth, unable to escape the coiling tension in her belly, unable to do anything more than submit to his erotic assault on her vulnerable flesh. Small, needy sounds escaped her lips.

"Damn, kitten, you are putting out a lot of cream." He lapped in earnest, wriggling his tongue into her core. He pressed two fingers deep into her and curled, brushing her inner flesh with delicacy and skill.

Her body gripped his fingers ravenously. Ruthless carnal greed became paramount and desperation for release stole every thought in her head. Helpless, needy sounds tumbled from her lips.

"You're good and hot now." He chuckled, a warm vibration that sent gentle shockwaves through her as his tongue danced against her flesh. Deep within her, his fingers flicked.

A sharp bolt of erotic delight jolted her. Her body

bucked hard enough to rock the glider. Climax rose and coiled unbearably tight. Her breath caught as she teetered on the edge.

His lips closed on her clit and he attacked the tiny swollen nub with his tongue.

She exploded, release slamming through her in a furious torrent of molten ecstasy. Her gasping cries echoed in the alley.

Sobehk released her clit with a satisfied sigh. "That's my kitten. Now you're ready to fuck." He pulled his fingers from her hungry core and grabbed either edge of the glider's saddle. The glider rocked as he stepped up on the running board and stood between her thighs.

Fallon panted for breath. She could barely think past the shudders wracking her body. *Bloody Fate . . .* She didn't think she'd ever cum that hard in her life.

He leaned over her back. "I can't tell you how much I'm looking forward to stretching your ass."

She sucked in a sharp breath as fear washed the heat from her body. Temper followed with blinding speed. "Why don't you shove it up your own ass?"

"Oh, you're just begging for a beating, aren't you? Don't worry; I'll get to that too." His body came down on top of hers, hot, heavy, and brutally exciting. His rigid cock pressed against the seam of her cheeks.

Everything in her focused on the hard cock branding her ass. In spite of the climax that had just torn the shouts from her throat, her body still hungered, and it hungered for a cock to fill it. Her cheeks heated as she realized that if she hadn't been tied, she would have spread her thighs for him, and eagerly. Her body wanted to be fucked that badly.

He gripped her hip. The broad slick head of his cock pressed tight against the small opening of her anus. "Push out and push out hard, because whether or not you want it, I'm coming up your ass, right now." Her anus began to spread under the insistent pressure.

She tossed her head and writhed, but his cock continued to press. The pain was sharp and immediate. She arched and twisted but the cables had no give. "Damn you! It hurts!"

"Of course it hurts!" His long nails dug into her hip. "I said, push out!" He slapped her ass hard.

She gasped under the burn of his strike and reflexively pushed out. The head of his cock slipped past the ring of her anus. She couldn't stop the small cry of surprise or the undignified moan that followed. Once he got past the tight muscle of her opening, it wasn't as bad as she had expected.

"Fuck yeah, the sounds of first . . . penetration." His cock pressed onward, stretching her with his hard length. He sighed with pleasure. "Not so bad once it's in there, is it?"

Fallon grit her teeth. *Bastard.* It would have been a whole lot easier to keep her over-excited libido at bay if it continued to hurt. As it was, the decadent feeling of his penetration was making her hotter — not colder.

"Keep pushing; you have a lot more cock to fit in there."

She gasped for breath and groaned as she pushed out. His hard shaft slowly forged deeper, stretching her impossibly wide.

He drew in a deep breath. "Almost . . . there."

Something blunt and rigid made contact with the outer lips to her cunt. She stilled in surprise. It didn't have the crisp hardness of plastic or glass, but rather the satiny give of leather, or flesh, and it was warm. The blunt broadness nudged between her slick folds, nosing into her hungry core. It felt like another cock.

"Oh yeah," he said in a soft growl. "You are soaking wet. My second cock is gonna slide right in."

Her head came up. *Second cock?* She had known that some races were . . . built that way, but she'd had no idea that Sobehk was.

"Oh, so you didn't know?" He chuckled, and it vibrated through the cock jammed up her ass. "Surprise." His hands closed on her waist. He pulled, driving both cocks all the way in. His hips slammed against her ass.

Fire scorched the abused ring of her anus even as her hungry core was finally filled. She howled and twisted, impaled on both cocks.

Sobehk groaned in obvious pleasure. "Fuck, your cunt is almost as tight as your ass!" He rolled his hips, digging his cock deeper into her ass while rubbing against something brutally exciting deep in her core.

She gasped as raw erotic pleasure mixed with the hot pressure of over-fullness. Her toes curled and shivers erupted all over her body. Her hips twisted under him in pure reflex.

"That's it," he crooned. "Feel those hard cocks stretching you open." He twisted his hips counter to her movements, working his cocks deep in her ass and cunt.

"Sadistic bastard!" Her voice was embarrassingly close to a whimper, but her body had a mind of its own and she continued to move under him.

"Nice of you to notice, but you are still gonna cum screaming on both my dicks."

"I don't . . ." She sucked in a breath, fighting to think through the sensual overload. "I don't cum that easily . . ." She groaned. "Not with a cock up my ass!"

"Is that so?" He pulled back slowly, sliding his cock a few increments from her butt. His other cockhead slid almost to the point of exiting.

She hissed in shock. His withdrawal wasn't painful at all; in fact, it felt distinctly pleasurable, but not in any recognizable way she'd ever felt pleasure before.

"Felt good, didn't it?"

Fallon dropped her head, annoyed that he'd figured that out so fast, but what really frightened her was her body's greedy hunger.

"More?"

She desperately did not want to give him the satisfaction, but her body had other ideas. She stiffened and her butt rose, just a tiny bit, in eager invitation.

"Oh yeah, you want more." His long nails dug into her hips. He thrust.

She choked as he filled her. Her ass burned even as her core clamped down in greedy delight. "Fuck! That hurts!"

"It hurts now because you're new to it." He leaned over her, and his voice dropped into a low growl. "Next time you'll beg for it."

A snarl erupted from her throat. It sounded utterly animalistic, like that of a hunting feline, and completely inhuman. She gasped, shocked. "Was that me?"

He choked out a laugh. "Yes, yes it was." He stroked her back with his warm hands. "It sounds like you're going to need that second dose soon." He pulled back, delivering more of that illicit pleasure. "No more mercy; you need an ass full of cum."

She stilled under him. "What?" He couldn't mean what she thought he meant . . .

He snorted. "Just relax and enjoy the ride. The faster I go, the quicker I get off, and the faster I can get you out of here." He pulled back and slammed back in with vicious speed.

She shouted with the hot brutal impact in her ass even as he struck something within her core that jolted her hard with erotic delight.

He grunted and pulled back only to shove right back in.

She shuddered, jolted across the saddle by the impact of his hips against her ass. And yet, heat coiled and tightened within her. A whimper escaped her lips.

He slammed in again. Then again, and again, increasingly harder in his thrusts . . . He grunted as he fucked her hard enough to rock the glider under them.

Powerful and cruel pleasure washed through her and coiled tight into a ferocious and rising wave. Her fingers splayed out as she twisted under him, overwhelmed. She couldn't stop her gasping cries of bright agony and dark delight.

He ground into her, hot, hard, and deliciously deep. "You're just about there."

He was right; she was going to cum, and cum horrifically hard. That last one was nothing compared to what was coiling in her belly. She could feel the scream building within her. Alarmed by the strength of her rising climax she struggled against it, burning with lust but more terrified of the fall.

"You stubborn little feral . . ." Sobehk growled over her. "Quit fighting it!"

Her body rocked and shuddered under his thrusts, burning and trembling with the need for release, but fear held her back.

Sobehk dropped on top of her and slid his hand around her hip and under. "Damn you, you are going to cum." His finger found her swollen clit and flicked. And thrust.

Liquid heat and fire erupted in a ferocious boil. Climax dug its claws deep into her, screaming for escape. She balanced on the edge. A howl of denial was ripped from her throat. "No!"

"Yes!" He ground his cocks into her as his fingers

worked her clit. "Cum, damn you!"

"No!" Fallon cried out, frantic with both need and fear, and still she held back from the edge.

He growled. "No more stubbornness." His open mouth pressed hot and wet on the long muscle of the throat.

She felt the points of his long teeth. A shiver of alarm raced up her spine. "Don't . . ."

He bit down.

Four small but fierce lines of bright hot pain tore her throat. She moaned.

His tongue swept across the small tears and he rose over her. "Now you'll cum."

A wave of overwhelming sensation slammed through her. Hot lust, intense pleasure and aching fullness mixed into a violent wave.

"Oh yeah, you're feeling it now." He thrust, and thrust . . .

She bucked, frenzied by the intensity of the sensations wracking her. It was too much. She screamed. Her body clenched tight with imminent release. Her breath stopped in her throat.

"That's it, kitten . . ." Sobehk groaned and thrust hard. "Cum, cum on my cocks and squeeze me dry!"

Release exploded within her. She fell shrieking and writhing into a maelstrom of orgasmic pleasure that washed her sanity from her mind. From far away she heard his triumphant howl and felt his final thrust. She shook under the final burning waves of orgasm as his cum filled her.

CHAPTER FOUR

Fallon was barely conscious as Sobehk unfastened the cables that held her down across the glider's saddle. She felt the cool edge of steel slide up the back of her legs. Two quick jerks tore the mangled remains of her leather suit from her body. He tossed it on the pavement. His fingers jerked at the buckles of her boots.

She tried to raise her head. "Not my boots." Those boots had been specially tailored for her. Most of her interneural infiltration tools were secreted in the leather and the lining. More than half of those tiny instruments accessed specially tailored breaking codes that she had programmed herself. Her entire profession was in her boots.

"The boots definitely have to go. Chaos only knows what kind of thieves' tools you have in them." He tugged the first off and threw it.

"No . . ." She struggled but simply couldn't get up the will to do more than shake her head. Her body shuddered and a wave of heat flushed her from head to toe. She groaned.

He tugged off her other boot and stroked her bare calf. "Shit. The fever has started. I have got to get you back." He pulled her up into his arms and threw his leg over the glider's saddle. Holding her crosswise in his arms, he frowned down at her and swept a hand across her brow. "Your eyes are starting to show signs of going."

She ignored his words; she was too busy staring at the sleek, silky black shirt stretched across his broad chest. He was also wearing a heavy leather coat that draped the sides of the glider. *He's dressed? When did he get dressed?*

He hauled her leg over his until she straddled him, facing his chest. She was just too damned tired to even attempt to move. His leather pants felt soft under her spread thighs.

Heat struck the back of her skull. It washed down her body, triggering a thorough soaking sweat. She barely noticed as he tugged her arms under his coat then around his waist. She was too busy trying to breathe past the wave of heat that flooded her limbs.

"Keep your wrists together around my waist."

A sizzling shimmer went through her arm augmentations, and her wrists locked together behind his back. Suddenly the heat passed and she could think again.

He tipped her head back. "Open your mouth."

"Huh?" She moaned softly. "Now what?"

"I said: open." His thumbs dug into her jaw and her mouth popped open. He tilted her head back and peered into her mouth. "Oh yeah, you got a nice set in there."

She shook her head and he released her. "Set of what?"

He smiled, and it wasn't pretty. "Fangs, kitten. You have a very pretty set of uppers and lowers."

Fangs? She explored her new teeth with her tongue. She pricked herself and flinched. They were sharp. *Fangs, great . . .* Her head fell against his heart and she closed her eyes. She was so tired. His warm scent washed over her. He smelled of clean sweat, male skin and sex. He smelled . . . good. She pressed her nose against him to smell him some more.

"It's time to go." He closed his coat around them both and buckled the glider's safety belts around them. "We're late." He pulled on the helmet and started the glider's air turbines, the vibration humming deep in her bones. He

35

leaned forward and grabbed the glider's handlebars. "We've been late." The glider lifted straight up on a wave of anti-grav.

"Huh?" She lifted her head. "Late for what?" The glider tipped up and lunged hard for the sky. She was slammed into his chest and the wind ripped her words away.

The howling turbo-glider and its two passengers lunged up from the manufacturing levels of the station's under-city. Sleek, narrow and built for power, the glider knifed into the flight stream arching over the corporate towers of the upper-city. Traffic lights gleamed on the aggressively edged side fins. Buoyant on a wave of anti-grav and pro-pelled by the glider's churning air turbines, the glider dodged nighttime flight-traffic at killing speed.

Fallon gripped Sobehk around the waist, her thighs straddling his, her bare feet hooked around his calves as they bucked over the conflicting air currents. Not that she could have let go if she tried with the force-cuffs locking her wrists around him. She clenched her hands into tight fists against his warm back and pressed her face into his chest. He had her under his coat, but he hadn't given her a helmet. The icy wind of the upper-city made her eyes wa-ter. It was a lot warmer in the deeps.

The glider suddenly dropped in speed and dipped.

Fallon jerked awake. *Huh?* She couldn't believe she'd ac-tually fallen asleep. Where were they? She turned to look. The colors were all smeary and too bright. She squinted into the wind to focus. They were circling the brightly lit open ring of a small, cone-shaped spaceport reserved for privately owned ships. She stared, wide-eyed. Blood and Fate, what did he want all the way out here?

Her eyes went out of focus. She squinted harder. They were very far away from the heart of the under-city where he'd finally caught her. Once she got away it was going to be one serious pain in the ass of a long trek back. Not to mention that she was stark naked. Getting something to wear up on the topside was going to be a problem all by itself.

The glider dove into the spaceport ring and slipped easily past slow-moving hover-barges towing freight and passengers as it skimmed deep into the lower levels.

Fallon bit her lip. She hadn't thought he would actually enter the spaceport. This was not looking good at all.

The glider took a sharp turn and dropped, landing on its cycle tires with a small bounce.

She yelped in surprise. "Don't get us killed!"

"Shut up and let me drive!"

They raced along the main passage that ran along the level's outer edge then took a sudden sharp turn into a small wedge-shaped berth. The dock lights illuminated the long, sleek and aggressive lines of a highly reflective black craft designed for space travel as well as atmospheric flight. It was only a little bigger than a frigate-class pleasure yacht, and it was armed with ports for energy pulse cannons and ballistics.

The howling roar of the ship's engines filled the berth. The deck vibrated under the glider's tires. At the berth's narrowest point was the door to the launch pit at the spaceport's heart. The door was closed, but the pit was already primed for lift. The massive superconductors deep in the very bottom were actively generating a massive wave of anti-grav. She could feel the shimmer of weightlessness under the glider.

Fallon stared at the craft and her heart thumped in her chest. She shouted over the noise. "Sobehk, that ship is about to launch!"

Sobehk shouted back. "That's right." He checked his speed, slowing as he approached the ship. "I told you, I'm behind schedule!" He turned the glider to the ship's rear where a narrow gangway led up into the yawning mouth of the ship's cargo hold.

Fallon stared at the ship's open cargo door and her blood turned to ice water. "But what about me?"

The glider roared up the ramp and into the ship. "What about you?"

Two tall, slender men in sculpted black armor came running up. Light gleamed on their silver hair and on their weapons. Both of them wore swords, and small blades were tucked all over their suits.

Sobehk unbuckled the safety belts and opened his coat, revealing Fallon locked around his waist.

One of them frowned. "Is that your catch?"

Sobehk pulled off his helmet and scrubbed a hand through his hair. "Yep."

The other scowled. "I hope she's worth it; we're late."

"It took a three-day hunt to catch her." Sobehk smiled. "I got the first dose in her and she already has a full set of teeth."

The first grinned at the second. "Sounds like definite Prime potential to me."

"Let me go!" Fallon jerked at her arms, pulling on Sobehk's waist in panic. "I need to get off!" Her body buzzed with tension as her muscles fought with her internal tech.

Sobehk snorted and smiled down at her. "You are not going anywhere."

Temper flared hot and she snarled at him, baring her teeth.

He grabbed the hair at the back of her neck and jerked her head back. His lips curled back, showing his far longer teeth. A growl rumbled in his chest. "Don't you dare bite me!"

She trembled in his grip, aware on a visceral level that

her throat was vulnerable to his teeth. Her gaze darted to the exit. Peter had said they took people—she hadn't thought he meant they took them *off-station*.

The ramp slid up, and the door irised shut and sealed.

Her breath stilled in her lungs. Her vision blurred completely. She could feel tears tracking down her cheeks. *This was not happening!*

She heard him speak as though from a great distance. "Hey, can you see?"

Fallon frowned. "What?" He seemed so far away it took her a moment to realize what he'd asked. She blinked, but he was one big watery blur. "No." *You big stupid brute . . .*"I can't see." *I'm too busy crying.*

"About time."

"Huh?" That didn't make any sense. In fact, nothing was making any sense at all.

"Blood tears," someone said right at her shoulder.

She felt heat begin to creep up her limbs. "What?" A humming filled her ears. The heat in her body pulled at her and made it difficult to think.

"Her eyes are going; she's late for her second dose." Sobehk sounded far away. "Let go, kitten."

Her arms dropped from around his waist. She was supposed to be doing something . . . going somewhere.

"She's going under."

"I see it." She felt Sobehk turn her and lay her across his lap. "Give me the syringe."

Sleep crashed over her.

Something punched into her heart, from very far away.

Fallon awoke disoriented and bent over on her stomach with her wrists pinned behind her back. It took her a moment to realize that she was being carried, draped over a warm broad shoulder, with her head down a muscular, naked back. Her gaze was irresistibly drawn down a long white braid swinging above a flexing muscular ass in skin-tight pants. It was a really nice ass, too . . .

Then her body started protesting, loudly. She groaned as every bruise, ache, and strain, from the last three days suddenly howled for attention. She shifted uncomfortably. For some strange reason, there seemed to be a hard knot at the base of her breastbone that was particularly annoying.

"Finally awake?" The deep voice was more than familiar.

Fallon closed her eyes. She *would* be ogling Sobehk's backside. *Terrific . . .*

"Before you get any thoughts about trying to leave the ship, we left the station about an hour ago and are currently in jump-space."

Oh shit! For a full breath, panic surged through her. The panic was abruptly squashed by practicality. She had known that her career would probably end in being caught by somebody. She just hadn't thought she'd get caught by someone she'd kissed. *Pain in my ass . . .* She flinched. Her ass was still sore from her reaming.

She seriously thought about wriggling out of his hold just on principle, but there wasn't any place to go, not on a ship this small. And she was just too damned tired. Her stomach gurgled. She winced. *And hungry.* She honestly hoped he planned to feed her sometime soon. She lifted her head and found that she was being hauled through a semi-dark, narrow, arched passageway walled in unrelieved black. "Where are you taking me?"

"The facility. You're incredibly filthy."

She snorted. "I should be; I've been sleeping in the under-city sewers for the past few days."

"Oh, so that's where that charming aroma came from?" He sounded revoltingly amused.

Fallon curled her lip. So she smelled like a cesspit; nice

of him to point that out. "I did it to avoid a big white-haired brute that wouldn't get off my ass." She felt a smile bloom with sudden memory. "When I dove into that last sewage pipe, the look of total disgust on your face was absolutely precious. You really hate getting your pretty armor all dirty, don't you?"

"*You* are in enough trouble already. Are you sure you want to add to it?"

"I figure I'm about as deep as I can get already, so why hold back?" Fallon's belly gurgled again. She shifted. Her stomach was not at all happy being draped over his hard shoulder. "Are we there yet?"

"As a matter of fact . . ." He stepped through a narrow oval door, knelt and tilted her back, depositing her onto her feet. "Yes."

Fallon teetered unsteadily on her bare feet. They were in a compact black-walled bathing facility with an enclosed water stall that would fit two, but no more. The commode and the sink were both lidded and designed for gravity and zero-g.

Sobehk set towels on the counter then turned and reached for her.

She back-pedaled into the wall where the door used to be.

He snorted. "Relax. I'm just checking your bandages." He peeled back the derma-strips with gentle fingers.

She looked up at him in alarm and felt her heart beat in her mouth for no good reason at all. "What for?"

"I want to make sure you didn't do any permanent damage."

"My arms work just fine, thank you." She suddenly focused on his handsome face and then his full mouth. A kiss would only be a small stretch away . . . She licked her lips. Her heart thumped harder. *What am I thinking?* She jerked away and almost fell against the smooth wall. Her knees didn't want to work properly.

He raised a brow at her. "Having problems standing?"

"No . . ." She was having problems being in the same room with him. She had to keep away from him, he . . . he smelled too good. What was wrong with her today? She'd been doing weird things, thinking weird things and now she was feeling weird things.

"Good. Turn around, put your hands on the wall and keep them there."

Fallon turned and set both palms on the wall. "Now what?"

"Hold still." His fingertips slid down her back. "I want to see if you took any other damage I didn't see."

She arched away from his light touch, but he persisted. It didn't feel bad; in fact, it felt kind of . . . nice. The hair rose all down her spine. Why was he being so . . . caring? Why couldn't he just stay a big loud-mouthed bastard? She could handle being yelled at. This . . . gentleness was scrambling everything in her head. Bloody Fate, she had almost kissed him!

"Chaos, you're filthy."

The breath exploded from Fallon's lungs. "If you hadn't chased me —"

"You *stole* my glider!"

"There was no reason to go after me once you got it back!"

He snarled, the primitive and completely inhuman sound of an angry predator. "We've been over all this! You lost, remember? That's why you are currently up against the wall."

Fallon couldn't stop her instinctive flinch. "Fine." She scowled at the gleaming black wall. "So, now what are you going to do?"

"Do? The same thing anyone does with a dirty stray—give it a bath." She could hear the insufferable grin in his voice.

"A dirty *stray*?" Fallon turned to glare at him over her shoulder. "What do you think I am, some kind of pet?"

Sobehk barked out a laugh. "Yes, actually." He jabbed a thumb over his shoulder at the oval door to the water stall. "Go on and get in." He reached for the fastenings to his pants.

She fled.

CHAPTER FIVE

The Vortex – Skeldhi brigantine class transport
Jump-Space

Fallon stepped into the water stall and looked around with interest. *Well now, this is rich territory . . .*

The stall was completely enclosed in sheets of semi-transparent silvery smoked material that looked like glass, with one whole wall that was mirrored. Lights and small-handled spray heads were mounted on each of the five walls; a dark-smoke chrome rail went all the way around the interior.

Fallon grimaced at her reflection. The brute was right; she was absolutely filthy. Her shoulder-length black hair was dull and matted with Fate only knew what, and her pale skin was barely visible through all the dirt. Her face had oily black smears across her forehead and one cheek, making her eyes look huge and really blue-green. She frowned at her face. Her eyes seemed bigger somehow, and she didn't remember having that much blue or green in them.

Warmth trickled down between her thighs and her ass. It was cum, from when he'd fucked her. She turned her back on the mirror in complete disgust. She had no idea how he had even touched her.

Sobehk stepped into the shower with his back turned, utterly and magnificently nude, giving her a mouthwatering view of his entire backside from shoulder to heel. His

44

long, frost-white hair fell in loose waves past his bone-pale shoulders to brush against his slender hips in an extravagant mane of white silk. He dropped a small collection of nubby white cloths on the shower's smooth dark floor and reached up to collect one of the chrome spray heads. The muscles in his back moved and flexed in an arresting display. He pulled the long hose from the wall and fiddled with something. Water sprayed from the nozzle in his hand.

Other than his brows and mane, he appeared completely smooth and hairless.

Unlike her.

Fallon dropped her arms and felt like crossing her legs to hide her rude feminine curls.

Sobehk turned to face her and raised his brow in amusement. His blue eyes looked enormous and brilliant against all that pale skin. "Ready for your bath, kitten?"

Fallon's eyes automatically dropped below his waist and her breath stopped in her chest. The broad expanse of his muscular chest tapered down into narrow hips that framed a pair of rigid erections in a nest of snowy curls, one cock right on top of the other. The upper cock was clearly larger, but the lower cock was not what anyone would call small. His plump pair of balls hung ripe and a little overlarge between his muscular thighs.

She couldn't catch her breath. She'd known he had a pair, she'd felt them slamming into her, over and over . . . *Bloody Fate, he'd had that top one up her ass?* A shiver shook her even as a spat of moist heat flooded her core.

Sobehk's chuckle echoed loudly in the small glass chamber. "Like what you see?"

Fallon looked up at Sobehk's grinning face in complete shock. She couldn't think of a single thing to say.

"You really had no idea until I fucked you?"

Completely speechless, Fallon shook her head.

Sobehk shook his head, his mouth open wide in amusement. His long teeth gleamed. "Chaos, you should see your face."

Fallon jerked as though struck. He was laughing at her, the bastard . . .

He waved his hand. "Come over here and hold onto the rail. It's going to take a lot of hard scrubbing to get all that filth off of you."

"I can bathe myself, thank you."

Sobehk snorted. "Bathing yourself is not the point of this little exercise." He pointed at the rail by his side. "Do it."

Fallon jerked her gaze away from his . . . extremities and walked over to where he stood, tall, pale and intimidating. He seemed to fill the whole shower with his big masculine presence. She ducked her head, chafing that she felt so small, helpless, feminine, and dirty standing under him. She turned away from him and wrapped her hands around the chrome rail that was just a bit higher than her waist. A shimmer went through her augmentation and her hands locked around the bar. She flinched. "So what *is* the point of all this?"

"The point is . . ." He leaned over her. "That you are mine to do with as *I* please, and at this moment, it pleases me to bathe you."

She was bitterly aware that the cuffs on her wrists gave him control of her body. And she was trapped on a small ship in deep space. He had all the advantages. For now.

Deliciously hot water sluiced over her from neck to toes. She moaned before she could stop herself. Black grime pooled at her feet and ran down the center drain. She hated being filthy.

"Tilt your head back and close your eyes." He sprayed her head down, soaking her hair. "Hasn't anyone ever bathed you before?"

Fallon shook the water from her cheeks. "No."

"No one?" Sobehk frowned as he attached the nozzle to the side wall, letting the water spray down over her back, rather than directly in her face. "Not even your parents, or a lover?"

Fallon stared at her hands. "I didn't exactly have parents." Her parents were a vague memory of people who shouted—and left. Her childhood had consisted of a windowless steel institution with hours spent strapped into a couch downloading crap she would never use. They called it education.

"You must have had at least one lover bathe you?" He pulled the soap dispenser from the wall and reached down to snag a cloth from the floor.

"No." Lovers were few and infrequent. Encounters were hurried and rarely happened in private quarters. They were only interested in scratching their itch and getting on with other things. A moist towelette did for bathing after. In a world of thieves, you couldn't trust anyone enough to actually fall asleep with them. She shrugged. "I didn't have . . . lovers like that."

"Considering the human vermin living on that station, I'm not particularly surprised." His expression was wry as he squirted creamy soap on the cloth. He set the soap back on the wall and faced her. "I'm going to make sure you get plenty of handling." He dropped the cloth on her back and started scrubbing her back and shoulders with brutal efficiency.

"Handling?" Fallon gripped the rail tightly as her body rocked under the pressure of his strong hands. He wasn't playing; he was scrubbing the burning fury out of her skin with vigorous attention to detail. Thick rich lather formed and spilled down her body in his wake.

"Being touched, being held . . ." He leaned over her back and whispered, "Being cared for." He knelt at her side and scrubbed at her flanks.

She ducked, her cheeks warming, and braced her feet to keep from getting knocked over by his sudden scouring assault on her legs. "What if I don't want to be . . . cared for?"

"I'm afraid you really don't have much choice in the matter." His cloth slid up between her legs and focused on her sore privates.

She turned away and hissed. The cloth was warm, and his hands were gentle, but it was painfully humiliating to have someone's hands on her, especially there.

"You'll just have to get used to the fact that . . ." He dropped the cloth and slid his soapy fingers over and into her tender flesh. "You don't get to make those decisions anymore."

She cringed. "Blood and hell, you are a bastard!"

He chuckled. "Yep." His shoved a soap-slick finger deep into her ass.

She froze, stunned by the sudden invasion. *He did not . . .* A snarl escaped her lips. Before she knew it, her foot had snapped out in a kick aimed at his kneeling side.

He twisted out of range and his hand whipped out. He smacked her wet thigh with a sharp crack. "Stop that!"

She yelped and pulled her leg back. The strike stung, a lot. She'd known it was a stupid move; her hands were locked on the bar, but she couldn't seem to stop herself.

"Behave yourself!" He stood up and reached for her shoulder.

Lightning blazed up the back of her skull and rage erupted in a hot red rush. She turned and snapped at him with her sharp teeth. "Don't touch me!"

He jerked his hand back. "What?"

Her eyes narrowed and a growl rumbled in her chest.

Her lips curled back from her teeth. If he tried to touch her again, she would make him bleed.

His eyes narrowed. "Oh, no you don't." His hand snapped out and his fingers knotted in her hair at the back of her neck, yanking her head back. He stared hard into her eyes and his lips curled back, baring his fangs only centimeters from her throat. "Get it through your thick skull, I caught you, I took you." His hand closed on her throat. "Your life is mine!"

She snarled and tried to jerk her head away. "Fuck you!"

His fist tightened in her hair. His other hand caught her chin, tilting her head back further and forcing her to arch back. He focused his cold angry gaze on hers. "Back down, kitten." A deep growl erupted from his chest. "You're already beaten. Don't make me prove it."

She focused on his mouth. His teeth looked really big, really sharp, and way too close. If he decided to rip her throat out, she was not in any position to stop him. Her growl died. She closed her mouth and swallowed, knowing he would feel it with his palm. Her gaze slid away from his and she trembled in his grasp.

"Good." He tugged at her hair. "Now, apologize."

She sucked in a breath. "What?" Her gaze darted to his.

His eyes were ice cold and his jaw was tight. "You heard me."

She cringed. He was seriously pissed. "I'm ... I'm sorry."

"Good girl." He pushed her back upright and released her hair. He cupped her shoulders and stroked her arms. "Now, keep that feral temper of yours in check."

Fallon hunched under his hands but the urge to bite him had completely fled. She had no idea where that urge had come from in the first place.

Sobehk released her arms and stepped away to retrieve

a fresh cloth from the floor. "You've got good reflexes. I barely caught that kick. You're going to make a damned fine *upuaht rehkyt*." He watched her as he coated the cloth with soap. "But the faster you learn to submit, the easier everything will go for you."

Submit? Her hands clenched on the bar and she shivered. "I don't take orders very well."

He snorted. "That is the understatement of the year." He knelt at her side and grabbed her ankle, turning her as far to the side as her hands on the bar would allow. "You'd better get used to taking orders." He looked up at her with narrowed eyes. "Or you will get beaten, a lot." His cloth swept across her belly and he began his merciless scrubbing across her hips then up toward her breasts.

Fallon rocked under his strong strokes. She'd been beaten before. It hadn't done any good then, she doubted it would do any good now. She suddenly tripped over the end of his earlier statement. "Wait a minute . . . you thought I'd make a what?"

"Took you long enough to catch that." He focused his scrubbing on her breasts. "An *upuaht rehkyt* is a bodyguard. *Upuaht* translates into Imperial basic as 'canine guard.' *Re-hkyt* means pet."

"What is with you and all the 'canine' and 'pet' stuff?" She bit her lip as the cloth rasped against her nipples, bringing them to abrupt and insistent life. "I'm not an animal!"

"Oh, but you are." Sobehk stood and lifted her chin to stare into her eyes. "Close your eyes." He ruthlessly scrubbed her face. "*Rehkyt* are what we Skeldhi call our human pets." He rinsed the soap from her cheeks carefully. "There, much better."

"A human *pet?*" Fallon had to blot her eyes against her shoulder as she couldn't release her hands from the rail.

"What? Are you going to put a collar and leash on me?" The idea was so silly a smile lifted her lips.

Sobehk scrubbed down her arms, pinking her skin in his wake. "Yes."

"Huh?" Fallon stared at him. "Are you serious?"

"Very." He tossed the cloth on the floor and reached for the soap dispenser. "Lift your chin and close your eyes. I'm going to wash your hair."

Fallon lifted her chin and closed her eyes tight. "A collar for people?"

His fingers dove into her matted hair and massaged her scalp. "The collar is for temperamental *pets*." Thick lather dripped onto her shoulders. "*Rehkyt* are designed to be sexually aggressive. Their appetites, or their tempers, occasionally get out of hand. The control collar, the *shen*, is jacked directly into your nervous system at the cerebral cortex. It does pretty much what force-cuffs do, only more so." He doused her hair with water to rinse off the soap.

She shook her head to clear her eyes. "You're putting a *control collar* on me?"

"Yep." Sobehk spread soap on his palms and trapped her gaze with his. "You'll be collared as soon as we are done here. As soon as I get to a proper enclave, I'm getting you a nice steel chain with a tag with your name and mine."

"A chain . . . *two* collars?"

He stepped behind her and his broad palms swept down, spreading soap along her waist and over her hips. "The control collar is for behavior. It doesn't come off. The chain is for the leash and the tag marks you publicly as mine — my pet, and my property."

Leashes? Tags? He really was treating her like a *pet*! Her mind reeled under the shock of what he was saying. Her knees jelled and threatened to give out. She stayed upright by will alone. Her throat constricted with alarm. "I don't like this game anymore."

His mouth caressed her ear even as his soapy hands swept across her belly. "It stopped being a game when I registered you and no one argued the claim, making you legally mine to collect."

Blood and Fate! Her knuckles whitened on the rail. "Sobehk, you can't make me your *pet!*"

"I already have." He pressed the rigid lengths of his erections against her spine and her butt. His soft groan caressed her ear, creating shivers. "You're already showing signs of impression."

Fallon shook her head as foam dripped down her body. *Impression?* What in burning fury was that?

He brought his soapy hands up and cupped her breasts. "Relax, kitten." He kneaded and caressed the warm softness in his broad palms. "I'll take very good care of you." He tugged the peaks of her nipples to rigid tautness with his strong fingers. "No more living in sewers."

Arousal scorched through her in a torrential wave of damp heat. Fallon felt her breath violently rush from her lungs. A small sound escaped her lips. He was doing it again, making her boil with need, and so easily. She was not used to getting excited so quickly, but then, she was not used to being completely in someone else's power either.

"It's done, it's over. Just let go, kitten," he whispered. He slowly rubbed both of his hot, rigid erections along the damp seam of her butt.

She found herself leaning back into him. She couldn't stop herself any more than she could stop the ache between her thighs. She took a deep breath to gain control and caught a nose full of his scent. She could smell the rich musk of his arousal even over the soap. A small, helpless sound came from her throat.

"That's it . . ." His hand slid sensuously over her belly, drawing tremors along the path of his fingers. "Don't try to resist." One hand slid up to cup her breast as the fingers of the other dipped lower, seeking the juncture of her thighs. "There's no need to resist."

Her body clenched in eagerness. She couldn't stop her legs from parting in invitation.

He squeezed her breast and a soft groan came from his throat. "I have you." The fingers of his other hand delved among the folds of her intimate flesh, exploring the damp softness with inciting skill. "Body and soul . . ." His fingers trapped her nipple and slid across her clit at the same time.

Fire, heat, urgency . . . She gasped, arching back against him, and bucked against his palm, so close to the edge of orgasm a breath more would take her over.

He chuckled. The sound held pure masculine triumph. "And you want me to have you." He pulled his hands away and stepped back.

Fallon shook hard with both fear of what was to come and raw carnal frustration. She set her forehead against the slick glass wall and fought against the lust howling in her body. *Bastard . . .*

He reached up and shut off the water. "You're clean. It's time."

Fallon felt her heart slam in her throat. He was going to put a collar on her throat and take control of her body. *Blood and Fate . . .* Sudden panic engulfed her. Her voice escaped in a tight whisper. "I wanna go home."

He grabbed the hair at the nape of her neck and jerked her head back. He stared hard and unyielding into her wide eyes. "You are home." His mouth took hers in a devouring and possessive kiss.

She moaned under his hungry assault, unable to release the rail and not all that sure she wanted to release his mouth. Pain crushed her heart in a tight fist of inexplicable and undefined emotion. A sudden sob exploded from her chest and tears abruptly fell from her eyes. She ripped her mouth away from his in mortified dismay. She was crying?

Sobehk caught her face in his palms. "There, that's what I was waiting for."

Fallon stared up at him in confusion.

"Let go of the rail, kitten."

She released the rail and scrubbed at her damp cheeks. The damn tears didn't want to stop. "You want me to cry?"

He pulled her into the circle of his arms. "Yes." With an arm around her waist, he turned and hit a switch by the door. Warm air filled the tiny glass room, drawing all the moisture from the shower stall.

Fallon wrapped her arms around herself and shook her head. "I don't get it."

He knelt down to catch her eye. "*Rehkyt* are affectionate by nature." He brushed away the tears that still slid down her cheeks with his thumbs. "You obviously don't give your affections easily, but you've begun to respond to me."

Fallon shook her head. "I don't want to be anybody's slave!"

"Ha!" He rolled his eyes and grinned broadly. "The way you kept dodging in and out of my reach, daring me to catch you? You were begging me to collar you!"

Fallon stared up at him in horror. All those times she had popped out just to see where he was, how close he had gotten . . . Had she been daring him to chase her, to catch her?

To keep her?

His blue gaze remained steady, knowing and amused.

She finally had to look away.

"You will make a very fine *rehkyt*." He leaned over to drop a kiss on her brow. "Trust me."

CHAPTER SIX

Clean, dry, and somewhat shaken, Fallon let Sobehk nudge her out of the water stall. Did she really want to be a slave—a pet? *Sobehk's* pet?

He strode past her to pick up a long silver-gray robe from the counter and shrugged into it, knotting the cloth belt at his waist. The long rich folds swept to the floor. He pulled his mane from the back of his collar then turned around and waved at the wall. A hole widened outward into an oval door. He stepped toward the opening. "Come on, let's go."

Fallon crossed her arms over her bare breasts and raised her brows. "Don't I get a robe?"

Sobehk turned to her and snorted. "You're *rehkyt*."

She looked at him in shock. "Are you saying I don't get clothes?"

"You get clothes when I decide to put them on you." His grin was slow in coming and malicious when it got there. "*If* I decide to put them on you."

Fallon lowered her chin and her temper burned with comforting heat. "If you think I'm going to walk around naked . . ."

"You'll crawl on your knees naked if I tell you to!" A growl rolled in his chest and he nodded at the door. "Are you coming, or do I need to make you?"

Fallon abruptly turned away to scowl at the open door. "Fine, whatever . . ." Stiff-legged, she marched toward the door.

Sobehk caught her shoulder. "Stay behind me and on my offside."

Fallon looked up at him, puzzled. The offside was his left, away from his weapon hand. "You're not carrying a sword."

His brows lowered. "Are you going to argue with everything I say?"

She shrugged. "Probably."

Sobehk sighed and pressed his fingers to his brow as though it pained him. "You really need a beating."

Fallon couldn't help but smile. "Probably."

Sobehk rolled his eyes and stepped out of the door. "Come on."

Fallon followed him out. The corridor was narrow, shadowed and empty, but there were doors on either side that anyone could suddenly walk out of. She eyed the closed doors with grave misgivings, suddenly glad that she had his wide back to hide behind. "Where are we going?"

"To see the *Sehnbay'syr* Tah, the master surgeon."

"What for?" She flinched and wished she could suck the words back into her mouth. They were going to medical to get her collared, obviously.

Sobehk glanced over his shoulder at her with a sly smile. "I'm taking my stray to the veterinarian to get a checkup."

Fallon growled. "Keep it up with the animal stuff, and I'm just going to have to bite you."

"I would not try that if I were you." Sobehk stopped at a closed door and waved his hand. "We have muzzles for pets that like to bite." The door opened under his palm and he stepped through.

"Oh, come on!" Fallon grabbed the edge of the door and stepped over the bottom edge. The door closed almost on her heels. "Muzzles for people?"

The medical bay wasn't particularly large, but it was

immaculately tidy. A black-and-chrome padded table commanded the very center and was stretched out under a well lit, state-of-the-art medical array designed for full emergency surgery. The slightly curved walls were the same silvery gray she'd seen everywhere else.

A man in a sleeveless smoke-gray robe looked up from behind his curved black glass desk, set against the right wall. His mane was the color of old bone and pulled back into a snug braid. The holographic projection display floating over the desk vanished. "Muzzles are for disobedient *rehkyt*." His voice was deep, crisp, and slightly amused. "Do you need one?"

Alarmed, Fallon ducked behind Sobehk and peeked from around his arm.

Sobehk shook his head and rolled his eyes. "I am considering it."

Fallon glared up at him.

"Indeed?" The medic stood and came around the desk to stand by the foot of the long table. He was very tall and painfully slender. His robe swept the hem of his long black kilt. His bare arms were roped with muscle. "So, what did you bring me, *A'syr* Sobehk?"

Sobehk turned to the side, revealing Fallon to the medic. "This is Isabeau."

Fallon kept her place as her face heated. "No one calls me that."

"Then I definitely will." He caught her around the shoulders and pushed her gently but firmly toward the long table and the waiting medic.

Fallon eyed the table and the medic uneasily but went where she was pushed. "Why do you have to be such a pain in my ass?" Her voice came out in a hoarse whisper.

The medic raised his brows at Sobehk in obvious question.

Sobehk snorted and returned the medic's speaking glance. "She's on the second dose and starting to feel it," he said very dryly. "Isabeau, this is *Sehnbay'syr* Tah. Be nice."

Fallon stared up at the master surgeon. Although his face was lined with age, he was still quite arresting. Electric blue gleamed in the heart of his stone-gray eyes, betraying his eyesight augmentations. Gold cuffs glimmered around the lobes of his pointed ears.

She closed her hands into fists to hide the shaking and couldn't think of a single thing to say.

Tah smiled and patted the table. "Let's have a look, shall we?"

For some undefined reason, every hair on Fallon's body came to sudden and alarmed attention. Her breath stilled in her throat.

The master surgeon raised a brow. "Shy?"

"Feral." Sobehk caught Fallon around the waist, lifted her, and deposited her on the edge of the padded table.

She gasped in surprise then bit her lip to keep from making another sound.

Sobehk sighed as he stepped back. "She's not used to handling yet."

"Ah, I see." Tah walked around the table and parted her knees to step between them.

Fallon trembled only slightly but didn't try to stop him.

The master surgeon smiled briefly and raised a small stylus. "Relax, this will not be painful."

"That's what they all say." Fallon flinched. Blood and fury, she couldn't keep her mouth shut if she tried!

Tah gave her a startled look and amusement flashed across his expression. He looked over at Sobehk. "How new?"

"Hours." Sobehk folded his hands behind him.

The master surgeon's brow shot up. "Indeed?" He caught Fallon's hand and turned the palm up. Gently he set the point of his instrument on her pulse. "And is this the reason you were a day late?"

"Yep."

"It took you that long?"

"Three, actually."

Fallon felt a small spurt of pride.

"Three?" Tah glanced over at Sobehk. "Your stubborn streak is showing." He smiled. "Mastered?"

Sobehk flinched only slightly. "Not quite."

"Ah, so not yet conditioned." Tah focused on the bandages on Fallon's shoulders. He raised a cool brow at Sobehk. "What happened?" He moved his stylus up to Fallon's right shoulder.

Sobehk suddenly flushed. "Isabeau decided to remove her force-cuffs with some exploratory surgery."

Tah blinked. "Surely that's an exaggeration?" He moved his stylus to her left shoulder.

Fallon snorted. "He's still pissed because it worked. I got one off."

Tah leaned back to look at her. "Did you now?" He turned to Sobehk.

Sobehk ground his teeth and glared at Fallon. "She got one off, all right, and bled out like a faucet, too. I had to patch her and dose her early to stop the bleeding."

The master surgeon sighed. "Triggering imprint vulnerability."

Sobehk nodded. "Pretty much."

Tah lifted his brow. "Considering your new acquisition, and the regulations against personal . . . possessions, were you planning on retiring from service?"

Sobehk gave a small shrug. "I've made enough to afford a small school on the coast."

"Ah, I see." Tah lifted the instrument from Fallon's shoulder and waved his hand by the head of the table. A holographic display bloomed into being. "Let's see what you have."

Fallon leaned over to look, but she couldn't make heads or tails of what she was seeing. None of the figures or lettering made any sense.

Tah began to recite in a voice laced with dry humor.

Fallon couldn't understand his language. Her internal translator didn't have anything to work with. Yet.

Sobehk's expression was grave as he nodded.

Fallon frowned. Was it bad?

The master surgeon stepped away from the table and went to his desk.

Fallon looked up at Sobehk's grim expression. "What was all that?"

Amusement lifted the corner of Sobehk's mouth. "Oh, '*Syr* Tah was just confirming my suspicions."

Fallon frowned at him. "What suspicions?"

Sobehk gave her a tight smile. "That you're a mongrel."

Fallon gasped. "Cheap shot, you big bastard!"

The master surgeon returned, and the amusement was back in his expression. "Her arm, please."

Sobehk took Fallon's wrist in his firm grip and held her arm out.

She looked up at Sobehk, startled. "What now?"

Tah took his place between her knees. "You are apparently somewhat undernourished. I'm giving you a vitamin supplement." He set the blunt end of an instrument against the vein near the crook of her elbow. There was a soft hydraulic hiss. He lifted the instrument from her arm and glanced at Sobehk. "That should keep you from having to feed her in the traditional manner during the rest of the process." He stepped away.

Sobehk frowned down at Fallon. "When was the last time you ate?"

Fallon opened her mouth, then closed it. She shrugged. "That depends on what you mean by *eat*." She was pretty sure that he wouldn't see nutrient bars as actual food, but it was all she had been able to carry for the past three days. They weren't good for much, but they were better than nothing, and they kept the hunger pangs down to a manageable level.

Sobehk rolled his eyes. "Never mind, I don't want to know." He hopped up on the table to sit next to her.

Fallon raised a brow at him. "What, are you getting a checkup too?"

Tah came back from his desk with a sleek black case twice as long as his hands. He looked up at Sobehk. "Make sure she has plenty of food as soon as she comes out." He opened the case and lifted out a smooth silver ring. It was open and one end was crammed with thousands of tiny pins. It was a collar.

Fallon froze. This was it.

Sobehk took the collar from the master surgeon. He turned his gaze to Fallon. "Lay face down across my lap, Isabeau."

Her gaze leaped to the closed door, but there really wasn't any place she could run to. The door was already gone, and the medical bay was too small to hide in.

Sobehk's hand closed tight on her wrist. "Isabeau, you have already done all the running you could possibly do. We are already a full jump from Dyson's Ring station. There is absolutely no way for you to return." His voice was calm but completely unforgiving. "That life is over. You have a new life now with me."

Fallon looked up into his hard gaze and her heart beat in her mouth. A new life? With *him*?

Sobehk patted his knee. "Lie down and this will be over quickly."

Fallon did not want to do this, but she couldn't think of a way around it. She pulled up her knees. She shook so bad she almost fell off trying to get into position.

Sobehk caught her shoulders and helped her lay face down with her head on his knee. "Isabeau, put your hands behind your back."

Fallon closed her eyes. She really, really didn't want to do this. She folded her hands behind her back.

"Keep them there."

The command sizzled through her augmentations and she jumped. She'd been expecting it, but she was so damned nervous.

Sobehk moved her hair to the side and over her shoulder, baring her neck. "Relax, kitten. I have you."

Cool metal went around her throat. It suddenly became hard to breathe. She closed her eyes tight.

He brought the ends together. With one hard jab, he pressed the pins into the base of her neck.

Fallon blinked. *Was that it?* The sharp stab from the pins was not that impressive. Stabbing herself in the shoulder had been far worse.

Sweat broke out on her body.

Huh? A blinding power surge went through the internal comp in the back of her skull. She gasped. The power surge traveled with appalling speed throughout the rest of her physical augmentations. Her entire body shuddered hard under the assault.

From far away, she felt both Sobehk and Tah grab her to keep her from falling off the table.

The massive surge spread down her spine and into places she knew for a fact no augmentation existed. Her skin tried to crawl from her bones and her fingers and toes twitched in reflex. She bit her lip to keep from screaming. A frightened whimper escaped instead.

It stopped.

"Shit . . ." Soaked in sweat, Fallon panted, shaking with exhaustion. "Is it over?"

Tah's cool hands closed around her wrists. "Not quite."

Sobehk wrapped her hair around his hand. He barked out something in a language her translator couldn't interpret.

Lightning blazed through her. She screamed and fought to get away. Both men worked to keep her in place.

The lightning stopped.

Fallon moaned and tears streamed from her eyes. "Son of a bitch . . . What in screaming fury was that?"

Sobehk released her hair and stroked her back with his palm "That was the command setting for punishment. This is the other one."

Fallon stilled. "Other one?"

Sobehk barked out another phrase.

Heat and lust burst in her core then clenched tight with terrifying strength. All thought fled but for the hunger in her cunt. She writhed across his lap, moaning in urgent need.

The vicious hunger abruptly relaxed its grip.

Fallon gasped and shifted restlessly. The urgency was over, but the need was not completely gone. A threatening heat simmered in her belly.

"Those were the two extremes of the collar." Sobehk stroked her back again. "The telepathic commands are programmed."

"Hold still." Tah daubed cool cream where the pins stabbed into her neck, easing the slight burn.

Fallon released a breath.

Sobehk's knee shifted under her cheek. "You can release

your wrists."

Her wrists separated and she struggled to sit up. "Is it over?"

Sobehk lifted her up onto her knees. "This is." He took her wrists and the force-cuffs came off in his hands.

She stared at her bare wrists. *He took them off?* She swallowed and felt the metal shift against her neck. She closed her eyes. *That's right, he doesn't need them; he can control all of me now.*

CHAPTER SEVEN

Fallon stepped from the medlab and padded after So-behk, gripping her elbows in a daze of shaky confusion. Her heart thumped in her chest and ached in a way she couldn't quite identify. Half of her wanted to run away screaming and find the smallest hole she could crawl into to hide in, and the other half wanted to lean up against So-behk.

Something surged in her heart and her breath hitched. A shudder passed through her and she stopped. What in bleeding fury was going on?

Sobehk turned back to look at her. "Isabeau?"

She took a breath. "I'm . . ." *Afraid.* She couldn't say it. She'd never admitted to fear in her life, but some part of her was desperate to be . . . comforted.

Sobehk smiled. "It'll be all right. I'll take good care of you." He held out his hand.

Fallon shook her head. "I can take care of myself, dam-nit." But she took his hand. His fingers closed warm and snug around hers. It felt far too good for her peace of mind.

"Yeah, but now you don't have to." He tugged. "Let's go fuck."

"Isabeau?" The sweet and eerily familiar voice whispered poisonously from the corridor behind them. "Izzie Fallon?"

Fallon's head came up in alarm. Every hair on her body stood at attention. There was no way in bleeding fury her boss's pet assassin could be on this ship. She turned around to look back up the corridor. They *couldn't* have let that nightmare of a cyborg onboard!

Metal struck hammer-blows against metal.

Sobehk jerked at her side. "What in bloody Chaos . . ." He turned around to head up the corridor.

"No! Don't!" Fallon grabbed Sobehk's arm. "If it's who I think it is, you'll only make him attack you. You don't stand a chance against him unarmed."

The shriek of tearing metal followed. Shouts echoed down the corridor. Then wet crunches and choked screams.

Sobehk tensed. "What the fuck is going on?"

Fallon's fingers tightened around Sobehk's arm. "If we're lucky, it's nothing you guys can't handle. If we're not lucky, it's a friend of mine."

"Isabeau, that doesn't make sense."

A smallish, gangling and completely naked human male came timidly down the hall. His face was plain with ordinary brown eyes and a mop of bland blondish-brownish hair. He was one of those people you never looked twice at. He lifted his chin and moved his head from side to side. He appeared to be looking for something or listening for something. A band of silver gleamed around his throat and blood painted his bare arms almost to the shoulders.

Sobehk frowned and set his hand on Fallon's shoulder. "Where in bloody Chaos are his handlers?"

Fallon stared at the blood-soaked arms and fought off a shiver. "They're probably dead."

"The collar is for controlling killing aggression . . ." Sobehk glanced down at her. "Is that your *friend*?"

Fallon swallowed and nodded. And she had thought her luck couldn't possibly get any worse. "He's a nano-based mimetic cyborg. I doubt your collar has any effect on him."

"The collar has some effect; he's obviously sightless."

Sobehk glanced down at Fallon. "Wait a minute, he's *mimetic?*"

Fallon nodded slowly. "He shape-changes."

"Who is this guy?"

Fallon winced. "Tusk is my company's assassin."

"A mimetic cyborg assassin." Sobehk rolled his eyes. "Great."

"And he's good. He's single-minded, single-purposed and never failed a mission." Well, he had failed, once. That was how she found out how to take him out if she ever needed it. The following week she'd had her augmentation upgraded for dexterity and speed.

The young man's head came up. He stared straight at Fallon with unfocused eyes. "There you are, Izzie!"

"Oh, hi, Tusk." She pasted a smile on her lips. "What's going on?"

The young man smiled. "Oh, the boss wanted to see you."

"He did?" Fallon kept her hands open and loose at her sides while slowly moving in front of Sobehk. "Why didn't anybody tell me?"

Tusk shrugged. "Couldn't find you."

"Oh, that's right . . ." Fallon rolled her eyes and glanced up at Sobehk. "Some guy was chasing me all over the station."

Tusk shuffled gracelessly toward her, smiling absently. "Rudi said you'd be here, so I waited for you."

Fallon frowned. "He did?" How in bleeding fury had Rudi known that she would end up here? "How long were you waiting?"

Tusk pursed his lips. "Three days, or so."

Three days? Fallon felt her temper surge. Rudi had set her up. *That back-stabbing son of a bitch . . .*

Sobehk glanced down at Fallon. "Who's Rudi?"

Fallon scowled. "This guy I made my last delivery to. New guy, stinks of the Imperium. He tipped me for the delivery and gave me a pass to the club where I met you—three days ago."

Sobehk frowned. "That sounds like a setup."

"Yep, it sure does." Fallon glanced at him. "The question here is why?"

Tusk tilted his head. "Rudi told the boss you didn't make the delivery."

"He . . . what?" Impending doom dried her mouth. You did not *ever* miss a delivery. "Tusk, he lied."

"Oh . . . That's too bad." Tusk's brows lifted then fell. "Because I gotta bring you back to talk to him or kill you." He sucked on his bottom lip. "But we're in space already and I don't know how to fly the ship, so we can't *go* back."

An icy sweat soaked her back. "Tusk, I'm sure something can be arranged . . ."

Tusk shook his head and eased closer. "No, I don't think so."

Sobehk stiffened and grabbed Fallon by the shoulder. "He's not terrifically bright, is he?" He pulled her behind him.

"No, but he *is* terrifically deadly." Fallon shoved back in front of him. "Do *not* get in front of his target."

Tusk sighed and smeared a hand across his cheek, staining his face with blood. "I'm gonna miss you, Isabeau."

Sobehk frowned. "Is he actually crying?"

Fallon winced. "Yes. He does that, right before he attacks."

Tusk shuddered violently.

Fallon licked her lips. "Now's a good time to get your knife out, and if you have a spare, I'd love to have it."

"I don't have a spare." Sobehk drew his long dagger from his boot and moved to Fallon's side.

Fallon dropped her voice to barely a whisper. "His only weak spot is at the base of his skull in the back just below the data jack. Nothing else will have any real effect on him."

"Got it." Sobehk flipped the dagger in his palm. "Just stay out of the way."

Fallon frowned at him. *Stay out of the way, my ass.* "Sobehk, he's really, really fast. I hope you have dexterity in your augmentation. You're going to need it."

"I'm not exactly a slow-ass." Sobehk snorted. "I got you, didn't I?"

Fallon flashed him a bitter smile. "Yeah, after three days of little food and less sleep."

Sobehk grinned. "That doesn't change the fact that you are currently wearing a collar."

Fallon rolled her eyes. "That ego of yours is going to get you in trouble." She shook her hands and bounced on her toes to trigger her augmentations. She did not want to be dealing with Tusk barehanded, but it looked like she didn't have much of a choice. Sobehk was going to need a distraction. She just hoped to the Maker that Sobehk was up to speed.

Shaking and twitching, Tusk flung his arms to the sides and his head fell back. He wailed and stretched and thinned. His arms extended and reshaped themselves from the elbow out into long curved blades. His feet lengthened until he stood on double-jointed legs, balancing on elongated, clawed toes. His head reshaped and stretched into a muzzle. His mouth split his head nearly in half, full of long jagged teeth. His skin hardened into pale skin-toned scales.

Sobehk curled his lip and dropped into a fighting crouch. "Oh, that's pleasant-looking."

"Personally, I was hoping to never see it." Fallon nibbled on her bottom lip and promptly stabbed it. *Damned fangs.*

Tusk's head came forward. He focused on Fallon and raised his bladed arms. "Time to die, Isabeau Fallon." The words were barely recognizable coming from that gaping maw.

Fallon took a calming breath and gathered herself. Time to see if her technician had done his job right. She lunged for the company nightmare.

Sobehk shouted.

Fallon dove, rolling under Tusk's swinging blade. She rolled up onto her feet behind him—and dodged Tusk's second swing as he turned with blinding speed.

Behind them Sobehk lunged into the fray, dodging swings and opening harrying cuts along Tusk's sides and flanks.

Tusk turned from one to the other, snapping and slashing at both. His foot lashed out and caught Sobehk in the gut, propelling him into a wall.

"Oh, shit!" Fallon lunged in and slammed her fist into where Tusk's kidneys ought to be then dodged his retaliating bite.

Sobehk climbed to his feet and came toward them, shaking his head. He was not moving well. Tusk's kick must have struck something.

Need a distraction! Need a distraction! Need a distraction! Fallon lunged toward the side wall, leaping up and catching it with her feet to shove herself toward the opposite wall, dodging another swing. She bounced off the wall and back, flipped out of range, drawing Tusk further down the hall and away from Sobehk.

The guy Fallon had spoken to hadn't been kidding when he said Tusk was fast. She only hoped she had enough energy to keep moving until Sobehk could take out Tusk's head.

Fallon ducked another swing and saw Sobehk grab Tusk around the slender throat from behind. The knife rose . . .

Tusk's arm moved into an impossible angle and stabbed backward and sideways — straight into Sobehk's side under the ribs and came out the other side.

Sobehk's eyes widened and he froze.

Fallon gasped. *No . . . It* didn't look real. The blade went in, the blade came out covered in red . . . but it didn't look real at all.

Tusk pulled his arm free and Sobehk dropped. The knife clattered to the deck.

Fallon stared in shock as blood pooled under Sobehk's body. *No . . .* Lightning seared up her spine and engulfed her skull. A white-hot blaze of rage erupted within her. "No!" Fallon focused on the nightmare, and the entire universe slowed to a crawling bloody haze. A liquid growl vibrated deep in her chest. "Kill you . . ."

She dove under Tusk's lazy swing. Skimming low across the floor, she snatched up the fallen knife. The handle was warm from Sobehk's hand. The smell of blood filled the hall with thick copper heat. She dropped to her knees, skidding into a turn then pushed off the wall for more momentum, and launched herself at the nightmare. She set the dagger in her teeth, biting down on the blade. *Kill . . .*

Tusk's movements seemed incredibly slow. It was almost easy to dodge his blade swings and get behind him.

She leapt up and scaled his long back by stabbing her fingers and toes through cool scaled hide into the warm wetness under it. Funny, she'd always thought his scales were harder than that.

Gripping him with her dug-in toes, she pressed flat against his cold back to avoid his blades. Taking the dagger from her teeth, she jammed the blade with all her strength up into the base of his skull. "Kill *you!*"

The blade went in just above the data jack, and up, sliding past a bony ridge to encounter some resistance within then slid all the way in to the hilt. She twisted the dagger deep in his skull. "Die!" White-hot blood sprayed, covering her chest with thick, slippery heat.

The nightmare collapsed, howling, and she rode it down, holding the dagger and screaming.

Voices shouted.

"Blood and hell!"

"Sobehk!"

"What the fuck happened?"

Her head came up. She could barely see through the wetness on her face. People with long white hair were running toward her with long blades in their hands. She grabbed for the dagger, but it wouldn't come free

"What in fury is that?"

"It's dead . . . whatever it is."

"It looks like she killed it."

She lunged for Sobehk and straddled him. She snarled in warning. If they tried to touch him, she would make them bleed.

The shouting people surrounded her. They all smelled wrong. She didn't know any of them.

"We have to get him to the medlab!"

"Watch out, she's in *rahyt*."

"Who's got the collar codes?"

"I do."

Lightning exploded in her skull. She fell to the deck screaming as sanity and consciousness were savagely torn from her grasp.

CHAPTER EIGHT

Fallon tried to stay asleep, but the nagging pounding in her head wouldn't let her. No, she did not want to wake up; something bad was waiting for her. She twisted, trying to go back to sleep, and discovered that she couldn't move.

Her eyes snapped open and she saw . . . blackness. She blinked. Still nothing but utter and unrelieved darkness. She rotated her wrists and shifted her knees. She was lying on her back naked and spread wide, harnessed into something that was keeping her completely immobile and suspended. A broad strap was all that kept her head from falling back.

She was absolutely helpless.

Terror washed through her followed by hot anger. "Sobehk!" She tugged harder. "Sobehk, what the fuck did you do to me?"

Memory crashed. Her breath stopped and her heart tried to stop with it. The nightmare, Sobehk being stabbed and falling, the blood . . . the killing.

Sobehk . . . A fist of pain and terror crushed her heart. He couldn't be dead! He couldn't leave her like this. He was all she had left. She threw her head back and shouted. "Sobehk, you better not be dead!"

But everybody always left . . . everybody.

Her breath rushed out on a sob then refused to return. She couldn't catch her breath, she couldn't breathe. Panic engulfed her. Her breath returned in a rush only to leave her on a scream. "Sobehk!" Tears burned down her cheeks.

"Don't leave me!"

Somewhere at her feet she heard hurried footsteps. Her heart leaped with hope.

"Isabeau?" The voice wasn't Sobehk's.

Disappointment slammed her back down. She swallowed past the ache in her throat. "Who's there?"

The footsteps moved to her side. His scent was rich and vaguely familiar.

"*Sehnbay'syr* Tah. Are you all right?"

Oh, right, the master surgeon. "Where's Sobehk?" She twisted in the harness and winced against the pain stabbing her skull.

"He's recovering from surgery."

She stilled. "He's alive?"

"Very much so."

"Thank the Maker." Every drop of energy washed out of her body and she collapsed into the harness's embrace.

A cool hand pressed against her face. "How do you feel?"

Like shit. Fallon groaned. "Do you have anything for a headache?"

"Just a moment."

Fallon felt something press against the inside bend of her elbow. There was a slight hydraulic hiss. Her headache faded. She sighed in relief. "Thank you. Can I see him?"

Tah took a deep breath. "Are you hungry?"

Fallon opened her mouth to say 'not really', and her stomach seized up on her. She bucked in the harness, trying to fold in half, and moaned. She was starving. Blood and hell, hunger never hurt this bad! She panted for breath. "Now that you mention it, do you have any deep-fried bovines on you? Preferably a whole one?"

The master surgeon chuckled dryly. "I have *A'syr* Mohr with me. He's brought you some dinner."

Fallon sniffed. Something smelled warm, meaty, and delicious. Her stomach gurgled in demand. She blinked into the darkness. How was she supposed to eat like this? "How come it's so dark in here?"

Tah's fingers brushed her arm. "It is not dark. You're temporarily sightless."

Fallon frowned. "You blinded me? What for?"

The master surgeon's cool hand grasped her fingers. "Blinding is standard procedure for all *rehkyt* in processing."

"Oh . . . When can I see Sobehk?"

Tah removed his hand and clothing rustled. "Tomorrow you will be brought to medical to speak with *A'syr* Sobehk."

Fallon's felt a sudden chill. "Am I in trouble?"

"No, you are not." Tah's voice came from the vicinity of her feet. "You were quite obviously acting on your impression." He sighed. "However, there are . . . complications."

That didn't sound good at all. "What complications?" And what in bloody fury was this damned impression thing they kept mentioning?

"Eat your dinner and be good, Isabeau. Everything will work out just fine." His footsteps receded.

Fallon took a breath to call him back. *What complications, damnit?* She groaned instead. "Why can't somebody just give me a fucking straight answer around here?"

Someone chuckled. "Hungry?" The masculine voice was at her left ear.

Fallon jumped. She didn't recognize the voice. *Oh, that must be A'syr Mohr.* He was the one with the food. She relaxed. "Starved, but . . ." She frowned and tugged at her bound wrists. "How am I supposed to eat like this? I can't even see!"

He chuckled. "I'll set you upright so you don't choke."

Fallon blinked. "Okay." Upright would definitely be an improvement over being flat on her back . . . and defenseless. She waited for him to do something about whatever was binding her wrists so she could sit up.

The rig vibrated, and the whole thing moved until her feet were in the direction of the floor.

"Better?"

"Uh, sure." She sucked on her bottom lip. Oh yeah, what an improvement. She was upright, but still bound hand and foot. Oddly, she didn't feel quite so defenseless.

"I'm putting the food to your lips. Open and swallow."

Something pressed against her mouth. She opened and a cube of something juicy and delicious was pushed in. *Food at last!* She attempted to chew, but her teeth wouldn't let her jaw move side to side. Her fangs overlapped, keeping her jaw locked in one position. She tried again and stabbed her bottom lip.

"Don't try to chew it!" Mohr chuckled. "Swallow it."

Fallon shifted it to the side of her mouth. "Swallow it? Whole?"

"Yes. Your teeth are not designed for chewing."

"Huh . . ." She struggled to chew what she had in her mouth then finally gave up and swallowed it. It lodged in her throat like a rock then something in the very base of her throat seemed to close around it, crushing it smaller. It passed into her stomach with ease. She sighed in relief. "So what *are* my teeth designed for?"

"Biting." Another morsel of food was pressed to her lips. "Open."

Biting? Great . . . She opened and swallowed. Eating swiftly developed into a new kind of torture. She couldn't chew and she couldn't wipe her chin when it dribbled. For some reason, the dribbling annoyed the piss out of her more than the inability to chew.

"You're scowling." A soft cloth swiped across her chin. "Is something wrong?"

Fallon turned her head away from the next bit of food and licked her lips. "Why am I tied up like this? Why can't I see?"

Footsteps moved away then returned. "All the *rehkyt* are blinded and harnessed. It's for their safety."

"I wasn't before."

"But you should have been on your arrival. *Rehkyt* are not supposed to see their captors."

Fallon turned toward his voice. "It was kind of hard to avoid seeing him. He tracked me for three days."

"So I heard." A warm moist cloth landed then slid across her shoulders.

She jumped and her heart thumped in alarm. There wasn't a damned thing she could do to avoid it. She heaved a sigh in defeat.

The cloth skimmed across her breasts. "Most targets don't even know they are being stalked until they're taken. We blind them at capture and set them in harness before we begin processing. You, on the other hand, were dosed by your taker before you arrived."

"Among other things." Fallon shivered with the visceral memory of being taken over the saddle of Sobehk's glider. Illicit heat stirred in her belly. "I understand the rig . . ." She was a prisoner, after all. "Why the blindness?"

"*Rehkyt* are blinded to avoid accidental impression." Mohr's hands drifted up to the metal band of her collar. "They're allowed their sight when they meet their masters for the first time."

Fallon shivered slightly. "What in bleeding fury is 'impression'? I keep hearing it, but I don't get it."

Mohr sighed softly and his fingers lifted from her throat. "Impression is the physical dependency a *rehkyt* has for their master."

Fallon stilled. Physical *dependency?*

His fingers slid down her arm to the straps around her left wrist. "We blind *rehkyt* because they will often imprint on the first person they see when they complete processing. The procedure makes them emotionally unstable and imprint-vulnerable. Compare it to hatchlings that will claim the first thing they see as their parent."

Fallon shook her head. "But I'm not a hatchling, I'm a human!"

"You are *not* human." Mohr snorted. "You are *rehkyt*. A creature designed specifically for carnal pleasure."

Carnal pleasure, my ass ... Fallon set her teeth. She'd heard enough. "Thank you for dinner."

"You're quite welcome. Are you ready to sleep?"

Fallon frowned. "I don't know if I can ..." A huge yawn interrupted her. "On second thought ..."

Mohr chuckled. "Sleep well and sleep deeply, Isabeau."

Fallon smiled sourly. "I'll do my best." Her augmentations buzzed just a tiny bit. *Was that the collar?* She was sucked under before her thought completed.

There were people talking.

Isabeau started awake.

"Oh, sensitive!"

"The chart says feral."

Hands stroked her arms.

She jumped.

"That would explain her reactions."

Hands closed tight around her upper arms.

"Relax; no one's going to hurt you."

They unfastened her and pulled her from the harness. The metal floor was warm under her bare feet. *Hot damn!* Her hands were tugged together at the base of her neck.

"Keep your hands there."

Fallon's augmentations locked them in place. She groaned in disappointment and stretched. She was still utterly blind, but at least she was out of the rig. "Am I going to see Sobehk?"

There was a shared chuckle. "Not just yet."

Abruptly they switched languages.

Fallon sighed. If they didn't want to talk to her . . . well, fine. Her translator had a hard time understanding their language, but the bulk of it came through pretty clearly. It wasn't anything momentous. They were chatting inanely about people and places she didn't know. Thank the Maker she had done some tinkering with her programs or she wouldn't have picked up a word.

Hands caught hold of her upper arms and tugged.

Now what?

They marched her out of the room and down the hall. She was turned to the left and they entered a room that smelled strongly of water and soap. *A facility?* She heard a hissing spray and then hot water spilled across her. She yelped in surprise and jumped under their hands.

"Watch it! Don't let her fall."

"I have her. Get the soap."

Hands and cloths moved over her entire body, cleaning every last finger and toe, and everything in between. It smelled like there were only two of them, and she only heard two voices, but it sure as damnation felt like there were a lot more. And she couldn't move a bleeding inch to avoid them!

Something was smeared in intimate places only to be rinsed away, taking intimate hair with it. Tubes went in to clean areas that had never seen cleaning before, triggering bodily functions of the most embarrassing kind.

One of them chuckled. "I don't think she likes this."

"Think not?" The other snorted. "She's only been growling since the water started."

Fallon stiffened. *Growling?* There *was* a low-grade rumble in her chest. She stopped it, but it took effort.

They stilled.

"Does she have her language downloads?"

"Not according to her chart."

One of them leaned closer to her ear. "Pet, would you like your nipples pierced with pretty little rings?"

My nipples pierced? Fallon jerked back, not that it did any good.

"Well, well . . . Someone has a talented translator."

Fallon winced. *Shit . . .* She shouldn't have moved and given away that she knew what they were saying. But, damn it, it was freaking hard to hold still. It was like something had scoured away every drop of self-control she ever had.

The other one chuckled. "Relax, pet, this is only a bath. Wait till they send you to the groomers."

"Don't scare her! The poor thing is a nervous wreck already."

Fallon scowled. *Poor thing, my ass. Get close enough for me to bite you, and I'll show you a nervous wreck!*

Her attendants continued bathing her with a disgusting amount of humor. She was moved this way and that as they scrubbed, pinched, prodded, and inserted oil-slicked fingers into embarrassing places.

They scrubbed her dry and rubbed some kind of scented cream into her skin, their strong fingers massaging her sore muscles. If it hadn't been so damned humiliating, she might have actually enjoyed it. They buffed her finger and toenails and trimmed her hair. For some odd reason, her hair seemed to be longer than just to her shoulders. From what she could feel, the stuff had grown long enough to reach almost the middle of her back.

When they finally headed out, Fallon was exhausted.

They walked down the hall and through a doorway, and she smelled her own scent, and cleaner. They had cleaned her room while she was gone. She did not want back in the harness, but she wasn't given a choice. *Fucking control collar.*

Someone walked in. It smelled like Mohr.

Fallon rolled her eyes. It was getting to be a serious pain in the ass identifying people by their body odor. Damn it, she wanted her sight back.

"Well now, that is much better." It was Mohr, all right, and he sounded insufferably cheerful.

"Thank you, we do try," one of them said dryly.

"Were you aware that her translator is picking up Skeldhi?"

Fallon ground her teeth. *Tattletale.*

"Really? How interesting." Mohr didn't sound cheerful anymore. "I wonder how much?"

"From what we could tell, quite a bit."

"I see." Mohr sounded positively annoyed.

Fallon felt a completely irrational sense of triumph. She bit down on her lip trying to hold back a sudden smile, and almost pierced herself with her fangs.

Mohr moved to Fallon's side. "Go to sleep, Isabeau. Now."

The command brought a sizzle through her augmentation. He'd used the damned collar. *The shit* . . . Fallon had time to take another breath and sleep sucked her under.

CHAPTER NINE

Fallon awoke stiff and fuzzyheaded for no good reason whatsoever. Her nose barely had time to register that Mohr was in the room with her, when she felt something being unplugged from her data jack. Swiftly and efficiently, he unfastened her from the rig. Groggy and blind, Fallon was shoved onto her feet and her hands pulled to the small of her back.

"Keep them there."

Her arm augmentations jolted slightly, locking her hands in place. *Damn it* . . . She groaned. There was a nagging bruise in the middle of her chest that she couldn't rub because her hands were trapped behind her.

Fallon rolled her shoulders but the ache in her body wouldn't go away. "What in fury did you do to me?"

Mohr's hand closed on her shoulder and he turned her. "Your third nanite dose. One more dose to go and your processing will be complete. Walk."

Fallon walked. "Where are we going?"

"Medlab."

Sobehk . . . Fallon stretched her stride.

Mohr snorted. "Are we in a hurry?"

Fallon frowned. "I'm going to see Sobehk, right?"

His fingers bit into her shoulder. "That's *A'syr* Sobehk to you, *rehkyt*, and yes."

Fallon gritted her teeth. *Bastard.* But he was taking her where she wanted to go.

A sharp turn to the left, a mechanical hiss, and Fallon

smelled antiseptic and blood. They were in the medlab. Sobehk's rich scent washed over her. He was somewhere close by. Her heart clenched then thumped hard.

Mohr tapped her shoulder. "Wait here." His footsteps moved to the right. He took a long, pronounced step.

Fallon frowned. He must have stepped through a doorway. She waited about four heartbeats then turned to the right and followed, sliding her feet across the floor to keep from tripping or knocking into something she couldn't see. Her toes encountered something hard. Lifting her knee and pressing forward told her that she'd either found the wall or a door. She caught a nose full of the medic Tah's scent . . . and someone else's.

For no good reason, every hair on her body shivered upright. *Danger* . . . Alarmed, she rolled to the right, pressing her shoulders back against what she hoped was the wall and not the door.

Voices murmured. Fallon focused on her hearing and waited for her augmentations to take over. The murmurs became distinct speech.

"Did you do any conditioning on that *rehkyt* whatsoever?" Mohr sounded annoyed.

She sucked in a sharp breath. They were talking about her.

"Why, did she bite you?" Sobehk's voice was soft, breathy, amused and cut through her heart like a knife.

Sobehk . . . Fallon blinked moist eyes. He lived.

"She's defiant, disrespectful, and flinches when she's touched!"

Bitch and complain. Fallon rolled her eyes. Mohr was whining like one of her damned instructors from the institution.

"She's feral! What did you expect?" Sobehk released a snarl. "She just needs proper care and thorough reconditioning."

"What she needs is a thorough beating."

Fallon snorted. Mohr was in a pissy mood.

Sobehk laughed. "She is a Prime! Of course she needs a beating!"

Tah chuckled softly. "An experienced *upuaht nehkyx* should have no difficulties."

There was that guard dog word again, but Fallon's translator completely tripped over the following word. Too many holes in her language context archives. She puzzled over it, but the translator refused to accept the word. There was no context for it. It had to be outside her experience.

"Proper care and training? That's all? You're sure?"

Fallon frowned. She didn't recognize that masculine voice at all.

"Damned sure, Khan. I followed her for three days. She's feral but not heartless."

Fallon couldn't stop the curl of warmth that bathed her heart. Sobehk didn't think she was heartless.

"It took three days?" Khan snorted. "Why didn't you leave her?"

Sobehk sighed. "I couldn't." His voice was so soft Fallon barely heard him. "That station was . . . awful. I couldn't leave her there."

There was something in Fallon's eyes. She was forced to wipe them against her shoulder.

"We've had a number of fear-based reactions, but she's shown no signs of overt aggression, merely a strong instinct for survival." Tah's voice seemed calm, but a thread of annoyance was also apparent.

"You're saying that she learned to fight like that for survival?" The disbelief was crystal clear in Khan's voice. "Even in *rahyt,* she displayed a suspicious amount of control. That leads me to believe that she is quite accustomed to dealing violence."

Fallon tilted her head. According to her context translator, that *rahyt* word seemed to be connected to 'rage' and 'insanity.' She had no clue where her internal comp had picked it up, but it was interesting to know.

"Did you look at the file on that rodent-run station? Of course she's used to violence!" Sobehk sounded like he was pissed. "But not once in three days did she attack anyone or anything that didn't attack her first!" A growl rumbled. "She's feral with damned good reason, but she's not a killer by nature."

Fallon felt a smile nudge her lips. He was defending her. *Damn . . .*

Khan sighed. "Even if everything is as you say, an internal inquiry must still be done."

"I'm not arguing with that." Sobehk growled softly. "Just be nice."

"Nice?"

"You heard me."

Fallon's brows shot up. *Nice? This from Sobehk?*

"I'll do my best." Sour amusement colored Khan's voice.

"You'd better."

Fallon heard footsteps approaching. *Shit!* She scooted along the wall away from them and bumped into something that felt like a chair. There was a subtle metallic hiss on her immediate right.

"Isabeau?" It was Mohr.

She turned to face him. "Here."

"You were supposed to stay where I left you."

Fingers dug into her upper arm. She winced as she was tugged and turned around.

"Not particularly obedient, are you?"

Fallon snorted. "Not my style." Never was, probably never would be.

"Now there is an understatement." Mohr sighed and

caught both her upper arms. He grunted, lifted her off the floor and took a long step forward.

Fallon bit back a small sound of alarm.

He set her down and released her arms. "Go on."

She took a small step forward. She could smell Sobehk directly in front of her. Tah's scent seemed to be coming from her right. She heard the softest rustle of fabric on her left. The other person, Khan . . . The hair on her neck rose. *Trap* . . . She froze and barely stopped herself from turning to face the sound. "I need my eyes." She wasn't moving a muscle without sight.

Silence ruled for about three breaths.

"Let her see." Sobehk's voice sounded tired but firm.

There was a subtle shimmer through her augmentations. Fallon shivered. What were they doing now? The deep darkness began to fade from her vision. She blinked in the sudden brightness and realized that she was staring at the foot of a chrome medical bed in a rather small steel gray room. The wall behind the head of the bed blinked with a holographic display covered in incomprehensible streams of data.

Sobehk sat propped upright under a pale gray blanket. His hair was unbound, a sweeping fall of frost that draped off the side of the bed. He was dressed in a cream robe open across the chest. Dark bruises stood out against skin nearly as white as the bandages around his middle. His face seemed hollow and dark smudges lay under his tired blue eyes. "Hey, kitten." He smiled. "You look good."

"I had a bath." Fallon stared, completely unable to look away from Sobehk's pale and bruised form. Blood and damnation . . . he was alive. "You look like shit." She winced. Why in fury had she said that?

Sobehk grinned. "Thank you. I feel like shit, too." He patted the blankets. "Come here."

She started forward, jerking at her hands pinned to her back. She needed them. She needed to touch him. A small distressed sound escaped.

Sobehk held out his hand and glanced to her left.

Fallon's augmentations shimmered and her hands were free. She lunged across the small room to the left side of his bed and grabbed his hand with both of hers. She pressed her nose into his warm palm then stared up at him. He was real, he lived. Her heart tried to shatter in her chest. His image smeared as her eyes overflowed.

"Hey, don't..." His arm curled and he leaned toward her, pressing her head against his chest with his free hand. "Everything's going to be fine."

She closed her eyes and heard the steady thump of his heart under her left ear even as the rich perfume of his skin filled her head. She opened her eyes and her gaze dropped to his bandages. He lived, but...

She jerked back but didn't release his hand. Her lips curled back from her teeth. "You big stupid bastard!"

Sobehk blinked then scowled. "What?"

"Don't you *ever* do that again!" Her fingers dug into his hand. "I told you he was fast! You should have let me handle him!"

Sobehk's lips curled back from his teeth. "You? I'm supposed to..."

"Supposed to what?" She shouted over top of him. "Supposed to get dead? I'm faster than you, you stupid, egotistical idiot! Don't you *ever* do that shit again!" She jerked one hand free and punched the mattress for good measure. "Do you hear me? Don't you *ever* put yourself in danger like that again!"

Sobehk's hand clenched tight around hers, and the dark heart of his blue eyes shifted to feline slits. His mouth opened and he released a coughing roar that rattled the instruments on the back wall. "You listen to me, you little pain in my ass!"

Fallon flinched back, but she refused to look away. She dug her fingers into his hand and the blankets.

"I'm the master—you're the *rehkyt*! I'm the one that's supposed to protect you!" A growl thundered in his chest.

Fallon opened her mouth, but her shout died in her throat. "What for?"

Sobehk blinked and gaped. "What *for*?" He rolled his eyes. "That has got to be the stupidest question ever to come out of that mouth of yours!"

"You and your big fat ego!" Fallon jerked on his hand. "You should have let me take him! I'm faster and better at fighting than you!"

"Better?" Sobehk curled his lip showing a long fang. "I caught you, remember?"

Fallon curled her lip and showed her teeth too. "It took you three days, and I almost made it that last time, too!" She scrubbed her free hand across her watery eyes and glared at him.

Sobehk grinned. "I still got you." He tugged her closer. "Come here."

Fallon sighed and let him pull her against his chest. She pressed her cheek against his heart and curled her fingers into his silver hair. Blood and fury, he smelled good. "I'm still going to kick your ass, as soon as you're well enough."

Sobehk wrapped his other arm around her and dropped a kiss on the top of her head. "We'll just see about that."

Laughter rang out. "What happened to 'nice'?"

Sobehk snorted. "Fuck you, Khan."

Khan's laughter softened to chuckles. "All right, I'm convinced." He sighed. "But I still need to do a map before I can release custody."

Custody? Fallon stilled then turned to look over her

shoulder. Only three strides away, a man sat in a small chair. He was draped from head to toe in the folds of a voluminous hooded robe that began as blood-bright scarlet and darkened to deep black where it reached the deck. Fallon couldn't believe she hadn't even noticed him.

Within the hood of his robe, bright copper eyes gleamed predator green within their feline-slitted hearts. A shimmering black circlet graced his brow. His sharply sculpted pale face was completely devoid of softness, and yet his mouth was surprisingly full and sensual. "Such a direct gaze." He raised a slender brow and looked over at Sobehk. "I'd say that you left off the conditioning altogether."

"There wasn't time." Sobehk sighed and brushed a hand against his bandages. "This happened within minutes of her collaring."

"I see." Khan rose gracefully from the chair, lifted his hands and dropped the scarlet hood, revealing hair the color of rich cream bound severely back into a complicated braided tail. The graceful curve of his ears had the same cuts in the lower arch as Sobehk, but the rings piercing his lobes were as black as the band around his head.

Fallon glanced around but neither master surgeon Tah, nor Mohr were in the small room. They must have left while she was still blind. And the door was missing. *Damned mimetic ship.*

Sobehk's hand squeezed hers. "Isabeau, this is *Mehdjay'syr* E'sey Khan. He's a lord-officer from the office of Security and Intelligence. Address him as *'Syr* Khan, or *'Syr.*"

Fallon swallowed hard. He was an investigations agent. An icy finger slid down her spine and every hair on her body shivered to life. She was in a small room with no door, with a wounded man and an investigations agent.

And she was a criminal that had just killed somebody. *Great . . .*

CHAPTER TEN

Khan stepped toward Fallon. The black hem of his silk robes whispered across the deck. "Hello, Isabeau."

Fallon automatically backed away. *Scary, scary man . . .* She could tell just from his gliding steps that he was augmented to the hilt and combat trained. He could kill her and easily.

Sobehk's hand tightened on hers, holding her at his side. "Isabeau, stay with me."

Fallon turned to see Sobehk's pale face. He didn't look well. She did not need to add to his stress. She took a breath and nodded then looked back at the lord-officer. "*'Syr?*"

Khan folded his hands behind him. "Isabeau, I need to map the contents of your mind."

Fallon sucked in a sharp breath. "You want my *mind?*" He wanted her to turn over her personal data, her private programs, her memories and experiences . . . everything that made her who she was? Was he *insane?* She bit back her initial comment. What he was, was dangerous. Pissing him off was probably not a good idea. "What for?" She cleared her throat. "*'Syr.*"

Khan glanced at Sobehk then focused on Fallon. "Somehow a rather nasty assassin ended up onboard this ship. It killed two men and severely wounded two more . . ." He looked down. "I was sent from the office of Security and Intelligence to find out who sent it and why." He shrugged with elegant precision. "We collected as much data as we could from the . . . assassin, but we couldn't collect much."

Sobehk smiled tiredly. "There was this big hunk of live-steel in the middle of his brain."

Khan's bright copper gaze locked on Fallon. "And the only person who currently knows anything . . ."

Fallon winced. "Is me."

Khan smiled fleetingly. "I'm afraid so."

Fallon took a deep breath. "How much of . . . my mind, do you need?"

Khan lifted his chin and tilted his head toward Sobehk. "All of it."

All of it? Her throat closed tight and her voice came out in a breathless whisper. "I don't know if I can do that, '*Syr*."

Khan took a deep breath and released it. He spoke quietly, gently and completely without remorse. "Isabeau, I'm not asking."

Fallon felt the icy chill of fear then the hot flash of temper surged. "You honestly expect me to let you take my *mind*?"

"Isabeau!" Sobehk's growl was a low rumble. "He's not taking it! He's just looking at it."

Fallon turned to glare at Sobehk. His blue eyes focused on hers. His expression clearly appeared angry, but his face was far too pale and his mouth nearly white. She clutched his hand and finally noticed how cold his fingers were. He wasn't angry, he was afraid. Something more was going on here. Her temper bled away under an icy wave of cold hard terror. "Sobehk, what's going on? What haven't you told me?"

"Quite perceptive." Khan sighed. "Do you want to tell her, or shall I?"

"I'll do it." Sobehk closed his eyes briefly. "Isabeau, you must cooperate with '*Syr* Khan, or you'll be . . . taken."

Fallon's heart tried to stop in her chest. She grabbed the edge of the bed to stay upright. "What?"

Sobehk stared hard at her. "When you took out the assassin, you were declared too dangerous for me to . . . keep. They want to impound you."

Fallon shook her head. "Dangerous? But, what about the collar?"

"He no longer has control over it." Khan very deliberately stepped away.

Fallon frowned. "Then who . . ." Her gaze focused on the red-robed lord-officer, and her blood froze in her veins. *Oh no . . . No, no, no . . .*

Khan turned to face her and a small smile appeared. "Very perceptive indeed."

Fallon turned to Sobehk, her fingers biting into his palm. "How do I get out of this?"

Sobehk sighed tiredly. "Let him in your head. All he wants to do is look."

Fallon closed her eyes and hunched her shoulders. *Blood and Fate . . . Why not ask for my soul while you're at it?* She opened her eyes to stare at Sobehk. He was the only person she knew on this ship and the only person who knew her. Did she really want to lose him? No. No, she didn't. She licked her dry lips. "Will it hurt?"

Khan moved to stand at the end of Sobehk's bed. "It hurts only if you try to keep the probe out. As long as you let it go where it will, you will feel nothing more than a slight tingling."

Fallon flinched. "Great." She took a deep breath, trying to control the pulse beating in her throat. "Can you make it quick?"

"I'll make it as quick as I can." Khan strode for the small table on the far side of Sobehk's bed. He opened up a small computational. The holographic projection behind Sobehk's bed shivered then changed.

She stared up at Sobehk. "How in fury did everything get so . . . complicated?"

Sobehk's brows rose then he smiled. "It got complicated when you saved my life."

Fallon snorted. "So it would have been a lot simpler if I'd let Tusk kill you?"

Sobehk nodded gravely. "I'd be dead, and you'd be in a holding cage on your way to the *Mehdjay* headquarters for Security and Intelligence where they would assign you to a trainer to see if you could be reconditioned and imprinted on someone else."

Fallon frowned, her fingers closing tight around his. "And if I couldn't be . . . reconditioned to like somebody else?"

Sobehk looked toward the lord-officer on the other side of the bed. "They destroy *rehkyt* that can't be recovered."

"Terrific." Fallon groaned. "You know, if you had left me on Dyson's, we wouldn't be going through all this."

Sobehk's brows rose. "So, this is my fault?"

Fallon snorted. "Damned straight it's your fault."

"If you hadn't taken my glider . . ." Sobehk smiled tiredly.

Fallon rolled her eyes. "You got it back the next day!"

Sobehk groaned. "I really need to beat that ass of yours."

"Probably." Fallon smiled just a little.

"Speaking of your ass . . ." Sobehk patted the blankets. "Get it up here on the bed."

Fallon jerked back. "Are you out of your mind? You're hurt!"

Sobehk glared at her. "Did I, or did I not, just give you an order?"

Fallon released a small sound. She desperately wanted to climb up there with him, but he was not in any kind of condition to deal with jostling. "Sobehk, I don't want to hurt you."

"Then be careful."

"Are you sure?"

His brows lowered. "Get up here. Now."

Fallon scowled as she moved to the foot of the bed. "What did I ever do to deserve a big bully like you?"

"You stole a glider," Sobehk said dryly.

Fallon climbed up at the very foot of the bed and faced him on her hands and knees. "I thought it was a kiss in a bar?"

Sobehk smiled. "That, too." He shifted toward his right with a wince and patted the side of the bed with his left hand. "Come here."

Fallon crawled to his side. His arm settled warm and comforting around her. She sighed and carefully set her head on his shoulder, snuggling into his embrace. His leg shifted under the blankets against hers. She lifted her knee and set it over his, pressing against his side. She set her palm over his heart. She felt his pulse steady and strong under her palm and stared up at him. "Don't let me hurt you."

His hand pressed atop hers and he smiled. "Your assassin couldn't get me. Think you can do any better?"

Khan came to the side of the bed in a whisper of heavy silk. "I'm going to set the probe in your data jack then I want you to turn over and face away from Sobehk."

Sobehk scowled. "Why?"

"Because you are wounded, and if my suspicions are correct . . ." He glanced down at Fallon and sighed. "She's going to need you to hold her, more than she needs to hold onto you."

Fallon swallowed. So, it *was* going to hurt. *Great.*

Sobehk set his jaw. "I can take it."

Fallon stared up at his tired and bruised face. No, he couldn't. She took a breath and smiled, though it hurt. "You and that big fat ego of yours." She looked over her shoulder. "Do it. I'll turn over."

Khan stared down at her, his brow rose and a slight smile curved his lips. He nodded. "I'll set the probe."

Fallon turned away. Fingers moved the hair from the back of her neck. Her hands closed into fists.

Khan pressed his device into the portal in the back of her skull. "It's in."

Fallon twisted her wrist from Sobehk's grasp and wordlessly shifted onto her back, and then her side, facing away. She dug her fingers into the blankets and mattress and focused on Khan.

Sobehk spooned against her back, his arms closing around her. His lips brushed the back of her neck. "I have you."

Khan held a small device in his hand. "Are you ready?"

She nodded, her mouth dry.

"Then we begin." Khan activated the device in his palm. "Relax and try not to fight it." He turned and faced the holographic projection at the head of the bed. "Take nice, deep, steady breaths. Don't try to think, just let it go."

A shimmer went through her augmentations, then something oily began seeping across her thoughts. Fallon closed her eyes.

"I understand how difficult this is. I've had to go through one of these too." Khan's voice was calm, soft and almost gentle.

Fallon frowned. The fact that he'd gone through the process of having his mind . . . probed, made him seem less threatening, though not by much. But why had he told her that? He hadn't had to.

There was a slight bump and what felt like a puzzlement in her mind. It was a request for entry.

Fallon released her personal firewalls and opened as wide as she could. The pressure eased.

Khan sighed deeply. "Good."

Breathe in, breathe out . . . Another bump in someplace unexpected. Fallon frowned, but there was nothing there to open. The bump persisted then abruptly shifted and moved elsewhere. Tension whispered through her body. Another bump . . . and shift. Tension tightened and pressure built. Heat flushed through her body and a cold sweat drenched her skin.

Sobehk's hand swept down her hip. "She's heating up but sweating cold." He sounded annoyed. "What are you doing in there?"

Khan turned to look at them with a frown. "Sweating *cold?*"

Fallon panted for breath under a wave of heat and opened her eyes. Sweat gathered and dripped. Pressure built in her mind and in her joints. She released a small sound of distress.

Sobehk hissed. "She's sweating ice cold, but her temperature is rising fast."

Khan stood over her his eyes hard. "How many doses does she have in her?"

Sobehk shifted against her. "Two."

Fallon tightened her fingers in the blankets. "They said three."

Both of them took a startled breath. "Three?" they chorused.

Sobehk's fingers bit into her hip. "Are you sure?"

Khan gripped the chrome rail on the side of the bed and shook his head. "Never mind that . . . How many times has she been ridden?"

Sobehk leaned up. "Isabeau, has anyone . . . fucked you?"

Fallon groaned under the ache building in her joints. "Just you."

Khan frowned. "How many times?"

"Once, right after the first dose."

"Once?" Khan bared his long teeth. "One of you had better be wrong." He strode for the wall and punched a button. "*Sehnbay'syr* Tah, how many doses are in this *rehkyt*?"

"Three." Tah's voice fizzled with electronic interference. "Is there a problem?"

Khan's hand curled into a tight fist and he stared at the floor. "Was she mounted after her last two doses?"

"No, I assumed *A'syr* Sobehk mounted her after her second . . ."

Khan looked over at Sobehk, his brows low over copper eyes that burned.

Sobehk's nails cut into Fallon's hip. "There wasn't time!"

Khan's mouth tightened to a white line. "Apparently not."

Another bump moved in Fallon's mind. This time the shift became another bump . . . and then another. Pressure intensified. She dug her fingers into the mattress hard enough for her nails to pierce it. The sound of ripping fabric was loud.

Khan stared up at the holographic display, bared his teeth and a growl rumbled. "This has been one farce after the other!" He punched the wall. "Get a mattress in here and bring me the fourth dose, now!" He moved away from the wall and pulled at the fastenings on his robe, opening it. He let the cream robe drop from his shoulders, revealing a long black robe bound with a scarlet sash.

Sobehk stiffened. "What are you doing?"

Khan tossed the heavy outer robe over a chair by the wall at the head of the bed. "I'm going to dose and mount your *rehkyt*."

"Khan, no!"

"No?" Khan turned to face him with his teeth bared.

"Then you'd rather she die?"

Sobehk jolted. "Die?"

"Yes, die." Khan drew several daggers from the folds of his scarlet sash. "Let me put this in clear detail for you. You have in your arms a newly primed *rehkyt*." He turned and tossed the daggers onto his robe. "A Prime *rehkyt* that has yet to be mounted after her second dose or after the kill that made her Prime, and yet was given the third course." He tugged his sash free. "A Prime *rehkyt* that is currently undergoing a mapping of her mind with boring probes." He pointed to the holographic display at the head of the bed. "According to that, she is riddled with sleeper codes that lead to one rather nasty trapdoor program."

Fallon's heart stuttered in her chest. A trapdoor program? *How in fury . . .*

Khan jerked the black robe from his shoulders, baring a pale chest marked with jagged sword scars. Small black rings pierced his pale nipples. "When those probes run out of places they can map, they are going to converge on that trapdoor." He threw the robe at the chair, leaving only his long black kilt. "Make no mistake — they *will* get in. And when they do, the pain will drive her straight into *rahyt*! Is that clear enough for you?"

Fallon shivered. *Rahyt* was madness, insanity and killing rage.

"*Rahyt*? Are you sure?"

"She has three doses and only been mounted once. What do you *think* will happen?" Khan sat on his robes and jerked at his boots. "If she isn't dosed and mounted, the *rahyt* will trigger regeneration fever. She will bleed to death from every pore in her body, *after* she tries to kill us once the rage hits."

"Bloody Chaos . . ."

"An apt description." Khan scrubbed his fingers

through his hair. "The only other option is killing her before she goes into regeneration fever."

Fallon scanned for the program and winced as her thoughts burned but found nothing. "I can't find it . . . I don't see it!"

"You're not going to. It's a trapdoor—a sleeper virus. You won't see it until it's active." Khan pointed to the wall. "According to what I'm seeing, you've been hacked." He waved his hand at the holographic display. "It's sloppily done and recent."

Sobehk shifted behind her. "Khan, she doesn't deserve to die!"

"No, she doesn't." Khan set his hands on his hips. "She's keeping her promise to cooperate, but every part of her that's still hers has already been mapped. It's tracking the sleeper traces, but it's running out of traces to find. We are running out of time." He turned to face Fallon. "*She* is running out of time."

CHAPTER ELEVEN

K han jabbed a finger at Sobehk. "Only you would have something like this!" He turned away, set his hands on his hips, and sighed. "I swear Fate and Chaos share a bed whenever you're involved!" He strode for the communicator on the wall and punched it. "*'Syr* Tah! Where's that mattress?"

"On its way."

Sobehk sat up in the hospital bed. "I'll do it . . ."

Khan curled his lip at Sobehk. "You barely have enough strength to sit up on your own. Do you honestly think you're strong enough to stop her when she goes to rip your heart out during *rahyt*?"

Fallon jerked. "No!" She moaned under the pressure building in her body and mind but turned to look back at Sobehk. "No, I would never . . ."

Sobehk pressed his hand over her heart. "*Rahyt* is not something you can control."

Fallon bared her teeth. "Watch me."

Sobehk's hand closed on her arm. "You can't. No *rehkyt* can; that's why you wear a control collar."

Fallon glared at him. "Then use it."

Khan shook his head. "We can't. The collar's signal will stop the probe and we'll only have to do it again. And you will still go into rage."

Fallon turned to glare at Khan. "Then wait until he can handle it."

"No." Khan's gaze hardened. "Other lives may be at

100

stake. We need answers now."

The door opened. Tah and someone Fallon didn't recognize in dark gray sleeveless robes carried a mattress roll between them. They dropped it on the floor. Tah held what looked like an antique syringe while the other Skeldhi unrolled the mattress and set a pale gray blanket to one side.

Khan strode to the side of Sobehk's bed. "Sobehk?"

Sobehk pulled his arms free. "Take her."

Fallon turned to look at Sobehk. "Sobehk, I don't want . . . anyone but you."

Sobehk's face was pale and drawn, but he smiled. "It'll be all right. You can trust him." He leaned over to brush his lips across her brow. "Go to him and be good."

Khan slid his arms around Fallon and lifted her against his heart.

Fallon flinched back. He smelled . . . wrong. She shifted uncomfortably, but his arms were hard and his hold firm

Tah looked at Sobehk then Khan. "Sobehk, if you let '*Syr* Khan take her on the fourth dose, it will change the DNA imprint from yours to his."

Sobehk folded his arms across his chest. "I know." He turned away.

Khan turned with Fallon in his arms, took four steps to the mattress spread out on the deck then knelt, setting her down on the mattress. He pulled up the skirts of his kilt and stepped over her, straddling Fallon's hips. He sank down on his heels. The black silk draped over her thighs. He held up his hand.

Tah slapped the syringe into his palm. His mouth was tight.

Khan checked the syringe then focused on her gaze. "Put your hands over your head."

Fallon hesitated. She didn't want to do this with him.

Tah frowned. "Did you tell her what this means?"

Khan scowled. "No."

The medic moved to stare down at the lord-officer. "*'Syr* Khan, she needs to know."

Khan's jaw tightened and his gaze chilled as he stared up at the medic.

Tah set his jaw as well. "This is a *rehkyt* that killed to save her master with only two doses in her before she hit Prime. That cyborg killed two fully armed Skeldhi and severely wounded two more and she took it down with only a knife." He folded his arms. "If you force this, how do you think she's going to react after the fact?"

Khan turned away and closed his eyes. "Fine. Bring me one of my knives. They're on my robe, over on the chair."

Tah nodded and went.

Khan turned back to stare at Fallon with burning copper eyes.

Fallon stared up at him, panting through the heat that rolled through her body while shivering from the cold sweat that drenched her. She could feel her body soaking the mattress under her back. She could also feel pressure building in a corner of her mind that nothing should be in.

Khan held up his hand for the curved, black-handled knife in Tah's hand. He bared his teeth at the medic and the other Skeldhi. "Out! Now!"

Tah nodded and they left, the door spiraling closed behind them.

'Syr Khan licked his lips and focused on Fallon. "Isabeau, what is happening to you will kill you. If I dose you and mount you, you will live, but my DNA will overpower Sobehk's. You will bear my mark on your body, not his. Do you understand what this means?"

Fallon's mouth fell open. "Are you saying that I won't be Sobehk's anymore?"

Khan glanced down, then focused on her. "That's

exactly what I'm saying. Physically and legally, you will be my *rehkyt*."

Fallon shivered hard and shook her head. "I don't want you. I want Sobehk."

Khan held her gaze. "He's not physically strong enough to mount you and control you during *rahyt*. That's what I have to do to save your life. The only other option is to kill you, now, before you fall into rage madness and kill us both."

Fallon shook her head and dug her fingers into the mattress. It was an impossible choice. Live and lose Sobehk or . . . die.

"Isabeau." Sobehk's voice was hoarse. "Khan is a good man. He'll be a good master. You can trust him to look after you, I swear it."

Khan looked up at Sobehk, his eyes wide then turned away and swallowed.

Fallon could barely draw breath past the ache in her heart. "But I don't know if I want to live without you."

'Syr Khan pressed his hand over his eyes. "Isabeau, I know you don't want me, and I'm not a particularly kind man, but . . ." He took a deep breath and opened his eyes. "I swear I will do my utmost to be a good master to you."

Fallon closed her eyes and turned her head, but the tears fell anyway. Fate and blood, it already hurt so much, maybe death would be easier. At the very least all the pain would stop.

'Syr Khan sighed and set his hands on his hips. His left hand held the syringe and his right the dagger. "If you want to live, put your hands over your head so I can dose you. If you'd rather die, put your hands under your back so I can . . . cut your throat."

"Isabeau, you stubborn little pain in my ass!" Sobehk's voice was tight. "Don't you dare give up and die on me!"

Give up? Fallon felt shock rock through her. Was that what she was planning? To just give up? She took a deep breath and scrubbed a hand across her wet cheeks. "I don't give up. I never have, I never will." She raised her hands over her head and clenched her teeth, glaring at the Skeldhi sitting on top of her. "Do it."

Khan arched his brow. "You're quite sure?"

Fallon loosed a growl. "Do you want me or don't you?"

Sobehk choked out a laugh. "This is your last chance to escape, Khan."

Khan smiled, displaying his long teeth. "Oh, I want you." He set the knife down at his side and caught her jaw, tilting her head back. He raised the syringe in his right hand.

Fallon had only a moment to realize that her hands were not locked into place by her augmentations then something long and sharp stabbed into her chest. She sucked in a breath but held still. Her heart stuttered painfully. The needle was withdrawn and her heart began to beat twice as hard. A fist of light seemed to close around her heart then expanded and exploded in a blaze of lightning that rushed through her. Her spine arched. Her nipples tightened and her core clenched with sudden urgency.

Khan rose to his feet and his hands went to the ties of his kilt. His eyes had expanded from feline slits to wide pits of darkness surrounded by bright copper. The kilt dropped to his feet, and he stepped out of it. His cocks were only half aroused and oddly shaped. Pronounced bumps marched from the flared edge of his cockhead to the root in a line along the top and the base of both cocks.

Fallon raised her brows. His cocks were not only ridged with small metal balls that had been invested under the skin, his cockheads were both pierced. Black metal balls the size of the tip of her pinky finger sat on the top and the bottom of both cockheads, marking a bar that had been thrust through them. "Kinky bastard, are you?"

"You have no idea." Sobehk snorted behind them. "Khan is a big-time pain junky."

Khan raised his chin and set his hands on his hips as he looked over at Sobehk. "You would know."

Fallon's breath stopped in shock. Sobehk . . . and *Khan*?

Khan dropped to a crouch and focused on Fallon. "I happen to enjoy both taking and delivering pain."

Fallon eyed his cocks. Oh yeah, he liked delivering pain alright.

He licked his lips. "Come up on your heels and spread for me."

Fallon lifted her knees, digging her heels into the mattress, and opened.

Khan nodded and reached for his fallen kilt. He pulled a small tube from a pocket and squeezed a dollop of clear gel onto his hand. He grasped his lower cock and smeared gel along its length.

Fallon swallowed. That ridged and pierced cock in his hand was getting shoved into her ass. All those bumps and that big hunk of metal at the end were going to be sawing in and out of her. And Sobehk had been a snug fit. *Shit, shit, shit* . . .

Khan's brow rose. "I am suddenly under the impression that you are not exactly looking forward to being fucked." His full mouth spread in a smile that was decadently sinful.

A bolt of lightning struck within her mind' and burned. She sucked in a breath and writhed. A hammer of heat slammed through her and she arched up from the mattress. A second bolt struck. She screamed.

Sobehk lunged up. "What the fuck . . ."

"The probes." Khan dropped on top of her to hold her bucking body down and wrapped her in his arms. "They've begun to work their way into her trapdoor."

Gasping and whimpering, Fallon wrapped her arms and legs around him. It burned! Oh, bloody Fate . . . her mind *burned*! She dug her fingers into him, and her claws cut into his back.

Khan hissed. "Oh yes . . ." He pressed her mouth to his shoulder. "Bite me, Isabeau. Bite hard."

Fallon opened her mouth wide, baring her teeth. Lightning struck again and she tore into his shoulder with her long teeth, biting down to keep the screams at bay.

Khan groaned and shuddered. "Chaos . . . Her venom is potent!" He opened his mouth and closed his long teeth on her shoulder. He bit down with merciless strength.

Fallon groaned as the pain in her body overwhelmed and eased the burning in her mind.

Khan moaned and released her shoulder. "Yes, that's it, pay attention to your body." He licked the jagged wounds he'd made in the meat of her shoulder.

Fallon released his shoulder and licked at the blood seeping from the tears she'd made. Urgent carnal warmth curled through her. She pressed up against him. His cocks were hot, hard, and exciting lengths against her belly. She had a moment to savor the feel of his arousal and then he reared back.

Khan stared into her eyes as he fit his upper cock to the slippery mouth of her body. He thrust and the bar in his cock head became a brutally hard pressure just within her.

Fallon gasped softly and arched upward only to feel his second cockhead pressing for entry into her ass.

He came down on one elbow over her. "This one is going to hurt."

Fallon swallowed. "I know."

He smiled briefly and pushed.

She moaned as her anus began to spread, catching on the unforgiving metal bar lodged through it.

He groaned and pressed, hard. "Take me."

Fallon took a deep breath and pushed outward. Her body opened and the bar surged within. She groaned as the ridges along the top and bottom of his cock followed, scouring viciously past her abused anus and then within the interior of her ass.

He grunted and shoved, sheathing both cocks within her.

She whimpered as her body closed tight around him. She could clearly feel both metal bars within her and writhed.

Khan held perfectly still and brushed the hair from her brow. "Are you all right?"

Fallon took a panting breath. "Yeah . . ."

"You're very tight." He smiled briefly. "Might I assume Sobehk has been the only one in your ass?"

Fallon felt heat flood her cheeks. "You might."

His brows rose. "Oh?" An unholy smile wreathed his lips. "Then my pierced cock is probably going to be quite an experience."

Fallon scowled at him, but a smile danced at the corner of her mouth. "Looking forward to it?"

"I think you are looking forward to it as much as I." Khan leaned over to look up at the display above Sobehk's bed. His smile faltered. "Isabeau, it's coming." He focused on her face and closed her tight in his arms. "When the pain comes, don't try to hold it back, and don't think, just let it wash through you."

Fallon shivered. "How bad is it going to be?"

"Very." He flashed a brief smile. "But we'll get through this, I promise." He focused on her mouth. "Isabeau . . ." His hot mouth covered hers and his tongue swept in to lay claim to hers. His clawed fingers dug into her ass.

She arched up moaning — and lightning exploded at the

back of her head, leaving a trail of fire. She closed her eyes and howled into his mouth, raking her claws down his back.

He pulled back and thrust his ridged cocks into her with horrific strength.

The ferocity of his stroke jarred her from what was going on in her mind, but the sensation was fleeting, and the fire in the back of her skull still burned. She arched up, writhing to feel more of his ruthless cocks, desperate to drive her searing thoughts away.

He grunted and drove into her.

She arched up to meet his thrust and snarled for more.

He groaned and his claws dug into her, cutting her skin as he thrust again, and then again.

She twisted under him. More, she needed more . . . Her mouth closed on his other shoulder, biting down.

He shouted and shuddered then grabbed the back of her hair and pulled her away, arching her throat back. His mouth brushed her throat and then his teeth closed on her. The canines sank in.

She arched her entire body and howled, grinding up into his ruthless and brutal thrusts. He released her head and she twisted sharply, rolling him onto his back.

He stared up at her in surprise then grinned as she proceeded to slam down onto his cocks. Her head dropped. Her teeth scored his breast and her tongue lashed across the rings that pierced his nipples.

He gasped but pressed her head against his breast.

She bit down.

He shouted, and pulled her head back then leaned up to take her nipple into his mouth. He sucked it into his mouth then opened wide and bit down on her breast.

She screamed and raked his chest with her claws.

The smell of blood and arousal mixed in a potent

perfume.

The fire in the back of her skull was suddenly eclipsed by a red heat that burned up her spine. She released a scream that raised the hairs on her entire body. The perfume of arousal changed to the rank scent of violence — and fear.

"Isabeau?" He rolled her under him and grabbed for her wrists. His eyes were fire bright with passion, but his mouth was hard. "Isabeau, stay with me!" He thrust hard into her body and struggled to hold her. "Stay with me, pet!"

CHAPTER TWELVE

She snarled up at the male holding her and writhed to escape his hands as the fire in her mind triggered a rage that hungered to tear the heart from his breast and drink the blood that raced under his skin.

A shadow fell over them. "Isabeau?"

She snarled at the second male then screamed with the lightning stabbing through her mind.

Yelling, shouting, struggling . . . The scent of freshly spilled blood and sex.

"Isabeau, please . . ."

She knew that voice. A warm, familiar scent curled around her. Need, want . . . *heartache* . . .

Fallon blinked up at Sobehk down on one knee at their side. She leaned toward him, searching for his scent. "Sobehk?"

Sobehk sighed and pressed his palm to her cheek. "I'm right here."

"Don't . . . go away." She turned her face into his hand. Tears streaked down her cheeks. "Don't . . . don't leave me."

Khan snarled. "Sit down before you fall down, Sobehk; in fact, why don't you go get your mattress and lay down here with us?"

Sobehk frowned. "Are you sure?"

Khan rolled his eyes. "You just pulled her out of *rahyt*. What do you think?"

Fallon whimpered and writhed as the fire in her mind

surged. "It hurts . . ."

Khan focused on Sobehk. "She is not talking about my dicks."

Sobehk groaned as he rose to his feet. "I'll get the mattress."

"Ignore it, pet." Khan began ruthlessly thrusting. "Pay attention to your body."

Fallon closed her eyes and arched up in an effort to erase what was happening in her head. Sobehk's rich perfume covered her and she opened her eyes to see him stretching out on a mattress alongside theirs.

Khan released Fallon's wrists and groaned. "You may as well be useful. Push up your sleeve and give me your wrist."

Sobehk's brows rose, but he shoved up his sleeve and leaned close, presenting his wrist.

Khan lunged at him, lightning-fast, and sank his fangs deep into Sobehk's forearm.

Sobehk shouted in shock. "Khan!"

Khan pulled back and licked his lips. "Lick the wounds. I need you hard."

Sobehk hissed in obvious pain. "What are you thinking?"

Khan smiled sourly as he ground into Fallon's body. "I'm thinking that there's a *rehkyt* that needs to drink a load of cum. Get busy."

Sobehk's eyes opened wide. "Are you serious?"

Khan bared his teeth. "Did I, or did I not, just bite you?"

Sobehk licked the wounds on his arm and yanked at the ties of his robe with his free hand.

Fallon writhed, caught between the agony in her mind and the cocks grinding harshly in her body. The base of his cocks began to swell into a ball of rock-hard flesh sliding in then out, passing deliciously against her clit. Liquid heat

111

flared in her core and began to build. She gasped in surprise then moaned under the rising wave of bittersweet and agonizing pleasure.

Khan grinned down at her and thrust in earnest. "You better hurry, Sobehk. She's rising."

Sobehk rolled his eyes as he tore the robe from his shoulders. "I would find one that likes pain as much as you do." He dropped onto his back, grabbed his cocks, and stroked them, groaning. "How did I get so lucky?"

Fallon leaned up and nipped at Khan's nipples.

Khan hissed as her teeth raked him. "I have no complaints." He grunted with his thrusts. "Are you hard yet? I'm just about to knot."

Sobehk sighed. "Yes. Your venom is fucking potent!" He sat up on his knees, framing Fallon's head.

"You think I'm bad?" Khan snorted. "Wait till *she* bites you." He caught Fallon's chin. "I need you to suck cock, pet."

Fallon tilted her head back to see Sobehk's rigid cocks only a breath away from her mouth. The scent of his arousal washed over her in an irresistible wave. She opened her mouth and stroked the underside of the swollen head of his larger primary cock with her tongue then opened wide to suck him in.

Sobehk hissed. "Shit!" He dropped, his hands framing her chest, arching over her body, and spread his knees to get lower.

Fallon tilted her head back to get more of him and lashed him with her tongue. He became even more rigid against her tongue. She moaned and suckled.

Sobehk groaned and thrust into her mouth. "Damn . . ."

Khan pushed up onto his hands, his thrusts slower, but hammer-stroke hard. "That good?"

Fallon moaned and sucked hard as Sobehk thrust into

her mouth even as Khan ground his torturous cocks into her body.

Sobehk moaned and panted. "That enthusiastic and I'm just as hard up as she is."

Hard up? Fallon growled and let him slide against her teeth.

He flinched. "Watch it with the teeth!"

Khan chuckled. "Can you cum first?"

Sobehk groaned. "Not going to be a problem, just about there." He sucked in a breath. "In fact . . . there." He groaned and shuddered. "Swallow it, kitten, drink me down."

Fallon felt him pulse on her tongue. Salty, musky cream filled her mouth, even as his second cock pulsed against her neck, spattering hot cum across her breasts. She swallowed, but there was so much of it, it dribbled past her lips.

Khan snorted. "She's missing some."

"Got it." Sobehk caught her jaw, tilting her head back and thrust his entire length down her throat. He gasped.

She couldn't breathe past the long cock jammed down into her throat. She whimpered and reached up to push him back.

Khan caught her hands. "No, swallow, pet."

Fallon struggled against his hold while cum pumped and pumped straight down her throat.

Sobehk moaned. "Mother Night, yes . . ." He sighed and pulled from her throat.

Fallon coughed and sucked air.

Sobehk fell on the mattress beside them and rolled onto his back, smiling. "Mmm, I needed that."

Fallon struggled to swallow what was left in her mouth and scowled at Sobehk's grinning face. "Dirty . . . trick."

"Is that so?" Khan dropped over her and thrust brutally hard. "My turn."

Fallon gasped as the metal at the end of his cock bumped something inside, something exciting and deliciously urgent. He struck it again, and then again . . . She groaned and shivered, arching up to meet him.

Sobehk rolled up on his side, set his chin on his hand and grinned. "I love watching you fuck."

Khan flashed him a smile then groaned while twisting his hips hard.

Fallon felt something swollen pass into both her ass and cunt, filling them brutally tight. She gasped.

Khan released a harsh breath. "I'm tied." He ground into her and moaned. "Mother, she's tight . . ."

Fallon felt something spark and shuddered as pleasure rose hot and fast. She writhed to reach it.

Khan smiled down at her. "Ready to fall, pet?"

Fallon panted and a small sound escaped her lips. She ground up against him. He was pressed right up against that delicious spot, but something was missing. "Please?"

Sobehk raised his brow. "Oh, begging? I like begging."

Fallon bucked up hard but got no closer. A whimper escaped. "Please . . . I need . . . I want . . ." She writhed and bared her teeth. "Bite me!"

Sobehk looked at Khan.

Khan smiled at Sobehk. "Bite her."

Sobehk's brows shot up. "Doesn't she have enough venom in her by now?"

Khan shook his head. "She doesn't need the venom, she needs the bite. She needs the pain."

Sobehk rolled his eyes. "Pain junkies . . ." He leaned over Fallon. "Where do you want my teeth, kitten?"

"Her breast, around the nipple." Khan grinned. "I took the other. Make them match."

Sobehk's brows rose as he stared at Khan.

Fallon squirmed as climax coiled in a boiling morass of

threatening intent. She was right on the damned edge and they were talking! "I don't care where, just bite me, damn it!"

Sobehk's mouth dropped over her nipple. His mouth opened wide and he sucked hard, his long teeth pressing into her skin.

"Maker, yes!" She grabbed Sobehk's hair to hold him and moaned as his sucking mouth burned a trail of delight from her nipple straight down to her clit. Her gaze locked on Khan's blood-orange eyes.

Khan held her gaze and ground his metal-laden cocks into her. "Now."

Raked by the delight within her body, Fallon arched up on a wail. Sobehk's teeth sank into her breast, delivering sharp slices of pain that pushed her over the edge into an exploding spiral of mind-shocking pleasure. She stared into Khan's eyes and shrieked.

Khan choked, his eyes went wide and he shook. "Bloody Chaos."

Fallon moaned; every part of her hurt. But the burning in her mind was gone. *Hot damn.* She opened her eyes and stared blearily at the steel gray ceiling overhead. Khan's warm but heavy steel and titanium weighted body was stretched out full length on top of her and nestled between her thighs. His breath feathered the left side of her throat.

Someone had pulled the pale gray blanket over them. It was actually fairly cozy, if it weren't for the fact that she was cuddled up with one of the scariest men she'd ever met.

And he owned her.

Her mind immediately shied away from that line of thought. She pushed at his shoulder. "Are we done?"

Khan opened one copper eye and tightened his arms at

her sides. He snorted against her throat. "We're tied." He moved his hips and the swollen base of his cocks tugged at the more than tender flesh he filled to capacity. He moaned in obvious enjoyment. "Tight."

She hissed and grabbed his bare butt to stop his movements. "I meant with whatever you were doing in my head."

Khan growled. "Be still."

Fallon froze then scowled. "I'm not the one that's moving!"

"No, you're the one that's talking. Be still." He opened his mouth and pressed his teeth against her throat in clear warning.

Fallon's breath stopped. Apparently, that pleased him. His wet tongue stroked where his teeth had been. She relaxed and fumed. *Just what I need, another bully.* She turned to look over at Sobehk . . . but he wasn't there. The mattress he'd been on was missing too. She tilted her head back to see if he'd gone back to his bed. The hospital bed was missing. The hair rose on her body. She was alone with Khan.

Khan's hand slid down the standing hairs on her arm. "What?" His tone was clearly annoyed.

Fallon flinched and promptly became annoyed with herself. "Sobehk . . ."

"Has been moved to my ship. We'll join him later." He nuzzled against her throat and ground his still-hard cocks into her. "Go to sleep."

Fallon winced and shifted under him. Great Maker, he was tight in her. *Sleep?* She rolled her eyes. *Right, sure, like that's going to happen like this?*

He growled.

She stilled then expelled her breath and tried to relax. His heart beat against hers in a slow, even rhythm. She found herself listening to it. Oddly, she found herself matching his slow breaths. Odder still, her eyes became heavy and she slid into sleep.

Fallon felt the weight on top of her move and opened her eyes to find Khan up on his elbows staring down at her. A slight smile curved his lips.

She blinked up at him in sleepy confusion. *What?*

He hooded his eyes and lowered his head slowly. His lips touched hers.

She opened her mouth to him, and his tongue brushed against her lower lip. The touch was surprisingly gentle. She touched his tongue with the tip of hers and he stroked lightly but more boldly against her. He tasted of warm male and slightly of copper. He tasted . . . familiar.

His head turned slightly, and he joined his mouth more fully to hers, his kiss slow and exploratory. She answered his kiss without thought. It just seemed . . . the right thing to do.

A sound vibrated in his chest. It was the strangest sound she'd ever heard. It wasn't a growl; it was more comforting in its rumbling, like a gigantic feline purr. The idea of Khan purring made a smile curve her lips.

He pulled back, releasing her mouth. Amusement softened the harsh lines of his face. "What?"

"You're purring?" Fallon couldn't help but smile more fully.

He snorted but smiled. "I do that when I'm pleased."

"Oh . . ." He was pleased. She'd pleased him. Something warm and alarming shifted in her heart. She flinched back from that warmth and her smile fled.

His brows shot up. "You don't want to please me?"

Fallon opened her mouth and then closed it. She did. She did want to please him. She looked away in confusion. This needful feeling was completely different from the protective urge she felt for Sobehk. It was more like she wanted

his protection, as though she wanted comfort from *him* —
Khan. She needed the comfort of knowing that Sobehk was
safe, but the thought of wanting Khan to be comforting . . .
The idea was alien and alarming. Her heart pounded in
fright and she jerked under him. She needed to get out
from under him. She needed to get out . . .

"Isabeau." His arm closed tight around her and his finger nudged her chin toward him, encouraging her to look
at him.

She turned to face him but closed her eyes. She didn't
want to see what was in his gaze. She didn't want him to
see what was in hers.

"Isabeau, look at me." His voice was soft but very firm.

She opened her eyes and braced herself.

There was a slight smile on his lips and warmth in his
odd copper gaze. He was very pleased about something.
"Your feelings have changed, have they not?"

Huh? Fallon grit her teeth. "No."

He snorted, rolled his eyes then his smile widened. "Toward me." His thumb brushed her bottom lip. "You feel
differently toward me."

Fallon opened her mouth to deny it but closed her
mouth instead. She didn't believe in lying.

He raised his brows. "Yes?"

She licked her bottom lip where his thumb had been and
desperately wanted to agree, just to please him. This need
for his approval was the most frightening thing she'd ever
felt. It honestly felt as if she would die without it. Her
breath stuttered in her throat and a fist crushed around her
heart. She couldn't make herself say no, but she couldn't
make herself say yes, either.

He smiled. "You do feel it. Don't you?"

Sprawled across his folded knees, her breath stopped
completely and tears streaked down her cheeks.

"Ah . . ." His arms closed tight around her. He crushed her to his chest and sat up, taking her with him. "You do."

Fallon wrapped her arms around his neck in complete dismay at wanting to be held just like this. He didn't smell wrong, he smelled right, and good . . . and strong. And it hurt. She could feel her heart ripping completely in half. She dug her nails into her arms and held her breath to keep the feeling at bay. Silent tears dripped down her cheeks and spattered down his back.

His lips brushed her ear. "It's all right. This is supposed to happen. You've taken an impression."

What? She had to gulp for breath before she could speak. "How can I have two impressions?"

He sighed and his cheek rubbed against hers. "You can't."

She froze and anger flashed at the back of her skull. Her tears dried instantly. "My feelings have not changed for Sobehk."

"I suspected that they hadn't." His hand swept down her spine. "I don't think you ever impressed on him."

"What?" She tried to push back, to look in his face, but his arms tightened. She finally gave up and set her arms around his neck again, letting him hold her. "If it's not . . . that, then what's going on?"

"Isabeau, what you feel for him is different from what you feel for me, yes?"

She frowned. "Yes." Very different, almost the complete reverse of each other.

"You want to comfort him, you want to care for him, you want to make sure he's safe. Yes?"

Her frown deepened. "Yes."

"But you want *me* to care for *you*, yes?"

She stilled in alarm. That was exactly what she was feeling.

119

"Isabeau, if you had impressed on him, you would not have yelled at him for being foolish. With no physical contact for almost two whole days, impression would have driven you insane to get him to bleed for you or fuck you."

Fallon shook her head. "That's stupid, he was hurt . . ."

He chuckled. "No, it is instinct for a *rehkyt*." He sighed. "What you feel for me is more basic, more physical, and very primal."

She shook her head. "I don't understand."

"Isabeau, you love him."

She froze and her heart turned over. *Love?*

"But you need me, physically. You want to be mine."

His? She frowned and shook her head slowly, even as her eyes filled and spilled over. *No.* She didn't want to be anybody's. So what if he'd put his DNA in her body? That was her *body*, not her heart, not her soul. *I'm still me, inside, where it counts.* Her arms tightened around his neck and her nails cut into her forearms. *I don't need anybody.* Anger was a refreshing heat that swamped the feeling of helplessness trying to overtake her.

He caught her shoulders and pushed her back to stare into her eyes. "No?" A smile played at the corner of his mouth. "You're quite sure?"

Fallon set her jaw and nodded.

His brow lifted. "Then you won't mind taking a shower by yourself?"

She glanced down. She was covered in brown smears of dried blood and other bodily fluids. She was seriously nasty. She grinned defiantly at him. "Are you kidding? I would kill for a shower and some privacy."

He nodded. "Very well." He pushed her up and his cocks slid from her body.

Fallon winced as the piercing bars at the end of his cocks slipped free. She stood up on the filthy mattress on shaky legs. Every muscle in her body ached and shivered. Thick gobs of moisture slid down her thighs. She grimaced. "Oh, gross . . ."

He rose to his feet, his long braid swinging at his hips. "You don't like being dirty?" He stepped behind her and tugged free the thing he'd put in her data jack.

She winced. "I hate being dirty."

"I see." He stepped past her and strode toward where Sobehk's bed had been.

Fallon turned and followed. She blinked. A massive and complicated tattoo sketched across his shoulders and swept down his back in swirls of dark blue ink. It was all sweeping lines and points, like thorns, but it didn't seem to be a picture. It was more a design . . . but something about it nagged at her. The shape was vaguely familiar, but she couldn't place it.

At the head of the room, Khan moved to the left of the colorful but completely incomprehensible holographic display. He pressed his palm on the blank wall. The wall spiraled open into an oval door. He turned to face her. "Take all the time you need. I'll shower after you." His smile held open anticipation, but a touch of cruelty seemed to hover on the edges.

Fallon grabbed her elbows and slipped past him. He was up to something.

CHAPTER THIRTEEN

Fallon looked around with interest. The small facility was very spare with plain steel walls, a covered sink and a zero-gravity commode commanding the back wall. A shower stall was set into the wall on her right with towels hanging on the left of the shower's sliding door. The towels seemed silly. There was a perfectly good water collector unit in the shower itself.

The chance to use the commode in utter privacy was near blissful. She pulled the shower door open and the interior light went on. The walls were highly reflective, but she was only interested in turning on the hot water. She wasn't interested in knowing exactly how filthy she was.

She got the water on and stepped under the spray with her eyes closed. The burning hot water poured down her head and spilled down her body in fierce rivulets. The scratches and bites on her ached under the water's heat, even as her muscles loosened and unknotted. She pressed her palms against the wall, moaning in sheer animal pleasure. She dashed the water from her eyes and reached for the soap.

Arm outstretched, Fallon blinked at her nude reflection. Her overlarge emerald green eyes widened and her deep red lips parted in surprise. *What the fuck . . .*

Frost-white streaks from her temples blazed in the midnight darkness of her well-beyond-shoulder-length hair. The graceful tips of pointed ears peeked out from her overlong mane. Her bruised and somewhat battered skin gleamed under the water like burnished gold.

She choked. *That's not me!* She looked down. The curved white nails on her feet looked more like claws than toenails. It *was* her. Scarlet nipples crowned her breasts, framed by livid gouges made from being bitten by long teeth — gouges that were already closed and appeared to be well on their way to healing.

She turned to look at the reflection of her back and muscle rippled. She did not remember having that much visible muscle. She investigated the bites on her shoulders and neck. Those bites were healing too — healing faster than she'd ever healed in her life. Fingers tipped in curved white nails drifted up to the points of her ears.

She frowned at her face. "Damn it, I do *not* have green eyes!" She had hazel eyes, kind of bluish, kind of greenish with brown mixed in them . . .

The four reflective walls stated otherwise.

She scowled and saw her fangs for the first time. *Damn, they're longer than I thought.* The small spurt of pride took her by surprise. She stepped back to look at her entire length.

She didn't look human at all.

But then, they'd been telling her she wasn't human. Not anymore. Her heart thumped hard. Sweat soaked her back. What had they done to her?

They had changed her. Just like Peter had said they would.

Fallon closed her eyes and took a deep breath. "I'm still me. That's just the outside."

Peter had also said that she wouldn't *want* to come back. An image of Sobehk flickered in her mind, followed by a stronger image of Khan's naked back covered with marks from her nails.

"No." She folded her arms tight against her stomach and

felt the bunch of muscle under her palms. "On the inside, I'm still me." She opened her eyes and reached for the soap in the wall dispenser, refusing to look at her reflection.

But she wasn't her on the inside either. Someone had jammed a sleeper program in her head.

Terror froze her where she stood, and the visceral desire to find Khan swamped her utterly. She had the shower door open before she stopped. She closed her eyes, took a deep breath. Damnit, she could handle this herself. She was a top-notch hacker in her own right. If she could get into her own head, she could disable the program — if she could find it.

But she wanted him.

"No, damnit. I don't need him." She slid the door closed and took several bracing breaths. She turned around and stomped back to the water to finish her shower. She didn't need him.

Not right then anyway. She could wait.

No, damnit! She slapped soap on her skin and lathered, shaking her head. She *didn't* need him. But part of her did. Part of her wanted to hear his voice, to feel his hands touching her . . . the perfume of his scent on her skin.

She scrubbed her golden skin with a vengeance, but the color didn't come off.

Fallon shut off the water, feeling more exhausted than when she had gone in. Tension sang in her bones. She wanted out of that bathroom. She activated the water collector and was dry in seconds. The scent of clean water and soap wreathed her skin. She smelled clean.

But she didn't *want* to smell clean. The absolute worst urge to bolt out of the shower stall to find Khan burned through her. Something in her desperately wanted to rub against him to change her scent to his.

No, damnit! Stiff-legged, she stepped out of the shower

and deliberately turned her back on the open door. Instead, she searched for a brush to do something with her overlong hair, but couldn't find one.

She faced the door and gripped her elbows to keep from running. She stepped out and automatically searched for him.

Khan was on her left with his back to her, using a small computational. His pale skin was marked by old sword scars, smeared in dried blood, and covered in fresh scratches. Sleek muscle shifted in his shoulders and arms, creating an arresting display under that strange and sweeping tattoo. His long braid fell down his spine in a creamy line.

He had a great ass too.

Her gut clenched. He was painfully beautiful to look at. She wanted to touch him, to be touched by him. She desperately wanted to get him to turn around and at least look at her. She set her jaw. *No, damnit.* It took everything in her to hold still and wait.

Khan shut down his computational, sighed, and raised his head, setting his hands on his hips. "You're very stubborn." He didn't turn around.

Fallon looked around. There was no one else in the room with them, so he had to be talking to her. A smile lifted the corner of her mouth, part relief that he had acknowledged her, but more in the fact that she had held out. "Stubborn is what I do best."

His head lowered and a small chuckle escaped. "I strongly suspect that we are better suited than I thought."

Fallon felt a small rush of elation. He thought they were suited. Then her heart clenched. *Sobehk* . . . She closed her eyes and turned her face away. Goodbye was coming. She took a breath and shook her head. Goodbye always came. It was just the way it was. She should be used to it by now.

"What is it?"

Fallon opened her eyes. Khan was at her side, less than a hand-length away. His hands were still on his hips. She hadn't heard him walk over. She took a shallow breath and yet the scent of his skin reached her. She turned to face him but crossed her arms and dug her fingers into her upper arms to keep from reaching for him.

What should she say?

How about the truth? That was usually unexpected.

She looked up into his copper gaze. "You're taking me from Sobehk."

His eyes widened just a hair, then his mouth set in a firm line. "I *took* you from Sobehk last night."

She flinched. The truth cut both ways.

Khan sighed. "Isabeau, it's better this way. Believe me. He couldn't have handled you. You're too much for him." He turned to the side and swept a hand across his jaw. "I don't think he has any real idea what you're actually capable of."

Fallon felt a spurt of anger. "And you do?"

Khan snorted then shook his head. "According to his report, you're a talented acrobat, a damned fine fighter, and quite a successful escape artist. You're listed as a thief." He turned to look at her. "But according to your personal data your real talents are not physical, they're mental. Just from the style of your personal programs, it's very obvious that you're one of the finest programming architects I've seen in a long time. You are definitely a thief, but not for objects — for information. You could make or break just about any code out there."

Fallon frowned, unsure how she felt about him knowing this. That he was impressed was obvious and . . . satisfying in a strange way, but it was also really unnerving to have someone know so much.

Khan raised a brow. "You also have one of the most sophisticated translation programs I've ever seen." He tilted his head to the side. "Most Imperial translators cannot grasp Skeldhi at all, and yet you seem to have quite a vocabulary and grammar list."

Fallon shrugged. "It's a context translator."

Khan shook his head. "But you've only been hearing Skeldhi for the past two days." He grinned. "Would you make me a copy of that program?"

Fallon felt the smile creep onto her face. "Sure, I can do that."

Khan folded his arms across his chest and leaned back on his heels. "You've been stealing data from landed ships. Yes?"

Fallon hunched her shoulders and her smile disappeared. He was an investigations agent; how had she forgotten? "Everybody stole something on Dyson's. I took ship secrets. It was how I made a living."

Khan nodded. "Yes, but you've been stealing it from within the ship. You've actually been breaking into the ships then leaving without detection."

Fallon shrugged. "Most of the really valuable data is hidden within the ship's sentience. The trick is not to disturb the sentience."

His gaze sharpened. "According to that data . . ." He pointed at the holographic display up on the wall. "The only reason you are still on this ship is because you were unconscious when it left the station."

Fallon looked away from the incomprehensible display toward the distant, invisible door. He was half right. "I don't have my tools. I'd have to make new ones before I could break out."

"But you could do it, even from this ship."

She nodded. It wouldn't be difficult either; a simple

matter of getting into their supply hold and digging around for appropriate parts to make new taps. The real key to getting into and out of ships was in her programming codes.

"Isabeau." Khan sighed deeply. "Sobehk would never understand you or your talents like I do. As his *rehkyt*, you'd only be someone that warmed his bed. I'm a *Mehdjay'syr*, a lord-officer of Security and Intelligence, a minister of investigations. A *rehkyt* with your talents is more valuable to me than just someone to fuck."

Fallon jerked back as though struck.

Khan walked past her and stepped into the facility.

She listened as the water went on, then walked over to the facility's doorway and sat down against the wall beside it. She pressed her cheek against her upraised knees and tried not to think or feel anything at all.

And failed miserably.

Sobehk. She closed her eyes and tried to swallow the lump in her throat. Sobehk *didn't* know her. Not really. But then, very few people ever had. Her boss had some grasp of what she was capable of, but even he had no idea how she did what she did. He only knew that if he wanted something, she could get it, and that she was near impossible to catch or stop.

But Khan knew her. It felt strange to be understood, to be accepted, even appreciated. But she didn't *like* him. Part of her wanted him, desperately. It was hard to admit, but there was no denying that something in her craved him. But the rest of her was scared shitless of him, and with damned good reason. He knew her. He could destroy her in ways that went beyond a few broken bones.

She sniffed and rubbed her damp cheek on her knee. Khan didn't seem inclined to cripple her like that; in fact, he seemed more likely to actually let her use her talents . . .

But that could change. And she'd never see it coming.

He knew her — but she didn't know him at all. And her life was in his hands.

She tightened her arms around her knees and shivered hard.

"Isabeau!"

Fallon jerked upright. *What in fury?* She leaned over to look in the doorway. Water splashed against the glass door. He was in the shower. "What?"

"Get your ass in here!"

CHAPTER FOURTEEN

Fallon got up and stepped into the facility. She jerked the sliding glass door open. Steam curled out along the ceiling. She stuck her head in.

Khan stood under the water with his head down and his hands braced against either wall. The shower stall was that small. His hair was still in its tight braid, but he was clean. Even the scratches on his back and flanks were practically gone. The blue tattoo on his muscular back was brilliant under the shower light. She could smell nothing but water and soap.

Khan raised his head and his copper gaze, reflected in the wall before him, caught hers. Tension sang in his body. "Come here."

She stepped into the shower and closed the door. Water splashed onto her as she approached. Her neck hairs rose.

He turned with blinding speed, caught her by the upper arms and slammed her against the back wall.

She gasped in surprise; he was fucking fast!

His mouth came down on her open mouth as he pressed the entire hard length of his body against hers. His cocks were urgently rigid against her belly. He growled and kissed her, taking her mouth as though starved, and with ruthless skill.

Fallon's nipples rose to hot, tight points and her belly clenched with sudden hunger. She moaned into his mouth and grabbed his forearms, digging in with her long nails.

He pulled his mouth from hers and his eyes blazed with

heat. "You are better at resisting than I." He reached down to catch her thighs, lifting her against the wall. "You would think I would have more control than a newborn Prime." He pressed her against the wall with his body and reached down to set his pierced cock against the entrance to her body. He snorted and a small smile appeared. "Ah, not quite so resistant after all. You're wet." He grunted and thrust.

Fallon gasped as the unforgiving metal bar at the end of his cock pressed into her snug channel. All too soon his second pierced cock was an insistent pressure against her anus. She grabbed him around the shoulders and groaned, pressing outward to let him in. He'd rubbed something on to make his second cock slick, but the bar still jammed against the ring of her anus. She writhed in discomfort. The pressure increased. She whimpered and arched. The bar passed within. She sighed as it slid deeper.

He grunted and thrust further in, the ridges of metal balls under the skin of his cocks scraping against tender flesh.

She bucked hard and sheathed him, all the way to the root. It hurt and yet the pain shoved all the aching in her heart out, making room for her body's pleasure.

He sighed against her right ear. "Mother Night, I don't know how in Chaos you held out. I was going insane."

Fallon locked her legs around his hips and writhed against him, feeling his rigid and pierced cocks moving in her depths. "You?" She moaned with the agonizing delight of having him within her. "I thought I was the one with the . . ." She panted. "The impression?"

He chuckled. "Impression goes both ways, master to *re-hkyt*, *rehkyt* to master. My body wants yours as much as your body wants mine." His hands closed tight on her thighs and his nails dug in. "And I really want to fuck you right now." He pressed his head against the wall. "Bite me, on the shoulder, hard and fast."

She stilled in shock. It went both ways? He wanted her?

"Bite me, damn it!"

She bared her long teeth and sank them into his shoulder.

He gasped and shuddered then sighed. "Mmm . . . yes."

Her eyes caught their reflection on the far side of the stall. His long muscular body with her legs wrapped around his hips, one of her arms around his shoulder, and the other gripping his upper arm. A thin line of blood slid down his back from where her teeth pierced him. She pulled her fangs from his shoulder and watched her reflection licking the blood from the wounds she'd made.

He pressed her hard against the wall and his hand came up to grab a handful of her hair. He tugged her head to the left.

Fallon watched his mouth open in the wall's reflection. His teeth gleamed white and then his head fell, lightning-fast.

Fire exploded in her shoulder. She shouted and bucked forward, her nails slicing into his back.

He sucked on the wounds, growling, then released her shoulder, licking his lips. His hands reached down to cup her butt, his nails digging in. He slid outward, the bars at the ends of his cocks keeping him from slipping completely free. He thrust back in brutally hard then again, and again . . .

She bucked in his arms, moaning and straining to meet his pounding rhythm. Her gaze was trapped by the reflection of his straining body fucking hers. Every muscle in his back, ass and thighs flexed as he took her with desperate violence against the wall of the shower. It was the most erotic thing she'd ever seen.

Pleasure sparked with incredible speed and coiled tight with boiling fury in her core. She dug her nails into his back as the scream built in her throat. She could see the blood running down his back from her nails. Slender but bright threads of blood slid down his thighs. It was hers, from where his nails dug into her ass. The sight inflamed her further. Her gasps became cries as pressure and need rose to the explosion point.

His grunts became gasps. "Yes, Chaos, you're going to cum . . . Yes!"

She writhed as her body came to the razor's edge — and refused to fall. Damn it. She moaned in frustration. "Oh, please . . ."

"Please what?"

"Please!" She shouted and bucked hard. "I need it!"

He groaned but the amusement was clear in the sound. "What do you need, pet?"

"Please!" She shuddered, tormented by the pleasure she couldn't reach. "Bite me again!"

His hands came up and closed on her upper arms. He pressed her back against the wall. Her thighs held him tight as he stepped back and stared her in the eye. Possessive heat flared in his gaze. "You need me." His lip curled, showing his long teeth. "You need *me*. Say it!"

Fallon shuddered on the edge of a chasm that was deeper than merely sex. Terror raised every hair on her body.

"You need *me*!" His eyes were burning pits as he shouted in her face. "Say it!"

She cried out and burst into tears. She didn't *like* him, but she did need him. She dug her claws into his arms as she fought against it, but the need for him burned in her heart as well as in her body.

Something like agony raced across his expression. "Say

it, damn you! *Say it!*"

"Yes, you bastard!" she screamed and collapsed, gasping for breath as the tears ran down her cheeks. She just couldn't fight it anymore. "Yes. I need you."

He expelled a long breath and set his brow against hers. "Bloody Chaos, you stubborn little bitch." His voice was heavy with exhaustion. He took a long slow breath. "Say it again."

She exhaled and sniffed, hanging limp in his embrace. "I need you."

He sighed. "Who do you belong to, *rehkyt*?"

She closed her eyes and shuddered, but she was too tired to bother fighting it. "You."

"That's 'you, '*Syr*.' Say it."

'*Syr*, according to her translator, meant 'master.' He was telling her to acknowledge him as her rightful master. Her rightful owner. She moaned but didn't put any real effort into it. "Do I actually have to call you that?"

"Yes, you do."

"Bastard."

He snorted. "That was not what I said."

She sighed. "You, '*Syr*.'"

He groaned. "You really *do* need a beating."

"Everybody says that." Her chuckle bubbled up unexpectedly.

"Then it must be true." He chuckled too. "And that's 'everybody says that, '*Syr*.'"

"Bloody Fate, you mean I have to use . . . that all the time?"

"Yes, you do."

"That sucks . . .'*Syr*.'"

He leaned back and smiled. "You'll adjust."

Fallon narrowed her eyes at him. "Now what?" She curled her lip. "'*Syr*.'"

His copper gaze hardened. "Who do you belong to, *re-hkyt?*"

Fallon swallowed. "You, *'Syr.*"

"Do you belong to Sobehk?" His gaze was absolutely merciless.

Fallon jerked and turned away. She was not going there. No way in fury . . .

His growl was low and thoroughly threatening. "Do you belong to Sobehk?" His claws cut into her arms. "Answer me."

She faced him and snarled. "Are you *trying* to rip my heart out, you bastard?"

He bared his teeth in a vicious snarl. "I didn't ask if you loved Sobehk. Do you *belong* to Sobehk?"

The whimper escaped before she could stop it. She couldn't do this, it hurt too much. She unlocked her ankles from around his hips and tried to pull off his cocks, but he was swollen tight within her. She writhed in his hold struggling to escape. "Let me go!"

"No." He caught her wrists and pressed her against the wall with his body. "We're tied."

She pulled and twisted, whimpering with the pain, even as he hissed and struggled to hold her still. She could not free herself. She couldn't unlock her body from his. She collapsed, panting with exhaustion. She had to fight herself to meet his gaze, but meet it she did, with every last drop of defiance she had. "I will not answer that!" She bared her teeth. "*'Syr.*"

"Yes, you will!" His voice was low and even but his copper gaze blazed with rage. He bared his teeth and a low growl rumbled.

Her gaze focused on the pulse beating in his throat, only centimeters from her mouth, and her fangs. She could make him release her. She could rip out his throat. She was close enough and fast enough to do it. She took a breath and tumbled the thought of killing him in her mind. She turned her gaze from his vulnerable throat. She just couldn't make herself do it. She just couldn't. She didn't want him dead.

He sighed and the anger went out of his gaze. His exhausted breaths panted in time with hers. "Answer the question, Isabeau. Do you belong to Sobehk?"

She closed her eyes and shook her head. She didn't want to answer. It would break something in her that would never be the same.

"Isabeau." He took a deep breath. "Answer me."

She laid her cheek against his shoulder, begging for comfort. "Please don't." She released a breath, and her tears. "Please, don't make me . . . do this."

"I have to." He released her wrists and wrapped his arms around her, supporting her weight. "We both already know the answer, but you have to say it."

She wrapped her arms around his neck and shuddered with the sobs that tumbled from her shattering heart. "You can't . . ." She had to take two breaths before she spoke past the pain. "You can't ask me to stop . . . loving him."

"I'm not asking you to stop loving him." He took an unsteady breath. "I'm asking if you *belong* to him."

"He wants me to. I want to."

He took a very deep breath and sighed against her throat. "Isabeau, he deliberately gave up his claim on you last night, when he told me to take you." His arms tightened around her. "When you decided to live, you knew you would not be his, but mine."

She closed her eyes and curled in tight. It hurt. It hurt . . . Blood and Fate, it *hurt*. "You can't make someone love you."

The angry tension went out of his body in a rush. "This

isn't about love. Impression is the Skeldhi instinct to hold on to and protect their mates. A Skeldhi female goes into compliance, breeding heat for two solid cycles, but only once every two years. Between seasons, they won't allow sexual contact. Without impression, males would not stay with them long enough to raise a family. Love is something else entirely."

"You're capable of mating for sixty days straight, but you only get to do it once every two years?" She winced. "That has got to be . . . frustrating." No wonder they were such a war-like race.

He chuckled tiredly. "That is the absolute truth. It would have been easier if males shared their seasons, but we don't. We're sexually ready at all times, so as to be available when a female goes into season. *Rehkyt* are specifically designed for fucking. They're concubines to keep the male half of the race from committing territorial genocide."

"And your females allow this?"

He snorted. "It was their idea. The first *rehkyt* was designed for a *Pshent,* a ruling queen, to keep her consort sane while she carried her children to term. There's your love. Queens originally killed their consorts after mating. She loved her mate enough to find a solution to territorial madness so he could live."

He pressed his cheek to hers. "Unlike humans, we are ruled by our instincts, not our emotions. As a *rehkyt,* you have our DNA and the instincts that come with it. You love Sobehk, but you've impressed on me. Your body knows who it belongs to, but I need you to admit it, to say that you accept it."

She bit her lip. She wanted him, but she didn't *like* him. "I don't want this . . . instinct." Her gaze caught her reflection behind him. Her burnished gold skin was bright under the light, and her eyes were overlarge and green in a way no human eyes could ever be. She looked away from her alien reflection and leaned back to stare into his copper eyes. "Why do you do this to people? Why was this done to me?"

His red-orange gaze focused on her. "Do you honestly think a human would have lived through what we did last night? I would have ripped your fragile human body apart from the inside out. Your *rehkyt* body is designed to not only endure but enjoy sex with one of us—sex that would kill a human."

"So you altered me, into . . . this."

"We alter all the humans that come into our hands. They live longer." His gaze pinned hers. "Isabeau." His voice was barely above a whisper. "Do you belong to Sobehk?"

It was done. It was over. There was nothing left to fight for. There was nothing left to fight with. "No, '*Syr.*"

His teeth sank viciously into her shoulder.

She screamed with the bright hot pain of his bite even as her body flared with an overwhelming wave of clenching carnal heat that threatened to eat her alive. She wrapped her legs around him and clawed his back with her nails in her violent urgency.

He released her shoulder and thrust, the blood running from his mouth as he slammed her into the wall with his merciless strokes. "Cum, for me. Cum now!"

Climax rose so fast she was screaming before it hit. Her body exploded from the inside in a release so profound it felt as though her heart burst. Lightning rushed up her spine and exploded at the back of her skull. Her screams stopped and she collapsed in his arms, barely conscious.

"Mine." He thrust into her, grunted, thrust again and then held. "You are *mine.*" He gasped, shuddering, his cocks pulsing in her body. A snarl escaped his blood-stained mouth. "No one else's!" His eyes closed briefly then he threw back his head and screamed with a voice that was not even remotely human.

Chapter Fifteen

K han trembled as he released Fallon from his arms, his softened cocks sliding from her body.

Fallon, burned and scoured, heart, soul and body, slid down the wall. Her shaking legs couldn't hold her.

He caught her under the arms. "Turn around and face the wall."

She panted softly and fought a losing battle to get her feet under her. "I don't think I can stand."

He grunted as he helped her turn. "You don't need to stand. Kneeling will do. Just keep your head up."

Fallon dropped to her knees and pressed her head against the reflective wall.

Khan knotted his fingers in the base of her hair, twisting it around his fist. "Head up and hold still."

Fallon winced. "I'm not going anywhere."

"No, you're not." He groaned. Hot liquid splashed her back, ran down her arms and spilled over her thighs. He reached down and hauled her up onto her feet, jerked her around and pressed her back against the wall, trapping her with his big, scarred body. "Who is your master, *rehkyt?*"

She dodged his stare and shivered hard. "You, *'Syr.*" The reply fell from her mouth before she knew she was going to utter it.

He caught her jaw and forced her to meet his hard copper stare. "I claim you by right of conquest as mine; my property, my pet, and my slave. Do you yield to my claim?"

She gasped in fright even as something else wrapped tight around her heart. The rank and inescapable smell of him burned in her nose.

His claws dug into her jaw, his gaze utterly pitiless. "Do you yield?"

She cringed and blinked as her eyes swam. "Yes, '*Syr!*'"

"Good." He took her mouth in a brutal kiss, his teeth scoring her tongue.

She whimpered in submission. There wasn't a drop of fight left in her.

He released her mouth and held her gaze. "I swear I will do my best to be a good master to you."

Her breath stopped in her throat and the tears tumbled free. She hadn't thought there was anything left in her to cry for. He'd already ripped out her heart, but this felt deeper. Like he was shoving something in the gaping hole he'd carved in her breast. It wasn't love. It was something older and more primal. And far more permanent.

He frowned. "Isabeau, breathe."

She choked and sucked air. She tried to hold back the sobs that burst free, but she just couldn't.

"Easy, pet." He caught her in his arms and held her against his heart. "It's done, it's over. Just let it go."

She wrapped her arms around his neck and dropped her head on his shoulder. "Oh, Maker, what have you done to me?"

"I've claimed you." He sighed. "Your head still isn't ready to accept what you are, but your body understands just fine."

She sniffed. "Understands what?"

"What you are, and what I am to you." His palm swept down her soaked back.

His touch felt good, and right. Too good, too right. "Instincts again?"

"Very much so." He dropped a kiss on her brow. "Let's get cleaned up." He pulled her under the shower's still-running water. His hands were gentle but thorough as he bathed her, touching every inch of her.

She sighed and relaxed, giving in to the comfort his touch offered. A small amount of shame coiled in the basement of her heart. She hadn't let Sobehk touch her this easily.

Fallon stepped out of the facility, stopped and shook hard. She swept her hands down her skin, still uncomfortable with the gleaming inhuman color.

Khan moved to the chair where his abandoned clothes lay. He picked up his black kilt and began to dress.

Fallon paced uneasily. She didn't want to think about what had happened in there, but she couldn't stop thinking about it. Her mind latched on the one thing she didn't get. "*'Syr*, why in fury did you piss on me?"

Khan turned to her as he closed his black under-robe. "It's part of the ritual of claiming." He wound his scarlet sash around his waist.

Fallon's mouth opened in shock. "But that's so . . . disgusting!"

Khan snorted and tucked his daggers into his sash. "No, it's male. Most males of any species piss to mark their territory and their property." He picked up his heavy black and scarlet hooded over-robe.

Fallon's hands fisted at her sides. "That's what I am? Property?"

He paused, staring hard at her. "Are you saying you're *not* my property?"

She turned her gaze away. She couldn't look him in the eye. "No, *'Syr*."

"Isabeau, just let it go." He shrugged into his over-robe.

"Trust your instincts. They'll lead you in the right direction." He sat in the chair to pull on his boots and a small smile appeared. "And keep you out of trouble."

Fallon glared at him. "And if my instincts tell me I should bite someone, '*Syr*?" She flinched. She was using that 'master' title a little too easily, but she couldn't seem to stop herself.

Khan's brows rose his smiled broadened. "Then it's highly probable that that person should be bitten." He stood and fastened his robe closed. "But be warned, to Skeldhi a bite is a prelude to sex or violence. You bite someone and they'll expect you to either fuck them or try to kill them."

Fallon rubbed her arms. "So far, I haven't seen much of a difference between sex and violence, '*Syr*."

Khan grinned. "To Skeldhi, there isn't much of one. If we can't fuck it, we want to kill it." He strode over to his computational and the holographic display on the wall dispersed.

She rolled her eyes. "Gee, thanks for the warning."

"You're welcome." He closed the small computational case and carried it back toward the chair. He set the case down on the seat then turned to her. He held out his hand. "Come."

Fallon moved toward him uneasily. He was fully dressed in his long robes of office, just as when she'd first seen him. Tall, dark and scary. And an investigations agent. But she couldn't stop herself from going to him. She stopped a single pace away, unable to look into his face.

Khan caught her chin and raised her gaze to his. His mouth was tight, and his eyes held something she couldn't begin to define. "There is nothing to fear. Anyone that wants to hurt you has to go through me first."

Fallon blinked and felt the most incredible urge. She

gave into it just to see what would happen. She tilted her head and rubbed her cheek against his palm. She had no idea why, but it seemed the right thing to do.

"Yes." A slight smile lifted his lips. "That's it. That's right." He sighed deeply, as though a weight had been lifted. His other hand came out of his robes. There was a distinct rattle of chain.

A chill raced across her skin and the hairs on her neck rose.

Khan released her and held up a chain between his hands. It was pitch-black, like the band on his brow, and made of links large enough to put her pinky through. A tag swung from the end. "This is my collar. Your blood carries my ownership in your DNA, but this chain marks you visibly as mine. The tag holds my name, and yours."

It *already* had her name on it? Fallon hissed in shock and sudden anger, smelling a deliberate betrayal. She stepped back. "You *planned* to take me from Sobehk before you ever met me." It wasn't a question.

Khan's gaze hardened. "Yes."

She dropped her chin and set her jaw, her hands fisting at her sides. "Why?"

His copper eyes ignited with anger and a warning growl rumbled from his chest. "Are you questioning me?"

Anger lashed through her in a white-hot bolt. "I don't *know* you! You don't make any sense to me! How can I . . ." She looked away then looked back. "How can I trust you?"

Khan took a deep breath, but the anger didn't fade from his gaze. "Isabeau, I have my reasons for what I've done, just as you had your reasons for choosing to live, knowing that you would be mine, and not Sobehk's."

Fallon winced in shame. He wasn't the only one that stank of betrayal.

"Isabeau, you do know me, better than you think. Trust

what you feel, not what you think. Impression doesn't happen without an instinctive connection."

Instincts again! Fallon stomped her heel on the deck in pure reflex, but there was nothing she could say to argue the point. Every time he opened his mouth, he hammered home the fact that she was not meant for Sobehk. And it was pissing her off! A growl rumbled in her throat.

Khan tilted his head and a slight smile lifted the corner of his mouth. "Blood or sex?"

Fallon froze. Every thought in her head ground to an abrupt halt. She looked at him. "What?"

Khan set his hands on his hips. "Right now, what would make you feel better, blood or sex?"

Fallon shook her head in confusion. "I don't understand, 'Syr."

"Don't think, *feel*. What do you want to do? Bite or fuck?" Khan moved the small computational in the chair behind him to the floor, tugged at his robes and sat down.

Fallon considered what she was feeling. She was furious. Wound tight with anger, and that anger definitely wanted something. She rubbed her jaw. It ached from clamping her teeth together. *Her teeth . . .* She looked at him. "Bite, 'Syr."

He nodded. "Blood." He pulled back his right sleeve, baring his forearm. "Come here." He stretched his arm out to the side, his hand fisted.

Fallon couldn't look away from the blue veins in his pale arm. She stepped toward him, drawn. She wanted to bite him with everything in her . . . and something else. She wanted something else too.

"Down, get down." His voice was hard, firm and oddly encouraging.

She dropped to the cold metal floor and crawled on hands and toes toward his bared arm. A breath away from his arm, she stopped. She could smell the blood pulsing under his skin. Her mouth watered and her jaw ached to sink her teeth into him. She looked at him.

He nodded. "Just your mouth, not your hands, and pull your teeth out to suck."

She licked the soft skin of his arm. The moan erupted from her throat before she could stop it. She pressed her teeth against his skin. His forearm was too broad to get her teeth into. She moved closer to his wrist. Her teeth sank into the thin skin with a slight pop.

He grunted and his fist tightened.

She pulled her teeth back out and closed her mouth over the holes. She sucked gently. It was salty, sweet, and right. She swallowed and liquid copper fire burned down her throat then warmed in her belly. Her thoughts drifted apart along the edges under a muzzy wave of warmth.

She blinked. *Am I getting drunk?* She swallowed again. The ache in her heart eased, washed away under the warmth spreading from her belly. *I am getting drunk.* She thought about stopping. A fist of pain closed around her heart. *No, I'm tired of hurting.*

She sucked harder, greedily. This was right, this was good, this was . . . comforting. *More . . .* Her thoughts subsided into a warm comfortable lull that pushed the pain away. She swallowed and swallowed. Something in her calmed, eased, unfolded, and a strange low vibrating sound came from the very base of her throat. It wasn't a growl, but it was a sound she'd never made before. It felt good to make that sound. She relaxed and let it happen.

"Ah, there we are." Khan curled his arm toward his body, slowly, pressing her backward toward him. "You needed to be fed."

She moved with his arm, too hungry to let go or resist, until her back pressed against the edge of the seat, sitting between his robed knees with his arm curved around her. Her stomach filled and her mind drifted toward the edge of what felt like sleep.

"That's it." His free hand swept down her hair. "Drink, pet, feed from me."

That sound in her throat became louder and her mind stilled, awash in a warm, safe place where nothing hurt. She took one last swallow and licked the wounds she'd made. Her head fell back onto his hard thigh and she looked up at him, her mind silent, her heart utterly at ease, and her body completely comfortable at last.

Khan smiled. "Better?"

She felt a smile tug at her mouth. She couldn't bring herself to even think of a vocal reply. She let her body reply for her. She nodded slowly.

"Feel good?"

She nodded again.

Khan raised his hands with the black chain between them.

A small shimmer of alarm slipped into her place of comfort. She swallowed and that sound disappeared.

He lowered it around her throat and gently encouraged her to lean forward.

She did so and closed her eyes. She didn't want to think about this. There was a subtle click. The chill chain draped loose around her neck. She flinched. There was a second click, and a weight tugged on the chain around her neck. She turned.

Khan held up his hand showing her another chain with a handle. It was a leash. He'd attached a leash to her collar. He leaned over to collect his computational, then rose to his feet. "Come."

Fallon climbed to her feet and stared at the chain between them. The meaning was simple: follow. There was meaning beyond this, but she didn't want to consider it. Beyond that was pain. Pain she didn't want to feel.

He turned toward the door and walked.

Fallon followed, automatically moving to the left, his offside, one pace behind.

CHAPTER SIXTEEN

The door opened and voices stopped.

Khan stepped through the doorway and two men in gleaming, iridescent black armor came to attention on either side of the doorway.

Fallon jerked in surprise, but she was just too . . . comfortable to feel real alarm. Her gaze darted around the dimly lit medlab's outer office. Tah turned to look at her from behind his smoked glass desk on her immediate right. A Skeldhi she didn't recognize in dark gray sleeveless robes, his pale hair pulled back into a long tail, leaned against the examination and surgical couch before them.

Khan turned to her and smiled. "It is done." He stepped back, encouraging her to follow him into the room.

Fallon stepped over the door's bottom edge, staring at his smile. He was pleased. Something lightened in her heart. She smiled and eased back into that warm place.

Tah rose slowly from behind his desk. "You succeeded in breaking her impression?" His voice was low, but tension tightened his mouth.

Fallon heard and saw but filed it all away for later consideration. At that moment she didn't want to think. It was more comfortable to just feel.

Khan's smile broadened, but his teeth remained hidden. "It appears that she didn't have one."

The other male, the one she didn't recognize, straightened upright, his eyes wide. "What?"

Khan nodded toward Tah. "Ordinary affection."

"Affection? That was all?" The other Skeldhi looked over at Tah. "Then how did she go into *rahyt*?" He shook his head. "Why would she . . . do what she did?"

Fallon frowned. The other Skeldhi's voice sounded familiar, but she couldn't smell anything beyond Khan's scent. She couldn't identify him.

Khan turned to look at him and frowned. "Calmly, she's just fed." Khan turned back to Fallon. He caught her gaze, pulling her attention back to him, and offered his palm.

She pressed her cheek into his palm and released a small breath. She didn't feel like making the effort to consider the somewhat recognizable Skeldhi any further. She was too busy being . . . comfortable.

Khan pulled his palm back and his gaze flicked from Tah to the other Skeldhi. "Humans have been known to accomplish some rather amazing things from the strength of their emotions." He tucked the handle of her lead into his sash and held his hand out to the left.

The left door guard handed him a length of red silk.

Tah looked over at the unknown Skeldhi. "Strong emotion has been mistaken for impression before." He looked over at Fallon. "In fact, emotion is normally the trigger for impression."

Khan opened the silk out, revealing a short sleeveless robe. "The telling difference is in the possessive display of the emotional state versus the possession display in impression." He stepped closer to Fallon and slipped it behind her, holding it up with the obvious intent to dress her.

Fallon put her arm into one armhole and then the other, focused on his pleased expression. She wanted to please him. She liked pleasing him.

Tah frowned. "When did you know?"

"The moment she touched him." Khan pulled the robe closed, folding one side over the other and knotting the side ties. "She didn't try to feed, she tried to comfort, and neither displayed the physical traits of impression abstinence."

The unknown Skeldhi tilted his head and frowned. "That was comfort?"

Khan held out his hand and another length of silk was handed to him, black this time. "Protective display. She was angry because he had gotten hurt. It was a purely emotional reaction, and he reacted in the same manner." He shook the silk open, revealing another robe, this one with long sleeves and embroidered, black on black, with a design similar to the one tattooed on his back.

Fallon tucked her arms into the sleeves. The hem fell to mid-thigh. She would wear his personal mark. That pleased her.

Khan folded the robe across her chest. He held out his hand and received a red sash. "My biggest difficulty was in getting through the emotional connection to get her to acknowledge the impression." He wound the sash around her waist.

Tah frowned. "The emotional connection was that strong?"

Khan sighed as he knotted the sash. "Quite. If there had been more physical contact between them, the emotion would most definitely have become impression."

Tah looked down at his desk. "Then is it wise to put them on the same ship? If the emotional connection is that strong, will this not cause emotional distress?"

Khan smiled, but his copper gaze chilled. "Absolutely." He turned to look at Tah. "May I have the ear clips?"

Tah frowned. "Yes, of course." He scooped up something from the top of his desk. He stepped out from behind the desk and approached Khan. "Would you like my assistance?"

"No. Thank you." Khan held out his hand but did not remove his gaze from Fallon's face. "I'm going to do this in the traditional manner. I do not wish to disturb her current . . . focus."

Tah dropped whatever was in his hand into Khan's palm. "And the traditional manner will not?"

Khan's smile drifted away. "She has come to expect . . . such, from me."

Tah glanced at Khan. "Is this what you wanted?"

"This is not a matter of want, but of need." Khan sighed and glanced down at his palm. "My needs are . . . complicated." He raised his palm toward Fallon's head. "As are hers, apparently."

Her gaze flicked to his raised hand. His fingers caressed the lower curve of her ear. She frowned. His touch was a little disturbing, but it seemed to be what he wanted. And she wanted to please him.

"Our natures are more closely suited than I expected." Khan smiled briefly then wrapped one arm around her and tightened until she was firmly pressed against him, chest to breast with her arms trapped between them. "Impression happened the moment she came with me in her body."

Fallon leaned into his warmth. She couldn't move her arms but liked being held by him. She felt safe. He brought his other hand up and encouraged her to turn her head.

Fallon felt him set something metal around the lower arch of her ear. His breath feathered her ear. She shivered. His lips caught around whatever was in her ear and his hand pressed against her head to hold her to his mouth. His tongue swept wetly across the curve of her ear and the metal piece. His flat front teeth caught hold of it. She heard a distinct crunch.

Sharp pain stabbed from her ear's lower arch. She jerked in his hold and cried out.

His arm tightened around her and his hand pressed her head still as he sucked on her wounded ear. A rumbling purr vibrated in his chest and into her.

She made small sounds of distress but leaned into him, comforted by the vibrating sound pressing into her. She hurt, but she'd pleased him. She liked pleasing him. She stilled.

He released her ear.

Weight dangled uncomfortably on the bottom of her ear. She frowned.

Khan caught her gaze. "Do not touch."

She nodded slowly. The weight shifted along the bottom of her ear and she winced.

Khan turned to look at Tah and raised his brow. A smile appeared briefly. "Tradition seems to suit her. Wouldn't you agree?" He turned Fallon's head the other way.

Fallon looked at Tah.

Tah's expression was perfectly placid, but tension showed in the corners of his mouth. "Her eyes are dilated very wide. I thought she seemed a little . . . quiet."

She leaned against Khan and sighed.

"Blood intoxication." Khan placed another piece of metal in the lower arch of her other ear. "I fed her for a good quarter, right before we stepped out."

Tah frowned only slightly. "In the traditional manner?"

"Yes." He shook back his sleeve to display the mark of her teeth, then cupped the back of her head to encourage her toward his mouth. His lips captured her ear and the metal piece in it.

Fallon felt his breath in her ear, his sweeping tongue and his teeth clamping on the metal in her ear. She closed her eyes. Pain was coming. A small sound of distress escaped.

Khan's chest vibrated against hers with his rumbling purr. He waited.

She took a small breath and leaned into him, seeking to keep that purr, that sign of his pleasure.

He bit down.

Crunch . . . *fire.*

She cried out but held still as he sucked on her ear. The pain mixed with his comforting purr and wrapped her in warmth. She blinked and felt something slipping away. Her knees buckled.

"She's falling." Tah's voice came from far away.

Khan bent to catch her under the knees then lifted her up against his heart. "She needs rest. This was a rough impression. For both of us."

Fallon blinked blearily up at him and curled up against his neck, snuggling into his warm hold and warmer scent.

Tah's mouth tightened. "I saw the bites."

"I have as many, if not more than she does." A chuckled vibrated in Khan's chest. "And she really likes using those claws of hers."

Fallon pressed her lips to Khan's throat in a brief kiss then set her chin on his shoulder and closed her eyes. That strange sound bubbled up in her chest and lower throat.

"She's purring." Tah sounded surprised.

Purring? Fallon frowned then sighed. *Oh, that's what that is . . .* She released the rest of her thoughts. She didn't want to think right then, she was too busy feeling warm, and comfortable, and sleepy.

"Some Primes can." Khan's voice was soft. "I need to get to my ship. I'll contact the captain with my new data on the incident as soon as I get this one settled." He started walking. Footsteps followed.

Fallon's eyes opened briefly to see the two guards about three paces behind them. She glanced to the side where Tah paced beside them. Khan's hand slid down her back. *Safe . . .* She closed her eyes and relaxed. *Warm . . .*

"Was this . . . separation between them necessary?" Tah's voice was very quiet, but his distress was clear.

Khan sighed. "*'Syr* Tah, even if they had imprinted, I would have had to separate them."

"What?" Tah's question was barely a breath of sound. "What is so terrible about the two of them paired? Is it because she's an *upuaht* level Prime *rehkyt*?"

Khan snorted in crystal clear derision. "No. It's because this *upuaht* level Prime *rehkyt* also happens to be the Fallen Star, one of the Moribund Company's code-crackers. She has a file about as long as this ship."

"Mother Night . . ."

"I was already on my way here to take custody when your call came through about the incident."

Fallen Star . . .

Fallon's mind struggled up from her warm, comfortable place of nothingness and into the place that pulsed with a hurt that felt like betrayal. She opened her eyes. She was being carried through one of the gray hallways. She swallowed and the purr in her throat disappeared.

Khan stiffened and turned to look at her.

She turned to look at Khan with that hurt pulsing around her heart. "You knew, all along?"

Khan glared briefly at Tah then looked at her. "Yes." Tension tightened his mouth. "It changes nothing. You are safe with me."

She wanted to believe him. Part of her already did. That part was loud and inviting and promised ease. She wanted that ease. She nodded and set her chin on his shoulder, then closed her eyes. But another part of her refused to believe.

The purr didn't come back.

A door buzzed closed.

Fallon's eyes snapped open. She was lying under a thick

black comforter in a pile of black and scarlet pillows. She jerked upright to discover that she was in a huge, circular bowl-like bed draped with sheer gold curtains that hung from a ceiling high over her head. She groaned. She was dead tired and desperate for sleep, but there was no way in fury she could sleep in this. It was too exposed, with too much light, and it was way too low.

She crawled to the edge of the bowl and shoved back the curtains. The damned bed was sunk about knee-deep into the floor! Her lips curled. There was no way she could fall asleep in this. Anything crawling along the floor or spilling across it would end up in the bed with her.

Beyond the edge of the bed, the room was long and fairly broad with gold carpeting. Though only a few of the sconces at the edges of the high ceiling were lit, there was a disturbing amount of light. Tall smoked mirrors on the dark red walls made the room look even more cavernous and bright. She would not be able to move an inch across that floor without being seen in those mirrors.

A massive set of black trunks sat against the left wall, a low but broad round table with four thick sitting pillows occupied the room's center, and a pair of huge doors were set into the wall on her right. Small tables with art objects were posted along the walls. She had no clue where the exit was.

There was barely cover at all.

However, the good news was that the room was so exposed she could tell in a glance that no one else was in it.

The bed she occupied appeared to be set in a small alcove and was the darkest part of the room, but it was far too open and exposed for comfort. Worse still, the whole setup led in a clear straight path to the bed. Anyone entering the room would come straight there.

If she was going to get some decent sleep, she needed to

find someplace a lot more secure, higher up, and dark. Her gaze drifted to the doors in the wall.

She moved cautiously from the bed, watching for any sign of movement. Her gaze darted to her own reflection moving in all the mirrors. It was unnerving as fury to be so visible.

She tugged open the tall door on the right. It was a wardrobe stuffed full with hanging robes, mostly black and red, and assorted trunks. She looked up. Above the hanging clothes, a broad shelf occupied the top quarter with the far ends concealed by the fact that the doors did not open the entire width of the wardrobe. There was a meter of shelf space concealed at either end even with the doors wide open. Boxes filled the center of the shelf, but the concealed ends appeared to be empty. *Perfect.*

She went back to the bed and collected two black pillows. Holding the pillows with her teeth, she grabbed onto the wardrobe's inner edge and climbed up. Hanging onto the top edge of the wardrobe with one hand — thank the Maker for augmentations that allowed her to lift twice her own body-weight — she pushed all the boxes out of the right corner then pulled herself up and shoved her feet into the empty space. Folding her legs tightly, she wriggled her butt onto the shelf. She turned over onto her knees and leaned out from the shelf to grab the top edge of the open door. She pulled it closed.

Darkness enveloped her. She wriggled back into the corner, tugging one of the boxes along the shelf with her. She set the box at her head to block her from view should someone open the door. Curled tight in the small space with her head nestled on one pillow and the other jammed against her back for comfort and warmth, Fallon sighed in complete ease. The shelf space was actually roomier than her bed at home. She snuggled into the pillows and promptly went to sleep.

CHAPTER SEVENTEEN

The Moon Blade – Skeldhi Mehdjay Battle-Cruiser
Outer Rim of Imperial Space
Local Space

Somebody chuckled.

Somebody else cursed. It sounded like Khan. "I know she's in here . . . somewhere." It *was* Khan, and he was seriously annoyed.

Fallon curled tighter into her dark corner, clutching the pillow under her head. If he was pissed, she was better off where she was.

"I'm sure she is, but I told you she wouldn't stay in the bed." Sobehk's voice was calm and very smug.

Fallon dug her fingers into the pillow. *Sobehk* . . . She did *not* want to face him. She was not ready to say goodbye.

"Why in Chaos not? She was dead asleep when I set her in it."

"Because she's feral." Sobehk sighed heavily. "Khan, she's been living in the bowels of a vermin-infested station run by cutthroats. She would sleep more comfortably in a blast hole high up in a wall before she would fall asleep in that bed. In fact, I found her more than once sleeping quite comfortably curled up in a disused drainpipe."

"I find it hard to believe that a talent like the Fallen Star would sleep in a drainpipe! She had to be earning her weight in Imperial credits."

"She probably did, and I'm pretty damned sure it's all

159

in her body. Did you get a look at the report on her augmentations? It's all state-of-the-art, elenium and titanium alloy. Her internal comp is worth a small craft all by itself, but it's obvious from her behavior that she didn't live in the station's topside. She probably had a snug hole somewhere in the deeps that she had to climb to reach."

Fallon frowned. That was a pretty damned close description of her cubby.

Sobehk chuckled. "My guess is that she's tucked into the smallest, darkest and highest place in here."

"Such as?"

"Try there."

The wardrobe's doors were pulled open.

Fallon froze.

The clothes below her were shifted about. "She's not in here." Khan's voice showed clear annoyance.

"Try looking up, not down." Sobehk sounded like he was barely holding back outright laughter.

"She couldn't possibly fit!"

"Oh, yes, she can. I watched her slide into a sewer pipe a child would have difficulty getting into."

The boxes shifted at the back of her head.

Fallon curled tighter into the corner, but she was already wedged in as tight as she could go.

"What in bleeding Chaos . . ."

The pillow was snatched from behind her and someone grabbed the collar of her robes. *Oh shit!* Fallon scrabbled for handholds as she was hauled headfirst from the shelf and into the light. The pillows spilled to the floor as she fell into Khan's arms.

Khan set her on her feet, one hand knotted in the back of her robes, and glared down at her. "What in the name of Chaos were you doing in there?"

Fallon rubbed at her eyes. "I *was* sleeping." She folded

her arms and looked away from his angry copper gaze. "*'Syr.*"

He slammed the wardrobe door closed with his free hand. "I have a perfectly good bed."

Fallon rolled her eyes. "It's in the floor, and perfectly visible! Anybody walking in here will go straight to it!"

Sobehk snorted then sighed. "Khan, I doubt she's ever slept in a real bed."

Fallon closed her eyes. She didn't want to see him. And no, she hadn't slept in an actual *bed* before. Too many things could find you there.

"Well, she's going to sleep in one now." Khan shook her by the collar of the robe. "No more sleeping in the closet!"

Fallon grit her teeth. *Fat chance.*

"You're going to have to tie her in the bed if you expect her to stay there." Sobehk definitely sounded amused.

Fallon opened her eyes and peeked at the mirrors. Sobehk was a tall, broad, and pale shimmer in the smoked glass. Long cream and gold robes draped him to the floor, and he appeared to be leaning on the curved handle of some sort of pale staff. His hair fell down his back in a loose fall of frost-white. Her heart lurched.

Khan swiped a hand across his jaw. "Mother Night, I cannot believe that one of the brightest minds in civilized space prefers the upper shelf of the closet to a bed!"

Fallon's brows rose. "You're supposed to be *civilized*?"

Both men stiffened.

Fallon clapped both hands over her mouth. Great Maker, where was her sense?

"Compared to you?" Khan's eyes narrowed, his lip curled. "*I* don't sleep in the *closet!*" A growl rumbled.

Sobehk smiled. "You're growling."

Khan snarled at Sobehk. "I *know* I'm growling!"

Sobehk shook his head and chuckled. "Khan, she's feral.

I doubt she even knows how to eat at a table." He looked over at Fallon. "Do you?"

Fallon's mouth fell open. "I've eaten at a table before." Well, at the counter of the diner, occasionally, when she wasn't in hiding during assignments.

Khan released a long breath. "How am I supposed to take her before the *Mehdjay* council if she doesn't know even the basics of polite behavior?"

Sobehk rolled his eyes. "I believe I already mentioned that she needed a lot of training?" He folded his arms and smiled. "I wasn't talking about *upuaht* skills. She knows how to fight. It's everything else that needs work."

"I don't have time for this!" Khan bared his long teeth. "I have duties!"

"I guess you should have thought of that before you took custody of a feral *rehkyt*." Sobehk grinned maliciously. "I feel so bad for you."

"Do you?" Khan turned to Sobehk. "Then you can help. I'll have the staff move you in with me."

Sobehk stilled. "What?"

"I can't have her disappearing into drain holes or conduits when my back is turned. You're merely a passenger, so you can help civilize her while I'm on duty."

Fallon jerked. Khan was having *Sobehk* watch her?

Sobehk moved closer. "Khan, are you out of your mind?" He stood a full head taller than the lord-officer and was nearly twice as broad, but he moved stiffly, supported by the thick staff clutched in his hand. He looked better, but he was obviously not well. "You can't expect me to stay here and not want to . . ." He bared his teeth. "That's cruel, even for you!"

Khan smiled and set one hand on his hip. "I didn't say you couldn't have her."

Sobehk's eyes opened wide and he looked at Fallon.

"Are you serious?"

Fallon stared at him, fully aware that her heart was beating in her mouth, afraid to think, and even more afraid to feel.

Khan turned to smile at Fallon. "Isabeau knows who she belongs to."

Fallon cringed and stared at the floor. And she thought Sobehk was a sadistic bastard?

Khan lifted his chin. "Since you'll be sleeping in my bed, you can help keep her 'tied' in it." He raised an insinuating brow. "Among other activities."

Sobehk folded his arms and smiled. "Missed me?"

Khan pursed his lips. "Perhaps a little."

"I see." Sobehk grinned, shaking his head then his mouth tightened. "I'll need a leash and a training whip."

Fallon turned to gape at Sobehk. *A leash and a whip?*

"You can use mine." Khan grinned and reached into his robes and pulled out a length of black chain with a leather loop at one end. "Start with voice training."

Fallon blinked. "What's wrong with my voice?"

Sobehk snorted as he took the leash from Khan. "The fact that you are using it for something other than answering direct questions." He took a step closer and set his hand on Fallon's shoulder. "I'll see she gets the basics."

Fallon couldn't help the warmth that coiled around her heart with his touch.

Sobehk snapped the leash onto the chain around Fallon's neck.

Fallon flinched, her gaze drawn to the black chain from her throat to Sobehk's hand. On second thought, maybe this wasn't such a good idea. Khan might know what was in her head and what she was capable of doing, but Sobehk understood her habits. Regardless of the fact that he had taken three days to catch her—he had somehow managed to stay on her ass all three days.

Khan shoved back his robe sleeve and raised his brow at Sobehk. "Think she'll be ready to eat at the table by dinner?" Coiled around his wrist was a length of braided leather that ended in a supple handle. He loosened the leather from his wrist, revealing a slender whip about a meter long.

"This stray?" Sobehk rolled his eyes. "She'll probably be more comfortable with a bowl on the floor."

"What?" Fallon set her jaw and glared at one then the other. They were *both* sadistic bastards.

Khan coiled the meter or so of leather, smiling tiredly. "It will be enjoyable having your company again." He handed the whip to Sobehk.

Sobehk took the whip and smiled as well. "If we can keep from tearing out each other's throats this time."

Khan turned away. "A great deal of time has passed since the academy. There is only one constant in life, and that is change." He looked down, then took a step away. "I'll assign crew to move your belongings." He strode for the far end of the room.

Four Skeldhi men in plain black skinsuits trooped through the oval door of Khan's room towing large red cases and matching smaller trunks. They set them in a neat arrangement beside Khan's black cases. One of the men went to the wall just past the double doors to Khan's wardrobe. He pressed his palm against it. The wall shifted as the mimetic material of the wall reshaped itself. Two more doors appeared, indicating a second wardrobe.

Sobehk orchestrated the arrangement of his belongings while kneeling comfortably on one of the large pillows by the low table in the room's center.

Her leash tucked into Sobehk's sash, Fallon knelt at his side on the bare carpet as ordered, her knees tight together, the tops of her feet flat on the carpeting, heels slightly out, and her palms flat on her thighs. It wasn't exactly the most comfortable position to sit in, but she'd been in far worse positions for far longer periods of time.

Under Sobehk's direction, the crew encouraged ledges to form from the mimetic walls and art objects were set on them. A few colorful hangings were posted on the walls between the tall mirrors. Clothing was unpacked and set in the new wardrobe. The four crewmen glanced at Fallon on occasion, but not one of them openly stared.

Fallon found the whole display fascinating.

"Isabeau, don't stare, it's rude." Sobehk's voice was soft but firm.

Fallon dropped her gaze to the carpet. "What? Am I supposed to pretend they're not there?"

Sobehk snorted in clear amusement. "Yes, as a matter of fact you are, and you will address me as *'Syr.'*"

"Not you, too?" Fallon looked up at him and hunched her shoulders. "*'Syr.'*"

Sobehk grinned. "Yes, me, too. In fact, you are to address anyone in possession of your leash as *'Syr.'*"

Fallon turned away. *Leashes, collars, 'Syr . . . Gross!* She suddenly had the most incredible urge to writhe on the floor in complete disgust.

Sobehk had the nerve to chuckle. "You'll get used to it."

Fallon cringed. "Do I have to?" She curled her lip. "*'Syr.'*"

Sobehk raised his brow and gave her a broad smile. "You'll get beaten a lot less."

Fallon opened her mouth to reply. *I haven't gotten beaten yet.* And closed her mouth just in time. There was a whip sitting on his knee. Tempting Fate when it was sitting right next to her was probably not a good idea.

The crew trooped out and made the door disappear behind them.

Fallon looked over at Sobehk. "Now what?"

He raised an expectant brow.

Fallon hunched. "*'Syr*."

Sobehk nodded. "Now, I teach you some manners."

Everything went downhill from there.

"Sit."

Fallon fumed as she sank down toward the carpet for what had to be the hundredth time.

"Roll on the balls of your feet. Keep your knees together, your shoulders back, and your back straight." Sobehk gestured with the uncoiled whip as he spoke. "Don't rush! Calmly."

Fallon eased onto her knees and was never so grateful for her internal augmentations. Without them, she would have fallen on her face more than once.

"Sit *down* on your heels. Set your hands on your thighs gracefully, chin up, and with poise." Sobehk nodded. "Better, much better."

Fallon let out a soft breath.

"Stand."

She stood.

"That's it. Roll back onto to your heels." The whip flicked out, tapping her thigh with a sting that was as fast and fleeting as it was accurate. "Thighs apart!

Fallon ground her teeth and parted her feet exactly shoulder-width apart. Sobehk was disgustingly free and painfully accurate with that whip.

"Chin up. Show some pride." Sobehk's eyes narrowed. "You are an *upuaht rehkyt*, a fighter, a rehkyt who defends her master, a pet with purpose, not a *saysehn rehkyt*, a flower, a pet that sits on her master's lap looking decorative!"

Fallon took a deep breath and lifted her chin.

"And get that look off your face!"

Fallon worked to school the annoyance from her expression. It wasn't easy.

"Sit."

And so on.

"Bow."

While kneeling. Fallon made a triangle with her thumbs and index fingers on the carpet and lowered her head. Her overlong hair fell in a straight black curtain around her face as her head lowered to only a few centimeters from the floor, her gaze concealed yet never leaving Sobehk's form.

"That was graceful, finally." Sobehk smiled tightly and raised his hand above his head. "What do I have in my hand?"

She flicked her gaze up without moving her head in any way. The mirror behind him showed her that he held one of Khan's back-curved daggers. "A knife."

"Describe it."

"Black-handled, eight-centimeter live-steel blade, back-curved. One of '*Syr* Khan's."

"Good." He released a deep breath and lowered his arm, setting the dagger on the table behind him. "At ease."

Fallon sat back on her heels as smoothly as she was able, her hands placed where they were supposed to be, open-palmed on her thighs, elbows slightly out.

Sobehk nodded. "Very nice."

Fallon released her breath and relaxed, a little. All this poise was a freaking pain in the ass.

"Stand."

CHAPTER EIGHTEEN

Sobehk leaned back on the thick sitting pillow, setting one elbow on the low table behind him. "Do you sing?" He unfolded his knees and extended his legs, crossing his slippered feet at the ankles. His movements were a little stiff, and his mouth tightened. It was obvious that he was tiring.

Sing? Fallon's brows shot up as she knelt before him in the proscribed manner. Her gaze slid from his. She wasn't supposed to look him in the eye anyway. "No, *'Syr.'*"

"Play a musical instrument?"

She found herself frowning and worked to get it off her face. "No, *'Syr.'*"

"Know any poetry?"

Poetry? Fallon's fingertips bit into her thighs. What *was* this? "No, *'Syr.'*"

"Dance?"

Fallon lifted her shoulder the tiniest bit. "Some, *'Syr.'*"

Sobehk snorted. "It's a good thing you're classified as *upuaht.* You'd need intensive training to be a successful *say-sehn rehkyt.*"

Intensive training? To be a *decoration?* Fallon felt the hair rise on her neck and had to fight the urge not to hunch down. He made it sound as though she wasn't good for anything.

"I know you know knives . . ." He rolled his eyes.

Knives? Fallon straightened immediately. *Oh, bloody Fate, yeah!* She bit back her comment. He hadn't asked a direct question.

Sobehk tilted his head to the side and a smile kicked up the side of his mouth. "Do you know anything about swords?"

Fallon flinched before she could stop herself. "No, *'Syr.*"

"Would you like to?"

Fallon's heart stopped, just for a second. She would kill to know how to use a proper blade like a real duelist. She looked directly at Sobehk. Screw manners. "I would love to learn the sword, *'Syr.*"

Sobehk nodded and his smile widened. "As long as you continue to do well in your other lessons, I'll see to your sword training as well."

Fallon blinked. "You know the sword?" She flinched. He hadn't asked a question. Too late now. "*'Syr.*"

"Yes, he does indeed." The doorway disappeared behind Khan. He moved toward them in a whisper of heavy robes. A small smile curved his lips.

Fallon jumped in surprise. She hadn't heard the door open.

Khan nodded toward Sobehk. "*A'syr* Sobehk was a very fine sword master before he ever became *Mahf'dhyt*, an enforcer." He smiled at Sobehk then raised his brow at Fallon. "He was my sword master at the academy."

Sobehk rolled his eyes. "And a more stubborn student I never had in my life!"

Fallon tilted her head. Sobehk taught *Khan*?

Sobehk smiled. "At the time, my father was the headmaster at the school, and he thought the young lord . . ." His gaze drifted toward Khan. "Would have an easier time dealing with someone closer to his age."

"More like he thought a little humility would do me some good." Khan curled his lip as he tugged at his overrobe. "Sobehk was already a master level swordsman at a good three years younger than I."

"You were master level at other things." Sobehk nodded at Fallon and tilted his head toward Khan.

Fallon nodded slightly. One of the things Sobehk had spent far too much time on was the intricacies of Skeldhi dress. She rolled to her feet and approached Khan.

Khan's brows shot up. He glanced at Sobehk.

Sobehk smiled. "I thought I'd teach her something useful."

Useful, my ass . . . Fallon barely stopped herself from growling.

Khan dropped his hands and raised his chin. "Indeed?"

Fallon tugged at the twist-fastenings of his robes. She slipped behind him to draw the robe from his shoulders and folded the heavy fabric over her arm.

Khan stepped away. "How has her civilizing progressed?" He tugged at his robes and rolled down onto his knees, dropping onto a sitting pillow at the low table with an unconsciously graceful ease that made Fallon instantly envious.

Sobehk sighed. "We have the very basics, but I haven't approached table manners yet." He caught Fallon's eye and nodded toward the wardrobe.

Fallon walked over to Khan's wardrobe to hang the robe.

"She has absolutely no cultural skills whatsoever."

She caught the shake of Sobehk's head in the mirror just before she opened the wardrobe door. Fate and damnation, he made her sound like a total barbarian. She struggled briefly with the heavy robe and the hanger, making damned sure to hang it with all the other robes like it. Order, precision and grace. *Bleck.* She closed the door.

Khan chuckled. "Good thing she's *upuaht.*"

"That's my opinion."

Fallon turned in time to catch Sobehk's smile.

Khan nodded. "The midday supper should be arriving shortly." He turned to face Fallon. "I guess we'll see if she can manage a table or will have to eat from a bowl on the floor."

Sobehk snorted. "Well, she knows how to sit and stand properly. I don't hold high hopes for anything else."

Fallon decided right then and there that she really, really wanted to bite Sobehk, and not in a good way.

The midday supper arrived on an anti-grav levitating tray escorted by two youthful and slender Skeldhi. They wore knee-length gray robes with white smocks cross-tied over them. The smell of something juicy, meaty and delicious wafted from the tray.

Fallon knelt on the carpet by the edge of the table, while Sobehk on her left and Khan on her right got to sit on nice cushy pillows.

The attending Skeldhi set a large smoked glass bowl holding a goodly-sized chunk of meat in a golden broth then two smaller bowls with other meats in broth in the center of the table. Square plates of exceedingly expensive black Shido porcelain edged in gold were set before Khan and Sobehk. Matching cup-sized bowls were set on the plates with snowy-white rolled cloth napkins bound in gold paper twists above them, and utensils above that. Crystal goblets and matching tumblers were set beside the plates and a carved crystal decanter filled with a deep gold liquid was set between Sobehk and Khan.

The arrangement was done in complete silence with swift efficiency and a formal elegance that Fallon found surprising. Watching their reflections in the mirrors rather than staring openly, Fallon found the whole thing fascinating.

One of the attendants bowed to Sobehk and presented

him with a rolled mat, a shallow bowl of red glass with some kind of lettering around the bowl's rim, and a broad spoon.

Sobehk nodded in thanks then raised a brow at Fallon as he set them on the far left. "In case eating at the table proves too difficult for you."

Fallon's cheeks flushed with heat, but she didn't growl. She dropped her gaze to the bare table before her.

At the last second, a square plate of plain clear glass was set before Fallon with a matching clear bowl. A napkin and utensils were added, and a simple plain glass tumbler was set beside her plate. A clear pitcher filled with what looked like water was set by the crystal decanter.

Fallon took a deep breath. Obviously she did not rate the good porcelain, but it wasn't a bowl on the floor, though that was still a distinct possibility. She eyed the rolled mat and the red bowl by Sobehk's elbow.

The attendants bowed and left, directing their floating tray between them.

Khan leaned forward and gestured for Sobehk's cup and plate. He scooped meat from all three bowls onto the plate and broth from the largest bowl into the cup then served himself.

Sobehk reached for the crystal decanter and filled both Khan's goblet and his, then filled his tumbler from the clear glass pitcher. He turned and filled her tumbler from the pitcher as well.

Fallon sniffed as discreetly as she could as he poured. It smelled like water.

Khan finally collected her plate and bowl and put food in them then set them before her. It smelled incredible. Her mouth watered and her stomach decided to protest its emptiness with a hard kick. She winced. She was hungrier than she thought, but she wasn't about to touch a damned thing until she saw how Khan and Sobehk did it first. She was not going to eat off the floor if she could help it.

Fallon watched as Sobehk reached for his napkin first then noted the way he placed it in his lap, then how Khan held the utensils. On instinct alone, she waited.

They began to eat.

Still she waited. Something told her it was the right thing to do.

Khan smiled at Sobehk then nodded at Fallon. "You may begin."

She blinked in surprise then reached for her napkin. She stopped before she touched it. Something was not right. What had she forgotten? She glanced at Khan. "Thank you, *'Syr.'*"

Khan grinned. "Very well done!" He nodded at Sobehk. "Definitely an improvement."

Sobehk grinned openly. "She figured that one out all by herself. We'll have her civilized yet."

Fallon flushed and collected her napkin. She'd pleased them both. Warmth wrapped around her heart.

It was the most nerve-wracking meal she'd ever attended in her life. Handling the utensils alone was an exercise in patience, but she did it. She speared a sliver of meat and sucked it into her mouth. It took two tries before she remembered that chewing was not an option. She finally noticed what was missing. There wasn't a single vegetable, just meat and broth.

Khan sipped at his goblet. "Something wrong, Isabeau?" Humor curved his lush mouth.

Fallon looked over at him. "No vegetables?"

Khan's lip curled. "Only food eats plant life."

Fallon froze. Humans ate plants. She stared at the unidentified meat on her plate. Great Maker, what was she eating?

Khan's brow rose and he snorted. "Before you go into a panic, no, we don't eat humans."

Sobehk sipped water from his tumbler. "We don't eat plants because they are poisonous."

Fallon frowned at Sobehk. "For me, too?"

Sobehk raised his brow at her.

Fallon flinched. "Sorry, *'Syr.'*"

Khan chuckled and shook his head. "Yes, for you, too. If it grew in the ground, you don't put it in your mouth."

Fallon stared at her reflection in the mirror across the table. No deep-fried potatoes? No bread, or noodles, which were made from wheat? Blood and Fate, there went every last one of her favorite foods. Great Maker, kaffa was brewed from a bean. She curled her hands in her lap. Chocolate came from a bean, too. She groaned. No *chocolate?*

Khan glanced at Sobehk and set his elbow on the table. "Something you're going to miss?" He smiled.

Fallon looked up at him in total misery. "No more kaffa or *chocolate?*" She sniffed. "*'Syr'*"

Sobehk rolled his eyes.

Khan laughed out loud. "You can still have both."

"I can?" Fallon sat up straight. "*'Syr?*"

Khan nodded, grinning then held up a finger. "But only in small amounts; they are still fairly toxic. Too much will make you very ill."

Fallon sighed in complete relief. "For a moment I thought my life was over." She clapped her hands over her mouth. "*'Syr.'*" Her voice was muffled behind her hands.

Sobehk groaned. "We genetically alter her, and she does just fine. We threaten her with the loss of chocolate and now it's the end of the world?" He looked away, pressing his hand against brow while closing his eyes.

Khan shook his head. "Do not underestimate the importance of chocolate to a female." He nodded at Fallon.

"Sobehk had brothers, I had sisters. I discovered quite early that chocolate makes an excellent bribe."

Fallon frowned at one then the other. She couldn't imagine either one being part of a . . . family.

Khan tilted his head. "Didn't you have a family?"

Fallon looked at her half-eaten dinner. "No, *'Syr.*" She had Peter and the lostlings, but that wasn't the same as having people that you actually belonged with.

Sobehk turned to face her. "Then who raised you?"

Fallon lifted one shoulder in a shrug. "There was the institution . . ."

Khan tugged his napkin from his lap and tossed it over his plate. "You did not learn to write code in an Imperial institution."

Fallon shook her head. No, she hadn't. Well, she wasn't on the station anymore and it didn't look like she was going back. She glanced at Khan. Ever going back. Peter's secret would still be safe. She hunched, just a little. "Peter taught me to write code."

Both Sobehk and Khan sat up. They traded glances.

Khan leaned on his elbow, cupping his chin in his palm. "Peter?"

Fallon nodded. "He's the station master."

Sobehk tossed his napkin on his plate. "You were raised by the station master? The Dyson's Ring station's artificial intelligence?"

"Peter isn't artificial." Fallon shot him a quick glare then looked back at her plate. "*'Syr.* He's a normal . . . well mostly normal, person. He has a body. It's hardwired into the station, but he has one."

Khan pursed his lips and glanced at Sobehk. "It was a very old practice that the humans used in their early days of jump-space travel. They originally hardwired a living body into the ship's computational to achieve quantum consciousness." He shook his head. "Your Peter must be quite old."

Fallon nodded. "He is, '*Syr*." Ages and ages old.

Khan's brows rose. "How did you meet him?"

Fallon sat up. She'd never told *her* story before. She'd prepared one, but she'd never actually said it out loud before. She looked over at Khan. "Can I tell it in story form, '*Syr*?"

"Story form?" Khan blinked, glanced at Sobehk then nodded. "Certainly."

Fallon tilted her head and nibbled carefully on her bottom lip. "I have to change the way I sit."

Khan sat back and waved his hand. "By all means."

Fallon rose to her feet, remembering at the last second how she was supposed to stand. She bowed to both Sobehk and Khan, stalked two paces away, grinned then twirled and dropped into the traditional folded seat of the storyteller. She loved storytelling.

She raised her hands in a sweeping gesture. "Once upon a time, in the heart of Dyson's Ring, there lived a boy who would never grow old, and his name was Peter."

Fallon recited the story she had rehearsed in her head but had never said out loud. It began with being strapped in an institution couch looking for anything but what they wanted to shove into her brain.

Peter had come as a welcome voice in the deep darkness. He told fascinating stories about far away worlds and showed her wonderful images from all over the universe. One day, he asked if she wanted to join him in Never-land and become a lostling.

Thrilled to find a way to escape her drab world of shouting voices, she had eagerly accepted. A map was dropped into her mind with fantastical instructions that marked an adventurous journey into the station's deeps. Her travels culminated in an open elevator shaft marked with a star.

Fallon pointed at the distant wall, caught up in her story. "First star on the left and straight on 'til morning!"

A leap into the darkness and she flew, buoyant on a cushion of wind, to Never-land.

Never-land consisted of a tiny maze of rooms crammed wall to wall with servers and couches where kids of all ages were wired in to play in the most incredible virtual reality fantasyland she had ever seen. It was there that she learned to build her personal fantasies with code and talent.

Eventually, she joined the hunting parties of older kids that made forays above ground to collect food. Armed with door codes, internal maps, and Peter within easy reach through any communications line, they slipped unseen through the station's maze of disused tunnels. Snatching and grabbing, the hunting parties provided the basic necessities for the rather motley group that lived deep in the station's heart.

Then kids started disappearing all over the station. Eventually, some of the lostlings started to go missing too.

Fallon, with her talent for code splitting, and a small collection of the savvier older kids went above to discover what happened to them. Armed with breaker codes for entry into doors and moving through hidden passages known only to the station master, they hunted through the station's bowels. Eventually, they found a small group of kids with a few of their missing companions locked in a warehouse. They had been collected to be farmed.

Sobehk shook his head. "Farmed?"

Fallon nodded. "Station kids are considered a crop of unskilled labor. This particular outfit collects them, 'harvesting,' they call it, then ships them off-world to sell."

Sobehk winced. "Oh . . . farmed."

Khan tilted his head. "Any idea who runs that

operation?"

Fallon bared her teeth. "The Moribund Company. The nastiest bunch of filthy pirates in the known universe."

Khan sat back. "You don't like the Moribund Company?"

Fallon let loose a string of foul curses that should have peeled the paint. She took a breath and smiled. "No, '*Syr.*"

Khan's brows rose. "But you code-cracked for them, yes?"

"No, I did *not!*" Fallon barely held back her snarl. She had to look away to get her temper back under control. "'*Syr*. The boss sold some of my stuff to them, I'm sure, but I didn't work for them. I broke into every ship of theirs I could find."

Khan smiled. "How very interesting. Please, continue with your story."

Fallon took a deep breath, closed her eyes briefly to get back into place and continued.

It became a regular mission to go out and find kids. It took time before she was able to get into ship holds as well as warehouses. Then one day, she ran into a trap-code that knocked her out cold. She woke up lashed to a chair facing the boss for the first time.

The boss was very curious as to how she had gotten into ships. He was not interested in the released kids, he assured her, but there were things he was definitely interested in getting out of the occasional ship. He'd be willing to ignore her forays to rescue the kids if she wouldn't mind picking up a few things for him along the way.

And so began her extremely lucrative job of breaking into ships for secrets. Every credit she earned went into her physical and mental augmentations to make it faster to get into ships and easier to avoid capture. With every upgrade, Peter taught her as much as her brain could hold. Peter wasn't exactly state-of-the-art, but he had access to every drop of information that went through the station's inter-star communications.

Rather than continue with how she had been caught by Sobehk, Fallon twirled up onto her feet and delivered a sweeping bow. "And so ends my adventures, gentlemen, of Peter, Never-land and the Pirates."

Khan looked over at Sobehk. "A most remarkable story."

Sobehk smiled. "I was impressed."

Fallon grinned. She'd pleased them. A small touch of sadness brushed her heart and tightened her smile. She hadn't been the only one that had gone on hunting forays for Peter, merely the most successful. With luck, another lostling would take her place and continue her mission, be-cause . . . she wasn't going back.

Khan poured some of the golden liquid from the cut crystal carafe into his goblet. "What pleases me the most is your profound dislike of the Moribund Company." He set the carafe down. "Because after a long and detailed look at your internal programs, it seems that the trapdoor pro-gram in your head is theirs."

Fallon gasped. "What?"

CHAPTER NINETEEN

The Moribund Company had planted something in her
head.

The rage closed around Fallon's heart into a fist of hate
so tight she had to gasp for breath. *How dare they?* She
folded onto her knees and dug her nails into the carpet,
shaking with violent rage. How *dare* they presume to put
their filthy programs in *her*?

"Isabeau?"

Fallon looked up, not caring if Sobehk saw her rage.

Sobehk tilted his head. "Would you like some water?"
He patted the floor beside him. "Come."

Fallon took a deep breath and eased back onto her heels
with exquisite slowness. She rose and stalked toward the
table. She folded her knees and dropped beside the table in
proper form. The amount of control it took to sit properly
actually helped to disperse the shaking rage trembling in
her limbs.

Only then did she notice Khan's perfect and dangerous
stillness. His copper gaze was ice cold, but a smile curved
his lips. "Isabeau, what do you want right now?"

Fallon could barely think past the hate boiling in her. It
took her two tries before she could get her desire into
words. She looked straight into Khan's eyes. How she kept
back the scream, she didn't know, but her words came out
even and fairly quiet. "I want to make them bleed."

"Good." Khan nodded. "So do I."

Sobehk pressed her water glass into her hand. "Don't

squeeze, you'll shatter it." He pushed the glass toward her lips. "Drink."

Fallon took a swallow, pretty sure she wouldn't need more than that, but drained the glass. She looked at the empty glass in surprise.

Sobehk smiled. "Better?"

Fallon nodded. The rage was still there, but it was far deeper. It took two tries before she could speak. "Thank you, 'Syr.'"

Sobehk looked over at Khan. "Can the program be removed?"

"It can, though not easily." Khan tapped the rim of his goblet with a finger. "Interestingly enough, I don't believe that whoever decided to put that program in Isabeau understood our Isabeau's actual capabilities, as it does not take advantage of them."

Fallon turned to look over at Khan. Her teeth clenched so hard her jaw began to ache. "What did they put in my head?" Screw manners.

Khan lifted his goblet. "It seems that whoever broke into your head made the same assumptions that Sobehk did." He sipped at the golden liquid.

Sobehk frowned. "What assumptions?"

Khan set the goblet down and focused on Fallon. "They assumed that you were a clever acrobatic thief because that is all the program accesses, your physical abilities."

Accessed her *physical* abilities? Fallon frowned. "For what? Am I supposed to do something, 'Syr?'"

Khan pursed his lips. "When the code goes active, it turns you into a mindless killing machine." His copper gaze hardened. "And then it kills you."

A killing machine? Fallon's mind came to a complete screeching halt.

Khan leaned forward and tapped a clawed finger on the

tabletop. "They have programmed you to be a sleeper assassin."

An *assassin?* Fallon shook her head. "But that's *stupid,* 'Syr."

Khan's lip curled. "As I said, I don't think they had any idea what your real abilities were."

"If she's supposed to kill someone . . ." Sobehk leaned both elbows on the table. "Then who is she supposed to kill?"

Khan raised a brow. "That is an excellent question. You see, she only has half the code in her head. The person with the other half of the code is the only one who knows."

Sobehk scowled. "How in bleeding Chaos do we find them?"

Khan tapped the tabletop with his finger. "It's simple, really. According to what you and Isabeau have told me, she was set up specifically for capture. The rest leads me to believe that the assassin was deliberately sent to push her into displaying her fighting skills."

The hair on Fallon's neck rose. Tusk *had* been sent to her, she knew . . . he had told her. But he had been sent to *die?*

"I don't believe they intended their assassin to be captured, but they obviously knew that Isabeau would be able to kill him." Khan tilted his head at Fallon.

Fallon shook her head. "I don't see how that's possible. I never told anyone I knew how to take Tusk down." She winced. "'*Syr.*" She was speaking out of turn.

Khan patted her wrist. "Whoever did your physical upgrades would know exactly what you were capable of. And also, they *were* in your head. They could have deduced it." He rolled his eyes. "Though I seriously doubt they were quite that bright, just from looking at the program they planted."

Fallon looked away. They had deliberately sent Tusk to

die at her hands. Tusk was deadly, true, and he had killed a lot of people, but mostly other bad guys. He'd never disobeyed the boss once. In fact, he adored the boss. And they had sent him to her to *die*? He had been betrayed, just as she had been betrayed. She closed her eyes as a fist of pain closed around her heart. All because someone wanted to show off her fighting skills.

Of all the stupid reasons to die.

Sobehk . . . Guilt stabbed right through Fallon's heart. It *was* her fault Sobehk had gotten hurt. She closed her eyes and took a deep breath, taking in his warm scent. He was alive. He lived. But he almost hadn't. She leaned over and pressed her head against his side. Screw protocol. "I'm sorry." Her voice came out in a tight whisper.

Sobehk's hand slid down her back and he sighed. "It's not your fault."

She rubbed her cheek against his side. "It *was* my fault. I should have taken the knife."

Sobehk's hand slid through her hair. "You're assuming that you could have gotten it from my hand."

Fallon sniffed. "I could have." She closed her eyes. "I *should* have."

Sobehk groaned. "I'm supposed to protect *you*, remember?"

Fallon wiped at her damp cheeks and looked up at him. "So?"

Sobehk glared down at her "So?"

Fallon simply smiled.

Khan rolled his eyes. "May I continue?"

"Yes, '*Syr*." Fallon took a deep breath and sat up. Oh yeah, she definitely wanted to know the rest of this.

Khan folded his hands on the tabletop. "If Isabeau had not taken three days to catch . . ."

Sobehk winced just a little.

Fallon snorted, amused in spite of herself.

Khan cleared his throat and raised his chin. "If Isabeau had been caught as most *rehkyt* are, what would have been her fate?"

Sobehk swept a hand across his jaw and flushed. "The auction at Port Destiny."

Fallon froze. Auction? A *slave* auction?

Khan nodded. "Then that is where the one with the other half of the code is waiting. We take them and we will know who the target is."

Sobehk shook his head. "But how do we find one person in that morass? There will be over a thousand Skeldhi attending that event!"

Khan lifted his glass. "We put Isabeau up for auction. The one who buys her has the second half of the code."

What? Fallon jerked back and nearly fell over. He wanted to put her in a slave auction?

Sobehk growled. "You can't be serious!"

Khan smiled and it wasn't pretty. "I assure you, I have no intention of selling my *rehkyt*. I was thinking more of merely tempting the buyer into coming out of hiding."

Sobehk's brows dropped low over his blue eyes and his mouth set in a white line. "How? Exactly."

"You set her up to be auctioned, and I pose as your *nehkyx*, your handler."

Sobehk shook his head. "You, as *my* handler?"

Fallon frowned. What the heck was a handler?

Khan raised his brow. "You are still recovering from an accident, are you not? I assure you, the news of the incident aboard the *Vortex* was not kept under wraps. So a handler would be quite appropriate, if not expected. As long as we keep the story as close to the truth as possible, it will be believed."

"They'll never believe she's still mine." Sobehk shook

his head. "Your DNA marks her . . ."

"So does yours." Sobehk smiled, and his copper gaze chilled. "She drank you down during the fourth course, remember? *'Syr* Tah says your mark is as prominent as mine."

Sobehk narrowed his blue eyes at Khan. "You did that on purpose?"

Khan waved his hand in dismissal. "Does it matter why I did it?" He focused on Sobehk. "Because of it, you can pose as her selling owner."

Sobehk frowned. "Khan, what are you up to?"

Khan's chin rose and his mouth tightened. "I am out to find the target of an assassination. If my suspicions are correct, then the target is among the council members."

Sobehk jerked back. "What?"

"Think!" Khan jabbed a finger toward Sobehk. "A *rehkyt* that kills an assassin like that creature where all can see? Naturally, she would have been marked for *upuaht* training. Therefore, she was deliberately set up to be so marked. How many Skeldhi can afford an *upuaht rehkyt*?"

Sobehk's hands became fists on the tabletop. "Only a lord could afford one."

"My point exactly."

"Night and Chaos . . . A lord is planning an assassination?"

"Not all that unusual. Lords kill each other all the time." Khan shrugged. "But Isabeau is a female. She could have been made to appear to be a *saysehn rehkyt,* a common pleasure pet if her conformation had not gone so obviously Prime. Though I doubt that will be a factor. Too many do not look beyond a pretty face to see if it has teeth."

Fallon felt a sudden curl of warmth. Khan thought she was pretty?

Sobehk shook his head. "What does Isabeau being

female have to do with anything?"

Khan set his elbow on the table and propped his chin in his hand. "Sobehk, in case you haven't noticed, our Isabeau is rather small and delicate in appearance." He looked over at Fallon.

Fallon tilted her head in confusion. *Delicate? Since when?*

Sobehk snorted. "But she's not!"

Fallon frowned. She wasn't exactly sure she was pleased that Sobehk didn't find her delicate.

"No, but she *looks* that way." Khan sat back up and pressed his fingertips together. "And the only place the big *upuaht rehkyt* males are not allowed to enter . . ."

Sobehk looked down at the tabletop with a frown. "The *Ehnyad* enclave—the council lords' personal chambers—have that restriction."

Khan nodded. "Correct. The *Pshent* enclave, the court of queens, does not allow *upuaht* or Primes of any type, male or female, but the *Ehnyad* enclave only restricts males from entering."

Sobehk straightened. "You think Isabeau has been set up to assassinate an *Ehnya'dhyt*? A council lord?"

Khan leaned back. "We won't know until I have interrogated the person with the other half of the code. But it *is* a possibility." He nodded toward Fallon. "Isabeau is an *upuaht* grade *rehkyt* capable of taking down a mimetic cyborg assassin. Whoever she's supposed to kill must have some pretty strong guards if they think they need someone with enough killing power to take down a fully grown male *upuaht rehkyt,* if not more than one."

Sobehk frowned. "But she's a Prime and wearing the ear-cuffs of an *upuaht* in training. Obviously, she's capable of killing."

Fallon started and recognized the weights dangling from the bottom edge of her ears, about a finger-width above the lobes. *So that's what he put in my ears.* She lifted her hand, but for some reason couldn't make herself touch them.

"You would think so." Khan sighed and shook his head. "However, too many males assume that a female cannot kill them, simply because they are smaller." He rolled his eyes and smiled slightly. "I had sisters, I know better."

Sobehk stared at Fallon. "Khan, I am in no condition to protect her from a lord and his guards when he comes to collect what he thinks is his property after the auction."

Khan smiled, showing his long teeth. "But I am, and I have a full coterie of *mehdja'dhyt* — security and intelligence officers — on this ship."

Sobehk turned to Khan. "Won't this ship give away the fact that the *Mehdjay*, the Office of Intelligence, is aware of this . . . conspiracy?"

Khan raised his finger. "Not if we proceed as though you never left the *Vortex*. I have spoken to the captain and he is going to make sure that the logs state that both of you are still aboard." He set his hands flat on the table. "The most obvious reason for the presence of *mehdja'dhyt* – intelligence officers — *is* the auction. I assure you, my ship will not be the only one there. The *Mehdjay* office is always looking to acquire high quality *upuaht* grade *rehkyt.*" He smiled. "Though not every *Mehdjay'syr* – lord-officer — has the resources to buy one such as Isabeau."

Sobehk shook his head. "There's a big gaping hole in this plan of yours, I can smell it. I just can't see it at the moment."

Khan rolled his eyes. "There are a number of gaping holes in it, one of which being that one look at our Isabeau will show that she's not only sighted but semi-trained."

Fallon sat up straight. "Does this mean I get to drop all the manners stuff?"

They both turned to her. "No!" they chorused.

Fallon cringed back. "Fine, whatever. Yes, *'Syr.'*"

Sobehk scrubbed his hand along his jaw. "I suppose I can say I had her trained somewhat to deal with her aggressive tendencies?" He looked over at Khan. "And perhaps drive up the price?"

Khan's brows rose. "Indeed. She *is* a Prime and your best catch to date, so it would be quite logical to try to get the best price for her." He frowned at Sobehk. "Are you in need of your medication?"

Fallon's gaze jerked to Sobehk.

Sobehk looked at the colored band around his wrist. "Yes, damn it."

Khan rose and approached Sobehk. "To bed with you." He held out his hand.

"I can get up on my own." Sobehk rolled forward. "I'm not that much of an invalid." He fell back on the cushion. A look of surprise widened his eyes.

"Is that so?" Khan leaned down to catch his arm. He frowned at the colored band around Sobehk's wrist. "You're late for your treatment." He reached down and levered Sobehk onto his feet. "Come on. I'll call the medic as soon as you're settled in bed."

Fallon jumped up and slid Sobehk's other arm over her shoulder.

Sobehk lurched toward the bed between them, his face pale and his mouth somewhat gray. "I hate this."

Khan snorted. "I'm sure you do, but I don't need you overextending yourself. No more waiting on the meds. I need you in the best possible condition by the time we get to Port Destiny."

Sobehk rolled his eyes. "Yes, *'Syr.'*"

Fallon dropped his arm and moved in front of him to pull off his sash and tug at his robes. Sobehk had been very clear that Skeldhi did not sleep clothed. Ever. She pulled his long robes from his shoulders, tossed them over her arm then dropped to one knee to tug at the ties to his kilt.

Khan nodded. "Remove your robes as well, Isabeau."

Huh? Fallon darted a startled look at Khan.

Khan smiled. "You're going to make sure Sobehk remains comfortable while he sleeps."

Yeah, right . . . Fallon curled her lip just a tiny amount as she unwrapped Sobehk's kilt. She would wait until Sobehk was asleep and then find someplace else to nap.

Sobehk snorted as he stepped out of his slippers. "I don't have the energy."

"Oh, no?" Khan chuckled. "That is simple enough to fix."

Fallon collected his slippers and turned toward the wardrobes to put Sobehk's belongings away.

"Khan!"

She opened Sobehk's wardrobe and caught a flash of movement in the mirror. She turned.

Khan faced her, holding Sobehk around the waist with his hand fisted in Sobehk's long white hair.

Sobehk grabbed Khan around the shoulders. "What are you doing?"

Khan jerked Sobehk's head to one side and sank his teeth into Sobehk's shoulder.

Sobehk shouted and shuddered. "Fuck . . . Khan!"

Khan stared at Fallon as he pulled his teeth free then licked the wounds he'd made. He leaned back, releasing Sobehk's hair. "How do you feel now?" He licked his lips and smiled.

Sobehk groaned. "Okay, that worked, you bastard." He bowed his head and chuckled tiredly. "Still up to your old tricks?"

Khan shrugged, just a little. "Perhaps one or two."

"Is that so?" Sobehk caught Khan's face in his palms. "Payback can be a bitch." He pressed his open mouth to Khan's, kissing him.

Khan's eyes opened wide then closed. His arms slid around Sobehk's waist as he kissed him back.

Their lips parted and they leaned against each other with their heads together. Khan turned and helped Sobehk step down into the knee-deep bed.

Okay . . . Fallon turned and tucked Sobehk's robe and kilt in his wardrobe. Perhaps the two of them together wasn't such an odd combination. She'd seen odder pairings, and there seemed to be some kind of romantic history between them. She just hoped it wasn't ugly history. Broken hearts made vicious enemies faster than cold-blooded murder.

CHAPTER TWENTY

"Isabeau!"

Fallon flinched. What in fury did Khan want now? Oh yeah, for her to get in that open target of a bed. "Coming, '*Syr*." She closed the wardrobe door and headed back across the room, tugging at her sash. She had her robes off her shoulders by the time she reached the edge of the bed. She would slip out as soon as Sobehk fell asleep.

Khan held out his hand.

Fallon gave him her robes and sash.

Sobehk was a pale and delicious vision among the tumble of red and gold pillows. His long sweep of frost-white hair glowed against the black silk sheets. He pulled back the black comforter and smiled. "Come."

Fallon dropped down into the bed and slid under the covers. Sobehk was almost hot against her bare skin. He smelled wonderful and precious. She leaned in close to sweep a hand across his chest and pressed a kiss over his heart.

Sobehk rolled over her and his mouth took hers with hunger.

She leaned up into his kiss. She'd missed him. Excitement washed through her body with sudden voracious heat. She moaned into his mouth as cream slicked her thighs.

His hand slid between her thighs, parting them. His fingers explored her intimate folds and he groaned in appreciation. His fingertips rubbed against her clit, inciting small bolts of delight.

Fallon moaned into his mouth and lifted her hips, pressing against his palm.

He released her lips and pulled his hand away to suck on his damp fingers. He smiled. Shifting his hips, he settled between her thighs and sighed. His primary cock nosed between her slick folds, pressing for immediate entry.

Fallon gasped. He was hard, both of his cocks. Khan's bite . . .

He thrust and sank into her with a soft groan, his secondary cock nudging for entry into her ass. It was slick with something. Sobehk chuckled. "Khan was kind enough to grease me. Open for me."

She looked up to see Khan watching them from the edge of the bed. An odd and hungry smile curled his full lips and heat darkened his copper eyes.

She frowned. Khan obviously wanted the two of them together . . . like this. He was pleased that they were together . . . like this. But Khan had made damned sure she admitted that she wasn't Sobehk's. What was going on?

Sobehk nipped sharply at her nipple.

She yelped and jumped.

"Pay attention when I'm fucking you!" Sobehk groaned and pushed. "Let me in."

Fallon arched and pushed, forcing her body open.

He surged hard and slid within, groaning in obvious pleasure.

Fallon moaned. Tight fullness, exquisite ache, dark pleasure . . . He filled her and her heart leaped to have him there. She closed her arms around his neck and locked her heels around his hips. *Sobehk* . . . She arched in eager hunger. She loved him. Great Maker, she *loved* him. And wanted him right where he was, in her body. Desperately.

He panted then surged again, seating himself to the root.

He groaned. "Mother Night, it's good to be back in here." He closed his arms around Fallon's waist and rolled, bringing her atop him.

Fallon sat up, straddling his hips, not wanting to put any pressure on his bandaged middle.

His eyes were dark wide pits outlined in sapphire brilliance. He smiled, then caught the back of her neck. He pulled her down to him, his mouth taking her nipple. He sucked with brutal tenderness. His teeth scored her breast.

Delight scorched from his mouth straight to her clit and throbbed. The scent of his arousal rolled from his skin, electrifying her. She moaned.

He released her nipple and cupped her breasts in his warm palms, pinching and rolling the swollen tips between thumb and forefinger.

Fallon whimpered with the exquisite fire stirred by his fingers.

He licked his lips. "Fuck me, kitten. Fuck me hard."

She rocked forward and up, leaning into his hands. The shafts slid outward. Decadent delight. She sat back and they slid within. The ripple of pleasure in her core was laced with the bright edge of pain in her ass. She rose and fell. It felt so good, it felt so right . . . More, she needed more.

She caught his wrists, holding his hands to her breasts, using him for leverage, rising sharply and falling hard in increasingly stronger lunges.

Sobehk groaned and moved under her. His knees came up, and he thrust in counterpoint to her driving plunges. His mouth opened, showing long teeth. He groaned. "Chaos." He sucked in a breath. "Almost there." His breath quickened and he increased his thrusts in speed and strength, grunting with effort.

Fallon felt the sudden and violent rise of heat and

tension that marked approaching climax. She was going to cum . . .

Sobehk arched tautly under her and his pupils abruptly changed from round to feline slits. A rumbling liquid growl vibrated through him.

A shiver of anticipation raced through Fallon. She felt the fullness in her cunt and her ass swell with alarming speed. She rose from him. She didn't want to get locked to his body.

"Oh, no, you don't!" Sobehk snarled and twisted, rolling her under him and grinding mercilessly within her. "Your tight little body will squeeze the cum from my knots in one long delicious orgasm guaranteed to give me an excellent night's sleep."

Fallon hissed and bucked as the tightness stretched her. Movement became uncomfortable.

Sobehk growled in masculine triumph. "Oh yeah . . . good and tied."

She twisted hard and yelped. He was lodged tight in her. They were locked. She glared at him. "Bastard!"

Sobehk leaned up and smiled hungrily. "Yep." His head dropped and his teeth sank into her shoulder.

Release exploded through her in a hot wet rush. She howled and bucked frantically under him, her nails scoring his butt and thighs.

His tongue stroked the bite on her shoulder. "Mmm, that was nice. Do that again." His mouth shifted and his teeth sank into her a second time, only a few centimeters from the first bite.

She gasped, shocked. The venom in his bite made the second bite sharper, harsher and hotter.

Climax knotted in her belly then rushed outward in a blaze of glory that burned up her arching spine and ripped a scream from her throat.

Sobehk ground into her, riding her bucking climax. "That's what I like to hear."

Fallon whimpered as she came down from her release and panted under him, soaked in sweat, the air perfumed with the rich musk of lust.

"Isabeau . . ." His mouth found hers in a leisurely but thorough kiss.

Fallon kissed him back, glad to her soul to have him exactly where he was, safe in her arms, though annoyed that she was stuck in the damned bed.

His arms closed tight around her, and he rolled to his side, their bodies locked in carnal intimacy and their legs entwined. His tongue swept deliciously against hers. A purr boiled from his chest. He pulled back and stared at her with eyes dark yet hooded with sleepy heat. "Isabeau." He brushed the hair from her damp brow then pressed a kiss there. He pulled her against his heart. "Go to sleep."

Fallon glanced up past Sobehk's broad shoulder to see that Khan still watched from the edge of the bed. His eyes were hot, but his mouth was tight. He rose and moved away.

Sobehk's heart pounded against her ear in a steady rhythm even as his purr closed around her.

Someone came into the bed.

Fallon started awake.

An unknown Skeldhi in long, sleeveless gray robes bent toward Sobehk.

Her entire body tensed, and a growl of warning boiled from her throat.

The gray-robed Skeldhi jerked back.

"Isabeau, no." Khan was suddenly in the bed at her side. He caught the chain around her throat and tugged slightly. "He's a *sehn'dhyt*, a medic." He looked up. "I have her,

A'syr. She's just being protective." He nodded toward Sobehk, who had not awakened. "Continue."

The *sehn'dhyt* leaned over Sobehk with a wary eye on Fallon. He applied a hydraulic syringe to Sobehk's throat.

Sobehk sighed but did not wake.

The *sehn'dhyt* lifted Sobehk's wrist to examine the band around it. He reached into his pocket and pulled out another hydraulic syringe. He darted an uneasy look at Fallon then applied that syringe to the bend in Sobehk's arm. He withdrew from the bed.

Khan released her chain and stroked her hair. "Go back to sleep." He moved from the bed.

Fallon snuggled up against Sobehk, putting an arm over his hip.

The *sehn'dhyt* looked over at Khan. "He'll need another treatment at the beginning of the night cycle and again in morning cycle." He glanced at Fallon. "He can begin exercise therapy the following day, *'Syr.*"

Khan nodded and lifted an arm, gently herding the medic toward the door. "I'll see to it that he stays on schedule, *A'syr sehn'dhyt.*"

Fallon pressed her nose against Sobehk's heart and curled tight up against him, listening to his slow and steady heartbeat.

Someone was in the room.

Fallon's eyes snapped open. She shifted and discovered that Sobehk was no longer locked in her body. She wormed out from under him.

He sighed heavily but remained asleep.

She moved as silently as she could across the blankets and pillows to the edge of the bowl. She lifted her head to catch a trace of scent. It was Khan.

"Isabeau." Khan's voice was barely a whisper.

An odd hunger tugged at her. She eased up over the edge and parted the gold curtains. There were fewer lights than before. Deep shadows filled the room's corners.

Khan sat cross-legged and facing her on a large pillow by the round table. He was barefoot and in only his black kilt. Sitting on the table by his elbow was a clear glass bowl half full of meat, a spoon, a folded cloth napkin and a clear glass tumbler of water.

"Come." He patted his knee, and muscle moved across his broad, scarred chest.

Fallon moved silently across the carpet, his scent drawing her. He smelled good. He smelled right. And a part of her wanted . . . *she* wanted . . . to touch him and be touched by him. She *needed* to touch him.

She stopped only a few steps away, trembling.

"Down."

She dropped to her knees.

He smiled. "Good. Lower, and closer."

She dropped to her hands and inched toward him. He encouraged her closer until she crouched nearly on her belly with her hands on his knees. She spotted the black chain leash coiled by his knee under the table.

He picked up the bowl, scooped food into the spoon and held it up. "Open."

Fallon cringed and made a small sound of protest. He wanted to feed her like a child? She knew how to eat properly.

His brow rose.

She flinched, opened her mouth and sucked the meat from his spoon. It was warm but tasted as though it was barely cooked. The copper taste of extremely rare meat was very strong. She sucked it down just the same, finally resigned to no longer chewing.

He smiled and picked up the napkin to dab at her lower

lip. In complete silence he spoon-fed her, stopping every now and again to offer her the glass of water or dab at her lips with the napkin.

He set the empty bowl and the spoon on the table and gave her lips a final swipe of the napkin. He leaned to the side, lifted the black chain leash from beside his knee and clipped it to the chain around her throat.

Fallon winced.

"Open my kilt."

Fallon reached into his lap to tug at the ties. The cloth parted to reveal his half aroused cocks.

"Lick. Don't suck, just lick."

Fallon set her hands on his thighs and dropped to her belly. She lowered her head into his lap, extended her tongue and stroked the bumpy underside of his primary cock. The metal balls under his skin rasped against her tongue. The flavor was strong enough that she was pretty that he wore titanium. It was a little odd, tasting so much metal in his cock. She licked.

He sighed and hardened.

She slid the point of her tongue around the flared edge of his cockhead and then across the sensitive tip. She flicked her tongue across and around the heavy balls that marked the bar that speared through the center of his cock-head from top to bottom.

Khan let his head fall back and groaned in pleasure.

The sound of his enjoyment and the scent of his arousal seared through her and cream slicked her thighs. She licked with increasing eagerness.

The electronic whisper of the door caught her attention.

The leash rattled in his hand. "Continue. Do not stop."

She continued to lick but proceeded to lave the top of his shaft so she could look above his knee to see who had entered.

The slender gray-robed *sehn'dhyt,* the Skeldhi medic from before, came in and bowed to Khan.

Khan waved his hand toward the bed. "Proceed."

Fallon watched him move toward the bed.

Khan tugged lightly on the chain. "Pay attention to me." He pushed her head lower.

Fallon licked at his lower shaft, her view completely blocked by his raised knees. His cocks stiffened considerably, and his breathing deepened. Liquid musk dampened her tongue. She lapped at it. Warmth curled and clenched in her belly and her nipples tightened to hard, hot points. Her clit throbbed. A small hungry moan escaped her.

She felt Khan's body shift and turn, but he held the chain too tight to allow her to raise her head to see.

He groaned. "All right, the *sehn'dhyt* has left." He pushed her back. "Sit up."

Fallon sat back on her heels and licked her lips.

Khan unlatched the leash, set it on the table and stood, his kilt sliding from his thighs. He lifted the fallen cloth and set it over the leash on the table. "Come." He strode for the bed, his rigid cocks waving before him.

Fallon rose and followed, her body trembling with hungry tension. He was going to fuck her. She couldn't wait.

Chapter Twenty-one

Khan pushed the curtain back and stepped over the edge into his enormous round bed. He turned and bent to pick up a black squeeze-tube that lay on the floor at the bed's rim. He squeezed a large dollop of gel into his palm then smiled at her as he reached down to stroke himself. "Come. Come to me."

Fallon eased over the edge into the blankets and pillows of the deep bed.

Khan seized her around the waist and flung her back onto the pillows.

She gasped in surprise.

Khan grinned down at her and then he fell on her, his hot body dropping onto hers and his mouth taking hers in a devouring kiss. His clawed fingers raked down her side.

She bucked, moaning under his mouth, and clawed his shoulders and back in retaliation.

He groaned and pressed his cocks against her belly then dug his claws into her butt.

She hissed with the bright, hot burn. Khan was apparently in the mood to play. Wriggling, she caught hold of his arm, insinuated her leg just right, and flipped him over onto his stomach. In half a breath, she climbed on his back to straddle his hips, and locked his arm behind him, pinning him.

He grunted in surprise.

Fallon dropped along the top of him and opened her mouth on his shoulder.

He stilled and his breathing quickened.

Fallon smiled. He was waiting for her bite. She raked her teeth and tongue across his shoulder instead, deliberately teasing him.

He growled, clearly disappointed. He rolled, trying to get her under him.

Fallon eluded his grasp with ease, rolling among the pillows and twisting out of his holds. Small giggles erupted as his frustrated growls increased. She darted in to nip at his pierced nipples, making him jump, then nipped the tender undersides of his arms. He pulled away but she pursued him, twisting around him to nip the sensitive insides of his thighs. She scored a nice nip on the cheek of his ass.

Khan jumped and twisted but he couldn't quite grab her.

Sobehk, spread out on his belly, groaned and opened one blue eye. "Khan, you are not going to win a wrestling match with her. She's augmented to the hilt for dexterity and . . ." He smiled. "She plays dirty."

Khan sat back on his heels among the pillows, panting just a little. His skin was marked by a full dozen tiny bleeding nips and more than a dozen scratches from her claws. "Is that so?" He grinned. He was obviously enjoying himself and brutally excited. He raised a brow at Sobehk. "Then how did you catch her?"

Sobehk chuckled softly. "I wore armor."

Khan's brows shot up. "Armor?"

Fallon snorted. "You try fighting him for three days straight when he's wearing armor, and you're not."

Khan tilted his head toward her and his eyes narrowed. "So, you like to fight dirty?" He came up on his feet but remained crouched.

Uh oh . . . Fallon instinctively backed away, but the bed was not all that large and Sobehk took up a pretty big portion of it.

Khan launched himself at her.

She threw herself back and rolled—and couldn't. Her foot was caught on something, or rather something was wrapped around her ankle. Khan landed on top of her. The breath was knocked from her lungs. She twisted her hands free and scrambled to get out from under him, but her ankle was caught fast.

Khan took no time at all to repay her nips.

She yelped and twisted but couldn't free her ankle.

Sobehk chuckled from the pillows. "Having problems, kitten?"

Fallon glanced down. Her ankle was trapped in his hand. She gasped. "Let go, you big brute! Let him fight his own battles!"

Khan locked his legs around her hips and pinned her hands above her head. "I'll take the back up, thank you." He sank his teeth into her shoulder.

Fallon shouted and arched up under him. She trembled, held still by the teeth in her shoulder. His venom raced through her, bringing every single one of his nips to bright, hot life while stirring the heat in her belly into an unbelievably ravenous craving. She moaned and lifted her knees to pull away from Sobehk's hold.

Sobehk's hand, a manacle around her ankle, tugged her legs apart.

Khan released her shoulder and grinned. "Yes, hold her open for me." He unlocked his legs and shifted between her spread thighs.

"Hey, no fair!" Fallon tried to buck him off, but Sobehk's grip held her open.

"You don't fight fair . . ." Khan came up on his knees, catching her under the thighs. His hands spread her wide. "Why should we?" He thrust. His primary cockhead surged into her slick interior.

They both gasped.

Fallon twisted her hips. The bar in his cock was a fierce and delicious pressure as it forged into her. The second cock pressed for entry. She sucked in a breath and pushed out. The slick head of Khan's second cock, and the bar that pierced it pressed into her ass even as his primary cock surged deeper into her hungry cunt. She groaned.

"Mother Night, ah . . ." Khan dug his clawed fingers into her ass, pulling her tighter to him. He thrust, hard, surging in to the root, and sighed.

Fallon wrapped her arms under his. She needed to be fucked and was not in the mood to wait any longer. She pulled him down to her and arched up to sink her teeth into Khan's shoulder.

Khan shuddered and hissed then moaned. "Spawn of Chaos, you're potent!" He ground his metal-laden cocks deep into her.

Fallon locked her legs around his hips, pulled her teeth from his shoulder, and stroked the tears with her tongue.

Khan sighed. "Mmm, yes." He locked an arm around her then pushed up with his free hand, sitting up on his knees with Fallon in his arms. His hands slid down to cup her ass. He lifted her to the very end of his cocks.

Fallon moaned as the cock in her ass delivered dark, rich pleasure on the retreating stroke.

He pressed her down onto him while thrusting upward.

She squeezed on the thrust and was rewarded as his pierced cock struck something deliciously exciting deep in her cunt. She released a startled cry and bucked hard.

Khan smiled. "Oh, liked that, did you?"

Fallon dug her claws into him and pushed upward. "Don't stop! More!"

Khan laughed softly and lifted, then shoved her down

on his cocks while thrusting as she fell onto him. Then again, and again . . .

Fallon twisted in counterthrust, and bright, sharp pleasure raked through her on each stroke. Delighted and desperate cries poured from her lips.

The rich scent of lust perfumed the small alcove.

Khan's breathing became labored, and sweat slid down his body. The base of his cocks hardened and expanded, slipping in and then out, pressing against her clit on each entry.

Fallon dug her claws into Khan's back as she bucked and cried out her building pleasure. Climax rose and tightened in a white-hot ball of tension waiting to explode.

Khan groaned and dropped down among the pillows, his body pinning hers. He caught a handful of her hair, pulling her head back and forcing her to arch under him. He lowered his head and nipped at her swollen nipples, scoring her breasts with his long teeth, while grinding deep within her. The base of cocks expanded further, swelling to tightness, locking her in his carnal embrace. His mouth centered on her nipple and opened wide.

She bucked frantically, right on the edge of falling. "Bite me!"

He held perfectly still.

She snarled and her nails scored his ass as she pulled him in tighter. "Bite me, damn you!"

He growled.

She stilled. "Please!" She shuddered in desperation. "'*Syr*, please!"

His teeth stabbed into her.

Fierce pain slashed across her breast in a burning rush of sharp-edged pleasure. Release detonated then shockwaved through her, setting her blood on fire. She screamed.

Khan locked her in his embrace, sucking hard on her nipple and drawing her blood into his mouth.

Fallon shuddered and bucked under him, releasing cry after gasping cry. The venom in his saliva increased the pleasure surging through her body and the burn from sucking at her wounds, extending the waves of climax to a maddening degree, drowning her in dark-edged pleasure.

Khan released her breast, his tongue stroking gently across her wounds. He released her hair and took possession of her mouth, stilling her soft cries.

She moaned and kissed him as the final echoes of her climax trembled through her, tasting her blood on his tongue.

He released her mouth and smiled. "Isabeau."

Panting and exhausted, Fallon looked up into his hooded copper gaze and couldn't think beyond the pleasure still curling through her.

He tugged the blankets over them and settled between her thighs, pressing her down into the bed. His arms slid under the pillows supporting them, cradling her body to his. His lips sought the base of her throat and a purr vibrated through him, signaling his contentment.

Fallon sighed, comforted by his deep purr. Her breaths timed to his and his heartbeat became loud in her ears. Her eyes grew heavy.

On the very edge of sleep, she turned to look over at Sobehk.

His blue eyes were open.

She reached out and caught his fingers.

A smiled flickered on his lips and his fingers tightened around hers briefly. His eyes closed.

Fallon released a long sigh and let sleep claim her, still grasping Sobehk's hand.

A small chime sounded.

Fallon jerked awake. Khan's long body was a heavy weight atop her, and he was breathing deeply, directly below her ear. Sobehk had rolled up against them in the night and flung his arm over both them for good measure. It was more than a little warm under the two of them.

The chime sounded again.

Fallon frowned. Was that noise some kind of alarm? She pushed at Khan's shoulder.

Khan groaned, his arms tightened around Fallon and he pushed his nose under her hair by the back of her ear.

Great. Fallon blew a hair from her nose. She took a breath and eased to her right, slowly working to get out from under his heavy and hot sprawling length.

The chime sounded again. And continued.

Khan groaned. "Fuck," he whispered in her ear then slid off to the right. He rolled over on his back, taking half the blankets with him while crowding Fallon up against Sobehk on her left.

Sobehk grumbled, tugging the blankets the other way and tighter around him while shoving her up against Khan.

Fallon shifted from side to side, trying to make some room for herself between both men. *You would think a bed this large would be big enough for everybody, but no . . . They both have to have the middle!*

Khan suddenly threw his arms up in a full body stretch.

Fallon found herself watching the blanket sliding down Khan's body, revealing the muscles all across his stomach and chest shifting in an arresting display. She licked her lips as she gazed in admiration. Khan's body was gorgeous in motion.

Khan took several deep breaths, sat up, and slapped her thigh. "Come on." He rolled forward and made for the edge of the bed.

Fallon groaned. She understood perfectly well that he had duties, but why did *she* have to get out of bed? She arched her back, stretching, then rolled up and climbed out after him. Her feet braced on the thick red carpeting, she twisted her hips and shook hard to make sure that all of her augmentations were awake and functioning. Fairly long periods of sleep had a nasty habit of occasionally sending one of her limbs into a mechanical torpor. She was not in the mood to fall on her face in front of Khan.

She looked down at her smeared thighs and grimaced. *Great Maker, I need a shower . . .*

Just beyond the red and black trunks arranged on the left wall, a doorway gaped open. The sound of running water was too much of a temptation to pass up.

She jogged toward the doorway and discovered a facility done completely in black. Even the chrome rails were black. Water splashed against the frosted glass wall on her immediate right. Apparently the entire wall was the shower. A long counter took up the left wall. She used the black commode in the center of the back wall with a profound sense of relief.

"Isabeau?"

Fallon looked over at the frosted glass. "Yes?" She rolled her eyes. "*'Syr.*"

"I don't have all day, get your ass in here!"

Fallon slid the glass door open and stepped into a black-tiled shower.

Khan leaned on his elbows against the right wall, his head back and long creamy hair loose from its braid. Water sprayed down from three showerheads, spilling across his tattooed back, over the curve of his ass then down his long muscular thighs. He groaned and lowered his head, then looked over at her. "About time." He turned over, pressing his shoulders against the wall, and held out his hand. "Come."

Fallon walked over to take his hand and he shoved her under the water. It was hotter than she expected. She flinched back, but he held her under the spray.

"Hold still." Khan picked up a cloth from somewhere and proceeded to scrub the living daylights out of every square centimeter of skin she had. Foam sluiced down her body.

"Close your eyes."

Fallon shut her eyes in time to have her head jerked back then his long fingers dug into her hair. In a very short time he had her hair thoroughly washed and rinsed.

Khan tugged her backward, by the hair.

Fallon winced. *He could have asked!*

His hand slapped the wall and the water cut off. Half a breath later, the water collectors powered up, drying them both in seconds.

Fallon was pushed from the shower into the main facility room and subjected to one of the most ferocious hair-brushings of her entire life. She hissed. "I could cut it . . ."

"Don't you dare! Only humans ruin themselves like that."

Fallon blinked. *Ruin themselves?*

Khan tugged and scraped her hair back and proceeded to braid it painfully tight. "A Skeldhi's hair is a measure of their personal attractiveness. Our women pride themselves on hair that can sweep the floor."

Fallon's mouth fell open. *Floor-length hair?* She couldn't imagine having to deal with hair that long. It had to take forever to wash it all.

Khan snorted. "To have your hair cut is to be shamed." He tugged sharply as he bound the end of her braid with a slender cord. "Only criminals have their pride shorn like a human."

Fallon frowned. "Sounds like you don't like humans

very much." She winced. "*'Syr.*"

"Oh, Skeldhi like humans just fine." Khan moved to the counter to brush and braid his own creamy mane. "They're as much fun to kill as they are to fuck."

Fallon froze. All of a sudden his earlier comment about humans living longer as *rehkyt* took on a completely different meaning. A shiver raced down her spine.

"You have nothing to fear, Isabeau." Khan smiled as he watched her in the mirror, but his copper eyes were hard. "You are not human."

His comment annoyed the piss out of her, but she was not about to argue with him. She *wasn't* human. Not anymore.

Fallon followed Khan from the facility to discover a number of Skeldhi moving around the chamber. A pair in silver-gray robes assisted Sobehk out of the bed while another two, far younger and in dark gray knee-length robes, pulled the blankets and sheets from the bed. Two more in floor-length black robes waited by the round table with clothes set out neatly across the dark, polished surface.

Khan headed for the two by the table. One lifted a long black kilt and the other a deep red under-robe. Khan held out his arms and they proceeded to dress him with blinding speed and methodical efficiency. In a matter of minutes he was fully robed, bound by a scarlet sash and strapped into his tall boots. His black-handled daggers were handed to him.

Fallon caught the reflection of Sobehk and the two gray-robed Skeldhi in the mirrors as they turned to enter the facility.

Sobehk stopped and looked up, staring straight into her reflected gaze. His nostrils flared, as though he'd caught an interesting scent. His eyes abruptly darkened as his pupils opened wide, the black centers swallowing the blue.

Fallon suddenly realized that Sobehk was not looking at her reflection, he was looking past her, at Khan.

Sobehk's brows dropped and his mouth tightened. He was clearly not happy about something.

Khan, for his part, was definitely, if not pointedly, *not* looking at Sobehk. He smiled slightly, his gaze locked on Fallon as he tucked the daggers into his sash. He gestured for Fallon to approach. "Hold your arms out and remain perfectly still."

Sobehk closed his eyes and disappeared into the facility.

Fallon did as ordered, and the two Skeldhi approached, holding a pair of short robes and a sash. They smelled utterly wrong and the hair on her neck rose. Her skin shivered under their fingers. Their scent wasn't bad or foul, but the urge to bite increased the more she breathed their scent.

Khan's gaze stayed hard on her.

Fallon held her breath to avoid smelling them even as panic made her heart pound. She couldn't hold her breath for long and took small breaths with her mouth. She could not believe how . . . *wrong* they smelled.

In swift order she was dressed as she had been before, though in clean robes. Fallon exhaled in a rush.

The two attendants bowed toward Khan then headed for the door with the two carrying bed sheets and blankets on their heels.

Khan lifted his chin. "We are breaking dock with the *Vortex*. As I'm monitoring the pilot during breakaway and the first jump, I thought you might like to sit with me and pair-view the flight."

Fallon blinked. "You're going to add me to your neural link, '*Syr*?" She was going to see space—as a pilot perceived it? *Great Maker . . .*

Khan tilted his head to the side. "I believe your computational array is sophisticated enough to do so."

Fallon bounced up on her toes before she could stop herself and grinned. "I'd love that!" She dropped to her heels, jerking her hands behind her, and felt her cheeks heat. She wasn't a child. "I meant, thank you, '*Syr*."

"You're welcome." Khan smiled and lifted the black chain leash from the tabletop. "Shall we go?"

Chapter Twenty-two

The corridor directly outside Khan's private chamber was narrow and black with bright chrome handrails along the walls. The ceiling curved overhead and everything shimmered slightly, indicating the ship's mimetic, atomic-level shape-changing nature. Fallon's brows rose. She hadn't realized that the entire ship was mimetic. A mimetic ship had to be a quite an advantage if someone shot at it. The hull could stretch to seal itself — as long as the holes were fairly small.

Fallon ducked behind Khan's back as Skeldhi in black skintight ship-suits or robes in differing shades of gray or black with the occasional bit of red trim passed to either side. Curious glances were sent her way, but their gazes retreated too quickly to be considered impolite.

The Skeldhi and their thing for manners... Fallon rolled her eyes. On second thought, being polite all the time could be considered a good thing in a society that was as quick-tempered and consistently armed as they were. It was much harder to take accidental offense if everyone followed the same rules.

The walk ended at a lift that opened onto another passageway. The corridors they passed through and crossed remained uniformly black but widened and held more foot traffic. Fewer robed Skeldhi walked these hallways; most wore ship-suits with the occasional fully armored and sword-armed pair marching in perfect step.

Another lift, and they entered another, broader,

passageway with oval windows that marched along the left wall.

Fallon frowned. The ship was a lot bigger than she thought. What in fury were they on?

The walk ended at an open doorway with two fully armed guards. The men came to attention, heels snapping together, shoulders thrown back and chins rising.

Khan nodded as he passed them with Fallon in his shadow.

Through the door, Khan halted.

Fallon peeked around his shoulder. A walkway opened directly in front of them, curving toward the right. A small four-step stairway was on their immediate right. She looked up the wall on her right. And up. The wall ended about two meters over her head, but there was a lot of open space past the wall. She'd seen a cathedral in an old holo-vid of Peter's. The ship's ceiling was about two stories away with a definite cathedral arch to it.

Whatever she was on was huge.

Khan led her up the small stair. His hand pressed on her right shoulder as soon as she cleared the last stair.

Fallon dropped to her left knee, setting her right hand to the floor and tucking her left hand in her lap, the way So-behk had taught her. It was hard to make out much with her eyes kept no higher than knee level. She could see little more than the bottom of a long curving desk to her left and the bottom of three black leather command chairs on her right set before a black wall.

"'*Syr* Khan, we are ready to release the *Vortex* on your command." The voice was deep and belonged to a pair of armored boot-toes protruding from under a long black kilt. A scarlet robe apparently left open, framed the sides of the kilt. The unmistakable bottom halves of two sheathed swords hung at an angle by his left thigh.

Khan shifted slightly, his leg pressing against Fallon's side. "You may release at will, '*Syr* Captain."

Captain? Fallon swallowed. They were on the ship's command center. She was kneeling on an actual ship's bridge. She frowned. But if he was the captain, why was he deferring to Khan?

The captain turned to the left and a second person was suddenly visible — well, from the knees down. He too wore an open scarlet robe framing his black kilt. The toes remained pointed at Khan.

"At your leisure, '*Syr* Khan." The heels clicked together. The voice was youthful and soft-spoken.

"Thank you, '*Syr* Commander." Khan tapped Fallon's shoulder and turned to the right.

Fallon rose to her feet and followed. From the corner of her eye, the captain appeared to be massive in size. His sleeveless robe of deep scarlet showed powerfully muscled arms with forearms riddled with active electronics. Both wrists blazed with electronic auras from the arrays embedded into his hands and forearms. Two swords were thrust through his black sash.

The other person was far more slender and dressed very much like the captain, with only one sword through his sash. His wrists were also aglow with active electronics. Fallon caught the hint of a smile on his mouth before she turned completely away.

Khan walked to the right then turned to walk along the back wall to the command chair on the far side. He turned to face the front of the ship.

Fallon turned with him and had to remember to breathe. Just past the captain and the commander, and a little below, a nav-pilot sat electronically enthroned and haloed in shifting gold light, indicating an active piloting array. Linked directly to the ship's sentience, the living mind of the nav-pilot created the quantum consciousness that folded space. Once jump-space was achieved, the ship would pierce through the vast forever of space in a blink of time.

Flanking the nav-pilot, two crewmembers in skin-hugging ship-suits were wired into chairs with holographic control displays spread out under their hands.

The viewscreen that took up the entire front portion of the pointed oval of the bridge showed the *Vortex*, which appeared to be parked *on* the end of the ship. Beyond the *Vortex* was an ocean of stars that literally went on forever.

The silence was deafening. No one said a single word, but Fallon's inner array hummed with interest as her programs responded to the signals from the active arrays all around her. She could almost make out what they were doing . . .

The *Vortex* suddenly lifted from the nose of the ship and kept lifting.

The captain turned to look at Khan. He was ruggedly handsome with a massive jaw in a broad face commanded by bright yellow eyes. His mouth was full and his smile wide. "We are ready to proceed, *'Syr* Khan."

Fallon shifted her eyes from the captain's face, barely in time to avoid his direct gaze.

Khan smiled just a little. "You may proceed, Captain."

The captain nodded. *"'Syr."* He and the commander turned to face the front of the ship and held out their hands. Their wrists blazed, wreathed in halos of shifting blue-white energy.

Khan tugged at his robes and sat in the huge and heavily padded command chair. He leaned forward a bit and allowed the interneural link in the chair's headrest to reach out and connect to his data port. He winced then sat back with a sigh.

Fallon winced. Sobehk had been adamant that *rehkyt* did not sit on chairs. The steel floor did not look comfortable. And the view from down there was going to suck big time.

Khan held out his hand and smiled. His copper gaze blazed with electronic blue radiating from deep within the pupils.

Fallon tilted her head in confusion but took his hand.

Khan tugged her into his lap, spreading his legs to let her sit on the seat with his chest as her backrest. His arms slid around her, and his lips pressed against her ear. "I trust you will not access anything in my head with that array and rather interesting collection of programs that is in yours?"

Fallon leaned into the press of his lips without thinking about it. "No, *'Syr.'*" She was not about to jeopardize her chance to view pilot-space. "You won't even know I'm there."

"Good." His hands lifted to the back of his chair and retrieved a slender link jack. He gently pushed her forward and affixed the jack to her port. "Lean back and close your eyes."

Fallon leaned back against his hard and warm chest.

"Ready?"

"Yes, *'Syr.'*"

Blackness, then ripples in the dark. The ripples became layer upon layer, upon layer, of velvety black cloth . . . all around. Space, rippling like a frozen ocean moving in tides immensely vast with an incredibly slow elegance. Flows of color bloomed into being, indicating gasses, temperatures, and matter. Sprays of color she had no name for shimmered and sparkled everywhere.

She bloomed into being, feeling the tides of space against her skin, tasting the different flavors of stars and hearing the harmonies of solar systems as orchestras of incredible grace. Ever changing, ever moving, ever harmonious . . . She could listen to it forever.

"Are you all right?"

She had to pull back into herself before she could respond and found that her cheeks were wet. Fallon wiped at her cheeks, still feeling the pull of the music of space. "Yeah . . . Yes, '*Syr*. It's so . . . beautiful."

His arms tightened around her. "Yes, yes, it is."

"Ready to proceed into jump-space on your mark, Captain." The nav-pilot's calm voice was a soothing ripple.

Fallon jumped. The nav-pilot's voice had come through her link to Khan.

"Begin." The captain's command was a deep bass through the link.

Fallon concentrated and realized that other voices chatted softly along the link. There was another voice murmuring under it all, but she couldn't quite hear it.

"Activating Phalrium hull grid and opening quantum teleological space-time manifold at factor eight." The nav-pilot's anticipation came through loud and clear.

The ship's skin seemed to shiver.

Fallon suddenly felt the fabric of reality shifting into a shimmering field of crushed star-space. It coalesced to spiral around the ship.

"Jump-space gateway open and stable, Captain."

The captain lifted both hands. "Advance drive, speed four. Proceed into jump-space."

"Proceeding into jump." The nav-pilot's voice echoed with deep calm.

Fallon took a deep breath. Tension shimmered through her inner array in echo of the ship.

The ship shimmied, collected itself and lunged, not forward, but through the quantum-folded layers of space as a needle thrusts through tight folds of cloth. Her mouth opened as the calm orchestra of eternity became a wild rushing concert of screaming, whirling stars—that swallowed her whole.

Something caught her, steadied her, and pushed her mind to focus on the harmonious melody in the center of a whirling storm of sound and color. The ship, sliding between the layers of folded space like a finely honed blade too sharp to even feel its passing.

Fallon's heart settled down to something less than complete panic. There was a hand pressed over her mouth. She sucked in a breath.

"Are you all right?" It was Khan.

Fallon could hear him, but he seemed to be very far away. She nodded. Her voice didn't want to work.

"I thought you said she didn't have a piloting array?" It sounded like the captain.

"There is no pilot's access," a soft feminine voice whispered. "Merely broad perception."

Fallon's curiosity surfaced. *Who . . .*

Attention and amusement became directed at Fallon. "I . . ." Presence echoed all around.

Fallon's breath caught. She was hearing the ship's sentience—and it was paying attention to her. The ship sensed her presence. *Oh shit!* Alarm raced through her inner array. Her pixie programming activated, shrinking her sensory signature to a tiny mote of light. Out of sheer habit, her spectral program activated, reversing her light into a mote of shadow, masking her signature.

"Oh!" The ship registered surprise. "Has she gone?"

"Isabeau? Are you still connected?" It was Khan. His concern echoed across their link. Curiosity poked her way but encountered nothing. Of course. "Where are you?"

Fallon froze. *Uh oh . . .* "Oh, I'm . . . right here." She turned off her spectral programming but kept her pixie program running, letting her sensory signature gleam like a tiny comet against the larger presence of Khan, and the ship. Hopefully, no one had noticed that she had disappeared completely.

The ship registered outright surprise.

Fallon bit back a groan. The ship had noticed. Time for some damage control. "I'm using my pixie program. It makes my signature too small to notice."

"I see that. I barely sense you at all." Khan's curiosity increased and suspicion entered the link. "However, there was no trace of you before. Nor was there a trace of any active programs."

Oh, shit . . . he noticed it. Her pixie program and the spectral programming at its heart were part of her secret array. Khan may have thought he'd mapped her entire brain, but in reality, he only had her surface programs. Without her personal coding language, they wouldn't even know that those programs were there—until she used them. And she had just used them.

Idiot! Fallon wanted to bang her head on something hard, but the only convenient hard surface was Khan's chest. She had a bad feeling that she was about to get into big trouble.

Khan's silence was deafening, and his suspicion was a growling pressure along the link. "Isabeau, why do I have the feeling that there is something you haven't told me?"

Oh yeah, trouble was coming all right. "I'm not used to being seen by ships, so I . . . panicked, and one of my programs kicked in."

"A program that makes you completely invisible to sensory detection?"

She took a careful breath. "Well . . . yes. I can't get into a ship's mind if they know I'm there."

Khan tensed under her. "A program that cannot be seen

when active, even though I am in direct link to your personal array?" The message slid across the link masked from everyone else — including the ship.

The hair on Fallon's neck rose and sweat formed all down her back. Oh yeah, she was in very deep trouble. "Yes."

Anger throbbed hot and heavy along their private connection. "Isabeau, are you going to tell me, or do I need to peel it from your skin with my whip?"

She held very, very still. "You have to be equipped with spectral programming to detect it."

"Spectral programming." Suspicion seethed through Khan.

Fallon was almost too scared to breathe. "It's a programming code that's made of absence or shadow, rather than energy. 'Spectral' was the only name I could think of that fit."

"You *built* it?"

"Well, yeah . . . I had to find some way to mask my energy signature while I was looking through a ship's mind, so I wouldn't be seen — and expelled. So I used non-energy, or reverse energy. Spectral energy."

"There is no such thing as spectral energy." Disbelief threaded through the anger that throbbed from Khan.

Fallon cringed. "True, it was something I made up. But it works pretty good for something that doesn't actually exist."

"There was no sign of this . . . spectral programming in your scan."

Fallon took a deep breath. "Of course not." Either he killed her for hiding this from him — or he didn't. "Because your scan couldn't read the spectral coding language either. Your scan saw what Peter made for me, all my basic programs. I doubt it found any of my real programs."

"When did you plan to tell me this?"

Fallon's mouth went dry. Truth or lie? *Shit . . . When in doubt, go for the truth. They rarely believe it anyway.* She released a breath. "I was hoping I wouldn't have to tell you at all."

"Isabeau." His entire body vibrated with tension. The link thumped loudly with restrained fury.

"Yes, *'Syr?"* He was really, really pissed. She hoped her death would be swift, but she sincerely doubted Khan had anything swift in mind.

"I am going to beat you bloody."

He wasn't going to kill her? On second thought, he was fully capable of coming up with something worse. "Yes. *'Syr."*

Khan grabbed her thick braid, shoved her forward and jerked the jack from the back of her head.

The stars dissolved and normal sight returned. Fallon winced.

In a single breath, Khan disengaged from his link and shoved Fallon from his lap and onto her feet. He did not let go of her hair. He turned to face the captain and the commander.

Both men abruptly saluted, their fists slamming against their hearts.

Khan nodded and marched Fallon down the stairs and into the hallway.

She marched, driven by the punishing grip on her hair. *I am so fucked.*

Oh, yes, you are, came across loud and clear.

She blinked. *What in bloody Fate . . .* Where the fuck had that come from?

Khan stopped and jerked her around to face him. *The collar allows telepathic contact if I so require it.* He smiled. *I am suddenly of the opinion that I should have been monitoring your thoughts all along, rather than occasionally.*

Occasionally? He'd been *in her head* occasionally? She narrowed her eyes at him. *Get out of my mind!* Lightning seared up her spine and through her augmentations. She knew that feeling. It was the punishment setting on the collar.

It stopped before she could take a breath to scream, but her knees gave out. Khan's fist was the only thing that held her up off the deck. She moaned.

Khan glared down at her. *Whose mind?* White-hot fury accompanied the thought. He didn't wait for an answer. He tugged her back onto her feet, shoving her before him as he marched in a long ground-eating stride. His heels thumped on the carpeted deck.

CHAPTER TWENTY-THREE

The grueling march continued through several broad corridors and ended with a sharp left turn into a small very plain chamber walled in black and carpeted in deep blood-red. The compartment was commanded by a broad black desk on the immediate left and a huge, nearly floor-to-ceiling window against the facing wall, showing space as it streamed by at jump speed. The door cycled closed behind them.

Khan unsnapped the leash and pushed her toward the desk. He tugged out the desk chair and shoved her into it. He slapped both palms on the desk's surface. A keyboard formed from the desk's surface and three holographic displays bloomed into being. A second keyboard, completely holographic, appeared and lifted to sit under his palms.

Khan's fingers flew across the holographic keyboard. "You will give me a copy of this spectral code of yours. Now."

"Yes, 'Syr." Fallon folded her arms and raised a brow at him. "I need a direct access jack and a rather specific Imperial interface script editor to make you that copy. 'Syr."

Khan curled his lip, showing a long tooth. "Name your program."

She did.

Khan tapped across his floating keyboard. The program appeared on the main display before her.

Fallon blinked. Great Maker, he not only had the program she needed, his version was newer than hers. She winced. Newer than hers *had been*. Everything she'd owned was lost back on Dyson's.

Khan leaned over the edge of the desk by her right knee, opened a drawer that hadn't been there before, and wasn't there again after he pushed it closed.

Fallon blew a strand of hair from her nose. He *would* have a mimetic desk.

Khan uncoiled a direct data jack, plugged one end into a port that appeared under his palm and then held the other end out to her. "Begin."

Fallon set the jack into the back of her skull and began writing code. Her spectral code activated and the music that ran it began to play.

Khan frowned. "Do I hear music?"

Fallon nodded, watching as the code on the holographic display began to shift into harmonious patterns. "I have a problem with math. Music is mathematically precise so I use it to memorize key phrases of coding."

Khan frowned at his display. *That explains the stylistic flavor of her coding.*

Fallon glanced at Khan, guessing that he'd meant his comment to be private. Apparently, the collar-induced telepathy went both ways.

Fallon felt her program shift and the text written before her abruptly changed composition. Her programming still saw it, but no longer existed as light.

Khan frowned. "What happened?"

Fallon frowned at her display. "I'm running it to check for flaws, '*Syr*.'"

Khan stared at her. "There is nothing on my display."

Fallon smiled tightly. "It's there, you just can't see it. You have to have the programming code downloaded to perceive it." Her internal program scan ended. It was functional. She turned to Khan. "It's ready, '*Syr*.'"

"Burn a copy."

Fallon shook her head. "It doesn't work that way. You can't save it the way you can normal programs. Once it's written in disintegrates. If you want it, I have to upload it to your internal array and activate it there. We need to tandem link."

Khan frowned and his gaze chilled. "A direct mind-to-mind activation?"

Fallon held his gaze and nodded. She could feel through their telepathic connection exactly how not pleased he was to hear this. "If you want this program, the only one who can give it to you, and activate it, is me."

Khan walked away to stare out the window at streaming space.

Fallon crossed one knee over the other. Either he trusted her, or he didn't. If he didn't trust her enough to go into his mind, install and then activate the code, that was perfectly fine with her. Without an active code, he couldn't see hers — and erase her programs.

Any other programs could be replaced with a bit of hacking, but not this one. If he took her code, she would not be able to replace it without going back to Dyson's for Peter's help. She could rewrite it, but she couldn't activate it. Peter was the only other one with an active spectral code.

She was betting he didn't trust her enough to let her set the code.

Khan clasped his hands behind him, and his head lifted. "Have you lied to me in any way?"

Fallon frowned. "About what?" She cleared her throat. "'Syr."

Khan turned to face her. His mouth was tight, and his entire body radiated tension. "About anything."

Fallon stared down at her right hand, thinking, and frowned. Had she? She'd omitted a few things, absolutely, but she couldn't recall a single thing that she'd lied about.

She looked up. "Not that I can think of. No, '*Syr*.'"

Khan nodded. "Very well then." He walked around the desk, opened another drawer that hadn't been there, then closed it, and it wasn't there again. He stood over her and held out a tandem jack. "Do it."

Fallon blinked. He was trusting her? "All right." Her fingers danced across her keyboard. "The code is ready for upload." She took the tandem jack and swallowed. The probe had exposed some of her — this would expose all of her.

Trust. He trusted her. She was going to have to trust him, too.

She got up out of the chair. "Please, have a seat."

Khan frowned slightly. "Will it hurt?"

Fallon bit back a smile. She'd asked him that about the probe. "Actually no, but it does knock you off balance when it's first activated."

Khan tugged at his robes and sat.

Fallon affixed the tandem link and readied the upload. She looked over at him. "Ready?"

He flashed a brief smile. "I am."

Fallon hit the mark key. "Beginning upload." She watched the code proceed down the page. "Nearly done."

"I don't feel a thing." Khan's voice was steady, but Fallon was pretty sure she could smell nervous sweat coming from him.

She smiled but kept her eyes on the screen. "You're not going to, your mind can't see it yet."

"How many people have this code?"

"Myself, and Peter, though I'm sure Peter's given the code to someone else, by now." Fallon tapped the keyboard and made an adjustment. "And you." She looked at Khan. "Ready to activate?"

Khan swallowed and took a breath. "Do me."

Fallon blinked then reached in and touched his code. The strains of the orchestral piece that held the activation key pulsed from her mind, directly into his.

He frowned. "Music again?"

Fallon didn't answer. She turned to the display. The code shifted, connected and came into harmony. It was active.

"Oh . . ." Khan sighed. He leaned back in the chair with his eyes closed. His eyes snapped open and he jerked forward, focusing on the display screen. His eyes narrowed. "I can see it."

Fallon swallowed. Oh, yes, he could.

His brow rose. "Can I disappear the way you did?"

Fallon glanced at the window of rushing stars and lifted her hands to remove the jack in her data port. "You said you wanted a copy, '*Syr*." She took a deep breath. "You can do everything I can, and you can tell if someone has that program active in their system."

"How?"

Fallon lifted her shoulder just a little. "They tend to . . . resonate, like tuning crystals."

Khan removed the jack from his skull. "Resonate . . . I see." He turned to her. "How do I work it?"

"When you sleep, it plays a kind of how-to file. When you wake up, you can use it."

Khan frowned. "I dream it?"

"It was the easiest way to do a tutorial, '*Syr*." She'd been a kid at the time. Dream-flight had been the *only* way to do a tutorial.

Khan pursed his lips. "And it cannot be tampered with, because no one can see it?"

Fallon nodded. "Other codes can't detect it, because the languages are made of opposite compositions."

Khan shook his head. "How did you come up with this

to begin with?"

Fallon looked at her toes. "I had a really vivid dream, '*Syr*.'" Inspired by one too many retellings of Peter's stories of flying children and a sparkling gold pixie, no doubt . . .

"A dream?"

Fallon nodded. "I was eleven at the time."

Khan turned the chair to look at her. "You wrote this when you were *eleven*?"

Fallon looked up and smiled. "No, '*Syr*. I had the dream at eleven. I actually made it when I was fourteen." Her smiled faded. "I was seventeen before it could do everything it does now." She hadn't needed to be completely invisible until she started breaking into sentient ships.

Khan rose from his chair in a rustle of black and red silk robes and set his palm on the broad black desk. The holographic displays winked out and the keyboard she had just used was absorbed back into the desktop. His eyes narrowed and a smile curved his mouth. "Are you ready for your whipping?"

The hair on Fallon's neck rose. "What?" She took a step back.

Khan lifted his hand and uncoiled the meter-long whip from his left wrist. "You need to be punished."

Fallon took another step back. "'*Syr*! I gave you my program!"

"Yes, you did." He set the whip on the smooth desktop and pulled his daggers from his sash, dropping them in his abandoned chair. "You also omitted telling me that it was there." His chin dropped and his copper gaze heated as he unfastened his over-robe, exposing his black under-robe. "But I think you are missing the point entirely."

Fallon searched her memory. *Point?* He had a point? She lifted her chin, exposing her throat in instinctive submission. "'*Syr*, I don't understand!"

Khan nodded. "I see that." His smile broadened, showing teeth as he peeled his black and scarlet over-robe from his shoulders. "Go around to the front of my desk and take off your robe." He began to unwind the scarlet sash closing his black under-robe.

Fallon hunched her shoulders and turned away, tugging at her red sash. It was probably better to just endure it than piss him off any more by trying to talk him out of it. She'd been cornered and beaten before . . . but not with a whip. She pulled the robes from her shoulders and took deep breaths. As long as she was still breathing at the end of it, she would recover.

Bare-chested in only his long black kilt, and whip in hand, Khan followed her around to the front of the desk. His long pale braid lay over his shoulder and across his breast, nearly falling to his waist. The black band around his brow and his matching black nipple rings gleamed with midnight rainbows under the light. He tugged her robes and sash from her fingers and dropped them on the desk. "Go to the window."

Fallon walked over the huge window and stared at the streaming stars of jump-space.

Khan stepped behind her and set his right palm on the glass.

A gleaming black rail oozed into being just below Fallon's chest height, forming directly from the window. The rest of the window darkened and became opaque then lightened to become reflective.

Fallon stared at her reflection, and that of Khan standing behind her, his arm extended past her right shoulder. She frowned. "A mirror?"

Khan smiled. "I want to watch your face." His smile broadened. "As you scream."

Fallon winced, hating the fear that widened her eyes.

Anger tightened her mouth. *Sadistic* . . .

Khan nodded. "Yes, yes, I know. I'm a sadistic bastard."

Fallon flinched. The collar. He was listening in on her thoughts through the damned collar.

Khan's eye narrowed. *Yes. No more secrets.* He moved behind her and his warm hands cupped her shoulders. The whip was a cool length dangling down the side of her arm. He leaned closer, his mouth brushing against her ear. "The point you were missing is that I am beating you because it pleases me to do so."

Fallon lifted her chin, exposing her throat, and swallowed. *It would please him* . . . A small shiver raced across her skin. She *wanted* to please him. To her complete surprise, her belly clenched with sudden hunger and moisture pooled.

"Yes, now you understand." His lips curved in a smile. His mouth slid down the side of her throat, his hot breath scorching her skin. His left hand slid down her arm then swept across her belly. "I fully intended to whip you all along." He pressed against her back. He was urgently hard under his kilt. His copper eyes gleamed with hunger in the mirror before them. "Your disobedience was merely a convenient excuse."

Sudden, demanding erotic heat scorched through her. Fallon shivered hard and her knees wobbled. She grabbed for the rail to keep from falling.

His hand swept up her belly to cup her bare breast. Her nipple hardened in his palm. He smiled. "Ah . . . yes." He closed both arms around her, his whip a cool length falling against her bare belly to curl around her feet. "You want to feel the kiss of my whip as much as I want to hear you scream." He pressed a soft kiss on her throat. *Mine.*

CHAPTER TWENTY-FOUR

Fallon shivered in Khan's arms. His cocks were hot rigid lengths against the small of her back even as the whip in his hand was a cool threat against her belly. And yet, erotic anticipation coiled within her and tightened. Her body both feared and hungered for what he was about to give her.

Reflected in the glass, Fallon's eyes widened to dark pits framed by thin rings of bright emerald, and color flushed her cheeks. There was no mistaking that her body was looking forward to the pain he was about to unleash. She vibrated with the feral need for pain at his hand, driven by an instinct that demanded he touch her, that he mark her with his possession. Some part of her needed him to prove to her that he wanted her. That she was his.

It was not love, it was instinct. And somehow, that hurt.

Khan's reflected gaze caught hers. His eyes were bright rings of copper around blackness. His cheeks were warm with color and his lips looked flushed and rich.

And she had caused it. She had brought the scent of arousal rising from his skin. He wanted her. She could see it in his hot gaze, feel it in the erections pressing against her backside and in the pressure of his fingers against her belly.

Impulsively, she turned toward him and lifted her mouth to his, pressing a sudden kiss to his lips.

Khan received her kiss and replied gently, and then hungrily. His arms tightened and he growled into her mouth, his tongue lashing and his teeth clicking against hers.

She replied with a trace of that odd vibration, her purr.

His hand left her belly. "Hold tight to the rail." His voice was deeper than usual and rumbled with a touch of a growl. "Stay upright but keep your head down and keep your feet together." He brushed her black braid over her shoulder, and it swept against the top of her breast. "My target is your back, ass and thighs." His lips pressed against the base of her neck. "If you wish the whip to kiss your breasts and belly, extend your arms."

Fallon nodded. She simply couldn't find the breath to speak.

He stepped back, and the whip snaked across the blood-red carpet as he placed himself behind her.

Fallon stared at what she could see of his reflection. Her hands closed tight on the rail. Moisture slicked her thighs and dribbled down.

The whip cracked loud and sharp.

Fallon jumped. He hadn't touched her.

Khan smiled. "Ready?"

Impatience and a touch of annoyance at her cowardice spurred her mouth before she thought. "Do I need to be?"

Khan's brows rose. "No, not really." His hand moved, just barely. The whip didn't make more than a whisper of sound as it flicked through the air.

Fire erupted across her left hip.

Fallon's head shot up and she hissed. "Shit!" She dropped her head and arched her back, stomping her foot in reaction.

The whip cracked.

Her right hip flared with pain.

Fallon choked but kept her head down that time. She could not stop the instinctive arch, then the twist of her spine.

"Oh, very pretty." Khan stepped to the side and smiled into her mirrored gaze. "You dance well under the whip."

Fallon clenched her teeth and shot a glare at his reflection. "Gee, thanks, '*Syr.*'"

He grinned. "You're welcome." He nodded. "Hold tight and try to stay still, I'm going to stripe you, shoulder to ass, very fast."

Fast . . . Fallon cringed. "Great."

His hand rose and fell and rose . . . over and over with incredible speed. The whip snapped almost continuously.

He stopped.

Huh? Fallon took a startled breath. She'd barely felt a whisper. Her entire right side abruptly bloomed with ferocious heat, and then blazed with fire. She took a deep breath. And then another. And then another . . .

"Isabeau, breathe!" His voice lashed through her, cutting through the white heat of her back. "Don't hold it! Let it go!"

Let it go? She threw back her head and shouted every obscenity she could think of. She arched and twisted to relieve the searing burn of her scorched skin, knowing damned well that it wouldn't do a drop of good. She didn't let go of the bar.

"Breathe!"

Fallon pressed her brow to the cool mirror before her and breathed. There was a slight tightening in the back of her mind — and then a loosening. Her entire body followed, her muscles releasing and relaxing. A calmness seemed to steal over her, and her thoughts drifted apart. It felt like she was getting just a little . . . high. The pain on her back didn't fade exactly, but it seemed to matter less. *Oh . . .*

"That's it. Breathe deep and slow." Khan's brow rose. "Ready for the other side?"

Fallon eyed his reflection and considered a number of

rude comments. She discarded them all. She was actually feeling too . . . relaxed to put any real energy into them. She pushed upright and braced herself. "Fast again?"

Khan's smile was slow and malicious. "Not quite. This time I want you feel each one."

He wanted her to *feel each one*? Fallon had to remember to breathe. Temper surged and slipped away. It was hard to be angry in this odd frame of mind. "Fine, whatever."

Khan grinned. "Good." He drew his arm back, letting the whip slide across the carpet. "Hold as still as you can, and shout or scream to let the pain go through you. Don't try to hold onto it."

Crack!

A thin line of fire sliced across the meat of her left shoulder blade. She gasped and gripped the rail tighter.

"Relax, don't hold it."

Fallon loosened her hands and took a breath. The pain faded.

Crack!

Another line of fire erupted exactly under the first. She gasped and squelched the small cry that tried to escape with it.

"Let the pain out with your voice." His voice was calm and firm. "Breathe."

She breathed.

Crack! Burn . . .

She yelped and arched, only a little.

"Let the pain out with your voice."

Crack! Burn . . .

She yelped louder and her toes curled.

"Better. Keep your feet flat on the floor."

She dropped to her heels. "Yes, *'Syr*." Her voice sounded a little high.

"Breathe deeper between the strikes. "

She sucked in a breath. "Yes, *'Syr*."

Crack! Burn . . .

Fallon cried out then gasped for breath.

"Louder and breathe deeper."

She took a deeper breath. She was definitely feeling light-headed.

Crack! Burn . . .

She shouted. He was right, the pain seemed to move faster through her with her shouts.

Crack! Burn . . . Crack! Burn . . . Crack! Burn . . .

She was forced to take deeper breaths between the strokes that slashed down her left side. One after the other, after the other, after the other . . . Her shouts gained in volume. Her spine curved slowly from side to side, not twisting to avoid him but simply because her body needed to move.

Crack! Burn . . . Crack! Burn . . . Crack! Burn . . .

She wasn't quite sure when her shouts became small screams. Nor was she sure exactly when she was forced to close her eyes because she couldn't see past the tears. She had no idea why she was crying. She didn't feel unhappy. It just . . . happened.

Crack! Burn . . . Crack! Burn . . . Crack! Burn . . .

Her screams increased in volume until she couldn't gain a full breath fast enough to scream loud enough. But she didn't ask him to stop, and she didn't let go of the rail.

He stopped.

She gasped, wavered, then dropped to one knee. "Oh shit, oh shit . . . Oh, fuck!"

Khan was at her side in two long steps. He knelt. "Are you still with me?" His palm swept across her damp cheeks then two fingers pressed into the pulse on the side of her throat.

Fallon nodded and winced. Her entire back was on freaking fire! "Shit!"

He caught her face and stared into her eyes. He smiled.

"Very bravely done."

Fallon's heart contracted and ached. He thought her brave. She closed her eyes. Fresh, hot tears slid down her cheeks in a sudden rush. She blinked in surprise. Tears? *What the . . .*

He smiled as his thumbs brushed her damp cheeks. "That's it, that's good." His voice was very soft.

"Good?" She leaned close and pressed her brow against his. "But I don't know why . . ." She sniffed. "Why I'm . . ."

"Why are you crying?"

"Yeah . . . that."

"It's release, catharsis. Everything you had pent up in you escaping. Pain does that. It releases all the emotions at once." He took a deep breath and released it on a sigh. "If the emotions run deep, sometimes pain is the only release."

She leaned back to look up at him. "You . . ."

"Of course." Khan smiled. "Let's put it this way, neither my nipples nor my dick piercings happened by accident."

Fallon cringed. "I couldn't imagine . . ."

Khan snorted. "I doubt you'll ever have that level of . . . frustration, to need that kind of pain." He caught her by the elbows. "Stand up. Stand up and look." He lifted her, holding her against his chest. "Turn and see."

Fallon brushed the tears from her cheeks and looked over her shoulder. In the mirror, she saw herself curled into Khan's embrace. Bright red lines framed her spine in a downward feather-like pattern, one atop the other, decorating her entire back from shoulder to upper thigh. It was actually somewhat . . . pretty, in a kinky kind of way. She frowned. "That's damned precise."

Khan smiled in the mirror. "Thank you." His palm slid across the welts that burned down her back.

Fallon's head came up and her breath exploded in a groan. "Oh, you just had to rub it, too!"

His cheek pressed against hers. "It feels wonderful. And

hot, very hot." His palm slid across her back again.

Fallon let a small whimper escape. "Yeah, I bet."

His arms closed around her, both palms wide open and pressing against the welts. "How brave are you feeling?"

Fallon panted for breath to hold back the moan. "How brave do you need me to be?"

"Good answer." Khan chuckled. "I was thinking that while we have thoroughly adorned your back, your front is rather naked."

What? She jerked back and stared up at him. "I don't think I can take that on my front."

Khan pursed his lips and raised his brow. "I was thinking more on the lines of three."

"Three?"

"On each side."

Fallon swallowed. Six then. "Where?"

He caught her elbows and pushed her back. Her back met the rail. It was icy against her overheated skin. It actually felt so good it hurt. She hissed.

Khan released her and raised his hands. "I was thinking here." His thumbs traced along the outer edges of both breasts. "And here." His thumbs slid under and up to the inside curve of her breasts. "And here." His gaze dropped and his hands fell to cup the gentle curve of her belly. "One on either side of the navel." He raised his eyes and caught her gaze. "These would have to be far lighter. The skin is far more tender. Can you take it?"

Could she? Fallon took a deep breath. And then another. She looked up at him. "And that's all?"

Khan folded his arms and raised a brow. "And then I fuck the shit out of you."

Fallon felt the weirdest bubble of humor erupt from nowhere. She almost laughed out loud.

Khan frowned. "What?"

Fallon dropped her chin and smiled. "I could really use the fuck."

Khan rolled his eyes. "I believe that goes without saying. You're dripping on the carpet."

Fallon looked down. Excitement was a wet trail down the insides of her thighs. Spots of damp marked the deep red carpeting at her feet. "Oh . . ."

"Can you handle more?"

Fallon looked up at Khan's face. His kilt was tented with his erections, but his knuckles were white around the handle of the whip and his gaze was very bright. He clearly wanted to inflict little more pain before he fucked her.

Fallon *wanted* to please him. She *liked* pleasing him. She smiled. "I can take it."

He smiled, showing his teeth. "Good." It was not a pleasant smile.

Oh shit . . . The hair rose on Fallon's neck and her chin jerked, up baring her throat. She knew it was submissive gesture, but she was too alarmed to care.

He caught the length of the whip in his free hand, caressing it. "Grab the rail behind you and tilt your head back."

Fallon did as asked, and did not bother to ask if he was going to go fast. She strongly suspected that he was going to draw this out very slowly.

The whip cracked.

A thin whisper of air caressed the outside of her right breast. Then it burned. A lot. She closed her eyes tighter, arched and moaned.

"Heels down, and don't hold it in."

Panting, Fallon dropped her heels on the deck.

The whip cracked.

A thin whisper of air caressed the outside of her left breast. Then it burned . . . even more.

Fallon opened her mouth releasing a gasp and its accompanying yelp. *Great Maker, when will I learn to stop while I'm ahead?*

The whip cracked.

A thin whisper of air caressed the inside of her right breast. Then it blazed white-hot. She shouted. "Son of a fucking *bitch*!" She stomped her foot twice for good measure.

"Oh, that was pretty, and it made your breasts jiggle nicely."

Fallon spat out another curse. "I'm glad it pleased you." She stomped her foot one more time. "'*Syr*."

The whip cracked.

A thin whisper of air caressed the left side of her belly. It felt like a knife slash.

Fallon gasped and gasped again while tears streamed from her eyes. She hadn't gotten enough air to scream. She very nearly dropped to her knees. Her grip on the bar behind her was the only thing that kept her up. Her breath exploded from her. "Bastard!" She dropped her chin to glare at him. "That fucking *hurt*."

Khan nearly laughed. "I see that, and you forgot to let your breath out. Chin up, two more to go, and breathe."

Two more . . . just two more to go. Fallon tilted her head back. *Great.*

The whip cracked, and then cracked again.

A thin whisper of air caressed the inside of her left breast quickly followed by a whisper along the right side of her belly. They both erupted into screaming agony at the same time.

Fallon found plenty of air to shriek.

Khan lunged for her. His hands closed on her upper arms. He pulled her against him and took her mouth, swallowing the last of her scream.

Fallon felt him propelling her backward, but she could

barely think past the burns on her body.

Khan pulled his mouth from hers and turned her around.

Fallon had about half a breath to see that she was facing the front of his broad black desk, when he pushed her down, bending her over it. Her hands and then her chest fell flat on the cool surface. Her scored breasts and belly protested the position. She gasped and tried to straighten up.

Khan grabbed her braid and pushed her back down. "Stay down." He kicked her feet apart. Fabric ripped. "Fuck . . ." The black silk of his kilt spilled across the desk to one side and he grabbed her thighs.

Fallon felt the nudge of his primary cock and the bar that pierced it, at her anus. It was slick. She didn't know when he'd had the time to grease himself, but she was thoroughly glad he had.

He pushed for entry. Hard.

She moaned and pushed out to let him in. He entered swiftly and without mercy, his second cock taking her slick cunt before she even knew he was there. She gasped.

He caught her wrists, pulled them over her head and pressed his chest against her burning back.

She howled and thrashed.

Holding both her wrists in one hand, he thrust his forearm under her mouth.

She bit him viciously.

He shouted and slammed his cocks into her.

Fallon shouted, releasing his arm from her mouth.

Holding her bucking body under him, he fucked her with brutal force and breathtaking speed.

Fallon exploded into almost immediate release. She shouted then writhed under his thrusts, gasping, only to feel the unmistakable clenching of another rise. She was going to cum again.

"Oh yeah," Khan grunted as he continued to power-slam into her. "I figure I'll get at least two more good hard orgasms out of you before I cum."

Fallon twisted under him, crying out with the force of his thrusts. Tension built with punishing strength, coiling tighter with each of his ruthless thrusts.

His sweat dripped down as he held her burning body trapped under his. "Mother Night, I love fucking you."

Climax ripped through her, burning straight up her spine and blazing at the back of her head. She screamed.

Khan gasped. "Oh shit . . ." He groaned and froze, panting for breath. "Damned telepathic link. Almost took me with you." He began thrusting again, slower, though no less hard. "One more, Isabeau. Give me one more."

Fallon panted and groaned. "I don't think I can."

"Oh, you can. Believe me, you definitely can." His mouth dropped onto her shoulder.

She froze. If he bit her, every mark on her body was going to hurt a whole hell of a lot more. "No, don't . . ." She twisted hard to get away from his mouth. "Don't bite me!"

He snarled and released her wrists.

Fallon shoved up onto her elbows.

Khan cupped her breasts and squeezed.

The whip marks on Fallon's scored breasts screeched in violent protest. She howled. Climax rose with angry speed and tightened with horrific force.

Fallon wasn't sure she *wanted* to cum this time.

"Oh, yes you do." Khan snarled.

Frightened by the force growing in her belly and near-mindless with the fire burning along her skin, she snarled and thrashed under him. "Get out of my fucking head!"

"It's *my* fucking head!" He slammed hard into her, driving her down onto his desk with his thrusts. "*Mine*! Do you hear me? You belong to *me!*"

His . . . Fallon's breath stopped, and she froze under him. Climax roared up in a fiery volcanic wave and exploded, ripping her sanity apart. She arched and shrieked, kicking and bucking with the force of her release.

Khan shouted atop her, slammed in hard and held her tight in a crushing grip. He gasped and then moaned, pulsing within her and pumping his cum into her trembling body.

CHAPTER TWENTY-FIVE

Fallon rubbed her cheek against the robe she lay on. The thick black silk was blissfully soft and cool under her naked body. Stretched out in the deep shadows under Khan's huge black desk, she felt more at ease than she had in the big open bed of his. The carpet under the robe was amazingly plush. Of course, she was amazingly spent, so a warmed steel pipe would probably have felt pretty comfy, too.

Slouched in his big plush desk chair, Khan tapped at his computational, working on something or other. His bare foot sat in the curve of her waist, one of the few places that didn't have a whip mark on it. Contentment hummed across the telepathic link between them.

He hadn't been kidding about pain being a big emotional release. She was really, really relaxed, mentally and physically. Except for the fire still burning on her back. For once she was thrilled to death that *rehkyt* did not sit on the furniture. She couldn't imagine trying to sit in a chair, not with all the welts heating her skin. All things considered, she was actually quite comfortable, as long as she remained on her side.

People came into his chamber and then went out. No one noticed her under his desk, and none of it concerned her, so she pretty much ignored them. It was rather nice.

The last person left the office and Khan rolled his foot on Fallon's waist. "I have excellent news for you."

Fallon half-opened one eye. "Good news? That makes a

nice change." She paused to yawn. "*'Syr.*"

Khan snorted. "It seems that the probe picked up your spectral coding, so I don't have to do another one."

Fallon stilled. "It did? How?"

"The probe is set to map the entire brain, biological and mechanical, as well as track program strings. Your spectral coding registers as somewhat biological, so it actually traced it to some degree. It is listed as a benign anomaly."

Fallon frowned. "Then you must have seen it . . ."

"No. Until I had your coding keys, the actual formation was still invisible. I had spotted the biological anomalies, but they didn't look like programming traces, so I didn't note them."

"Wait a minute, my program looks *biological*?"

"The pattern it makes is completely biological, rather like blood vessels." His foot rolled against her waist absently. "Which leads me to my other bit of good news."

Fallon rolled her eyes. "Great." Her invisible programming code wasn't invisible after all, and he had more 'good' news. *I can hardly wait.*

"Apparently your spectral programming also acts biological in nature."

"Huh?"

"Your coding appears to be defending itself. It's attacking the program the Moribund Company placed in you. Given enough time, it appears that it will eventually dismantle it."

Fallon's mouth fell open. Her coding was dismantling the trapdoor in her head? "Yes!" She slapped the carpet. "Now that *is* good news! Then, if the other half of the trapcode ends up in my head — it won't work!"

"It would still work."

"But you just said . . ."

"I said your code is dismantling it, but it appears to have

only made progress along the edges. It's entirely possible that should the other half of the trap-code end up in your head, it will restore the entire thing."

Fallon groaned. "Shit."

"Quite. When we get to Port Destiny Station, you are to allow no one, and I mean absolutely no one beyond Sobehk and myself, to physically touch you."

Fallon snorted. "I may have to bite a few people, '*Syr*."

Khan chuckled. "You're an *upuaht* Prime; they'll expect you to bite them."

Fallon smiled. "Oh, goody, more good news."

"You will bite no one, Isabeau."

"What? But you just said . . .?"

"Do you know how this trapdoor got into your head?"

Fallon frowned. "No. I don't remember being unconscious at all. I collected the data, handed the memory crystal to Rudi, took my tip, and left. There isn't even a blip on my internal chronometer. No missing time at all."

"Then the program was either passed by skin to skin contact or some other way that involves physical contact, so no biting. I don't want anyone close enough to make contact."

Fallon's temper flared. "If I stay out of hand range, they're going to think I'm afraid of them." She thumped her fist on the carpeting. Damnit, she wasn't afraid of anyone. Her gaze slid to the foot sitting on her waist. Khan didn't count; only an idiot wouldn't be afraid of him.

"Why bite them when you can stab them?"

Fallon stilled. "Huh?"

"Sobehk says that you are quite skilled with knives, and I do believe he's going to show you how to handle a sword."

Fallon's mouth went dry. "You're going to let me carry a *sword*?"

Khan chuckled. "You're an *upuaht* Prime; you're supposed to carry blades. That's what those clips in your ears are for. They allow your ears to heal with the assassin's split. As a *rehkyt*, you do not scar, so to maintain any kind of mark, metal has to be inserted into the cuts to prevent them from healing closed. Anyone who sees the clips, or the resulting cuts, will know immediately that you have weapon skills."

Fallon blinked. *Oh, so those cuts in everybody's ears actually meant something.* Her mouth fell open. She was going to carry *blades*! "Hot damn!" She choked. "I meant, thank you, *'Syr.'*"

"Thanks are not needed. Regardless of the situation we are currently involved in, I would not let you walk anywhere unarmed. Simply being my *rehkyt* is hazardous enough."

Fallon swallowed. "Hazardous? *'Syr*?"

"I am an investigative lord-officer. There are a number of people who would take great delight in killing a helpless *saysehn rehkyt*, simply because they could not kill me instead."

Fallon felt a chill rush down her skin. "Shit . . ." Then she frowned. "I'm not helpless, *'Syr.*"

Khan chuckled. "Very true. However, I intend to keep quite a tight leash on you. I do not believe in taking risks."

Fallon set her chin on her hand. A tight leash . . . *Great.*

"Speaking of leashes, crawl out from under there; it's time to meet Sobehk for midday supper."

Lunch! Fallon's stomach gurgled, loudly.

Khan laughed.

Following Khan back through the populated hallways at the end of a leash, Fallon didn't quite limp. The screaming agony in her back had finally settled down to only a moderate seething. She did, however, make a conscious effort to keep her steps as smooth as possible and absolutely avoided bumping into anyone, or anything. While somewhat endurable enough to walk, the slightest of jarring step or sudden change in direction was punished with slashing pain.

The fact that Khan had insisted on tying her sash snugly over her robes did not help. She could not wait to get naked.

By the time Khan opened the door to his chamber, Fallon's jaw ached from clenching her teeth against inadvertent sounds. One did not growl, hiss, snarl or whimper around unknown Skeldhi.

Sobehk was a welcome sight sitting at the table. A small, bright blue ceramic pitcher of steaming something or other sat on a tray with two small and equally blue handle-less cups. A third cup sat in Sobehk's palm. He caught sight of Fallon, frowned and set his cup down. "What happened?"

Khan turned and released Fallon from the leash. "My whip happened." He coiled the chain, set it in his robe pocket and began unknotting Fallon's sash. "It seems that Isabeau had secret encoding that she didn't bother to mention."

Sobehk's brows rose. "Coding your probe didn't find?"

"Oh, it found it, it just didn't recognize it as coding." Khan pulled the sash free. "I now have a working copy of it." He turned her around and gently drew the over-robe from her shoulders, leaving the thin red sleeveless under-robe on. "But the omission presented the perfect opportunity to carve a little respect into Isabeau's back."

Fallon gasped. He wasn't kidding about the carving. The silk of her under-robe was sticking to her back. She hadn't thought he'd actually cut her skin. Apparently, she was wrong.

He tugged on the robe just a little.

Her back exploded with pain. A small cry escaped her lips.

Khan stopped. "Damn."

Sobehk growled. "Just how bad did you carve her?"

"Apparently deep enough to seep." Khan sighed and set the silk back up on her shoulders. "We're going to have to wait until I can get you in the shower to soak the silk before we attempt to take that off."

Fallon stomped her foot, jarring her back, and her temper more. "What? You're not going to just rip it off? I thought you liked hurting people?" She knew as soon as the words left her mouth that she had made a huge mistake, but she was too tired and in too much pain to care.

Khan caught her shoulders and turned her to face him. His copper gaze was narrow and heated. "I do not hurt others by accident. When I choose to deliver pain, be assured that it is quite deliberate." His frown deepened. "You need to be fed."

Fallon blinked. "Huh?"

Sobehk frowned. "Dinner is already on the way."

Khan turned to Sobehk. "She needs blood."

So she could get drunk and stupid again? Fallon jerked back. "I'll be fine, thanks."

Khan turned her toward the table. "Sit."

Fallon dropped to her knees on the carpet next to Sobehk. She gasped then hissed through her teeth. "Shit."

Sobehk caught her elbow before it could smack the tabletop. "She doesn't look good, Khan."

"And I have a migraine trying to split my skull wide open." Khan dropped onto the pillow beside her and pulled up his sleeve. He presented his forearm. "Bite."

Fallon stared at his arm and felt a deep longing. She turned her face away. "No, thank you, *'Syr.* I'll deal with it."

Khan growled. "I prefer not to deal with the severe headache that comes from *not* feeding you."

"What?" Fallon turned to stare at him. "You get headaches?"

"Migraines. In times of stress or pain, impression drives you to drink my blood, and my blood pressure rises to match your need." Khan winced and a vein throbbed at his temple. "If you do not feed, we both suffer."

Fallon frowned. "And if you're in pain or stress?"

Khan smiled briefly. "Then you get the migraine and I drink your blood."

"Drink it." Sobehk poured whatever was in the blue pitcher into a small cup. "His blood doesn't just knock out the pain, it helps you heal faster." He pushed the cup toward Khan.

Khan chuckled. "I keep telling you the same thing."

Sobehk's brows dropped. "She's already bonded. I'd rather not be."

Khan scowled. "Sobehk, you've been . . ."

"Khan, don't!" Sobehk's blue eyes widened then shifted to feline slits. "Just don't."

Khan growled and turned to face Fallon. "Face Sobehk, now."

Fallon flinched back from his anger and turned her back to him as he'd asked.

Khan curled his arm around her and thrust his forearm under her nose. "Drink, now."

The scent of his skin, and the blood pulsing under it was more than Fallon could bear. She opened her mouth on his forearm and bit down.

Khan released a small gasp and groaned. "Chaos, her venom . . ."

She pulled her teeth back out and covered the puncture from her teeth with her mouth. She sucked in a mouthful of copper-sweet fire and swallowed. Heat burned down her throat and expanded in her stomach. The blaze in her back faded almost immediately. It wasn't gone, it was just ignorable.

Khan sighed. "Much better." He caught her upper arm. "Lie down. Put your head in my lap."

Fallon let him pull her down, his arm curled around her with his forearm tight against her mouth. She eased down on her side with her head turned up, resting on the silk between his thighs. She had a nice view of the chamber's ceiling and Sobehk's face. If she tilted her chin up, she could see Khan's, too. They were both here, with her. They were both safe. It was . . . comforting.

Khan released her upper arm and stroked her brow. "Good, keep drinking."

She sighed and relaxed. The heat in her stomach curled up into her mind and pulled cohesive thought further apart with each swallow.

Khan used his free hand to lift the small blue cup. "Sobehk, she may have caused my blood pressure to spike, but my blood pressure has been high since I first saw you on the *Vortex*."

"No," Sobehk growled.

Khan growled right back. "Yes, damn you. I know you feel it. I can smell it on your skin!"

Sobehk curled his lips back from his teeth, but his chin lifted to bare his throat. "I denied recognition when I left the academy, I deny it now!" He made a visible effort to drop his chin.

Khan sneered, his head low and his long teeth flashing. "You can deny it all you like. That doesn't change the biological fact that it's there!"

"Khan, I will *not* submit!" Sobehk snarled openly, baring the full length of his teeth., but his eyes were wide. "Not then, not now!"

"Sobehk . . ." Khan sighed, the snarl fading from his expression and from his voice. He took a deep breath and released it. "You already gave me your submission years ago." He set the cup down. "All that's left are the legal formalities."

"No. I don't want to . . . serve." He turned away.

"Why is this so difficult for you? Your father was *dhe'syah* to mine, it's only right that you are *dhe'syah* to me. Why do you think your father put you with me?"

"I said no." Sobehk shook his head, then turned to glare at him. "If you push this, I will return to my original quarters."

Khan's brow lifted and a very nasty smile curled his lip. "Sobehk, this is my ship and my crew. You go nowhere that I do not approve of."

Sobehk jerked back. "What?"

Khan's eyes narrowed, but his smile remained. "I prefer to have your voluntary admission, but I have no difficulty waiting for your body to make that decision for you. And don't think I won't make you kneel for it."

Sobehk glared, but his chin began to lift. "You wouldn't . . ."

Khan's brows rose and his smile broadened to show teeth. "I told you before, the only constant is change. The academy was a long time ago." He sighed and his smile disappeared. "I need you. I need you with me, Sobehk."

Sobehk dropped his gaze to the table. "Please, don't force this on me."

Khan picked up the small blue cup. "I'd rather not, but I am . . . tired of being alone. Of having no one I can . . . trust."

"Trust." Sobehk groaned. "That was a foul shot."

Khan snorted. "You've always been a pain in my ass, but

you have never been untrustworthy." He sipped.

Sobehk rolled his eyes. "You had to have at least one . . ."

"No." Khan set the cup on the table very carefully. "This . . . occupation is not conducive to anything but ambition."

Sobehk looked up and smiled just a little. "And greed?"

Khan groaned. "Go ahead and say it."

Sobehk assumed a completely innocent expression. "Say what?"

Khan glared at him.

Sobehk's smile broadened. "Well, if it will make you feel better."

Khan rolled his eyes.

Sobehk set his chin on his hand and smiled, just a little sadly. "I told you so."

"Ah . . ." Khan snarled. "I hate it when you're right."

"Oh, come on!" Sobehk snorted. "You hate it when anyone is right — but you."

Khan stared hard at Sobehk, his mouth tight. "Sobehk, I need my *dhe'syah.*"

Sobehk turned his head sharply, as though he'd been slapped. "Khan, please . . ."

Khan glared at him and spoke through clenched teeth. "I have waited long enough. We have *both* waited long enough!"

"Don't!" Sobehk turned completely away, presenting his shoulder. "Khan, I'm asking you . . . please don't push this, at least not now."

Khan sighed. "Very well. Not now."

CHAPTER TWENTY-SIX

Supper arrived, was laid out, and eaten by Sobehk and Khan with only a few sparse comments that passed right over Fallon's head. Stretched out on her side with her head in Khan's lap, she was in a haze of physical contentment. Her mind was completely still, and she drifted on the very edge of sleep.

The supper dishes were gathered and removed.

Khan gently pushed her upright. His hands firm around her forearms, he rose, lifting her onto her feet. "I have to get her in the shower and the robe off while she's still intoxicated."

"You fed her for quite a while." Sobehk rose as well. "Do you need help?"

Khan's head came up. "Are you strong enough to?"

Sobehk smiled. "I start exercise therapy first thing tomorrow. Keeping her upright in the shower shouldn't be too taxing."

Khan flashed a smile. "Then perhaps you should get undressed?"

Fallon stood perfectly still, perfectly calm. The scents of Sobehk and Khan curled around her. She smiled and went where she was led, barely noticing the deeper shadows of the facility or cool tile under her bare feet.

Water hissed on with loud force and steam curled.

Hands pushed her under the water. The sudden heat spilling down her head and shoulders jarred her away from her calm place. The thin silk robe she wore soaked up the warm water and slid against her skin. Her body began nagging her to notice something. She pushed to step away from the water.

"Where do you think you're going?" Sobehk's hands curled around her upper arms to hold her firmly under the water. "It's not wearing off, is it?"

Khan swept his hands down the silk soaking against her back. "It shouldn't be." His fingers plucked at the neck of her robe. "Hold her."

"I have her."

The robe began to peel away. Stinging along her back began to penetrate her fog.

"It's coming free."

She made a small sound of distress and pressed her nose into Sobehk's chest to breathe in his comforting scent.

"Khan?"

"She's just reacting to the water's heat. I'm monitoring her through the collar." He pulled the robe free. "Ah, only some of them seeped. Hold her while I wash her."

"Mother Night, her back . . ." Sobehk's arms tightened on her arms.

Fallon lifted her head to look at Sobehk's face. His mouth was tight, and his gaze fixed past her shoulder. He was staring at her back.

"Sobehk, keep your voice down. If you alarm her, she will wake."

"Khan, what did you do?" His voice was hoarse.

Hands slid gently down her back. "What I did to you." Soapy foam slid down her hips and thighs.

"Khan, she's half my size!"

"You were a lot smaller back then, as I recall."

Sobehk lifted his head and glared past her. "Not this small!"

"Sobehk, she likes pain. She came almost as soon as I

entered her, and then twice more."

"Blood and Chaos . . ."

"Actually, no. I didn't cut her." His hands left her back. "Turn her around, so I can wash the front."

Sobehk turned her and stepped back to lean against the shower wall, holding her away from his body. "Fuck . . ."

Khan cupped her chin and stared into her eyes. "She's still under."

"I don't believe she endured this."

"She never asked me to stop." Khan smiled. "When I tagged her ears in the traditional manner, she barely flinched."

Fallon focused on Khan's smile. He was pleased. Her lips lifted in echo.

Sobehk took a deep breath. "It looks like it's healing."

"She's healing very quickly." Khan swept his hands down her shoulders and over her breasts. "By the time we get to Port Destiny, there won't be a trace of it." He knelt and soaped her thighs.

"Thank the Mother."

Khan looked up and his hands slid up to cup her crotch.

Fallon took a deep breath and parted her thighs for him.

He smiled and his fingers explored her gently, washing away the traces of his possession. "Actually, I was hoping to keep some trace of it."

"What? Why?"

Khan stared past Fallon's shoulder. "As clear warning that she is not merely decorative." He stood. "I don't want some young idiot getting ideas."

Sobehk chuckled. "She'll kick his ass for him."

Khan's head lowered and his gaze hardened. "I'm deadly serious. No one touches her but you and I."

"Are you going to let her wear a blade?"

Khan's smile turned malicious. "Absolutely."

"Good."

Khan looked down at Fallon. "I need to bathe, do you?"

"No, I'm good." Sobehk turned Fallon to face him and lifted her chin to look in her eyes. "She is quite deep under."

Khan stepped away. "Impression deepens blood intoxication."

Fallon turned from Sobehk to watch Khan step under the water. His blue tattoo blazed under the shower lights. She turned and leaned her shoulder, and then her side against Sobehk's warmth, riveted by the sight of water beading and then spilling down Khan's muscular body. He was so beautiful . . .

Khan stiffened.

Sobehk's arm slid around her waist. "What?"

Khan's head dropped under the spray then he shook the water from his face. "I picked up something from her collar."

"What?"

"It's . . . nothing." Khan reached for the soap.

"Khan, you are a lousy liar."

Khan scrubbed at his skin. "I'll have you know I am a very good liar."

Sobehk snorted. "You have never, ever been able to lie to me."

Khan lifted his head and a smile curved his mouth. "There's a reason for that."

Sobehk sighed. "Not that again . . ."

"You brought it up, not I." Khan turned to face him and slowly smeared soap across his muscular chest. His black nipple rings and the matching posts in his cocks gleamed under the light. Lather snaked down the ridges of his belly and dripped down his thighs.

Sobehk swallowed hard. "Tell me what you picked up

from her."

Khan stopped looked away and continued to rub soap across his skin. "She thinks I'm . . ." He winced. "Beautiful."

Sobehk swallowed again. "You are."

Khan choked. "What?" He lifted his chin and his mouth twisted into a sour smile. "I know what I look like. I'm scarred all to Chaos."

Sobehk looped his arms around Fallon's shoulders then set his chin on her head. "It's part of your charm."

Khan looked over at Sobehk, his eyes wide and his mouth slightly open. "Charm?" He laughed, then shook his head. "Mother Night, and you called me a lousy liar?"

Sobehk growled very low. "I don't lie, Khan. I don't need to."

Khan folded his arms across his chest and dropped his chin. "Prove it."

"Prove it?" Sobehk's head lifted. "How?"

Khan's mouth tightened. "Kiss me."

"I did, yesterday."

Khan snorted. "That was not a kiss to prove you think I am anything beyond a bastard."

Sobehk chuckled. "Well, you are."

Khan rolled his eyes and stepped under the water. "There, you've proved *my* point."

Sobehk released an exasperated breath. "Khan, my hands are full. I can't kiss you if you're way over there. You have to come over here."

Khan froze. He turned slowly, his eyes wide, his cheeks flushed. His gaze dropped to Fallon then lifted back to Sobehk.

Sobehk chuckled. "Well? I'm waiting."

Khan moved toward them in that dangerous glide of his.

Fallon sighed softly. He was freaking gorgeous in motion.

Khan stopped briefly, his gaze flickering to Fallon.

Sobehk snorted. "What's she thinking now?"

Khan released a breath and a smile flickered across his mouth. "She likes the way I move."

"I do, too." He snorted. "Now quit delaying and get your gorgeous ass over here so I can kiss you."

Khan moved in a sudden rush and framed Sobehk's shoulders with his hands pressed against the wall.

"Let's not flatten Isabeau while we're doing this." Sobehk took a deep breath. "And I'm supposed to kiss *you*, remember?"

Khan snorted then rolled away to the side. He leaned back against the wall on Sobehk's immediate right and smiled. "Good point."

Sobehk turned to face Khan, curling his arm around Fallon and pressing her against his left side. He smiled. "Which point was that?"

Fallon wrapped her arm around his waist and looked up.

Khan grinned. "Both, of course."

Sobehk leaned toward Khan, his smile warm and his blue gaze gaining in heat. "Can you control yourself?" He stood a full half a head taller and he was far broader than Khan.

Khan actually had to lift his chin to look at Sobehk. His smile slid away, and his copper eyes widened. "Control myself?" His voice was a touch breathless.

Sobehk turned to face him and set his right arm on the wall above Khan's head. "Remember, *I'm* kissing *you*."

Fallon looked up and watched both men. Their cheeks flushed, their lips blushing.

Sobehk smiled and lowered his mouth. "Don't forget."

Their lips touched.

Khan's eyes widened and he pressed back against the wall.

Sobehk smiled then pressed his mouth firmly against Khan's. His throat moved. A small groan escaped, and his eyes closed. His head tilted to gain a closer fit.

Khan's eyes closed and his chin lifted higher. His throat moved as well. A groan came from deep in his chest.

Sobehk's kiss gained in aggression and he pressed closer. Khan matched him until they kissed with blatant hunger. But they didn't quite touch.

Fallon blinked, feeling a trace of something echoing in the back of her mind. It was coming from Khan. It gained in strength until the feelings transferred with force. *Hideous need, deep hurt . . . love.*

Unable to endure it, she tightened her arm around Sobehk and slipped her arm around Khan's waist, embracing them both. She rubbed her cheek against Khan's side, blinking past the tears to watch.

Khan tried to pull away but Sobehk pursued him, pressing closer. Sobehk's stance squared until he had Khan trapped hip to chest, tight against the wall. His hips shifted. A growl rumbled.

Khan moved sharply, shoving Sobehk back with one arm.

Both men were violently erect.

Sobehk caught Khan's hand on his shoulder. His gaze was hard, hot and determined. His knuckles whitened.

Khan sucked in a breath and licked his lips. "Sobehk . . . I really don't think you're ready for sex while standing." Khan smiled but his mouth was tight. "I do, however, possess a rather large bed just outside."

Sobehk blinked as though awakening from a dream. He released Khan's hand. "I guess I got carried away."

Khan's smiled widened and he shook his hand. "I

wasn't complaining." He glanced down at Fallon. "But I think we distressed our *rehkyt*."

"Huh?" Sobehk looked down at Fallon, huddled against Khan's side. "Mother Night . . . tears?"

Khan frowned slightly. "This time I don't have a clue."

Sobehk looked over at Khan. "It had to be something she heard from you."

Khan snorted and dodged Sobehk's gaze. "I assure you, I couldn't hold a damned thought in my head during that."

"Yeah?" Sobehk grinned. "Then I did it right."

Khan raised his brow. "I was impressed." He slapped the wall and the water stopped. "Shall we continue this outside?" The water collector hummed to life.

Sobehk's cheeks flushed hot pink.

Fallon walked between them as they left the shower and discovered the slender gray-robed medic waiting.

Sobehk groaned. "*Now*? You have to medicate me right now, *A'syr sehn'dhyt*?"

The young man smiled. "I'm afraid so, *A'syr* Sobehk."

Khan groaned dramatically. "Well, there go *my* plans for the afternoon." He dropped his head and sighed. "But since you are here, could you see to something for me after you've seen to *A'syr* Sobehk?"

The *sehn'dhyt* bowed briefly. "Of course, *'Syr* Khan." He stepped toward Sobehk, and pointedly kept his gaze well above Sobehk's waist, ignoring his rather impressive erections. "Your arm, *A'syr*?"

Sobehk smiled bitterly and held out his arm. "Of course, *A'syr sehn'dhyt*."

The medic applied two hydraulic syringes to the heavy blue vein in the bend of Sobehk's arm.

Sobehk's erections faded. He groaned. "Damn . . ."

The *sehn'dhyt* turned to Khan. "*'Syr*?"

Khan caught Fallon by the shoulders. "I need a salve for

this, *A'syr*." He turned her around so he could see her back.

The medic gasped softly. "Right away, *'Syr!*" He fled out the door.

Sobehk frowned after him. "Well, that certainly killed the mood." He teetered on his feet and his eyes widened.

Khan caught his arm. "To bed and to sleep with you." He turned him toward the bed.

Sobehk groaned and walked, guided by Khan's grip. "I think I have about ten more minutes of 'awake' left."

Fallon followed a few steps behind.

Khan helped him to the bed and shoved the curtains back with a snort. "If you're lucky."

Sobehk fell back among the pillows and abruptly yawned.

Khan climbed in to pull the covers up and over him. "I don't think you are going to be lucky."

Sobehk's lids drooped. "Apparently not." His breathing deepened and his eyes fluttered closed.

Khan rolled his eyes and climbed back out of the bed. "Oh, joy, I actually get to do some work today."

The *sehn'dhyt* came back through the door in a rush of rustling silk.

Fallon turned to see him heading for Khan at the bed. She frowned and took a single step toward him.

The medic's gaze darted to Fallon. His eyes widened and he froze in mid-step.

Fallon stopped, her gaze locked on him. He didn't move, so she didn't move either.

The *sehn'dhyt* swallowed. "*'Syr?*" His voice was soft, but a little high.

Khan turned toward the medic. "Yes?"

The medic did not approach Khan, he simply held out his hand. His gaze remained locked on Fallon.

Khan walked over and collected the squeeze-tube he

held out. He examined the tube. "Ah . . . This is perfect, my thanks, *A'syr sehn'dhyt*."

The medic bowed, slowly. "Yes, *'Syr*. Anything else, *'Syr*?"

Khan focused on the *sehn'dhyt*, and then followed the medic's wide gaze to Fallon. He smiled briefly. "Thank you, that will be all, *A'syr*."

The *sehn'dhyt* bowed again and fled in a sedate hurry.

Khan shook his head and sighed. "Half their size and the terror of the staff." He collected one of the sitting pillows by the round table and walked toward the bed. He tossed the pillow down on the left side of the bed's rim then leaned over to tug one of the black sheets free.

Sobehk grumbled but remained asleep.

Khan smiled briefly then knelt to spread the sheet out over the pillow and the floor. "Isabeau, come."

Fallon moved to Khan's side. She impulsively pressed her lips to the side of his throat.

Khan jumped, smiled, then caught her hand and guided her onto the sheet, turning her to face the bed. "Down. Lay down."

Fallon knelt then spread out on the sheet, her head resting on the pillow.

Khan and bent over her and smeared something cool and smooth across her back with long delicious swipes. "You are to stay here. Don't leave Sobehk's side until I return, or he wakes."

Fallon nodded, too comfortable to form a reply.

"Good."

Lulled by the warmth of his palms, Fallon closed her eyes and loosed her rumbling purr.

CHAPTER TWENTY-SEVEN

The door to Khan's chamber opened.

Fallon's eyes snapped open. The dozens of small chamber lights were cut down to sparse three, making the room quite dim. Deep shadows filled the corners. According to her inner chronometer, it was well into ship's night. She lifted her head from the pillow.

Sobehk moved among the pillows but did not awaken.

Khan stepped in and moved toward the round table. His shoulders were slumped, and he seemed tired, but he carried a tray.

Fallon sniffed. *Food.* Her stomach growled.

Khan set the tray down on the low round table in the room's center, looked over at her and gestured that she come.

Fallon didn't need a second invitation; she was starved. She lunged off the pillow and bolted. She stopped at the last second, nearly skidding on the carpet.

Khan rolled his eyes and gave her a tired smile as he tugged off his over-robe.

Fallon lifted her hands to help him with his robe.

Khan shook his head. "Eat. I'm going to take a shower."

Fallon sat as she was supposed to, on the carpet rather than one of the kneeling cushions and applied what manners she had. At least until Khan disappeared into the facility. As soon as he was out of sight, she lifted the small bowl to her mouth and wolfed the food down as fast as she could shovel it in. She could not believe how hungry she was. It was good, too. So good she used her tongue to get the last of it from the inside of the bowl.

Somebody chuckled behind her.

Fallon froze. *Shit . . .* She calmly set the bowl down, applied her napkin then turned to face the bed.

Sobehk was bent over the edge of the bed, half in and half out. His chest rested on the carpet with his arms folded and his chin propped up on his palm. His eyes were only half-open, but he was grinning. "Hungry?"

Fallon swallowed. "Starved, actually, '*Syr*."

He chuckled tiredly. "I could tell."

Fallon looked back at the tray. She had eaten every scrap. *Uh oh . . .* She turned back to face him. "Was I supposed to save any . . ."

Sobehk snorted. "No. I had supper, you didn't."

Fallon frowned. "But, that was hours ago . . ."

Sobehk waved a hand. "The medication I'm on kills my appetite." He smiled. "Tomorrow night, however, you'd better keep a close eye on your bowl, or I'll finish it off for you."

Khan came out of the facility, completely nude with his rich, creamy mane unbound brushing his hips. "I am burning with exhaustion, and the both of you *would* be in the mood to chat."

Fallon stared at the long fall of silk streaming over Khan's shoulders and wondered what it would feel like in her hands and against her skin.

Khan stopped and raised his brow at Fallon. He turned on his heel and disappeared back into the facility.

Fallon looked at Sobehk in confusion.

Sobehk rolled his eyes and shrugged.

Khan emerged from the facility and walked over to Fallon. He held out a bone-white round hairbrush. "Would you mind brushing my hair for me?" He smiled.

Fallon's mouth fell open. "I'd love to!" She snatched the brush from his hand.

Khan sat down on the edge of the bed next to Sobehk. "Since you're both awake—" He stretched his legs out onto the blankets and crossed his feet, "—we might as well discuss our respective parts once we get to the station."

Sobehk sat cross-legged among the pillows and tilted his head to look up at Khan. "What do you need me to do?"

Fallon sat cross-legged behind Khan and ran her fingers through his creamy hair. It slid through her fingers like water. She picked up a double handful and buried her face in it. It smelled clean and of Khan. It smelled . . . sexy. She brushed at the ends then climbed higher, stroke by stroke.

Khan's brows rose and he glanced back at Fallon. "Sobehk, you need only be yourself, a *Mahf'dhyt* enforcer on sick-leave with a *rehkyt* to sell. Isabeau is your rather unstable and only half-trained *rehkyt* . . ."

"That's not even stretching the truth." Sobehk smiled.

Fallon took a moment to shoot Sobehk a narrowed glance. She drew the brush down Khan's mane in long sweeping strokes. She swept her other hand after it to smooth it down.

Khan sighed in obvious enjoyment. "I have a suite reserved for our use in the main enclave one door away from the *Mehdjay* chambers where my officers will be housed." He leaned back on his hands. "As your handler, I'll be beneath notice."

Khan's creamy mane spilled across Fallon's thighs and into her lap. She was forced to shift back to keep brushing.

Sobehk snorted. "You could never be beneath anyone's notice."

"You'd be surprised." Khan' voice soured. "I'm a certified *nehkyx*, because I spent a full year tracking down an illegal drug ring by posing as a student. They certified me four months after I broke their ring because they never un-covered my actual identity."

Sobehk's brows rose. "I'm impressed."

"So was the home office. It was my first assignment." Khan smiled. "I've been working in secrecy ever since. I have four separate DNA-coded legal identities, including my original as a fully trained *nehkyx*. Luckily, I was known as Khan in that one, too, so we're less likely to have an ac-cident. My actual identity is rarely used anywhere but in the *Mehdjay* main office and heavily encrypted."

Sobehk's smile disappeared. "No one knows who you are, even on this ship?"

Khan looked away. "The senior officers are aware that the *Moon Blade* is my personal transport. Beyond that?" He shrugged. "I do not occupy the master suite and I do not wear my rank and status visibly, so the majority of the ship's staff assumes I am simply a *Mehdjay* lord-officer, and nothing more." He tilted his head. "A few lords within the *Mehdjay* offices know my true identity. I'm generally rec-ognizable only in one of my other identities."

"Great Mother, I can't imagine living like that. Hiding who you really are."

Fallon swept the brush down Khan's hair and smiled tightly. She could. She'd been hiding all her life. It was safer that way. If they didn't know you, they couldn't find you.

Khan smiled. "It's really not that bad. It makes my func-tion easier to accomplish."

Fallon frowned. Function? Just what did Khan do? She figured he was a high-ranking cop, but what existed be-yond that?

Sobehk shook his head. "What about friends or lovers? Do you use a false identity for those, too?"

Khan looked away. "It is far simpler and safer to simply do without."

"You? Do without *sex*?" Sobehk frowned. "I find that hard to believe."

Fallon's brows shot up. With Khan's appetite? She found it hard to believe too.

"Considering my . . . position, I am not a *safe* person to know." Khan looked down and took a deep breath. "And personal security remains an issue. I have too many secrets."

Sobehk winced. "That can't be doing good things for your temperament."

Khan abruptly smiled. "It has been recently remarked that I have been almost pleasant in the past few days."

"I bet." Sobehk smiled grimly. "So, when do we arrive?"

"The day after tomorrow is the auction."

Sobehk frowned. "One day doesn't give me a whole lot of time to train Isabeau."

"You labeled her as feral." Khan snorted. "I sincerely doubt they'll expect very much."

Thanks for the vote of confidence. Not. Fallon tugged hard on the brush.

Khan winced and flashed a narrowed glance back at her. "Of course, I expect her to exceed expectations."

Fallon smiled and brushed in long smooth strokes.

Sobehk focused on Fallon and flashed a sudden grin. "I'll see to it."

Fallon stopped briefly, remembering her last training session with him — and the whip.

"I'm going to give you her collar codes."

Sobehk's smiled disappeared.

Fallon stilled. He would have control over her again. She wasn't quite sure how she felt about it. It was odd, a mix of happiness and wariness. Happiness that she would have a direct connection to him, but at the same time . . .

She lifted the brush and dragged it through Khan's silky

hair more slowly, frowning. Khan didn't use the collar, much. She distinctly remembered him using it to punish her but beyond that . . . She didn't think he had. Sobehk, on the other hand, had used the collar a lot. And yet he hadn't punished her with it, not once. Well, he'd set the punishment control, but she had the feeling that he'd found it . . . distasteful.

Khan sighed. "She's really quite good at this."

"Khan, you need her codes."

Khan snorted. "Sobehk, I'm giving you access to her codes, not autonomous control."

Fallon couldn't stop the odd feelings of both security and betrayal that spilled through her. She wanted to be with Sobehk, but she felt safer with Khan having control. She tilted her head and sucked on her bottom lip. Her feelings weren't making any sense, whatsoever!

Khan turned his head and caught Fallon's eye.

She stopped.

He leaned back and lifted his chin, focusing on her mouth.

Fallon blinked. It looked like he wanted a kiss. She set the brush down and shifted to his side then leaned toward him and brushed his lips with hers.

He smiled and his tongue stroked her bottom lip.

She opened her mouth to taste him.

Khan pressed more fully into her mouth. He gasped and pulled away to stare at Sobehk. "What in Chaos . . ."

Fallon jerked back, startled.

Sobehk lifted his head from between Khan's legs. "What? I wanted to see what you tasted like with all that metal in you."

Khan scowled. "You could have warned me."

"Now, where's the fun in that?" Sobehk grinned. "You never complained before."

"I'm not complaining now, just . . . surprised." Khan smiled and lifted his brow. "Are you suddenly feeling energetic?"

"I wish." Sobehk rolled his eyes. "I don't know what the medics have put in me, but it kills my appetites." He sat back on his heels and looked down at his completely uninterested anatomy. "All of them."

"I see." Khan shook his head then smiled. "Your mouth seems to have plenty of energy."

Sobehk smiled sourly. "That's about the sum total."

"I could bite you?"

Sobehk jerked back and his eyes narrowed. "No. Thank you."

Khan's brow rose. "Very well then, how about putting that mouth of yours to good use?"

Sobehk frowned. "I thought I was?"

"I was thinking more along the lines of . . ." Khan twisted sharply and caught Fallon around the waist. "Using it on Isabeau?" He pulled.

Fallon yelped and sprawled facedown across Khan's lap. She kicked out. "Hey!"

Khan knotted a hand around her braid to keep her there and gave her ass a light swat. "Be good."

Fallon choked in shock. The swat hadn't hurt—but it should have. She frowned. Her back felt warm, and a little stiff, but it didn't burn. It didn't even sting. What had he put on her?

Sobehk's brow rose. "That's not a bad idea. I haven't had a taste of her since she went Prime."

Khan grinned. "Can you make her scream?"

Sobehk smiled broadly, showing teeth. "Absolutely." He raised his brow. "You should have heard her when I had her tied over my glider."

Fallon gasped then turned and growled. "You didn't

have to mention that!" She snapped her long teeth at Sobehk. "You bastard!"

Sobehk eased out of range and smiled. "You say that like it's a surprise." He looked up at Khan. "And you?"

Khan twisted sharply, pressing Fallon down onto the carpet beneath him. "I've been dying to fuck her tits." His head dropped and he nipped at her nipple.

Fallon yelped and bucked under him.

"Oh, that sounds nice!" Sobehk pursed his lips. "This will be a lot easier if we tie her down."

Fallon twisted under Khan to look at Sobehk. "What?"

Khan laughed, his eyes bright copper and gaining in heat as he held Fallon down. "Now, there is an excellent idea!"

"Guys, this isn't funny!" Fallon tugged, but she couldn't move much at all. Her arms had been pulled down and her knees bent to bind her wrists to her ankles. They had laid her out and tied her to the handles on either side of a long narrow black trunk. A thick pillow was set between her back and the trunk's hard surface, but her butt hung slightly off one end, and her head hung off the other. Her neck was cushioned from the trunk's edge by a small tubular pillow.

Khan grinned and tugged at the pillow at her neck, apparently making sure it wouldn't slip. He licked his lips. "Oh, I don't know, all that wiggling is quite entertaining."

Fallon tugged at her wrists and growled. "I will *so* get you both for this!"

Khan chuckled. "You'll only be punished for it."

Fallon twisted and got absolutely nowhere. She glared at Khan. "It'll be worth it."

Sobehk stood between her splayed thighs and stared down at her opened and exposed flesh. "Her cream is going to get all over that."

"It can be washed." Khan straightened then walked around to check the bindings on her wrists. "It was the only thing narrow enough to be comfortable and low enough for you to sit—" He smiled. "—while you dine."

"I'm actually more worried about her breaking it."

"It won't break." Khan cleared his throat. "I've used it before."

Sobehk's brows rose. "Have you?"

Khan's cheeks flushed. "Once or twice. On a layover."

"For them, or for you?"

Khan swallowed and looked away. "Only two of my identities are as lords; the others are . . . not."

Sobehk chuckled, and his blue eyes narrowed. "Well then, perhaps this masquerade of yours will prove more entertaining than I thought."

"We'll see." Khan lifted his chin and gave Sobehk a sly smile. "I think she's ready. Shall we begin?"

CHAPTER TWENTY-EIGHT

Strapped down on the narrow black trunk, Fallon had to lift her head to see a damned thing, but she could feel anticipation humming from Khan. Excitement threaded with anger, satisfaction and desperation seeped through the link made by her collar.

Khan was definitely up to something.

Sobehk dropped a thick pillow at the foot of her trunk and knelt down. His warm hands cupped her thighs.

Khan lifted his leg and straddled her hips then sat down.

Fallon grunted. He wasn't that heavy, but that wasn't the point. She was completely helpless. She hated being helpless.

Khan leaned over her and his long mane spilled down her side. He smiled. "I have seen how you handle pain. Let's see how you deal with pleasure, shall we?"

"Pleasure?" Fallon's brows shot up. "Think you can do that?" Her mouth curved into a sarcastic smile. "'Syr?"

Sobehk laughed. "I think she has your number, Khan."

Khan grinned. "Oh, but I have hers, too."

Fallon raised one brow. "Think so?"

"Simple observation frequently reveals more truth than outright torture." Khan lifted his chin and turned his head sharply. His creamy mane spilled across her belly and breasts. He fingered a lock from his eyes then spread his palms over her breasts with his hair trapped under them and against her skin. He slid his palms around her breasts, across her torso and over her belly. "What do you think?"

Fallon inhaled as her nipples tingled and tightened. It felt like she was being massaged with the finest silk imaginable. Her toes curled and she groaned. "I think . . . you're . . . evil."

He chuckled warmly. "I can be."

Sobehk's hot wet mouth descended onto her intimate flesh and his tongue swept across her tender folds, drawing shivers. He pulled back and smacked his lips. "Damn, she tasted good before, but . . ." He lapped then smacked his lips again. "That is one incredible flavor. I could eat her all night." He pressed his entire mouth to her and sucked.

Fallon gasped and tried to buck, but she was tied too securely. "Shit!"

Khan dropped down on her, trapping his long hair between their bodies. He cupped the back of her head and lifted her mouth to his. His lips brushed lightly, his tongue sliding in slow sweet forays against hers. And then he moved, his chest and belly sliding across hers, side to side in a slow, sensuous and stirring massage of warm, hard flesh and silk. The rings on his nipples flirted with her nipples. His brutally hard erections rubbed against her belly with delicious intent.

Sobehk sucked on her wet flesh with tender sweetness and moans of appreciation. His palms opened on her inner thighs and stroked in stirring circles against her skin. His tongue flicked and pressed across her clit with devastating skill.

Fallon moaned into Khan's mouth as the hair rose on her limbs. She was literally being bathed in raw sensual pleasure. She could feel her body responding with rich cream.

If they kept this up, she was definitely going to scream.

Khan lifted his mouth from hers. "Such a quick response." Satisfaction purred in his voice. He tossed a glance over his shoulder at Sobehk. "I think we work well together."

Sobehk released a sinister chuckle, but his tongue did not stop its sweet torture.

Khan's head dropped to her breast and he caught her nipple in his flat front teeth. He pinched the swollen flesh, very slowly, in a bite of exquisite tenderness.

Fallon shuddered, racked by the intensity. Her core tightened with agonizing hunger. Her hands tightened into fists and her back bowed up.

Sobehk caught her clit in his teeth and tugged, very lightly.

Her breath caught. The intense pleasure from her nipple and the searing bolt from her clit met in her belly. She exploded into climax before she knew it was there. Her breath released in a scream.

Khan groaned and lifted his head. "Oh, that was very nice."

Sobehk sucked noisily and moaned in agreement.

Khan smiled. "Again."

Again? Great Maker, she barely survived that one! Fallon gasped for breath. "I'd rather not . . ."

"Oh, that's too bad." Khan's smile broadened. "As I insist that you cum again." His head lowered to her other nipple. His teeth captured her and began to bite down with devastating tenderness. His body moved against her in sensual sweep of silky hair and hot skin.

Sobehk pressed his mouth tighter and inserted two fingers. He curled them and flicked.

Still shuddering from her last climax, she rose hot and fast — and much too intense . . . She shuddered hard in resistance.

Khan chuckled against her breast. "Oh, yes, resist. I like it when you resist."

Sobehk focused his attack on her clit, sucking while

flicking deep within her.

Fallon gasped and arched, her hands in tight fists and her toes curled hard. She moaned and tried to shift under Khan's weight.

Khan sat up and slid forward until his rigid cocks nestled between her breasts. He cupped her breasts and squeezed, capturing his lower cock and plump balls between them. He rocked forward, slowly pumping his cock between the fullness her breasts. He moaned. "Oh, very nice." The tips of his thumb-claws grazed her swollen nipples.

Fallon gasped as Sobehk's mouth on her clit and Khan's claws tenderly biting her nipples built a hot molten blaze in her belly. She was going to cum . . .

"Isabeau." Khan sucked in a sharp breath and leaned over, cupping the back of her head in one palm. "Lick me. Lick me as I fuck your sweet tits."

Fallon opened her mouth and stroked the swollen flared crown of his primary cockhead brushing her lips. She lashed her tongue and tasted the titanium balls marking the bar piercing him. Liquid musk pearled on her tongue.

Khan groaned and slowly pumped his secondary cock between her breasts as she licked his primary. "Sobehk, she's going to make me cum very soon."

Sobehk lifted his mouth from her flesh. "Are you sure you want to cum? You don't want to sleep in her?"

Khan's gaze blazed red-hot and his smile was full of teeth. "Oh, I definitely want to cum."

"Damn, I can't see, even with the mirrors."

Fallon caught movement in the mirrors and saw Sobehk rising to his feet. She looked up at Khan.

Every muscle on Khan's body stood in sharp relief as he pumped his secondary cock very slowly between her breasts, while the head of his primary cock slipped in and out of her mouth. He licked his lips and his eyes narrowed.

Fallon's brows drew together even as she licked. Whatever Khan was up to, he was about to get what he was after. She could feel his excited anticipation burning across the telepathic link.

Sobehk leaned over Khan's shoulder. He sucked in a breath.

Fallon's hips bucked in time to Sobehk's fingers, still lodged within her.

Sobehk's blue eyes widened and the round pupils shifted into feline slits then expanded into darkness. "What I wouldn't give for a hard pair of dicks."

Khan raised his brow. "If I bite you, you could take her mouth."

Sobehk groaned. "If you do, I'll probably cum right away, just from your combined scent." He took a strong sniff and his eyes closed briefly. "Bloody Chaos, the smell . . . you're both right on top of cumming."

"Yes, yes we are." Khan groaned. "Make a decision now."

Sobehk held out his forearm.

Khan snarled and bit down, hard.

Sobehk gasped. "Mother Night, Khan!" His eyes closed and he sucked in a sharp breath. "Bloody Chaos, your venom works fast."

Khan released Sobehk's arm and slid his tongue across the punctures. He slowed his thrusts and groaned. "Hurry, we're right there."

Sobehk moved to Fallon's head.

Khan let Fallon's head fall back onto the pillow at her neck. "Give her your secondary and take her tits; I'll get her cunt." He released her breasts and leaned back. His fingers sought then found her slick opening. "Mother Night, she's wet." He drove two fingers into Fallon's flesh.

Fallon gasped and shuddered with the swift invasion.

Sobehk frowned. "My primary will spill all over you."

Khan snorted. "So?" he glanced down. "Isabeau, open your mouth and close your eyes."

Close her eyes? Oh yeah, four dicks and three of them were going to unload on her breasts and neck. She did not want to get cum in her eyes. Fallon closed them and opened her mouth. Warm hard cock slid across her tongue. She knew that flavor. *Sobehk* . . . She closed her lips and suckled.

Sobehk groaned and his palms closed on her breasts, enclosing Khan's cock between them. "Gods, her mouth . . ." His hips jerked, driving his cock deeper into her mouth, then he pulled back.

Fallon swallowed to keep from choking and sucked in a swift breath.

Khan groaned and shoved hard between her breasts. His fingers plunged within her, pressing insistently against her inner sweet spot.

Fallon moaned around the cock in her mouth as Khan's thrusting fingers stirred the coiling heat in her belly to an angry throbbing frenzy. She was right on the very edge.

A hungry growl was followed by a yearning moan.

Sobehk began a frenzied but shallow thrusting.

Khan, seated atop her and thrusting between her breasts, matched Sobehk's swift rhythm. The sound of wet kisses and soft moans filled her ears.

She opened her eyes.

Khan had Sobehk's hair in one fist and his mouth locked to Sobehk's, kissing him with desperate ferocity. Sobehk was kissing him back, just as fiercely. Khan moaned, and pressed his thumb on her clit, mercilessly hard.

Pleasure so intense it was actually pain, and it hammered her. Fallon's breath stopped and she froze. Release exploded in a hot wet rush then slammed up her spine in a cascade of fire. She closed her eyes and arched hard under them, her mouth opening wide on a muffled wail.

Khan gasped, froze, then shuddered. His hot cum spilled across her throat and spattered her cheeks.

Fallon jolted hard as his release speared straight into her mind and slammed her up and over into a second and brutally violent orgasm.

Sobehk choked, shuddered, and froze. His cock pulsed in her mouth and he came. His hot cum spilled into her mouth and across her breasts and belly.

"Fuck . . ." Sobehk's cock retreated from Fallon's mouth.

Khan chuckled. "You made quite a mess all over me." His voice was very soft.

"I . . ." Sobehk sighed. "Yeah, I did."

Khan groaned and climbed off Fallon. "We better get her loose, and all of us in the shower and then, most definitely to bed. I don't know about you, but I'm dead tired."

Sobehk was utterly silent as he helped Khan release Fallon from the trunk.

Fallon sat up and rubbed at her wrists.

Khan rolled up the thin cable they'd used, and a smile played on his lips. Cum was smeared all over his belly. It smelled like Sobehk's.

Sobehk's shoulders were slightly hunched and his mouth tight. He smelled of Khan. He took the cable from Khan without looking at him then turned away to set it on one of the red trunks piled against the wall.

Fallon frowned. Khan was very pleased with himself; she could feel it through the collar, but she could see that Sobehk was clearly unhappy about something.

Khan led the way into the facility and turned on the three showerheads. Steam filled the small glassed-in room. He reached for the soap and began washing with undisguised enthusiasm.

Sobehk washed at a distant showerhead and kept his back to Khan.

Fallon tugged her hair from its braid and then washed it, and her body, mercilessly.

Although all three of them occupied the shower, no one spoke. The facility held only the sound of splashing water.

Sobehk rinsed the last of the soap from his muscular body then set his palms flat on the back wall. He sighed and pressed his brow against the wet metal, letting the water fall on his shoulders.

Fallon stared at Sobehk. Her heart ached for him. Khan had to have done something. She turned to Khan and leveled a glare at him. She focused on their telepathic link and projected as clearly as she could. *What did you do to him?*

Khan looked over at Sobehk and sighed very softly. *I made him face a truth he didn't want to see.* He walked to Fallon's side and dropped a quick kiss on her brow. *You're a good pet.*

Fallon blinked. *Huh?*

Khan approached Sobehk. He leaned back against the wall, his gaze focused on the water swirling down the center drain. "Do I need to ask?"

"I . . ." Sobehk released a breath and his hands slid down the wall. "No." He groaned. "Bloody Chaos, Khan, I'm not a fucking submissive!"

Fallon stiffened. *What in fury . . .*

Khan rolled his eyes. "Sobehk, did you never think that perhaps I wasn't asking you to be one?"

Sobehk turned his head to face Khan. "What?"

Khan snorted and crossed his arms. "Do you remember that time we came back from class early and we found our fathers . . . in their compromising situation?"

"Oh, yeah." Sobehk winced then smiled. "That was a little . . . unexpected."

Khan raised his brow. "You did notice who *wasn't* on top?"

Sobehk froze. He frowned. "Now that you mention it . . ."

Khan chuckled softly. "Apparently it runs in the bloodline, though from what I've seen, it's actually pretty common between blooded lords and their *dhe'syah*."

Sobehk's brows shot up. "You're joking."

Khan walked over to the door and hit the wall, starting the water collector. "You'll get to see it yourself at the next *Ehnyad* conference."

Sobehk groaned. "I'd rather not."

Khan grinned. "I would be a fool to go anywhere without my *dhe'syah*."

Sobehk rolled his eyes. "Oh, this is going to be loads of fun. I can tell."

Fallon stared from one male to the other. What in fury was a *dhe'syah*? Some kind of bodyguard?

Khan opened the sliding glass door. "Look at it this way; you get to keep your pet." He stepped out of the shower.

Fallon looked at Khan in shock. *What?*

Sobehk turned to look at Fallon. His blue eyes were wide and his mouth slightly open. His mouth snapped closed and his jaw clenched, as did his fists. "That manipulative little shit!" He lifted his chin and closed his eyes then suddenly dropped his head. His breath left him in a rush. He pressed a hand to his brow and a chuckle rumbled from him. "I am definitely going to ream his royal rump for that one." He raised his head and smiled tiredly at Fallon. "You going to stand there all night?" He held out his hand. "Come on, it's bedtime."

Fallon moved cautiously toward Sobehk. "Is somebody going to tell me what's going on?"

Sobehk winced. "I'll tell you tomorrow."

Fallon raised her brow at him. "You better."

Sobehk snorted and snatched her hand. "Or what?"

"Oh, I don't know . . ." Fallon closed her fingers tight around his warm hand and smiled. "But, I'm sure I'll think of something."

Sobehk rolled his eyes as he led her from the shower. "Knowing you, yes, you will."

CHAPTER TWENTY-NINE

A small chime sounded.

Fallon's eyes snapped open. She was on her side in the bed, nearly buried in pillows with Khan spooned hot and solid against her back. She frowned. She'd actually slept through the night cycle rather than awakening to climb out. *Huh.*

Sobehk groaned, on the far side of Khan.

Fallon turned to look over her shoulder just in time to see Sobehk stretch out across the sheets, catching all that heavy muscle moving and shifting. He really was a handsome brute.

Sobehk sat up, yawned, scratched, and turned to grin over Khan's back. "Come on, kitten, time to get dressed."

Fallon's mouth fell open. "Me?"

Sobehk climbed up onto his knees. "You want to learn the sword, right?"

"Hot damn!" Fallon twisted out of Khan's hold and lunged out of the bed.

Sobehk smiled and rolled out far more sedately.

Khan chuckled and rolled onto his back. "Have fun. Don't kill each other." He snagged a few pillows then grabbed the comforter and pulled it up to his chin.

Fallon frowned at him. "Don't you have to get up, too?"

Khan set his arm behind his head and grinned. "Not for another hour."

Fallon checked her internal chrono. *Oh, for the Maker's sake . . .* It was a full hour and a half before full ship morning. She glared at Sobehk.

Sobehk moved toward his wardrobe, scratching the small of his back and refusing to look her way. "I think I have something you can wear . . ."

Khan rolled onto his side. "If you will wait about five more minutes, the staff will be here with practice garb for both of you and a small rising meal."

Sobehk frowned. "What, did you take care of everything?"

Khan yawned. "Rank has its responsibilities."

Fallon tilted her head. What in fury was that supposed to mean?

A double chime sounded.

"There." Khan lifted a hand, and the door appeared in the blank far wall and cycled open.

Two youthful attendants in dark gray robes came in with a floating tray. They placed a pair of small, steaming bowls on the table, along with a pair of dull, plain steel practice swords. They turned to Sobehk.

Fallon's gaze focused on the black chain leash coiled in the center of the table.

Sobehk nodded and held out his arms.

The attendants dressed him in a short but heavily padded sleeveless red robe. The robe was tucked into very full, pleated black trousers that were gathered tight at the waist. A red and black sash was wound around his waist.

Sobehk bowed to his attendants and grabbed for one of the small bowls on the table and a rolled napkin. He tilted his head toward Fallon. "Get over here and get dressed."

Fallon swallowed. She took several deep breaths and walked over. She bowed politely and held her arms out from her body. She released her breath very slowly and took tiny breaths to keep their scent from sending her into a panic.

Sobehk frowned slightly, watching Fallon while forking meat slivers into his mouth.

The attendants were swift. In a very short time, Fallon was dressed in a smaller version of what Sobehk wore.

Fallon bowed again and thanked all those years spent in the sewers that taught her to breathe amazingly shallow. She walked over to the table and picked up one of the small bowls and snapped open a napkin. Whatever it was, it smelled delicious. She scooped a piece of barely cooked meat into her mouth, trying not to drip on her nice clean robe. It was wonderfully tangy.

Sobehk frowned at her. "Is there a problem with being dressed?"

Fallon shook her head and swallowed what was in her mouth. "They smell wrong."

Sobehk's brows rose then he rolled his eyes. "Oh." He shrugged. "I'd heard that some Prime are nose sensitive."

Fallon swallowed. "Nose sensitive?"

Sobehk sucked in a piece of meat and nodded. He swallowed. "Some Prime can differentiate between people by scent alone."

Some Prime? Fallon froze with a piece of meat halfway to her mouth. She set it back in her bowl. "You're kidding, right?"

"Nope." Sobehk upended the small bowl into his mouth. He swallowed and applied his napkin. "Some Prime can actually track by scent, though it's not common."

Apparently, her sense of smell wasn't exactly 'normal.' Fallon focused on eating, unsure whether she should say anything.

Khan groaned in the bed and turned face up. "Sobehk, could you come here please?"

Sobehk rolled his eyes at Fallon then walked over to the

bed. "Yeah, what?"

Khan chuckled. "I thought you might find this useful."

Sobehk sighed. "Oh, thanks."

Khan shifted among the pillows. "I suggest keeping the telepathic link open. She has some rather interesting thoughts going through her head on occasion."

Fallon frowned. *What the . . .*

Sobehk turned around and grinned, showing his long teeth. "Oh, yes! I have you now!"

Fallon frowned in suspicion. "What?"

Sobehk's stride positively bounced as he approached her. He leaned in close. "I suggest you be a very good pet." He waggled his brows as he leaned past her to pick up the leash on the table. "Khan just gave me your collar codes."

Fallon winced. "Great."

Sobehk chuckled and handed her a gray-sheathed practice blade. A black cord had been wrapped around the sheath only two fingers from the hilt.

Fallon held the blade with both hands for an entire breathless moment.

The sword was a weapon from a more romantic time when ships sailed the seas rather than the stars. However, instead of archaic tempered steel, the modern blade was made of live-steel and practically hummed with nanites. Live-steel would return to shape from a forty-five-degree bend, would never lose its edge, and could withstand extremes in temperature, such as the absolute cold of space, without shattering. It would hold the perfect shape of its making for as long as it existed. Live-steel was said to be born, not made.

The practice blade in her hands was very likely made of ordinary steel and dull, but still . . . a sword.

Sobehk lifted the other practice sword. "Shove this through your sash, like so . . ." He demonstrated by shoving the sword through the broad folds of his sash then angling it at his hip.

Fallon shoved the sword into her sash, and very nearly straight into her pants. She got it on the second try.

"Here, like this . . ." Sobehk leaned forward and set the sword at her left hip, angled just a bit toward the center. He tugged at the dangling black cord and showed her the wrapping knot that kept the sheath from sliding from her sash.

He lectured a bit on the proper hand positions to carry the blade in a public area then tucked the black chain leash through his sash and turned for the door.

Fallon stared after him. No leash?

At the door, Sobehk turned back to her. "Are you coming, or what?"

Fallon's brows shot up. No leash. *Hot damn!* She grinned and strode toward him and the door. "Let's go!"

Fallon discovered very quickly that walking through the ship's somewhat narrow hallways with a sword jammed in her sash was more complicated than it looked. The long end kept getting caught in her long full pants and the grip kept getting tangled with her robe. She was constantly shifting it away from her clothes and out of other peoples' way. For some odd reason, people kept trying to walk into it, as though there were a magnet at the end designed to draw knees.

Sobehk tossed the occasional smile her way but other than that, he strode through the early cycle halls ignoring her presence at his heels.

Fallon followed Sobehk into a lift and then out into a huge and somewhat empty shadowed room. The distant steel walls and the very distant ceiling were supported by immense girders. Massive crates were stacked and secured in seemingly random areas, and the plate steel deck was painted with gridlines. Lighting was focused straight down on the piled crates and nowhere else.

Fallon followed Sobehk past several stacks of boxes. "This looks like a warehouse."

"It's cargo storage and the designated practice area." He stopped, turned to the right and pointed. "That's our spot over there."

Fallon took another look around. "I don't see anyone else practicing." She rolled her eyes. "Oh yeah, everyone else is still asleep."

Sobehk smiled as he led the way toward a blank area between two rows of cargo. "Do you really want people watching you stabbing yourself?"

Fallon scowled. "I am very good with blades."

"I'm sure you are." Sobehk stepped into the cleared area. Light snapped on overhead and poured down into the empty space. "But a sword is not a knife."

Fallon set her hands on her hips. "A sword is a really long knife. How hard can it be?"

Sobehk raised his brows. "Draw."

Fallon pulled the sword from its sheath – and got stuck, with half the blade still in the sheath.

Sobehk did not laugh; he didn't even smile. He tilted his grip down, angling the sheath. "Try it this way."

It took more than one try just to get the stupid thing free of her sheath. Finally free and in her hand, Fallon found that the practice blade was actually balanced, but it was awkwardly lengthy.

Sobehk nodded. "Good. Sheathe it."

Fallon swallowed. "Okay." Getting that big long piece of steel back into its sheath in her sash was even more problematic. Her arms were just too short.

Sobehk nodded. "Hold your grip like so and return like

this." He tilted the sheath down and to the side.

Fallon nibbled on her bottom lip and repeated his motions. The blade slid home.

Sobehk nodded. "Good. Draw and return."

Drawing the sword then returning it without striking the floor or her shins, or oddly, jamming her elbow into her side, turned out to be far more of a challenge than it had looked. Eventually, she got it right. Of course, her memorization program didn't hurt.

A sword was nothing like a knife.

"Draw."

Fallon drew the blade and held it extended before her in the one-handed position he had shown her, one foot slightly forward in a balanced stance.

Sobehk nodded. "Good. Now . . ." He drew his blade with disgusting ease and stood at her right side in the same exact position. "All you have to do is copy what I do. When I say 'hold,' freeze in place, so I can adjust your stance. Got it?"

Fallon took a small breath. "Yes, '*Syr*."

He moved, slowly and gracefully, lifting the sword above his head while his right foot slid back, taking nearly all his weight, and his left hand rose to the level of his heart.

Fallon followed.

"Hold."

Fallon froze.

Sobehk stepped behind her and adjusted her head, her shoulders, her arms and her feet. He caught her by the hips and moved her back just a bit. "Weight back here. Balance here." He returned to place and then changed positions.

Fallon followed and followed, and followed . . .

Sobehk called out position changes and watched with a small smile on his lips, but he didn't laugh, or make any nasty comments, or get upset when she took forever to do something. He was calm, relaxed and . . . centered, even patient. He seemed like a whole different person.

There were a lot of 'holds,' but somehow, Fallon found the whole thing rather relaxing.

Sobehk dropped into a relaxed stance and slid the sword into his sheath with a snap.

Fallon followed, and her sword actually went where it was supposed to go, the way it was supposed to get there, on the first try. She blinked in surprise. "Oh!"

Sobehk nodded and smiled. "Good." He stepped forward and set his hand on his sword grip. "Assume the ready position. We're going to do the entire pattern again."

Fallon stepped back, copying his movements, and frowned. "That was a pattern?"

Sobehk grinned. "Yep, and we're going to do it over, and over, and over until you can do it without me."

Do it *without* him? Fallon's mouth fell open. "Sobehk, that's a long freaking pattern. It's going to take forever to learn it!"

"It only took me four years to learn that one." Khan strode around the edge of a pile of crates bordering their space. He was dressed in matching red and black practice garb with a dulled practice blade in his sash.

Fallon's mouth fell open. "Four *years*?"

Sobehk grinned. "Khan was an unusually quick student."

Fallon rolled her eyes, groaning then frowned. "Wait a minute . . . you said 'that one.' There are more of them?"

Sobehk nodded. "Eight."

Fallon rolled her eyes. "I'm doomed."

Khan chuckled and moved to Fallon's other side. "And this is the short one if I recall correctly." He stepped back into position, his hand on the sword grip.

Sobehk chuckled. "I figured I'd start her on something

easy."

Pain stabbed through Fallon's heart. He might be starting her lesson, but after the auction . . . He wouldn't be finishing it. She took a deep breath to deal with the ache in her chest.

Khan sighed and came forward. "Sobehk, are you paying attention?"

Sobehk frowned. "To what?"

Khan's brows dipped and his eyes narrowed. "To your *rehkyt*?"

Sobehk looked down at Fallon. "Isabeau, is something wrong?"

Fallon looked straight ahead, avoiding the heavy stares from both men. "No, I'm good."

Khan rolled his eyes. "Turn on the telepathic link, you idiot."

Sobehk rolled his eyes. "Fine, whatever . . ." He froze then released his breath and winced. "Ah . . . shit."

Fallon glared at Khan. "Thank you, '*Syr*. Now you've made us both miserable."

Khan folded his arms and stared hard at Sobehk "Tell her."

Sobehk stared hard at the floor and took a deep breath. "I won't be leaving after the auction. I'm staying, with Khan and you."

Fallon stared at Sobehk. "What? I don't get it. Why?"

He rolled his shoulders and looked away. "It's . . . complicated."

She turned to Khan and glared. "What did you do to him?"

Khan's brows shot up.

Sobehk chuckled.

Khan lifted his gaze to Sobehk. "Do you want me to tell her?"

Sobehk sighed and turned to face them. "I'm Khan's *dhe'syah*. His . . ." He frowned then looked up at Khan. "Is there an Imperial equivalent for this?"

Khan looked down at Fallon. "Sobehk is my liege man, my most trusted companion."

Fallon frowned in concentration. "Is that like a squire to a knight?"

Khan smiled. "More like a knight to a prince." He lifted his gaze to Sobehk and frowned. "Though he has yet to make his formal oath."

Sobehk rolled his eyes.

Fallon choked. "You're a *prince*?" Her voice came out in a breathless squeak.

Khan pursed his lips and shrugged. "Yes."

Sobehk snorted. "He's a blood prince. If he has a daughter, she'll be in line to the throne."

Khan grimaced. "I doubt she'll ever make heir, not with my four bloodthirsty sisters ahead of her."

Fallon's brows shot up. "Not you? You're not in line to the throne?"

Khan shook his head. "My race is ruled by queens."

Sobehk nodded. "The men fight, the women govern."

Khan looked down at Fallon. "The point is, Sobehk is not leaving. You're going to have us both."

Fallon stilled. Sobehk wasn't leaving. Somehow that made the ache around her heart worse.

Sobehk stepped back into the ready stance. "Shall we get back to work?"

Khan nodded and took position on Fallon's left.

Fallon stepped back and set her hand on her sword's grip. Khan was a prince and Sobehk was his knight? It was like something out of one of Peter's old story vids. All of a sudden, Sobehk's reluctance to 'serve' made an awful lot of sense. Sobehk wasn't exactly the submissively obedient type. She smiled grimly. Served him right, though. If she had to wear a collar and have an "owner," it was only fair that he had one, too.

Sobehk scowled down at her. "Clear that head of yours, I can't concentrate with all that noise coming out of you."

Fallon growled before she could stop herself. But she bit back her retort. If he hadn't been listening, he wouldn't have heard her.

"I heard that!" Sobehk swatted at her.

Fallon ducked his swing easily. "It's *my* head! *You*, get out of it!"

Khan turned and glared at her. "Whose head?"

Fallon groaned. On second thought, having the two of them might *not* be the best idea in the world.

Deep in the ship's hold, the three of them moved in unison, slowly stepping to the beat called out by Sobehk. Their blades rose and fell with arms outstretched, stepping, turning, and shifting from stance to stance in a very, very slow martial dance.

All three sheathed their blades in unison.

Fallon blinked as though slipping from a trance. "Whoa . . ."

Sobehk nodded. "Knew I'd find a practical use for that telepathic link sooner or later."

Khan nodded and stretched. "I think that worked rather nicely."

Fallon frowned. "What?"

Sobehk stepped back and waved his hand. "Take two steps forward."

Fallon did.

"Draw."

Fallon drew. The blade came from her sheath in a fluid motion and she held it up in perfect position without even thinking about it. *Huh.*

"Turn around."

Fallon turned.

Sobehk leaned back against a large crate with his arms folded. He smiled. "Begin."

Khan lunged at her with his blade low, held two-handed, and driving for her stomach.

Fallon engaged, twisted to the side and back, and slid her blade up his blade, riding it to get to Khan's throat.

Khan wove out of the way.

She followed, her blade snaking after him.

Khan twisted sharply to avoid her then lunged at her, snapping out a lightning-fast countermove.

Fallon's blade rang out as she met him. She lashed out with her foot.

Khan dodged her kick and snapped out his fist.

She blocked and brought up her blade to parry the steel headed for her outer thigh.

"Hold!"

Fallon froze.

Khan grinned and laughed. "That was damned impressive!"

Sobehk laughed. "Yeah, and she even used some of the moves from the pattern!"

Fallon's brows shot up. He was right. She *had* used a few of Sobehk's fancy moves.

Khan turned to face Sobehk. "That wasn't *all* from the pattern?"

Sobehk shook his head grinning. "Khan, there was no way in hell I could have imprinted that whole pattern in her head . . ."

Fallon turned to face him. "What?"

"I projected the moves straight into your head to help you learn what I was doing." Sobehk smiled. "Apparently some of it stuck."

Fallon frowned, thinking. "Huh . . ."

Sobehk lifted his chin at Khan. "Most of that was Isabeau's natural fighting style."

Khan's brows shot up. "Really?" He sheathed his blade.

Sobehk stepped away from the crate he'd been leaning against. "Now you know why it took three days to catch her."

Fallon sheathed her blade and grinned. "It took him three days to tire me out enough to actually beat me."

Khan chuckled. "I don't think she's going to have a problem with the assessment."

Sobehk smiled and dropped a hand on Fallon's shoulder. "I never thought she would."

Fallon frowned at one and then the other. "What assessment?"

Khan dropped his chin. "It's nearly time for midday supper. Shall we go?"

Sobehk nodded. "I'm starved." He caught Fallon by the shoulders and turned her toward the break in the crates. "Go." He shoved her forward.

"I'm going!" Fallon rolled her eyes and followed Khan from the alcove created by the stacked crates. "Sobehk, what assessment?"

Sobehk fell into step beside her. "The one at the auction."

Fallon shot him a narrowed glare. "I figured that much out."

Khan led the way toward the lifts. "Now is not the time to talk." He smiled over his shoulder. "Supper is waiting."

CHAPTER THIRTY

Following in Khan's and Sobehk's wake up in the lift and then through the black-walled hallways, Fallon found carrying the sword far less embarrassing. Even though the halls were far more crowded with many more people in long flowing robes, the ends of her sheathed blade didn't get tangled in her clothing or in anyone else's.

They arrived at Khan's quarters and found that supper was indeed waiting.

Seated between Khan and Sobehk, Fallon found her table manners painfully annoying. She was starved, and yet she could only eat one slice of the succulent meat at a time, and she couldn't lick the bowl after. Of course, the headache wasn't helping any, either. Fallon pressed a hand to her pounding temple and leaned over the table so she wouldn't drip on her robes.

Khan looked over at Fallon then looked at Sobehk. He nodded at Fallon. "Are you monitoring?"

Sobehk grimaced. "I feel it."

Khan leaned back. "That's not from me."

Sobehk frowned. "What?"

Fallon looked up, wincing through her headache. "What?"

Khan lifted his brow.

Oh, bloody Fate . . . Fallon scowled. "What, *'Syr?'*"

Khan tilted his head toward Sobehk. "Do you remember what I said about migraines?"

Fallon blinked. "Then this isn't just a headache?"

"No." Khan lifted his chin at Sobehk. "You're Sobehk's *rehkyt* as well as mine, and he is in pain."

Fallon jerked back from the table and glared at Sobehk. "Why didn't you say something?"

Sobehk glared at Fallon then glared at Khan.

Fallon looked back at Khan. "What do I do?" She winced as a particularly nasty throb stabbed her temple. "'*Syr*."

Khan raised his brow at Sobehk. "You need to feed."

Sobehk shook his head. "I need too much. She's too new to . . ."

"From me." Khan's brows lowered over his copper eyes. "Once you start feeding, the pressure to feed will leave her."

Sobehk winced.

"Sobehk . . ." Khan lowered his chin. "Enough." A growl threaded through his words.

Sobehk closed his eyes and took a deep breath. "I'll feed."

Khan nodded. "Good." He rose from the table and began unwinding his sash.

Sobehk staggered to his feet. "Damn . . ."

Khan nodded at Fallon. "Help him undress. Leave the garb on the table for the attendants."

Fallon nodded, rose, and went to Sobehk.

Sobehk held out his arms, his eyes a glassy bright blue, and hot.

She tugged his sash free then began unwinding it.

He took a deep breath and froze. His jaw clenched and his hands fisted. "Shit." He closed his eyes and lifted his head.

Fallon looked up. "What?"

"Just . . . hurry. Please." His voice was hoarse.

Fallon looked over at Khan.

Khan smiled. "He needs to feed, and you are who his

body wants to feed from."

Fallon hurried. She untied the short robe and tugged it from his shoulders then unfastened the pleated trousers. They fell to the floor and she scooped them up, setting everything on the table.

Sobehk's breathing had deepened and became labored. He was also rigidly erect.

Nude and also magnificently erect, Khan raised his brow at Sobehk. "Can you get to the bed yourself, or do you need help?"

"I can do it." He turned and walked to the bed, weaving only slightly. He fell among the pillows and groaned.

Khan walked over to one of his black trunks and pulled open a drawer. He took out a squeeze-tube, shoved the drawer closed. He looked over at Fallon and frowned. "Disrobe." He walked over to the bed and stared down at Sobehk as he squeezed gel onto his palm.

Sobehk stared up at him. "That's going to hurt."

Khan stoked his gel-coated palm over his primary cock. "Yes, it very likely will." He raised a brow. "Do you plan to resist?"

Sobehk swallowed. "No."

"Good." He dropped the squeeze-tube on the floor by the edge of the bed and stepped down into the blankets. He dropped to his knees at Sobehk's side.

Fallon slipped out of her trousers and set her clothes on the table then walked over to the bed.

Khan held out his hand. "Come."

Fallon stepped down into the bed and took his hand.

Khan tugged and she fell against his chest and into his arms. He caught a handful of her hair and tugged her head to the side. His teeth sank into her shoulder.

She yelped. "Shit!"

He sucked hard, taking a mouthful of blood.

Fallon's headache immediately relented. She relaxed.

Khan pulled his teeth from her shoulder. He licked his lips, caught her chin and covered her mouth with his.

Fallon gasped in surprise and his tongue surged in to engage hers. Her senses reeled, and she kissed him back. Her nipples tingled to sudden life and her core gave a hungry throb. Moisture slicked her thighs. A small moan escaped.

He released her mouth. "Mount him."

Fallon was more than ready. She threw her leg over Sobehk's hips and caught his primary cock in her palm. She pressed the hot cockhead against her moist entrance.

Sobehk groaned and caught her hips.

Fallon eased down onto him.

Sobehk's mouth opened, and he thrust. His cock stabbed hard up into Fallon.

She threw back her head and gasped. His secondary cock was a hot, hard pressure against her anus.

Khan moved behind her. "Hold."

Fallon held still. The cock pressing at her anus shifted and she felt a slippery finger pressing into her. She pushed and the finger passed within and moved around.

Khan sighed. "Good pet." His finger slipped out of her.

Sobehk grunted.

Khan set his palm on her shoulder. "He's prepared; mount."

Fallon lowered herself. Her anus gave, opened, and let him in. She groaned. She kept forgetting how big he was.

Sobehk thrust upward, hard, spreading her wide and seated himself fully.

Fallon groaned.

Khan moved back. "On your belly."

Sobehk groaned and rolled, carrying Fallon with him. His eyes were wide and very blue as he stared down at

Fallon. He spread his knees, opening her further.

Khan swept Sobehk's silver-white hair from his broad back. His palms lingered on his skin. "I have missed you." His voice was soft. He leaned over Sobehk's back and presented his forearm. "Drink."

Sobehk focused on the arm and his pupils widened to dark pits. He opened his mouth. His long white teeth gleamed. He bit down.

Khan grunted and spread out along Sobehk's back. His arm curled around Sobehk's waist.

Sobehk's eyes drifted closed. He swallowed and moaned. He ground his hips into Fallon.

Khan drew Sobehk's head back. Khan's lips curled back, showing his long teeth. He thrust hard.

Sobehk's eyes flew open. He swallowed. A soft sound escaped, but he didn't release Khan's arm.

Khan drew Sobehk back, forcing him back onto Khan's lap until he was sitting up on his knees.

Sobehk grabbed for Fallon's thighs, pulling her with him, and forcing her body to arch, her thighs spread over his until only her shoulders were on the mattress.

Fallon groaned. It wasn't an uncomfortable position, but it was somewhat awkward. She was pretty sure she could feel Khan's secondary cock resting against the seam of her butt.

Khan locked one arm around Sobehk's waist and thrust, slowly but with incredible strength.

Sobehk's eyes closed and he tensed. And he swallowed.

Khan sucked in a deep breath and his head fell back. He thrust, and thrust . . .

She was right. It was Khan's cock. She could feel it sliding against her ass with each of his thrusts.

Sobehk moaned and shuddered. His hips bucked in sudden counterthrust. His fingers tightened on Fallon's thighs and his cocks surged into her then he retreated to press back onto Khan's cock.

Khan's mouth opened on a feral smile. "Yes, *Dhe'syah*, fuck me. Fuck us both."

Sobehk groaned and began shoving forward hard into Fallon then shoving back onto Khan. A thin trickle of blood slid down his chin and dropped onto her belly.

Khan grunted with Sobehk's thrusts, and his hand opened on Sobehk's stomach, his claws digging into his belly. His breath quickened and his lips curled back, baring his long teeth. His gaze focused on Fallon and his eyes blazed with heat.

Every muscle in Sobehk's body strained and flexed, his claws digging into her thighs.

Fallon grabbed the pillows around her. The sight of Sobehk being fucked by Khan scalded Fallon to the core. It was the most erotic thing she'd ever seen. Her core clutched at him even as her ass ached with him pumping within her. Heat and pressure built within her.

Sobehk's thrusts quickened and he turned his head, obviously to release Khan's arm.

Khan jerked his arm tighter against Sobehk's mouth, refusing to let him go. His gaze dropped to Fallon. "Isabeau . . . hold his wrists, don't let him go."

Fallon grabbed Sobehk's wrists.

Sobehk twisted his hands in Fallon's hold, but her hands held most of her real strength. He couldn't pull free.

"No, *Dhe'syah*, you have denied this long enough." Khan began thrusting faster and harder, encouraging Sobehk to buck between them at a quicker pace. "You will submit to your body's needs." He panted for breath. "And mine."

Fallon writhed under them. Sobehk's flesh was hardening within her. He was knotting — which meant Khan was too. The idea of Khan knotted tight within Sobehk's ass brought a hot illicit thrill racing through her blood. She trembled, and a spat of fresh moisture filled her core.

Sobehk's gaze went completely out of focus, his thrusts becoming far less controlled. He groaned and tried to pull from Khan's arm.

Khan held his arm fast to Sobehk's mouth and thrust harder. "Let go, *Dhe'syah*. Let go."

Sobehk moaned and his eyes widened. His flesh tightened to solid balls of hard flesh sealing his cocks within Fallon's body. His body stopped straining and he stopped fighting Khan's thrusts. His head fell back onto Khan's shoulder.

Khan sighed. "Yes." He groaned and his arm tightened around Sobehk's waist. "Mother, yes . . ." He ground in deep, his thrusts a steady driving force.

She groaned and her hips bucked against Sobehk's unresisting body. He was pressed up against something within her that jolted her with a harsh bolt of raw urgent pleasure with each of Khan's thrusts. It was driving her insane.

She was going to cum, and cum hard.

Khan groaned. "Isabeau, release him."

Fallon released Sobehk's wrists.

Sobehk's hands fell limp to his sides and his body slumped back against Khan.

Khan disengaged his arm from Sobehk's mouth. He pushed and they toppled over.

Sobehk's head hit the pillows to Fallon's left and his weight pressed her down into the blankets.

Fallon groaned. Bloody Fate, she was right on top of cumming, and they had to stop! Damn it!

Khan tugged Sobehk to the side and lifted his head above Sobehk's shoulder. "Isabeau, give me your wrist."

Fallon lifted the arm that wasn't trapped under Sobehk. Khan's warm fingers caught her wrist. "When I bite you, I want you to bite Sobehk at the same time. Ready?"

Fallon eyed the erect masculine nipple only a kiss away. She smiled at Khan. "Yes, '*Syr.*"

Khan lifted her wrist to his mouth. His tongue stroked her wrist.

Fallon pressed her mouth against Sobehk's nipple.

Khan smiled briefly and bit.

Sharp pain stabbed from her wrist, and then fiery release slammed through Fallon in a hot wet wave. She sank her teeth into Sobehk's breast. She moaned under the assault and closed her eyes, bucking hard and trembling under Sobehk's heavy body.

Sobehk gasped and convulsed above her and Khan groaned.

The blazing erotic waves of their climaxes slammed through her telepathic link. Her body clenched hard and shoved back up into a second climactic tempest and then over, only to grab her by the gut and thrust her over again . . .

Her screams were muffled by Sobehk's chest.

Fallon released Sobehk's chest and trembled under his heavy weight.

Khan groaned and slid to Fallon's right. His copper eyes were half-lidded and deep contentment radiated from him.

Sobehk groaned and rolled over to the left. His eyes were closed, his breathing labored.

Fallon could feel something leaking through the telepathic link from Sobehk. It felt like . . . despair, threaded with a strange sense of relief.

Khan's contentment faded into concern. He lifted up on his elbow. "Sobehk . . . I . . ."

"Khan . . ." Sobehk sucked in a deep breath and released

it. "I knew it was . . . over. I knew the moment you showed up on the *Vortex*, that this . . . would happen."

"Sobehk, I . . ." Khan winced and sat up, closing his arms around his knees. "Shit." He scowled. "I won't say I'm sorry. I'm not." He sighed. "I couldn't let you leave me again."

Sobehk snorted. "I know. Manipulative little shit."

Khan set his cheek on his knees and smiled just a little.

Sobehk groaned shifting uncomfortably. "I don't believe you fucked me up the ass with that . . . thing in your dick!" He shot a glare at Khan.

Khan snorted. "That thing is *in* my dick because I couldn't think of anything else painful enough to stop from missing you."

Sobehk's brows shot up. "You're kidding."

Khan lifted a brow. "Actually, no I'm not. I had it done about a year after you left."

Sobehk frowned. "And the nipples?"

Khan shrugged. "A month after you left."

Sobehk winced. "Couldn't you just visit a lot of bars and beat the snot out of anyone stupid enough to get in your way? That's what I did."

Khan smiled sourly. "I tried that, among other things. It didn't work." He flashed a smile. "It was you I wanted to beat the snot out of." He rolled his eyes. "I took up this occupation as an outlet for my . . . aggression. However . . ." His gaze drifted to the door. "I discovered that I have less of a stomach for it than I expected." He sighed. "I prefer to use a less torturous style of inquiry than many of my . . . colleagues."

Fallon jerked upright. "Torture?" She choked. "'*Syr*?'"

Sobehk chuckled softly. "Khan is a *Mehdjay'syr*. He's a lord-officer of Intelligence and Security appointed by the queen to investigate high-level crime by any means necessary. Torture is part of his . . . function."

Fallon stared at Khan, wide-eyed with shock.

Khan shrugged. "Torture is the established method of gaining facts from . . . the unwilling." He smiled sourly. "But I have discovered that uncovering the facts ahead of time saves me the need to do more than gain their admittance and send them straight to judgment. I prefer to send only the truly deserving to the bowels."

Fallon swallowed. "The bowels, *'Syr?'*"

Sobehk stretched and winced. "You'd call it prison, but it's a bit more . . . involved."

Khan rolled his eyes. "It involves a lot of very painful and messy equipment that does quite horrible things to the body and mind."

Fallon stiffened as a chill rolled up her spine. "Great."

"You have nothing to fear, Isabeau." Khan reached out a hand and swept it across the top of Fallon's head. "I'll take care of your punishments myself."

Fallon hunched her shoulders. "Is that supposed to make me feel better?"

Sobehk barked out a laugh.

Khan shrugged then grinned. "Not really."

"Terrific." She rolled up onto her feet and left the bed.

Khan frowned after her. "Where are you going?"

"The facility! I'm a mess!" And she really needed to go. Sobehk had been resting on her bladder, and it wasn't happy. She stopped and groaned. Damn it, she'd forgotten to ask permission. She turned around with her hands in her hips and raised a brow at Khan. "*May* I have permission to use the facility, *'Syr?'*"

Sobehk chuckled. "You better give it to her. She *is* feral."

Khan rolled his eyes. "Yes, of course, by all means."

Fallon nodded. "Thank you, *'Syr.'*" She turned and fled into the facility.

After a fast trip to the commode, Fallon stepped into the glassed-in shower. Within minutes, hot water was pounding the hell out of her back and shoulders, forcing the tense muscles to relax.

So, she was the pet of a prince and his knight. She tilted her head. Well, that was certainly different. And there were worse places she could have ended up, like the prison pits . . . She shied away from that line of thought.

She stretched her arms, working the aches out of them from swinging the sword. The sword work was hard, but it was also very . . . relaxing to her mind. She hoped she'd get to do that a lot more. She'd always felt better with a weapon in hand, and a sword was a very cool weapon to know how to use.

Fallon left the facility feeling a whole lot better.

Khan and Sobehk were curled up in the bed talking quietly. They started and looked over at her.

Fallon raised a brow. They almost looked . . . guilty? They must have been talking about her. She rolled her eyes. Fine, whatever . . ."All right, you two, don't you think it's time you told me what I'm supposed to do? We're going to get to the station tomorrow. I'd kind of like to know what to expect."

Khan pursed his hips. "You are a *rehkyt* up for sale. You are not supposed to know."

Fallon rolled her eyes again. "But how am I supposed to know who to stab and who to just growl at?"

Khan shrugged. "If anyone approaches you, attack them."

Fallon's mouth fell open. "I don't want to attack innocent staff!"

Sobehk chuckled and looked over at Khan. "I told you."

Khan growled. "Fine, rub it in."

Sobehk shook his head. "Don't worry, kitten, you'll be

with us the whole time."

Khan's eyes narrowed and his smile sharpened, showing teeth. "We have a vested interest in anyone that might approach you, so naturally we have no plans to allow you out of our sight."

Fallon folded her arms across her chest. "Great."

CHAPTER THIRTY-ONE

The Moon Blade – in space dock with the Vortex
Imperial Space – Outbound Corridor
Morning Cycle

Fallon gasped at her reflection in the mirror beside So-behk's wardrobe. "I can't wear this in public!" The black leather suit hugging her from ankle to shoulder gleamed as though polished and was as soft as heavy silk against her skin. It was also incredibly supple and slightly elastic. Completely sleeveless, the suit gave her complete range of arm motion.

It was also open a full hand span wide, from the high collared throat to the very top of her crotch. It barely contained her nipples. It didn't even try to contain her breasts. The slender belt that buckled directly under her breasts was the only thing keeping them from falling completely out. The belt crossed behind her then continued around to just above her navel. A second belt framed her hips. The two thin belts were the only thing keeping the suit from gaping open when she moved.

The wide opening ended in a vee barely a finger-width above her feminine cleft. The only reason her pubic curls didn't show was because Khan and Sobehk had seen to the removal of all her bodily hair in their last shower. Among other incredibly embarrassing cleaning procedures.

Khan smiled from where he stood between the two attendants buckling him into studded leather. His creamy hair was once again bound into a snug braid, though black beads had been introduced along the braid. The black band that normally rested around his brow was gone, and the black rings in his ears had been traded out for gold, as had the rings in his nipples. "Would you rather be naked?" He tugged his jacket sleeve over the slender black band around his wrist, covering it.

Fallon bared her teeth at her reflection. "I'm seriously wondering if complete nudity would have been more modest!" Her hair had grown to reach the center of her back and had been scraped back into a simple but neat black tail. Her very green eyes looked huge and the delicate points of her ears were displayed with the gleaming silver clips. Her lips were very scarlet. "Great Maker, I look like . . ." She looked like a sex toy. Which, of course, was what she was — a sex toy.

Khan shook his head, grinning. "You look like a *rehkyt* that will tear apart anyone that gets too close."

Fallon turned to glare at Khan. "What an amazing coincidence, I *feel* like tearing apart anyone that gets too close." She crossed her arms over her spilling breasts.

Sobehk chuckled as his attendants wound a bright blue and silver sash around his waist over his heavy silver and white robes. "I think you look spectacular, but if nudity is what you prefer . . ."

Fallon shot a narrow glance at Sobehk. "Thanks, and no thanks." She curled her lip at Khan. "If this thing falls apart on me, I swear I'll bite you, and not in a nice way!" She growled, just to show she meant every word.

All six attendants froze where they were.

Khan blinked in surprise then burst into laughter. Sobehk's laughter was only a breath behind.

Fallon sighed heavily. "What am I going to do with you two?"

Both men exchanged a speaking glance and laughed harder.

The attendants exchanged glances. They were forced to wait until the laughter died down to gasps and both men were able to stand upright before they could continue dressing them.

Four fully armored *Mehdjay* guards left their quarters towing several of Khan's black and Sobehk's red trunks behind them. The trunks were headed for the *Vortex*, docked alongside the *Moon Blade*. The *Vortex* would carry the three of them to Port Destiny Station, as though Sobehk had never left. On arrival they would occupy a suite in the Skeldhi enclave.

The plan was that the *Moon Blade* would dock in a private hold as opposed to the public docks. Khan's men would quietly occupy the suite next to theirs in the Skeldhi enclave and arrest the man planning to buy a *rehkyt* sleeper assassin as soon as he was uncovered at the auction.

Neat, tidy, efficient and simple.

Fallon rolled her eyes. This whole plan was simply begging for something to go terribly wrong.

She turned to gaze at her men and sucked in a slow breath.

Sobehk looked very regal in heavy layered robes of pale silver and bright blue over a midnight blue kilt. His silver-white hair had been brushed into a thick mane and dressed with thousands of tiny braids that flashed with sapphire beads. He leaned on the carved handle of a heavy white cane.

Next to Sobehk's broad-shouldered and robed elegance, Khan looked small and slender, but very menacing in overlapping and body-skimming studded black leather. More than half the studs on his breast, his sleeves, and down the sides of his boots, were, in fact, the pommels of small knives. A rather long knife had been sheathed against his spine and two decorative back-curved daggers were tucked into the blue and black sash around his hips.

His jacket opened all the way down, showing his muscular stomach to perfection. The skintight leather pants lovingly displayed his muscular thighs—and his delectable ass. His semi-armored leather boots hugged him up to his thighs.

The attendants offered both men long hooded robes. They bowed and left.

Sobehk whistled softly as he slid into his over-robe of deep charcoal gray velvet lined in white silk, taking care with the full sleeves of his dress robes. "Khan, if I wasn't already sleeping with you, I'd rape you myself. Damn."

Fallon grinned at Sobehk. "He has a very bite-able ass."

Sobehk grinned back. "Oh, yes, he does."

Khan arched a brow, but his cheeks tinted with pink as he shrugged into his supple black leather robe. "I'm glad you both approve." His voice was very dry. He motioned toward Fallon. "I need to change your collar."

Fallon walked toward him and very quickly discovered that the suit she wore had a tendency to rub against her nipples and her clit. It wasn't painful or even annoying, but it was quite clear that she was going to have very hard nipples very fast. And wet panties—if she had been wearing any sort of panties. "I don't get a robe?"

Khan reached for the black chain she wore. "Your skin will not burn under station daylight." The chain came apart in his hand and slid free. "Ours will." He dropped it in the open drawer of his trunk.

Fallon felt an odd sort of loss without Khan's chain.

Sobehk walked over to stand at their side. "Port Destiny

was made to reproduce the conditions on human Terra. Skeldhor Prime does not have as strong a sun as the human world. We sunburn within minutes."

Khan lifted a short chain of plain steel links and fastened it around her throat.

The heavy steel was a cool weight at the base of her throat. Fallon shivered. "I thought you guys healed faster than humans?"

Khan turned away to pull a steel chain lead from the drawer in the trunk. "Oh, we do, but sunburn is still damned uncomfortable." He handed the lead to Sobehk.

Sobehk looped the long lead and tucked it halfway into his sash, leaving the steel chain clearly visible. "Ten seconds of blistered skin is still blistered skin for ten seconds."

"I see." Fallon stared at the steel lead in Sobehk's sash and clenched her teeth. They were about to begin a dangerous game of bait and trap to find out who wanted a sleeper assassin, and why. And she was the bait. She had known this all along, and yet she hadn't been bothered by it before. Now it bothered her.

She wasn't worried about herself; she was more than capable of taking care of herself, but she wasn't so sure about them. Sobehk was still wounded and while Khan was clearly deadly, his augmentations appeared to be strictly for physical strength. He didn't have anywhere near her speed or dexterity.

Khan caught her face and dropped a swift kiss on her lips. His bright, copper gaze bored into hers. "Everything will be just fine. All you have to do is not let anyone touch you physically, and resist anyone's attempt to part you from our company, no matter how slight."

Fallon licked her lips. He must have picked up her concern. "Yes, *'Syr.'*"

Khan released her and turned to Sobehk. "Ready?"

Sobehk smiled grimly, his silver mane spilling down over his breast. "I'm more than ready for this hunt."

Fallon's hands closed into fists. So was she. But this time, she wasn't taking chances on anyone getting hurt because of her. She would make damned sure both her men stayed safe if she had to tear the weapon from their hands to do it.

Screw obedience.

Khan led them through the ship's black-walled corridors and into a lift. Fallon found it interesting that while she and Sobehk drew curious glances, no one looked twice at Khan.

They stepped out of the lift into the ship's cargo hold where she had learned to use the sword.

Khan's strides were long and ground-eating. He led them through the maze of stacked cargo to a circular airlock in the middle of the far right wall. Two fully armed guards stood on either side of the door. The guard on the left held out a sword in a white sheath to Sobehk and the guard on the right, handed Khan two black-sheathed swords, one slightly longer than the other.

In an uncertain universe where thousands of races interacted, some friendlier than others, no one walked unarmed. However, in the sealed environment of a ship or a space station, where a pinhole could mean the deaths of thousands, energy weapons were tightly controlled; swords, though, were perfectly permissible. Even a state-of-the-art blade of live-steel could not cut through armored plating and release atmosphere.

Sobehk shoved his sword into his sash.

Khan followed suit then turned to Fallon with the shorter blade.

Fallon raised her brow at him. She wasn't wearing a sash.

Khan scowled. "Shit."

Sobehk chuckled and unwound his midnight blue sash from around his waist, leaving only the white. "Good thing I thought ahead."

Khan snatched the sash from his outstretched palm. "You're going to be a pain in my ass, I can tell."

Sobehk arched a brow and his smile became decidedly predatory. "Absolutely."

Khan snorted and wrapped the sash around Fallon's hips with swift efficiency then tucked the ends in. He held the sword out to Fallon. "With this live-steel blade, I grant you the right to defend to the death."

Fallon bowed and took the sheathed blade from his hands. "I accept the responsibility of life and the consequences of death."

Khan blinked and looked over at Sobehk. "Did you teach her that?"

Fallon grinned as she slid the sword into her sash. "What? I saw it in a fiction vid."

Sobehk chuckled and rolled his eyes.

Khan nodded at the guards.

One of the guards turned to the side. His fingers danced on the wall keypad. Machinery rumbled, air hissed and the thick airlock door rolled to the left, revealing another door. Sobehk stepped in, then Khan and Fallon. The door rolled closed behind them.

Khan stepped back to stand on Fallon's right.

The door before them opened and Sobehk stepped into a pale gray corridor.

Sehnbay'syr Tah nodded and smiled. "Welcome back to the *Vortex.*" He blinked at Khan. "Oh, I didn't recognize you, *'Syr.*"

Khan smiled grimly. "With all due respect, *Sehnbay'syr* Tah, I would be most pleased if you continue to not recognize me and address me as *A'syr*. In fact, I must insist that you deny any form of recognition whatsoever."

Tah frowned slightly but nodded. "As you wish, *A'syr*." He turned to their right. "This way, please."

Tah led them through the gray-walled hallways straight to the gleaming medical bay. Sobehk lifted Fallon onto the padded surgery table and Tah did a swift check on Fallon's transformation progression. One booster shot later, Sobehk was confirmed by blood type as her legal owner.

Tah turned to Sobehk at the foot of the table. "This will only last two days. After that . . ." He glanced at Khan, who stood by the table's far side, away from the door. "The other DNA code will very visibly reassert itself as being primary."

Sobehk nodded. "Understood."

"Let me make sure everything is in order." Tah passed by Sobehk and sat at his desk. A holographic display bloomed into existence above the surface of his desk.

Fallon hopped down from the medical table, landing on the far side by Khan.

The door spiraled open on the far side of the room.

Fallon froze.

A tall, slender Skeldhi entered the medical bay. He wore his pale hair pulled back into a long tail and a dark gray sleeveless robe over a dark blue kilt. He continued past them to stand before Tah's desk and bowed slightly. "We are in final approach to dock within Port Destiny Station."

Fallon frowned. She knew that voice. She sniffed. She definitely knew that scent. She focused on the Skeldhi. He smelled like . . .

Tah nodded. "Thank you, *A'syr* Mohr."

Fallon nodded. *Ah, so that's what he looks like.*

Mohr turned and his sharp gray eyes passed right over Khan to focus on Sobehk standing at the foot of the medical bed. "*A'syr* Sobehk! So that's why we stopped, to pick you up."

Sobehk smiled. "Only for a bit, before going on medical leave."

Mohr's gaze drifted to Fallon on the far side. He frowned. "I thought that *Mehdjay* officer took custody of her?"

Fallon's brows shot up. Mohr didn't recognize Khan.

Sobehk waved his hand. "Turned out that she wasn't who he thought she was." He shrugged. "I got her back." He smiled. "He gave me a *nehkyx* handler by way of apology."

Mohr's frowned at Khan, leaning against the table with his arms folded across his chest. "Nice." Mohr looked away, clearly dismissing him.

Fallon snorted. *Idiot.*

Mohr looked back at Fallon. His smile was thin and tight. "I guess since she didn't impress, you're taking her to the auction?"

Sobehk nodded. "She's worth a fortune."

Fallon scowled at Sobehk.

Mohr's smile sharpened. "She's going to make you a very wealthy man."

Fallon decided at that moment that she definitely did not like *A'syr* Mohr.

Sobehk pursed his lips. "I certainly hope so."

Tah came out from behind his desk. "*A'syr* Mohr, I need to check on a few of the other *rehkyt*. Would you be so kind as to accompany me?"

Mohr nodded and followed Tah out of medical.

Sobehk looked at Fallon. *You recognized A'syr Mohr by scent?*

Fallon started and looked at Sobehk. His voice had echoed in her mind, not her ears. He had used the collar's telepathic link. *Uh, yeah.*

Khan tilted his head slightly. *I told you her thoughts were interesting on occasion.*

Sobehk glanced at Khan. *Why, so you did.*

Fallon frowned. *Must you have your conversation in my head?*

Sobehk set his palms on the table and arched his brow smiling. *Whose head?*

Not you, too! Fallon very nearly growled her frustration.

Sobehk frowned at Khan. *Does she need to be fed?*

Khan looked over at Sobehk then focused on Fallon. *Since yesterday. I chose not to feed her so that she will appear to be the unimpressed* upuaht rehkyt *she is supposed to be.*

Sobehk raised his brow at Fallon. *That does explain her temper displays.*

Fallon scowled. *What temper displays?*

Khan smiled. *Her need to feed, coupled with her nose sensitivity should make her less likely to allow anyone to get close enough to touch her.* He pursed his lips and gave Fallon a measuring look. *A little added frustration should keep her nice and aggressive.*

Fallon felt the hair on her neck rise. *What do you mean by "added frustration"?*

CHAPTER THIRTY-TWO

Port Destiny Station
Imperial Space — Outbound Corridor

Sehnbay'syr Tah came back into medical and left the door open behind him. "It is time."

Sobehk moved toward the door and Khan followed with Fallon at his heels.

The sound of marching boot heels and whimpering gasps came from the hall, as did the rank smell of fear-sweat.

The hair on Fallon's neck rose and she stilled. She did *not* want to go out in that.

Sobehk stopped at the door and turned to look at her. "Isabeau?"

Khan turned and caught her gaze. His copper eyes narrowed. *I'm right here.* He set his warm palm on her shoulder.

Under the pressure of Khan's palm, she walked to the door. Several pairs of armored *Mahf'dhyt* marched past the door leading blind, naked, and frightened *rehkyt* between them.

Fallon shivered hard.

Sobehk stepped out into the hall.

Fallon followed, propelled by Khan's hand. She made an effort to stay within the draft of Sobehk's scent, but the smell of fear was overpowering. Her skin dampened with sweat.

317

A'syr Mohr abruptly stepped out of a side door right at Fallon's left elbow.

Fallon started so hard she was on the far right side of the hall with her back against the wall and one of Khan's small knives raised in her fist before she knew what happened. She closed her mouth over her long teeth, shutting off her frightened snarl.

Sobehk turned sharply, his eyes wide. "Sorry about that, *A'syr.*"

Mohr's startled expression dissolved into a frown. "Still quite feral, I see."

Sobehk lifted a cool brow at Mohr, his mouth tight. "Very feral and *upuaht.* You're lucky she didn't stab you."

Mohr's frown deepened to a scowl. "You would think that would have been tempered by now."

Sobehk snorted. "I'm sure her Master will see to her tempering."

Khan turned and held his hand out to Fallon while staring pointedly at the dagger in her fist.

Fallon felt her cheeks heat and approached Khan, offering him the dagger. "Sorry, *'Syr.*"

Khan smiled as he took the dagger from Fallon's palm. *Good reflexes.* He sheathed it against his heart.

Fallon winced in embarrassment. *Thanks.*

Sobehk nodded at Mohr. "If you will excuse us, *A'syr*?"

Mohr's scowl deepened. "Of course."

Sobehk turned and began proceeding down the hall, leaving Mohr behind.

Fallon breathed a sigh of relief.

The hallway opened onto a loading bay that looked familiar. Fallon glanced around and saw Sobehk's glider, the one she had stolen a very long time ago, fastened against the right wall by two others. This was where she had first come onto the *Vortex.* Dead ahead, the back hatch was wide open, and darkness lay beyond it.

Fallon followed Sobehk down the ramp that led off the ship and into the station. Light was sparse and shadows were everywhere. Ships of every kind and description were docked everywhere she looked. Their landing floods provided the bulk of what little light the dock had. The deeply shadowed dock ceiling was a very distant half a kilometer away and curved slightly downward with gigantic struts ribbing the curve like the exterior of a barrel. A quick glance down showed that the floor was curved slightly, like the bottom of a huge bowl. The floor's gentle curve matched the ceiling's distant curve. Apparently, the dock was shaped like a hollow ring.

Soft sounds from the far right brought Fallon's attention to the *Mahf'dhyt* herding *rehkyt* with swift efficiency into an unmarked bulky gray hover transport.

Sobehk continued away from them toward a hovering steel gray shuttle car at the end of their dock space.

Fallon released a soft breath. She would not have been able to deal with all that fear.

A'syr Mohr has followed us. Khan's thoughts shimmered with annoyance.

Fallon's heart began trying to hammer its way out of her chest for no apparent reason whatsoever.

Sobehk glanced behind them. *I'll handle it.* He stopped and sharply turned to face them.

Fallon stopped and Khan stopped at her side. Out of the corner of her eye, she could see that Mohr was only half a length away. He caught up fairly quickly.

Sobehk lifted his chin and smiled. "Why don't you take that shuttle, we'll wait for the next?"

Mohr blinked then frowned. "But . . ." He glanced at Fallon. "The shuttle will fit all of us . . ."

Sobehk smiled. "I'm sure it will, *A'syr*, but I wanted to

take care of something." He tiled his head at Fallon. "Privately, if you don't mind?"

Mohr's brows shot up and then he smiled thinly. "Oh, of course." He continued past them and climbed into the small shuttle.

Fallon kept track of Mohr from the corner of her eye. Then she noticed that Sobehk and Khan were watching him indirectly, too. They waited in a small tight knot until the shuttle lifted and moved away.

Fallon exhaled then glanced up at Sobehk. "What in fury was his problem?" She crossed her arms.

Khan lifted his brow and tilted his head at Fallon. "Very likely *A'syr* Mohr didn't want to ride with the *rehkyt* any more than you did."

Fallon rolled her eyes.

Sobehk frowned at Fallon. "Do you need a beating?"

Fallon felt a smile tug at the corner of her mouth. "Probably."

Khan smiled at Sobehk. "Of course she needs a beating, she's a Prime."

Fallon bit back a sudden chuckle.

Sobehk rolled his eyes and shook his head. "Come on, you two, there's a taxi stand not far from here." He strode off

Fallon followed in her proper place on Khan's left.

The docking bay was humongous. Fallon had been in spaceports before—Dyson's was technically one big spaceport—but the variety of ships that she strode past—size, color, shape—was mind-boggling. Dyson's was technically a backwater station, well off the trade routes but pretty deep in Imperial space. Most of Dyson's traffic was human. Port Destiny occupied a crossroads. And it showed. There had to be hundreds of sentient species represented in this corner of the dock alone.

Every now and again a monstrous mechanical noise would fill the bay followed by an icy breeze, announcing that a new ship had been lifted into the dock.

It was not a short walk to the taxi stand. Sobehk was actually leaning on the white staff he carried as he pointed to the three small bright yellow taxi shuttles parked against a wall. A ramp onto to a two-lane station shuttle-way was only a few meters away from the parked hovercraft.

One of the three drivers, a tall human dressed in rugged gray trousers and a matching padded jacket, tossed his smoldering cigarette and waved a hand toward them. "Need a ride?" His Imperial basic held an odd twang, an accent.

Sobehk lifted his hand. "We do, if you don't mind."

The man grinned. "Great!" The driver's hatch to the first shuttle opened, and the man slid into the seat. The shuttles turbines rumbled, and the craft lifted from the steel deck to hover about two hand spans above it. The back doors on the shuttle popped open.

Sobehk moved between the wall and the shuttle and got in on the right. Khan stood by the left door and gestured to Fallon.

Fallon lifted her sword out of the way and slid onto the padded bench seat next to Sobehk. Khan slid in after her. She frowned. She hated sitting in the middle of a vehicle; it was impossible to see anything.

The shuttle interior was heavily cushioned and upholstered in soft black plastic. There was a plas-steel glass window between the driver and the passenger area. Fallon smiled slightly. The safety glass made perfect sense since everyone walked around armed.

Directions were given and the shuttle moved forward on its cushion of air. The craft dove into the right lane of the tubular shuttle-way and ramped upward. Unlike the dock, the two-lane shuttle-way was very well lit. Broad bands of bronze were painted along the walls.

Kahn leaned back to look over at Sobehk. "We're going to the Garden District?"

Sobehk smiled. "Trees."

Khan frowned and his mouth opened.

"Trees?" Fallon looked over at Sobehk "As in real ones? Living ones?"

Sobehk smiled. "As in bigger than a four-story house ones."

Fallon's mind blanked briefly. She simply could not picture a plant that large. "I know it's possible, but . . ."

Khan touched her shoulder. "You mean you've never seen a tree?"

Fallon looked over at him. "Sure, a few times. But not up close." Only the very wealthy could afford the space for a real tree, and they were jealously guarded. "I saw a huge one once. It was inside one of the bigger corporate buildings. You could see it through the building's glass walls. It was a whole story and a half tall."

Khan's brows shot up and then he smiled. "I think you're going to find the Garden District quite . . . interesting."

The taxi merged onto a four-lane shuttle-way painted with broad green bands then turned and exited the lighted tunnel, diving into a darkness that shimmered with lights and oddly shaped moving shadows.

Fallon frowned at the passing scenery. Darkness meant it had to be station night, but what was with all the odd shadows? She couldn't quite figure out what the heck she was seeing. There wasn't a straight line anywhere.

The shuttle scooted along a lighted shopping area teaming with pedestrians.

Fallon suddenly realized that she was looking at plants

with branches and leaves that spread wider than Khan's whole chamber. Trees. They were trees. She sucked in a sharp breath and lunged across Sobehk's lap to press her face against the window. "Great Maker . . . how many are there?"

Sobehk laughed and caught her hips. "Mother Night, sit down!" He pulled her down onto his thighs. "The station is about eight kilometers long and a full two-thirds of the interior surface is forested. The rest is lakes and cropland."

"Lakes?" Fallon stared at the passing shadows, trying to get an idea of what she was seeing. "Can I see one?"

Sobehk choked. "A lake?"

Fallon rolled her eyes and smiled. "I'll settle for a tree. Can we stop and look?"

Khan snorted. "You'll have plenty of time to touch a tree and any number of weeds when we get to the enclave."

Fallon looked over her shoulder at him. "We will?"

Khan smiled. "There are about a dozen trees including a rather large Terran oak in the garden attached to our suite."

"Oh . . ." A real live tree. She was going to see one up close, and possibly touch it. The whole idea was . . . shocking.

The shuttle stopped at the very end of the shopping district near a pair of lifts. The doors popped open.

Fallon crawled over Sobehk to get out and look. Tall ornate cast-iron posts shed light on the walkways, illuminating shop fronts and brilliantly garbed people of every species. Potted trees and plants were everywhere. People were actually sitting under them on small white benches.

There was so much space . . . everything looked so far away. And green, even in the dark of station night, everything looked and smelled green and alive. And healthy. There was not one touch of mold or rot or rust in the air anywhere.

She looked up and saw stars. No . . . not stars, lights. They were lights shining from buildings very, very far away directly over her head and far into the distance.

Dyson's was a biosphere, a city wrapped in a bubble. Up was up and down was down. This station was something completely different. The whole station was shaped like a barrel and turned to generate gravity. Directly overhead, people were walking around and doing things, and she was the one upside down.

Khan cleared his throat. "Can we go now?"

Fallon looked back. The shuttle had left and both men were hovering by the lift. "Oh . . . sorry."

Khan shook his head and rolled his eyes, but amusement shimmered across their link.

Sobehk stood by the lift door leaning on his staff. He was smiling and clearly amused, too, but he also had dark smudges under his eyes.

Fallon walked over to stand by Sobehk, but her eyes hungrily devoured the unguarded trees that were only a short walk away.

The lift door opened behind them, and they stepped within the lighted and windowless space large enough for six.

As the doors closed, Fallon leaned up on her toes to catch the last little bit of view until it was sealed away completely.

CHAPTER THIRTY-THREE

The lift doors sealed closed with a soft sigh.

Fallon dropped onto her heels and straightened.

Sobehk leaned against the left lift wall and smiled.

Impulsively Fallon stepped over to Sobehk and wrapped her arm around his waist. She pressed her head onto his shoulder. His robes smelled of exotic spices, and of him. "Thank you."

"You're welcome." Sobehk's arm went around her, and he held her close. "Actually, it was Khan's idea."

"Me?" Khan folded his arms across his chest and leaned against the opposite wall. "This trip through the Garden District was all *your* idea."

Fallon knew darn well whose idea it was. She lunged for Khan and wrapped him in a hug anyway. "Thank you." She kissed him on the cheek for good measure, too.

Khan sighed then smiled. "You're welcome."

"Yeah, the little side trip was my idea." Sobehk smiled. "But the whole idea to have a garden suite with live plants and trees was yours."

Fallon blinked up at Khan. "Really?"

Khan took a breath and released it. "Sobehk and I were talking about this station and the . . . conditions on the one you came from."

Sobehk snorted and curled his lip. "It was a garbage dump."

Khan's cheeks pinked and he shrugged. "And I thought one of the small garden suites I have on retainer would make a nice change for you."

Khan had arranged to have a garden suite for . . . her? Fallon stared at Khan, shocked. It was the nicest thing anyone had ever done. Impulsively, she closed her arms tight around him and pressed her face into his shoulder. The leather of his robe was soft under her cheek. Unfortunately, it didn't absorb tears too well. She watched them run down his shoulder.

Khan jerked in her hold. "Isabeau, what is this? Tears?"

Fallon had to take a breath, and still her words came out tight. "That was so . . . sweet, of you."

Sobehk choked out a laugh. "She's right. It was awfully sweet. You must be mellowing."

Khan growled. "Blood and Night! Give me a fucking break, will you?" He pulled Fallon away from him by the upper arms. "Isabeau, I just . . ."

The doors opened. Two fully armored Skeldhi guards glared in, their weapons at the ready.

Fallon jerked away from Khan, wiping at her cheeks.

Khan glared at the guards. "What?"

"Nothing, *A'syr Nehkyx!*"

The guards stepped back and stood to either side, two paces back from the door. The one on the left raised a small device.

Sobehk stepped out into a darkened hallway and raised his left fist to shoulder height.

The guard touched the small device to the back of his hand then peered at it. He nodded. "Thank you, *A'syr.*"

Khan stepped out and raised his hand. He was scanned and nodded to.

Fallon followed and raised her hand. The hallway was narrow, with charcoal carpeting and pale gray walls softly lit with frosted glass sconces set high along the walls. The scanner was cool against the back of her hand. Her internal computational array registered that she was being scanned for biomechanics as well as blood type.

The guard frowned at his reading.

Sobehk lowered his chin and eased his hands to the side in a clearly aggressive pose. "I trust everything is in order, *A'syr*?"

The guard nodded. "Your rehkyt has some very sophisticated computational augmentations for an *upuaht* Prime, *A'syr*."

Sobehk's brows dipped. "Yes, she does."

The guard on the right started. "Pardon my asking, but are you *A'syr* Sobehk?"

Sobehk turned to face him. "I am."

The other guard's mouth fell open. "This is the feral?" He choked. "I mean, the one up for auction?"

Sobehk's frown deepened. "Yes."

The guard on the right frowned. "I thought she'd be . . . bigger."

Fallon scowled. *I'll show you bigger . . .*

Khan darted a stern look at Fallon. *Hold onto that temper of yours.*

Sobehk looked from one to the other. "Is there something I need to know about?"

The guard on the left winced. "Well, there's a . . . wager riding on which councilor is going to end up with her, *A'syr*."

Khan sucked in a hard breath. "Which *councilor*? There are *Ehnya'dhyt here*?"

The guard on the left smiled at Khan, carefully hiding his long teeth. "Three arrived for this auction, and all three have come to bid on *A'syr* Sobehk's Prime."

Sobehk's mouth fell open. "Three *Ehnya'dhyt, A'syr*? How did they get involved?"

The guard on the right shrugged. "They probably saw the ship vid from the attack on the news broadcast like everyone else."

Khan stilled. "The ship vid was on a news broadcast?"

"According to report, the broadcast hit the news-net about twenty-four hours after the attack." The guard on the left smiled at Sobehk. "Your feral is famous, *A'syr* Sobehk."

Sobehk winced. "Great."

"From what I saw . . ." The guard on the left gave Fallon a long cool look. "Whoever acquires her is going to possess one bleeding fury of a bodyguard."

"You saw the vid?" Khan's anger shimmered across the link.

The guard on the left shrugged. "Everyone has. It's all over the station."

The guard on the right nodded solemnly at Sobehk. "You are going to be a very wealthy man, *A'syr*."

Sobehk's cheeks pinked. "Thank you. May we be excused?"

Both guards straightened.

"Yes, *A'syr*!"

"Of course, *A'syr*!"

Sobehk stepped past them. "Good day, *A'syrs*."

"Good day, *A'syr*!"

Fallon's hands tightened into fists as she followed Sobehk down the shadowed hallway. *Three* councilors? Here? Great Maker, what if the assassin wasn't going to present himself? What if the one who was supposed to die by her hand simply bought her instead? She shook her head. *What a freaking mess!*

Khan brushed her right elbow. *They still have to plant the second half of the code. We'll just have to watch who tries to approach you before the auction.*

The hallway ended at a pair of arched, frosted glass doors heavily etched with vines and flowers. Sobehk grasped the ornate silver handles. He looked over his shoulder at Khan and Fallon. *Ready?*

Khan glanced at Fallon. *If anyone gets too close, do not be afraid to pull your sword.*

Fallon flinched. *I'd rather not hurt anyone accidentally.*

Sobehk snorted. *You won't. They've been using a sword longer than you have. Most of them since childhood.*

Fallon ground her teeth. *Great. That makes me feel a whole lot better.*

Khan grinned. *It will add to your aggressive reputation.*

Fallon glared at Khan. *You are not helping.*

Relax. You'll do just fine. Sobehk chuckled and pulled the doors open.

Fallon stepped out onto a black marble floor veined with silver. The room was gigantic and perfectly round. To the left and right, ornate, jewel-bright carpets had been laid out with graceful divans and plush lounging chairs of black velvet. Broad smoked glass tables at knee height perched atop black marble statuary. Skeldhi in long colorful silk robes occupied a few of the divans and chairs.

The distant walls held tall smoked mirrors draped with swags of black velvet, and arched doorways with etched glass doors. The light was soft and came from frosted glass fixtures suspended from ornate hooks that arched from the walls between the mirrors and doors.

Fallon looked up and gasped. The entire ceiling was a glass dome that showed deep space.

Khan leaned close. "You can view the local nebula through the dome at station dawn."

Fallon stilled. A nebula?

Khan smiled. "It's quite . . . colorful."

Sobehk looked over his shoulder. "Khan, are you being nice again?"

Khan scowled. "I don't *do* nice."

Sobehk grinned. "Could have fooled me!"

The path they were on led to a circular open area in the center of the room. A small group of seven Skeldhi in ornate black armor stood to one side, talking quietly among themselves. Their floor-draping, silver-furred black cloaks fell from the left shoulder down to the right, leaving the right arm free.

Fallon's attention was caught by a small burst of laughter on her immediate right. She turned to see a small, gold-skinned and completely nude figure scurrying across one of the ornate carpets on hands and knees. It was a female *rehkyt* with her bright red hair pulled back into a thick tail of curls. She stopped and picked something up with her mouth then turned and looked up at Fallon. Her eyes were a brilliant azure and she held a golden ball in her mouth.

Fallon's gaze was drawn to glitter. A small fall of diamonds dangled from her pierced nipples.

The *rehkyt* turned away and scurried toward one of the tall wing-backed velvet chairs.

A Skeldhi man in bright blue robes reached down and took the ball from her lips. He patted her on the head and rolled the ball across the floor.

The *rehkyt* chased after it on hands and knees, her curly tail bobbing with her motions.

The man laughed.

Looks like fun. Khan's thought was laced with amusement.

Fallon shot a quick glare at Khan. *No, it does not.*

Sobehk chuckled then abruptly stopped. *Here they come. Get ready.*

Fallon's head came up. *Here who comes . . .*

Dead ahead the small knot of armored Skeldhi had noticed them. The seven men had spread out across their path and four of them had dropped their cloaks to the floor. They were all fully armed and tiny blades jutted all over their armor.

Fallon stiffened. *Are they going to attack?*

Khan tilted his head one way and then the other. *Yes and*

no.

Fallon felt the pressure of a growl in her chest and lightning sparked at the back of her mind. *Is that so?*

Sobehk darted a glare over his shoulder at Khan. *Isabeau, they're going to attack you, not us. We'll be fine.*

Me? Fallon's red-tinted anger bled away in a sudden rush and she nearly tripped. *What in fury for? I don't know any of them!*

Sobehk sighed softly. *It's more of a test to see how good you really are.*

Seven of them . . . Fallon's jaw set. *This is the assessment, isn't it?*

Khan grinned. *Yes.*

Fallon rolled her eyes. *Great.*

Khan set his palm on her shoulder briefly. *Let no one touch you, but don't go out of your way to kill any of them.*

Sobehk nodded at the armored men. They parted to let him pass.

Fallon felt her temper surge. *Seven of them, armed to the teeth, and I only have one short sword . . .* Her gaze dropped to the pommel of Khan's blade jutting from the side of his robe at his hip.

Khan stepped up to the line of armored men.

Two men unsheathed their blades.

Fallon grabbed for Khan's blade and spun, blade out and away from Khan, forcing the entire line to part in front of them.

Khan kept walking as though nothing had happened, but his amusement echoed through their link.

Fallon backed away, drawing her shorter blade from its sheath at her hip as six of the men closed ranks around her. She tossed both blades straight up and, spinning, caught them in opposite hands so that the shorter blade was in her left hand. It was a well-practiced knife move. If the swords hadn't been so well balanced, she would not have been able to do it.

She spread her arms, blades out and smiled. "'Can I help you, gentle '*Syrs*?"

An older Skeldhi with a bright blood-red sash smiled grimly. "That is an unseemly amount of attitude, *rehkyt*."

"Is it?" Fallon raise a brow. "I thought it was exactly the right amount." Her smile broadened, baring her long teeth. "I can give you lots more if you prefer?" She caught a hint of movement behind her and turned on her heel, catching a descending blade aimed for her shoulder at the neck.

The young man holding the blade grinned, his aqua green eyes blazing.

Fallen smiled right back, dropping her left hand and her shorter blade, slicing into the back of the knee joint in his armor. The idiot had forgotten that she was armed with two swords.

The young man's eyes widened, and he twisted sharply, moving away before she could do more than nick his skin.

Fallon scowled. *Damn it . . .* She'd been aiming for a deeper cut.

He lunged at her, his sword point first.

Fallon spun under the blade, slashing out with her longer sword.

The young man dodged unbelievably fast, only to dart back in with a knife in his left hand.

Fallon was forced to drop and roll completely under him. He had too much reach on her to roll out of the way in time. *Faster. I need to go faster.* She needed to activate her dexterity augmentations. She slashed for the backs of his knees in passing.

He saw it coming and sidestepped.

She was just a touch faster than he was and scored a second nick to the back of his knee.

Blood spattered the floor.

The young man cursed and backed away.

Fallon frowned. Still not fast enough, but her dexterity was increasing. Her biomechanics had finally kicked in.

Two more came at her, one from behind and one from in front, both with knives in their off hands.

Fallon lunged onto her feet in a smooth spinning rise and was forced to exchange a small flurry of lightning-fast sword blows with both of them. She simply could not get out of their way. One shifted closer, ruining her ability to use her longer blade. She lashed out with her foot and kicked him hard in the knee to get him out of her personal space. There was a nasty wet popping sound.

He choked and dropped.

Fallon feinted a kick at the other and he dodged. She took the opening and spun out of range, gaining more space to use both her blades.

Two more men came at her.

Fallon gasped. "Three? Three, against one?"

The older Skeldhi in the red sash smiled. "Are you saying you yield?"

Fallon bared her teeth at him. "I don't yield that easy."

Sobehk chuckled on the far side. *That's certainly the truth.*

CHAPTER THIRTY-FOUR

Fallon surveyed her three attackers and the older Skeldhi, smiling from the sidelines. She'd had enough. "Fuck this shit . . ." She snarled and lunged at the one closest to her. She caught him in the bend of his arm, slicing deep.

Blood spattered the black marble floor.

His sword went spinning out of his hand. He bit out a foul expletive and jumped back.

She did a quick check on the two left. Neither one wore gloves. *Good.* She lunged, blade extended, for the one to her right then twisted and slashed at the one on her left trying to close in on her. She nicked his unprotected wrist.

He choked and his sword went spinning. More blood hit the floor. He backed away.

Fallon smiled grimly at the man before her. "Just you and me. Care to dance?"

The older Skeldhi rushed her from behind.

Fallon ducked and dodged his blade. *Oh, like I didn't see that coming a mile away.*

A blade lashed toward her face.

Fallon dodged it, but only barely. She turned sharply, spinning low on the floor, blades out, forcing the young man to jump or get his ankle sliced open.

The older Skeldhi had two swords, both long. And he was grinning.

Fallon frowned in concentration. The old guy was good. She'd need all her concentration to get him. That meant getting rid of the other one fast. She whirled and backflipped to gain distance then dropped into a deep crouch to get under the younger man's swinging blade and behind him. A sharp slice to the back of his knee dropped him.

Fallon spun away and lunged straight for the older guy. She had dexterity on him, but not by much and he was really practiced. With swords. She didn't stand chance against him using a sword.

He grinned.

Fallon closed in at top speed and tossed her blades to either side.

He brought both blades forward but not quite close enough.

She twisted sideways, dodging both fully extended blades, and caught his left wrist in her right hand. She punched the side of his left elbow hard then dropped into a low crouch to get out of the way of his other blade.

He shouted as he released his blade. His kick took her in the left side. He was definitely not smiling anymore.

Fallon grunted with the impact and dropped to her hands, swinging her left foot hard. She caught the outside of his knee on her left side with the top of her foot.

He grunted but didn't go down. His blade stabbed downward.

Fallon rolled onto her back, moving just enough to avoid the sword point aiming for her face, while getting close enough to punch him hard in the kneecap of the knee she'd just kicked.

There was a wet pop.

"Son of a fucking bitch!" His shout was crystal clear and in unaccented Imperial. He fell heavily to his side, grabbing for his knee with his right hand, his sword still out in his left.

Fallon rolled out of the way and came up in a low

crouch, ready to go after him again if she needed to. She shook her hand. His damned knee had been armored and her hand hurt like holy burning fury.

"Hold!" Sobehk's voice echoed with force.

Fallon froze.

Sobehk approached the kneeling and panting older Skeldhi. "*Mahfeht'syr* Loran? Are you all right?"

The older man sat up, sheathed his blade and grabbed his knee with both hands. He nodded and winced. "Yeah, fine."

I guess it's over. Fallon straightened up from her fighting crouch, shivering hard. It was more a reaction from the speed of the fight than anything else. Her dexterity augmentations taxed the hell out of her muscles.

It's over. Khan winked at Fallon from behind Sobehk. *Good fight.* He left Sobehk's side to collect his fallen swords.

Two gray-robed Skeldhi medics came trotting from the small crowd that had gathered. They dropped to one knee on either side of the older Skeldhi. One tugged at his leg armor, peeling the shin greave and the boot back to get to the wounded and swelling knee. The other unbuckled the arm armor on his other side.

Loran grimaced under the medic's hands. "Mother Night! That *rehkyt* of yours is worth her weight in fucking gold!"

Sobehk smiled. "I'm glad you approve, *Mahfeht'syr.*"

One of the medics looked up. "The knee is dislocated, but not broken."

The other medic poked at the elbow she'd punched. "Heavy bruising, some strain. You'll have full use of it to-morrow."

"Oh, is that all?" Loran rolled his eyes then focused on Sobehk. "Name your price and I'll pay it. Screw the *Ehnya'dhyt!*"

Sobehk smiled. "And if I asked you to empty your account, *Mahfeht'syr?*"

Loran wiped at his face and grinned. "I'd do it and gladly, *A'syr* Sobehk. She'd make every credit back in the pit within a few weeks."

The pit? Fallon blinked. *What pit?*

Sobehk grimaced. "There's a tiny little hitch in that plan, *Mahfeht'syr.*"

Loran frowned. "What?"

Sobehk shrugged. "She doesn't like to kill."

Loran's mouth fell open. "You're joking."

"Afraid not." Sobehk tucked his hands behind him. "She only fights when cornered. She's very good at running away and better at hiding."

Khan came to Fallon's side. *You're shaking.* His sword was back in his sheath. He slid her sword back into her sheath. *Are you wounded?* He lifted her chin and peered into her eyes.

Fallon smiled at the worry plainly visible in his copper gaze. *Nope, just an augmentation reaction from the fight. It'll stop in a bit.*

The *Mahfeht'syr* looked over at Fallon. "You're saying that she's non-aggressive?"

Sobehk chuckled. "Oh, she's quite aggressive, *Mahfeht'syr.* Unfortunately, she is absolutely uncompetitive. She'd make a terrible gladiator."

Fallon started. *Gladiator?*

Blood-sports are big business on the Imperial rim. Khan stepped behind her, his hands passing over her arms and down her flanks, obviously looking for cuts she might have missed. *Many of the less stable rehkyt find great satisfaction as cold-blooded killers.*

Fallon flinched and her gut twisted. *Not me.*

Of course not. Khan stepped in front of her. *You prefer to hang onto control rather than wallow in blood madness.*

Mahfeht'syr Loran looked up at Sobehk. "I guess she's better off as a bodyguard." He sighed. "Pity, she would have a brilliant career . . ."

"Brilliant but short." Sobehk sighed dramatically. "It's possible she'd allow herself to die rather than kill for money."

The two medics levered Loran up onto his one good leg.

Loran groaned and scowled. "That altruistic?"

Sobehk nodded sadly. "Afraid so."

Khan looked into Fallon's eyes. *Headache?*

My head's fine. Fallon opened and closed her fist, wincing. *But my whole hand hurts from punching his knee.*

I'll bet. Khan smiled fleetingly. *Let me see.*

Fallon gave him her hand. Dark splotches spread from her main three knuckles. *Shit . . .* Bruises this fast normally meant a bone was broken or fractured.

You're a rehkyt, not a human. Khan's fingers felt cool as he explored her hand. *Just bruising, nothing broken.* He turned to look at Sobehk. "No sign of *rahyt.*"

Mahfeht'syr Loran's mouth fell open. "She did that cold?"

Khan curled his lip. "I would think that would have been obvious, *Mahfeht'syr.* You're alive."

Loran raised his brow at Khan.

Shit . . . Khan bowed respectfully and turned back to Fallon.

Mahfeht'syr Loran eyed Sobehk. "Your *nehkyx* suffers from an overdose of attitude, *A'syr* Sobehk. Apparently, that's where your *rehkyt* is getting it. He needs to be disciplined."

Sobehk glared at Khan. "My apologies, *Mahfeht'syr.*"

Khan's eyes widened. *Discipline?* His mouth tightened. *I'll show* him *discipline . . .*

Fallon grinned at Khan. *Temper, temper, 'Syr. You're supposed to be a respectful subordinate, remember?*

Khan raised his brow curled his lip. *Sobehk's right. You do need a beating.*

Fallon chuckled.

Mahfeht'syr Loran gripped the two medics holding him upright around the shoulders and grinned. "Apology accepted." He nodded toward Fallon. "I award the steel and the blade. Congratulations on a fine *upuaht rehkyt, A'syr* Sobehk. I hope you find a satisfactory home for her."

Sobehk's smile faded. "I certainly hope so, *Mahfeht'syr.*" He bowed.

The two medics turned Loran toward the door.

Khan patted Fallon on the shoulder. *There, you have official permission to carry a sword.* He grinned. *And wear clothing.*

Fallon stared at him. *I needed permission to wear clothing?*

Loran stopped the medics and turned to face Sobehk. "You know, I may buy her anyway, *A'syr.*" He grinned. "She'd make a hell of a sparring partner, and I bet her bedsport is phenomenal."

Sobehk smiled. "Absolutely, *Mahfeht'syr.* She's very satisfactory at both."

Fallon scowled at Sobehk. *Satisfactory?*

Sobehk glanced her way and smiled. "If you will excuse us, we're headed for some much-needed rest."

Mahfeht'syr Loran waved his hand. "And me as well. Good night, *A'syr* Sobehk."

Sobehk bowed again. "A swift recovery to you." He marched over to Fallon's side and glared at Khan. *Khan, your mouth . . . Are you trying to spill your identity?*

Khan rolled his eyes. *Relax.* Mahfeht'syr *Loran has no idea what or who I am.*

Sobehk growled. *Just get us to that damned suite so I can bitch at you out loud!*

Khan grinned and started walking. *I think you're doing just fine with thought.*

Sobehk released a snarl. Mahfeht'syr *Loran is right. You do need a beating.*

Fallon shot a cheeky grin at Khan. *Ha!*

Sobehk grabbed Fallon's braid and yanked her to his side. *Don't get all cocky,* rehkyt. *What in flaming Chaos were you thinking, diving at him without your swords? I almost had a stroke!*

Fallon winced as she was hauled sideways down the aisle. *What? I knew what I was doing!*

Sobehk tugged on her braid. *Suicidal idiot!*

Fallon gasped and grabbed for his wrists. *It wasn't suicidal, damn it! It worked!*

Sobehk released her. *That's it! I'm beating the both of you!*

Khan snorted.

You think I won't? Sobehk smiled grimly.

A pair of etched glass doors opened to reveal a softly lit hallway carpeted in midnight blue, with slate blue walls and an arched ceiling with frosted glass globes shedding amber light. There was a deep blue door on the right, a matching door on the left and another pair of doors made of deeply smoked glass at the hall's far end.

Khan moved forward in a determined stride and shoved open the double doors of glass to softly lit night. The sound of crickets bloomed sharp and sweet.

Fallon felt a cool breeze scented strongly with green. "Oh . . ."

Khan turned and held out his hand to Fallon. "Come."

She shivered then bolted. She stopped at the edge of the door. Small lights lined the base of an enclosing wall two meters high. The contained space was not as large as the main enclave hall she'd just been in, but it was still big enough to support . . . She stopped to count. Eight . . . There were eight trees and they towered impossibly high, all around. There were smaller bushes with spots of color . . . Were those flowers?

The wind whispered and the air rustled with thousands of living green leaves. Everything moved, even the ground. The ground? The entire floor was covered in a carpet nearly as high as the top of her foot. It moved under the breeze.

Khan smiled. "Well? Go on."

"But the floor is . . . moving."

"Grass." Sobehk chuckled behind her. "It's just grass."

Grass was a plant. "It's alive?" It was shocking. It was terrifying. "All of it?"

Khan rolled his eyes. "Yes, it's all alive."

Fallon jerked back. "I shouldn't step on it if it's alive . . ."

Sobehk didn't bother hiding his chuckles. "It's supposed to be stepped on. That's what it's for!"

Khan groaned. "Great Mother — she's afraid of hurting the grass!"

Sobehk snorted. "She'll get over it."

Fallon felt a hard shove between her shoulder blades and was propelled forward out into the enclosed garden. The grass bent and gave under her foot. The scent of green sharpened. She froze. She was standing on living things.

Sobehk and Khan walked out behind her. They wandered about, examining the various bushes and flowers, tromping heavily and carelessly all over the grass.

Sobehk stopped by a blooming vine and reached out to touch an open white flower. "Terran Moonflowers, very nice."

Khan walked past him, his arms folded behind him. "I told the gardeners I wanted flowers that bloomed in the dark."

Fallon gathered her courage and approached the broad column of a gigantic plant dead center in the walled enclosure. She leaned back but the broad canopy of branches and leaves spreading over her hid the top. She reached out to touch it. It was rough and uneven under her palm, and very solid. It was also cool. She had thought it would be warm. She knelt to touch the grass under her feet. It was cool, too. Living things, but no warmth. *Huh* . . .

Impulsively, she tried to measure its diameter with her hands. It was too big to get her arms around and very unmoving. She looked up. The whole top of it moved, but the main column didn't budge.

Khan chuckled. "So you like the oak that much?"

Fallon released the tree and put her hands behind her back. She turned to look at him. "I was just . . . measuring it." Her gaze drifted upward. The leaves were too far away to touch.

Sobehk smiled. "You should be able to climb it."

Fallon's mouth fell open. "Oh, I couldn't . . ."

Sobehk choked on a laugh. "Oh, come on! I watched you scale a steel wall! A tree should be easy!"

Fallon stared at him. "Steel walls aren't alive."

Khan rolled his eyes. "As long as you don't step on a branch too weak to hold your weight, you won't hurt it."

Sobehk raised a brow at Khan. "We may have to chain her when the mowers come through."

Fallon froze. "Mowers?"

Khan grinned. "To cut the grass, prune the trees and pull up the weeds."

Fallon felt the hair on her neck rise and a low growl rumbled in her chest. "You don't mean that."

Sobehk dropped his head and started to laugh.

CHAPTER THIRTY-FIVE

Amid a lot of amused ribbing, Khan and Sobehk finally coaxed Fallon back into the suite and then through the door on the right. The chamber was done in white marble veined with midnight blue and slate gray. The mirrors on the walls were bright glass rather than smoked, with silver mesh curtains closing off the oval nest of a bed against the back wall. A large desk of clear glass and bright chrome occupied the left wall and both Khan's and Sobehk's trunks occupied the right.

Fallon gazed at the whole thing and frowned. The suite was supposed to be one of Khan's but it was clearly unlike Khan's taste. It looked more like something Sobehk would choose. She looked over at Khan and raised her brow.

Khan scowled at her. "Don't you dare say it."

Fallon pressed her fingers to her heart and opened her eyes very wide. "Say what?"

Sobehk looked around and nodded. "Very nice." He grinned at Khan. "Thank you."

Khan's shoulders hunched. "It wasn't nice. It's *supposed* to be your suite."

Sobehk rolled his eyes and strode over to Khan, catching him by the shoulders. "I know what it's supposed to be." He lifted Khan's chin, dropped a kiss on his lips, and grinned. "Learn to suffer a little gratitude."

Khan flinched back. "You are taking this dominant role a bit seriously."

Sobehk snorted. "What are you talking about? I've

always been dominant."

Fallon rolled her eyes. They were flirting again. She could feel their rising arousal through the telepathic link. Time to make herself scarce, before they started ripping each other's clothes off — and hers too.

She walked over to the door on the right wall and discovered an opulent white marble and midnight blue facility. A frosted glass and chrome shower occupied the left wall.

She stripped out of her sweaty suit in seconds.

The water was hot and delicious on her fight-strained muscles. Fallon leaned against the wall and let the water pound relaxation into her body. *Spoiled, I've been spoiled rotten by all this water.* And good food. And constant affection.

She sighed. She was disgustingly happy. She had no idea how in fury it had happened, but she was. Both men were infuriating in their demands — ask permission, be respectful . . . She curled her lip. Be polite. *Bleck!*

She pressed her forehead against the marble wall. She knew she loved Sobehk, but for some strange reason, she was beginning to love Khan too. He drove her up the walls, and down again, and he *wasn't* nice. Not in the usual sense of the word, but then, he could be terribly . . . sweet. And he cared for her. She could feel it pulsing against her heart. She smiled. She wasn't the only one with interesting thoughts on occasion.

Sobehk . . . Sobehk loved them both. She could feel that too. Sobehk would kill for either of them in a heartbeat, just as she would kill for both of them.

And Khan? She felt a chuckle bubble up. The Maker help anyone who even thought about harming Sobehk . . . or her. Her heart ached suddenly and violently. She did love them. Both.

Fallon was pitifully grateful for the shower spray

running down her cheeks.

Fallon stepped out of the shower with her suit over her arm, wrung out and more than ready to pass out.

The curtains over the bed's alcove were parted, showing that both men were naked and already in bed and under the midnight blue covers among the white silk sheets and pearl gray pillows.

Sobehk had Khan spooned against his chest and wrapped in his arms with Khan's head tucked under his chin. Sobehk opened one eye. "If you want to watch station dawn in the garden, your fighter-practice clothes are on the top of my trunks."

Actually, she'd love to see the garden in full station daylight. Fallon walked over to the trunks and lifted a deep blue padded short robe and the black pleated trousers. A narrow white sash went with it. Sobehk's colors. She looked over at Sobehk. "Thank you."

His eyes were closed. He waved then snuggled against Khan, who was apparently fast asleep.

Fallon dressed and went out into the garden barefoot. The grass was still surprisingly cool and damp. She eyed the oak in the center of the walled garden and wondered what the view would be like from up there.

It took less effort to climb than she thought it would, but the branches thinned sharply the higher up she went. She stayed very close to the main trunk to avoid damaging the smaller branches. She stopped about halfway up. The tree definitely felt alive as it swayed under her body. The trembling leaves were a loud rush in her ears. It was exhilarating. She climbed higher.

Her head reached the upper branches and suddenly, she could see past the leaves . . . a million lights in the darkness, everywhere, all around.

The air brightened and became tinted with pink. Mist

curled and eddied up from the trees.

She looked up and saw clouds. The station was large enough to actually possess real clouds. Light bloomed brighter just beyond the clouds. Pink lightened to gold.

A chorus of fluting sounds burst out around her. Small feathered flying creatures burst into flight. Birds . . . Real living birds.

Bright yellow flowers exploded from the tops of the trees and fluttered madly. They were joined by other colors, all fluttering in huge colored clouds. They were butterflies as big as her outstretched hand.

The mist thinned and parted, revealing an entire world of green and blue crawling up the sides of the horizon and arching all the way over her head. There were lakes directly above her head. And birds flew everywhere — where anyone could see them.

It was incredible. It was paradise.

Fallon sat down on the branch and held onto the tree's trunk with both hands as her heart burst from within. Great gasping sobs exploded from her chest, and she let them. There was no one up here to see. She was alone in this moment of perfect beauty. She would remember it and treasure it for the rest of her life.

Stretched out and perfectly at ease sprawled across one of the stronger triple-forked branches of the oak, Fallon napped. The tree rocked soothingly under her with birdsong and rustling leaves wrapping her in a sweet green lullaby.

"Isabeau!" Khan sounded annoyed, but she could feel his amusement through her link. "Are you still up in that tree?"

Fallon didn't bother opening her eyes or shouting back. *Yes, 'Syr.*

"Don't you think it's time to come down and get some

sleep?"

Fallon smiled. *I was sleeping, 'Syr.*

"You need to eat, too."

Fallon's stomach rumbled. Damn, he was right. She groaned and sat up. *On my way down.* She slipped down the branches and dropped to the ground from the last branch. The grass was much warmer under her feet, and so was the direct station sunlight. Halfway to the door, she stopped under the heat of the station sun and stretched, coming up on her toes. She dropped to her heels and jogged to the door.

Just within, Khan leaned against the right wall in a long black dressing robe. His brow lifted, as did the corner of his mouth. "Enjoy the dawn?"

"It was . . ." Fallon couldn't think of a single word to describe the wonder of it—and he had arranged for her to have it. She lunged at him and grabbed him around the shoulders. She pressed a kiss to his mouth, trying to express straight from her heart what he had given her.

Khan started under her mouth then grabbed her shoulders and turned suddenly, pressing her back against the wall. His mouth opened as he kissed her back, answering her with a spear of feeling that stabbed her straight through the heart. Heat and physical need flashed white-hot through her body. Cream soaked the crotch of her trousers.

He groaned into her mouth and his hands dropped to her sash, unknotting it then untying her trousers. The pleated black fabric dropped to the floor. His hands cupped her ass and he lifted her up against the wall.

Fallon wrapped her arms around his neck and lifted her legs, locking them around his hips.

His fingers delved into her core.

She was wet—she was far more than wet, she was running down the inside of her thighs. She sensed rather than felt him rubbing her cream on his secondary cock and then she felt his primary cock and the bar that speared it pushing for entry. She released his mouth and arched back against the wall to let him in.

His primary cock surged halfway in. He gasped. His second cock nudged at her anus.

She moaned and pushed to open for him. His broad cockhead and the metal bar that pierced it pressed past her tight ring.

He shoved hard and buried himself fully.

Fallon gasped . . . filled, taken, possessed.

Khan groaned, set his feet and gripped her ass with clawed fingers. Taking her full weight in his hands, he surged hard and fast into her body. Then again, and again . . . fucking her with merciless strength. His lips pulled back from his long teeth as he slammed into her.

Fallon moaned and bucked against his thrusts. He felt so good. Each stroke filled her and struck a spark of fire that led toward glory. He felt so right. He belonged in her body.

A potent cocktail of confusing emotions washed from Khan across the link . . . possession, affection and blinding need. He wanted her body with obsessive hunger, but he wanted more. He needed her to care for him.

She opened her heart as wide as it would go . . . she did care, she did.

He wanted her love. He wanted her to love him. Desperately.

Fallon wanted to give it, but she was afraid. What if she lost him?

He snarled. Determination and a hot wash of possessive rage answered her. They would not be separated. He would not allow it. He would kill anyone, anything that tried.

Fallon clawed his back and snarled right back. She too, would kill anyone, anything that tried to separate them. Her thoughts shifted abruptly to Sobehk and discovered that he was included in Khan's thoughts.

Khan saw Sobehk as his, too. More than merely instinct and affection, they fit together. They belonged together. They would stay together. Khan would have it no other way.

Climax rose higher, surging upward to crest in a white-hot wave, stopping right on the very edge. Fallon cried out with the ache in her body and in her heart.

Pain ached from Khan's heart. He would not ask for her love. He wanted it given. His teeth sank into her shoulder.

Release exploded through Fallon in a roaring wet wave that tried to rip her apart. She cried out as her mind shouted that she did love him. She did. Barely aware under the roll of pleasure, she buried her teeth in his shoulder, determined that he feel her answer.

Khan shuddered hard and choked as climax took him. His thoughts disappeared under a white wave of intense pleasure.

Fallon was slammed hard up and then over into a second burning orgasm. She screamed. A third climax roared out of nowhere and ripped through her with violent force, washing her mind clean away.

Panting in Khan's arms Fallon grasped his braid and tugged. "Did you hear me?"

Khan groaned. "Hear . . . what?"

Fallon tugged harder and sucked in a deep breath. "That I love you, you thick-headed, white-haired, kinky-assed pervert."

Khan smiled tiredly and pressed his sweaty brow to hers. "Yes, I heard you. But I wanted to hear your mouth say it."

Fallon choked on a tired laugh. "There, my mouth said it, too."

Khan chuckled as his heart slammed against hers. "That has got to be the most disrespectful, unromantic declaration of love I have ever heard uttered."

Fallon groaned and smiled. "Yeah, well, what did you expect? I *am* disrespectful and unromantic."

"Mother Night . . ." Khan released her legs to let her stand but wrapped her in his arms and pressed her against the wall. "I *really* need to beat you."

Fallon smiled. "Beatings have never made all that much of an impression on me."

Khan grinned and flashed long teeth. "Perhaps not, but I impressed you."

Fallon rolled her eyes. *Oh, please . . . Hello, ego.*

Khan pressed his brow to hers. "And beating you makes *me* feel so much better."

Fallon chuckled. "I'm glad my beatings do someone some good!"

Khan's head jerked back. "Beatings? You've only been beaten once!"

The door opened on their immediate right and Sobehk stuck his head out. "You're both going to get beaten if you don't get in here now! The damned food service is on its way here to deliver dinner!"

Fallon grabbed her fallen trousers and bolted through the door.

Khan followed at a more sedate pace, tucking his robe more closely around him.

Sobehk closed the door and curled his lip. "I don't believe you just fucked in the hallway! Blood and Chaos, you two, there was a perfectly good bed only a few paces away!"

Khan gave Sobehk a long, cool look. "Don't even try to

pretend that you weren't masturbating the whole time we were at it."

"So?" Sobehk's cheeks bloomed with pink. "It would have been a hell of a lot more entertaining if you had been in the room with me."

Khan's chin dipped and his smile turned feral. "It was entertaining enough that you sent Isabeau into a third climax."

Fallon looked up in surprise. That had been Sobehk's release?

Sobehk shrugged then grinned. "It's nice to feel how much you're loved."

Khan froze, staring.

Fallon grinned at Khan. It was nice to see him shocked.

Sobehk raised his brow at Khan. "What? You think I hadn't noticed?" He rolled his eyes. "Oh, come on, I know when people are in love with me." He smiled at Khan. "Just as I knew when Isabeau started falling in love with you."

Fallon stared at Sobehk.

Sobehk aimed a sly smile at Fallon. "Shall we dress for dinner?"

Chapter Thirty-Six

A chime rang.

Khan finished tying a midnight blue robe over his black kilt. "Ah, dinner is ready in the hospitality chamber."

Fallon looked up from the black sash she was knotting over a matching midnight blue robe that fell to mid-thigh. "There's a hospitality chamber?"

"It's the room across the hall." Sobehk turned, tugging at the bright blue sleeves of his over-robe. "The service comes in, serves, then rings the chime to announce when they leave."

"The hospitality chamber is generally used to receive and entertain guests." Khan walked over to Sobehk and pulled up the collar of Sobehk's white under-robe so it folded properly over his blue over-robe. "This is one of the smaller residences. I have a much larger one with three bedchambers and a full office as well as a dining room and an audience chamber."

Fallon blinked. "For one person?"

Khan snorted and tugged at the folds of Sobehk's robes. "You'd be surprised how much of it I use when dealing with official business."

Sobehk grinned at Khan. "You know, you're very good at this. You'd make an excellent servant."

Kahn smiled right back at him and flashed a long tooth. "Of course. I actually know how retainers are supposed to behave."

Sobehk frowned.

Khan turned away. "Shall we go?" He led the way out of the bedchamber and opened the door across the hall.

The deep, wide, pale blue chamber was carpeted in pearl gray. A low, smoked glass table framed on three sides with a pair of plush blue velvet lounging chairs occupied the immediate left, with a long sofa stretched behind it against the wall. A very extensive entertainment center occupied the wall on the immediate right.

At the far end of the chamber, plates were laid out for three on a table covered in white damask that could easily have served eight. The plates were silver-edged midnight blue, crushingly expensive Shido china accompanied by equally expensive cut crystal goblets and matching tumblers. Steam curled up from four elegant warming tureens of bright silver. A pair of cut crystal carafes sat between the three place settings. One was filled with a gold liquid and the other with what appeared to be water. Live flowers in three shades of blue graced the center of the table.

Sobehk went to the back of the table and Khan took the chair on the right.

Fallon stared at the third chair, facing Sobehk. *Rehkyt* were not supposed to sit on the furniture.

Sobehk grinned. "Isabeau, you may sit in the chair to eat."

"Thank you, '*Syr*." Fallon dropped into the chair. It felt so strange to be in an actual chair after eating so often on her knees.

Khan raised his brow and gave her a smile. "If we were entertaining guests, you would have been fed already and left in the other room until dinner was through."

Fallon stilled. Left in the bedroom like a canine that couldn't be trusted not to beg from the table.

Sobehk nodded. "Yes, like the pet you are supposed to be."

Khan poured water into her glass. "Or you would stand behind our chairs in the personal bodyguard's position, though you would be equally ignored."

Fallon's brows dipped. "I wouldn't mind being treated like a bodyguard. It's being treated like something . . . decorative, or entertaining, that I have problems handling."

Sobehk chuckled. "But you *are* decorative and entertaining." He served himself from one of the heated tureens set on the table.

Fallon raised her brow. "But only satisfactory?"

"Isabeau." Sobehk leaned both elbows on the table and focused his bright blue gaze on her. "*Mahfeht'syr* Loran is incredibly wealthy and immeasurably powerful. The last thing I wanted was his real interest in buying you. There is a very real chance that he could succeed in outbidding everyone else. If he did so, Khan would have a great deal of difficulty getting you back from him."

Khan set some fragrant meat on Fallon's plate. "Make no mistake, I would get her back, but it could take over a cycle to do so." He lifted his brow at Fallon. "However, *Mahfeht'syr* Loran is not known for his forgiving nature. Once he discovered the reality of your ownership, he would make sure to carve his displeasure from your skin every spare moment he had until I succeeded in getting you back."

Yikes . . . Fallon hunched her shoulders. "But what if he was the one that . . . um?"

"Had you programmed?" Khan shook his head. "*Mahfeht'syr* Loran does not need a half-trained *rehkyt* for an assassin. *Mahf'dhyt* are fully trained legal assassins."

Fallon froze with a piece of meat halfway to her lips. Sobehk was *Mahf'dhyt*.

Sobehk's brows rose. "You didn't know?"

Fallon set her utensil on her plate and frowned. "I just

thought you were a hunter."

Sobehk shrugged. "I am . . . was . . . a hunter. But I'm also a fully trained legal executioner. Rather like a street cop." He tilted his head to the side. "Where Khan is like a detective."

"Oh . . ." Fallon picked up her utensil.

Khan raised his brows. "Though I can legally torture detainees to obtain answers and you have the legal right to kill someone that cannot be safely taken in."

Fallon swallowed. "Why do I have the feeling that I'm so deep in the dark I feel blind?"

Khan snorted. "*You* don't need to worry about anything but pleasing Sobehk or me." He nodded at her untouched plate. "And right now, eating would please us both."

"Yes, '*Syr*." Fallon sucked a piece of meat into her mouth. It was really, really good. She had two helpings before she could think past her stomach. She sipped at her water then turned to Khan. "Um, '*Syr?*"

Khan nodded.

Fallon set down her glass. "When exactly is this auction I'm supposed to be in?"

Khan lifted his wine glass and examined the golden liquid within it. "The auction for *upuaht rehkyt* is at station sunset."

Fallon swallowed. "Tonight?"

Khan nodded. "Tonight."

Fallon couldn't eat another bite.

Sobehk frowned at Fallon then looked at Khan. "Considering the preparations both you and I have to make for tonight, I think perhaps a nice long nap may be in order."

Khan glanced at Fallon and nodded. "I think you may be right."

Fallon jerked in her chair. "A *nap?*"

Stripped nude, Fallon dropped into the bed, falling back among the white sheets and pearl gray pillows. And proceeded to pout.

Khan snorted and pulled the midnight blue coverlet up to her chin. "You'll be perfectly safe in here. Sobehk and I will be right across the hall."

Fallon opened her mouth to protest that she didn't need to *sleep* . . .

"Isabeau." Khan caught her chin and stared hard into her eyes. "Sleep, *now*."

Bastards! Masculine chuckles accompanied the smothering darkness that washed her under a thick blanket of sleep.

Fallon was jarred from deep sleep. She surfaced with a gasp. *What in fury* . . .

Isabeau. Khan's mental voice was loud and a touch angry.

She frowned. *Yes?*

I need you to dress quickly and go out into the garden. Khan was definitely angry.

Fallon got out from under the blankets and grabbed the short midnight blue robe she'd worn to dinner from the top of Sobehk's trunk. She knotted the white sash, focused on Khan. *Okay, I'm heading out.*

Good. Go. There was a thread of triumph in his mental voice.

Fallon darted out and into the hall. Voices were coming from the other room. She recognized Khan and Sobehk but there were other voices coming from in there, too. Neither Sobehk nor Khan sounded pleased. *Uh oh* . . . She bolted for the garden.

The garden was awash in bright sun and shadows. On impulse, she headed straight for the big oak. She looked up into the swaying branches. She leapt up, grabbed onto a lower branch, hauled herself up then climbed to just a bit higher than Sobehk could easily reach. On a likely and broad forked limb, she sprawled out, full length.

She's in the tree again. Sobehk's amusement carried across the mental link.

Khan released a soft sense of relief. *Good, very good.*

The glass doors from the hallway opened and someone stepped out, swathed in a long gold and white hooded robe. "*Rehkyt?*" The voice was male and very youthful.

Fallon blinked. *A kid?*

A prince, and a very high-ranking councilor. Khan's mental voice simmered across her mind threaded with anger. *Do not harm him, but do not let him touch you.*

A prince? Fallon watched the youthful figure. *Great . . .*

The prince moved deeper into the garden then walked toward the tree. He walked all the way around the trunk, stopped, and looked straight up at Fallon. The young man's face was beyond pretty. His eyes seemed to be violet. "Hello."

Fallon froze. Great Maker, what should she say?

Why not try being polite? Khan's sour amusement was crystal clear.

Fallon swallowed. "Hello, '*Syr.*"

The prince frowned and his braid slipped from his hood, revealing hair as gold as his robe. "What are you doing up there?"

Fallon lifted her brow. Good question. She smiled. Let's see how he deals with the truth. "Staying out of reach, '*Syr.*"

His violet eyes widened. "Why?"

Fallon pursed her lips. Hmmm . . ."Because I was told to?" She cleared her throat. "'*Syr.*"

The prince smiled, and it was breathtaking. "They're trying to keep you from impressing, aren't they?"

Fallon blinked. That sounded like as good an excuse as any. She smiled. "Of course, '*Syr*."

His expression turned serious and very adult. "I'm bidding on you tonight."

Fallon frowned. "Do you need a bodyguard, '*Syr*?" She winced. She'd spoken out of turn. He hadn't asked a question.

The prince sighed. "Yes, I do. Pretty badly, too." He tilted his head. "I've seen the vid. You're very good." He smiled. "And pretty."

Fallon leaned up a little. He thought *she* was pretty? She grinned. "I'm not half as pretty as you are handsome, '*Syr*."

He sighed and rolled his eyes. "That's the whole problem. No one takes me seriously."

Fallon leaned back down on the branch. "Oh, I'm sorry. I'm sure that'll change as you get older, '*Syr*."

The prince looked away and scowled. "*If* I get older."

Fallon's claws dug into the branch. "Is someone trying to kill you?"

He snorted and looked up at her. "They've been trying to kill me since I came of age. Now that I have my father's council chair, it's gotten worse. You would not believe the things my staff has found."

Fallon frowned. "It sounds like you need a trained professional, '*Syr*. I seriously doubt I'd be good enough for you."

The prince shrugged. "Oh, I have lots of trained professionals for everything." He looked up at her. "Everything but the bedchamber." He folded his hands behind him. "I need someone to protect me when I sleep."

Fallon winced. "Oh . . ."

The prince aimed that breathtaking smile at her again. "I'd like to see the rest of you. Why don't you come down here?"

Fallon sucked in a sharp breath. Great Maker, his smile was lethal. "I . . . can't, *'Syr.*" She aimed a sharp panicked thought at Khan. *Can you come get this kid, please?*

You're doing just fine. Khan was clearly amused. *Keep talking to him, you've gotten more out of him than Sobehk or I.*

The young man's brows lifted. "I smell . . . fear?" His smile turned feral. "You're ready to impress, I knew it!" He headed straight for the tree and grasped one of the lower branches, clearly intending to climb.

Fallon sat up on her branch. "*'Syr!* What are you doing?"

The prince flashed a hungry smile. "Ensuring my purchase." He pulled himself up onto the branch. "If you're already impressed, *A'syr* Sobehk will have to close off all other bids."

Oh shit! Fallon grabbed one of the upper branches and climbed higher. "This isn't a good idea, *'Syr!*"

The prince followed her. "I think it's a perfectly acceptable idea."

Fallon moved around the trunk to the far side and climbed higher. "I thought impression needed sex to happen? Isn't it kind of hard to have sex in a tree?" Speaking of trees, she was running out of tree fast. *Khan! Help me, damn you!*

I'm coming. Khan's mental voice held determination. *That little sneak . . . he promised he wouldn't do this!*

The prince laughed. "You *are* new! Impression can happen on contact, that's why you've been told to stay out of reach." He peeked at her from the other side of the trunk. "There you are." He reached out.

Fallon released the branch she held and dropped, catching the branch below her with her palms. She pulled sharply and brought her feet up onto the branch to perch. She looked up at him. "You're cheating!"

"So?" He grinned. "You *are* good." He started back down. "I definitely have to have you."

"Isabeau!" Khan's shout sounded like salvation.

CHAPTER THIRTY-SEVEN

Fallon dropped as fast as she could, swinging from branch to branch. Not an easy thing to do since the whole tree was moving and it was highly irregular in shape, not to mention the fact that the bark was rough on the palms. She landed on the grass in a crouch.

Khan had his leather robe on and his hood up. His mouth was tight. *Are you all right?*

Fallon stood up. *Fine, and I stayed out of hand contact. What took you so long?*

"Oh!" The prince moved back down the tree at a considerably s lower pace. "*A'syr Nehkyx*, do you have to call her in?"

Khan looked up and folded his arms. "Yes, my prince, she needs to get dressed for the auction."

The young man landed on the grass gracefully. "Pity . . ."

Fallon darted behind Khan.

The prince grinned. "*A'syr Nehkyx*, would you be kind enough to tell *A'syr* Sobehk that I am quite determined. I will empty my account if I have to."

Khan bowed. "I will do so, my prince."

"Thanks!" The young man leaned to the side to smile at Fallon. "It was nice to meet you, Isabeau."

Fallon sketched a deep bow. "It was my honor, '*Syr*."

The prince turned and jogged for the glass doors.

Khan turned to look at Fallon. *I believe you made an impression.* He smiled.

Fallon frowned at him. *Funny, that's what he was trying for.*

Khan's smile became grim. *So I saw. The little sneak.*

She looked at the closed doors where the prince had disappeared. *Khan, I have a bad feeling that he's the intended target.*

Khan sighed. *I do, too.* He started toward the doors.

Fallon followed him with her arms crossed. *But we still don't know who wants him dead!*

Khan snorted. *Unfortunately, I do.* He grasped the door handle. *Fully half the council wants him dead.*

Fallon shook her head. *What! Why?*

Khan shrugged and tugged the door open. *Oh, the usual reasons, power, greed —*

The prince was right inside the door.

Khan raised his brow. *Precociousness is another.*

Fallon jerked back from the door, stepping into direct sunlight. Her skin gleamed like metal — and warmed, very quickly.

The prince focused on her and his mouth opened. "Oh, gold . . ."

Khan cleared his throat. "My prince?"

The prince's gaze widened as he focused on Khan. "Oh! Excuse me, *A'syr Nehkyx.*" He hunched his shoulders and turned to walk down the hall. Waiting at the far end were two older Skeldhi in long brilliant robes, along with six fully armored *Mahf'dhyt* enforcers. The prince joined them, and they all trooped out.

Fallon came inside and rubbed her arms. "It was getting warm out there."

Khan smiled. "Your *rehkyt* skin can take more sunlight than ours, but you will still burn if you stand directly in it long enough."

Sobehk stepped out of the left doorway. "Mother Night, three *Ehnya'dhyt! Three!*" He grimaced. "Remind me *not* to do that again!"

Fallon's mouth fell open. The other men in robes had been councilors, too?

Khan stepped into the hall with Fallon at his heels. "You handled them very gracefully."

Sobehk snorted. "Yeah, right. More like they handled *me*!"

Khan shook his head, then raised his brow. "It seems that the prince was quite taken with our Isabeau."

Sobehk frowned. "I missed part of that earlier sending, one of the councilors was yammering in my ear. Did you say that the prince tried to climb the tree to get to her?"

Fallon curled her lip. "He didn't just climb it; he chased me up and down it!"

Sobehk snorted. "Determined kid."

"I think he's a *scared* kid." Fallon raised her brow at Khan. "Can we do something about getting him a proper bodyguard?"

Khan scowled. "Not you."

Fallon snorted. "Obviously not me, but there has to be somebody . . ."

"I'll see what *rehkyt* are available." Khan rolled his eyes and headed toward the bedchamber. "Come, we need to get dressed."

Fallon followed. "Just us?"

Khan nodded then turned to let her pass. "The dressers will be here very soon to dress Sobehk in court garb."

"Fancy togs, huh?" Fallon grinned at Sobehk. "That ought to be interesting."

Sobehk pointed at the bedchamber. "Go."

Khan leaned back against the right side of the lift and crossed his arms. He was back in his black leather arsenal-laden jacket and skintight pants with his long sword shoved in his sash.

Fallon paced in the lift. She was back in her belly-exposing sex toy leathers, including Sobehk's blue sash and Khan's short sword. Khan had also taken the time to drag her hair back into a tight tail and set a silver ring to hold it very firmly in place.

Sobehk, however, looked majestic. The dressers had done quite a job on him. His hair had been completely redressed into a very full lion's mane with thousands of tiny sapphire beads on tiny braids, and his robes were fit for a prince. He wore three layers, beginning with sheer frost-white under sapphire blue damask. A midnight blue heavily brocaded over-robe hung open and draped him to the floor and a bit beyond.

The blue sash peeking out from under the long over-robe was heavily embroidered with silver thread and nearly scraped the top of his pointed boots. Broad silver bracelets were on his wrists and his nails had been manicured sharp, then dipped in silver.

Sobehk turned to look at the lift's floor reading. He was clearly not thrilled. His knuckles were white as he clutched his white staff.

Fallon's eye was drawn to the broad design embroidered in silver thread across his shoulders and down his back. It looked something like a gigantic oval moon with six ornately clawed rays. *Weird symbol.* She went back to pacing. Great Maker, she hated waiting.

Khan eyed Fallon's pacing. "Calm yourself. You have already passed the difficult part, the assessment. We need only arrest anyone that approaches you with the second half of the code."

Fallon clutched her upper arms. "And how are *we* supposed to know when *they* have it—*before* they stick it in my head?"

Khan lifted his hand and peeled back his sleeve, revealing the black band on his wrist. "Part of my work, while you were napping, was to complete the programming on this. With the help of your spectral code, I will be able to detect its presence. I had it halfway completed when we left the ship." He examined the black band. "Your coding is not as simple as it appears."

"Oh, thanks." The compliment to her work was as startling as it was warming. Fallon's brows shot up. "Is that why we had to be so careful about anyone coming near me, because you didn't have it ready?"

Khan lowered his chin. "Of course."

Sobehk chuckled. "*And* because Khan is a possessive bastard. He doesn't like others touching his property."

Khan snorted. "And you are not?"

Sobehk opened his mouth on a retort.

The lift doors opened, revealing guards stationed on either side.

The chamber beyond was a huge round auditorium with tiered seating packed nearly solid with people in brilliantly hued robes. Dim globes shed light on either side of the doors to over a dozen lifts lining the curved walls. Stepped aisles led downward to the center.

At the very bottom was a large, oval, chest-high stage that gleamed like black water. The force-grid had been activated around it, blocking anyone from climbing onto, or off the stage without clearance. In the middle of that black expanse, someone paced. Light poured down on his golden skin and long dark hair. The auction was apparently well underway.

Khan stepped out and lifted his fist, presenting the back of his hand for scanning. He received a nod and stepped down, then turned with his arms crossed.

Fallon frowned. Unlike the other aisles, the carpeted

steps leading down from their lift were lined on either side with clear safety-glass walls. She wondered if it was needed to keep back the audience?

No. Sobehk pushed Fallon out of the lift. *The glass is to keep unimpressed and frightened* rehkyt *from attacking someone that accidentally gets too close.*

Fallon rolled her eyes, lifted her hand and presented her fist for scanning. *Same thing.*

Seated Skeldhi stood up to peer at her through the glass with flyers or data readers in their hands. The chamber echoed with whispers.

Fallon felt the hair on the back of her neck rise. Suddenly she was very glad that glass was there.

The guard nodded.

She stepped forward to wait by Khan's side.

Sobehk received his nod and glanced about as he proceeded down the steps toward them. *I do not remember there ever being this many people at an auction this far out of Skeldhi space.*

There's a wager, remember? Khan moved down the stairs, leading the way two steps ahead with his hand on the pommel of his sword, clearly stating that he was acting as guard. *On who will lay claim to our Isabeau?*

Ah . . . yes. Sobehk's mouth tightened. *A lot of money is going to be lost when that fourth* Ehnya'dhyt *steps in.*

A fourth councilor? Fallon frowned at Khan's back. *What fourth* Ehnya'dhyt?

Nothing you need to worry about. Khan's amusement was matched by the sense of anticipation wrapped around it.

Fallon followed Khan to the very bottom of the steps. A second set of stairs led onto the stage.

Khan held out his left fist. "Hold."

Fallon stopped and looked over at the chest-high stage. Stalking back and forth across the black expanse was a heavily muscled gold-skinned male in skintight leather pants. Tall boots climbed halfway up his muscular thighs. His straight black hair was an unbound spill of darkness that fell to the center of his back. The steel chain was bright against his golden throat and silver clips gleamed in the bottom curve of his ears.

Abruptly, he stopped, then turned sharply to face Fallon. His eyes were enormous and pitch-black, not one speck of color. His mouth and nipples were as red as hers.

Her heart thumped. He was an *upuaht* Prime, like she was.

Khan frowned at Fallon. *Don't get any ideas.*

Fallon started. *Ideas about what?*

Sobehk chuckled. *Don't give her any ideas.*

A bell rang.

The male started hard and turned sharply toward the center of the stage, his body tense and very still. The bitter scent of fear-sweat washed from the stage.

A man dressed in leather half-armor came up onto the stage from the far side with a chain lead in his hand.

A far smaller Skeldhi male in pale orange and gold robes followed. His mane was a full creamy fall that glittered with gold beads. His face was youthful, and his eyes were as pitch-black as the *rehkyt's*. He held his hands out toward the golden male and smiled.

The *rehkyt* moved cautiously toward the robed man, his chin up and his body tense. He towered head and shoulders over the smaller Skeldhi. The *rehkyt* took the smaller man's hands and trembled hard then dropped to his knees as though felled by a blow.

The Skeldhi sucked in a sharp breath and closed his eyes, gripping the other man's hands.

Khan nodded. *Fast impression. Good match.*

Fallon blinked. *Wow . . .*

The leather-clad Skeldhi handed the robed man the

chain lead.

The rehkyt released his new owner's hands and lifted his chin so that the lead could be attached to his chain collar.

The entire audience murmured.

The *rehkyt* rose to his feet and walked off stage following the smaller man.

The bell rang again.

The energy grid blocking the stairs disappeared.

Khan held out his hand. "The sword."

Fallon jolted hard but pulled the sword from her sash. "It's my turn?" Her mouth went dry and she had to swallow. "'*Syr?*"

Khan took the sheathed sword from her hands. "Go up the stairs. You're permitted to look at the audience in this instance."

"Great . . ." Fallon wiped her damp hands on her blue sash.

Sobehk rolled his eyes. "Oh, I almost forgot. That has to come off, too." He leaned forward and tugged the sash free from Fallon's hips.

Fallon's chest tightened. Without Khan's sword and Sobehk's sash, she suddenly felt naked and exposed in a way that had nothing to do with bare skin.

"*A'syr* Sobehk?"

Fallon, Khan and Sobehk froze. All three looked up the glass-lined aisle steps.

A pair of older men came toward them. One man wore pale yellow and cream robes with a heavy bronze over-robe, and the other was in copper and scarlet with a black over-robe. They reeked of money and power.

Fallon frowned. They looked . . . familiar. They *were* familiar. They were the two men with the prince.

Sobehk straightened and pasted on a smile. "*Ehnya'dhyt*

Dhuet and *Ehnya'dhyt* Sehnby, I'm honored."

Fallon eyed Sobehk. He wasn't honored; he was suspicious as fury.

Khan casually examined the band on his wrist. He gave Fallon a look of complete triumph. *Get behind me and do not let them touch you.*

Them? Fallon moved behind him and frowned. *It* can't *be that simple.*

Most crimes committed are incredibly simple. Khan lowered his chin and stepped forward, next to Sobehk. *And for the most mundane of reasons.*

Both councilors stopped a full sword-length away. The councilor on the right tugged on his black robes and lowered his chin, peering directly at Sobehk. "I would like to restate my original offer to buy your *rehkyt.*"

Sobehk politely lifted his chin and briefly flicked his gaze away. "I'm honored, *Ehnya'dhyt* Dhuet, however . . ."

"I'll double my offer."

Ehnya'dhyt Sehnby, on the left, settled his bronze robes closer around him and smiled at his companion. "I'll triple mine."

Sobehk straightened to his full height, but his eyes widened. "'*Syrs,* I don't understand, why do you want my *rehkyt* so badly?" A thought speared toward Khan. *You'd think they'd have figured out by now that their money and positions are not going to impress me into selling her to them.*

Khan's mouth tightened briefly. *It normally works on the lower ranks. Most A'syr would sell to them just for the right to brag that they sold to a councilor. They're not used to dealing with your sheer stubbornness.*

Ehnya'dhyt Sehnby smiled briefly and tilted his head in a slightly less aggressive posture than his black-robed companion. "The prince is my nephew, my sister's son. He has spoken of nothing but her since he saw her . . . I thought she would make the perfect gift."

Ehnya'dhyt Dhuet curled his lip and folded back the sleeves of his black robe, revealing the scarlet sleeve under it. "That's all well and fine, but the boy needs a proper bodyguard that he will actually remain with." He gave Sobehk a sour smile. "The prince has a habit of locking his guards out of his rooms." His smile disappeared. "Sooner or later, this habit will cost him his life."

Fallon frowned. They didn't *sound* like they were looking for an assassin.

People lie. Khan's thoughts shimmered with derision.

"Oh, and one other thing." *Ehnya'dhyt* Sehnby lifted his brows and smiled. "It seems that there is some question to the validity of your ownership, *A'syr* Sobehk. Would you be so kind as to allow your *rehkyt* to be tested?" He stepped to the side.

A'syr Mohr was revealed behind them in his gray medic's robes. He stared hard at Sobehk, his mouth tight, his hands firmly behind him.

Fallon felt a growl rising in her chest. He must have finally recognized Khan and figured out what they were doing.

Sobehk narrowed his gaze on Mohr. "The ownership of my *rehkyt* was tested at the doors of this hall."

Mohr's gaze focused on Fallon, bypassing Khan completely.

Fallon's frown deepened. Mohr wasn't acting like he recognized Khan. But, if he *didn't* recognize Khan, and one of them had the other half of the code, then . . . What in fury was going on?

Ehnya'dhyt Sehnby's gaze chilled. "Yes, but how thoroughly?"

Ehnya'dhyt Dhuet rolled his eyes.

Fallon felt some kind of tense communication pass between Sobehk and Khan, bypassing her completely.

Sobehk smiled coldly. "May I suggest another way to determine rightful ownership, councilors?"

All three men focused on Sobehk.

Sobehk deliberately lowered his chin and smiled, baring his long teeth. "Purchase."

Khan grabbed Fallon by the arm and propelled her up the short flight of stairs and onto the stage. The energy grid snapped closed behind her, locking her in.

CHAPTER THIRTY-EIGHT

A sea of shadowed, staring figures and their hushed whispers washed and eddied all the way around the circular stage.

Fallon suddenly and viscerally understood why the *re-hkyt* male had paced and smelled of fear. The complete attention of all those people and the total lack of any place to hide brought the hair up on her neck and soaked her back with sweat.

She reached out to Khan and Sobehk, wondering what was going on, and touched . . . nothing. They were gone.

Fallon's heart hammering in her chest, she moved back toward the stairs. They weren't there either. The aisle was empty. *Shit . . .* She was alone.

Alone with a million people staring at her.

She started pacing from one end of the stage to the other, just to keep from screaming. She had no idea what was going on. If they were bidding—or fighting, there was no way of knowing. There was no sound but whispers and the clicking of her boot heels. For an eternity.

The bell sounded.

Fallon nearly jumped out of her skin. It was over. Her inner chrono stated that only thirty-five minutes had passed. Her head lifted and she looked around. There was no trace of anyone headed for the stage. Where in bleeding fury were they?

Movement at the back of the stage caught her eye. Someone came up the steps swathed from head to foot and beyond in a long heavy crimson and gold court robe tied with a black and gold sash. A deep hood obscured the face completely.

The energy grid parted.

The pungent scent of warmed silk and heavy spice obscured the scent of his body, but Fallon could tell it was definitely a Skeldhi male.

He stepped onto the stage. In a calm smooth stride, he moved toward the center of the stage.

Oh . . . shit . . . She backed away, bared her long teeth and growled in warning.

He stopped in the center of the stage. He extended his arms forward and turned his left wrist up. A knife flashed.

The sea of whispers became a hushed sighing of expectation.

Blood spattered the smooth black floor. The perfume of warm copper richness filled her nose.

Fallon froze and her growl stopped cold. She *knew* that scent.

The figure tilted his head up and she saw copper eyes. Khan smiled and whispered. "Come."

Mindless with relief, Fallon lunged across the stage. *Thank the Maker, I was going freaking insane!* The overwhelming scent of his blood filled her head. Urgent raging hunger for the taste of his blood exploded within her. The sheer physical intensity was as terrifying as it was sudden. She stopped a pace away and trembled. She *needed* . . . A small whimper escaped. She needed . . . *him.*

Khan spread his other hand flat out and lowered it. "Down, get down."

Her eyes locked on the rivulet of crimson dripping from his wrist, she dropped to her knees and opened her mouth. *Want . . .*

Khan pressed his bleeding wrist to her mouth.

She grabbed him around the legs and sank her teeth into

his wrist around the cut. She swallowed a burning mouthful. Something around her heart unknotted. She moaned.

Khan gasped and staggered just a little. He caught the back of her ponytail with his other hand and turned her head toward the audience.

The audience released a collective sigh.

Fallon barely saw the people staring with rapt attention. She leaned her cheek against his thigh, sucking hard. She swallowed a second mouthful. Every drop of fear and tension disappeared. She slumped just a little against his legs.

Enough. Khan groaned and pulled his wrist away.

Fallon made a sound of protest, but she released him.

Khan grinned and lifted his wrist to his mouth to lick the wounds. *Any more and you'll be intoxicated.*

Fallon licked her lips for the last taste. *So?* Her gaze was drawn to the drops of scarlet on the shining floor.

Khan's eyes narrowed. *Don't you* dare *lick the floor.* He pulled his black chain collar and matching lead from his sash.

Fallon smiled and lifted her chin. *I'm not that* feral.

With you? One never knows. Khan unfastened the steel chain from around her throat and tucked it into his sash. *You continue to surprise me.* He snapped his black chain collar and its matching lead around her throat. His gaze slid to the people all around. *Shall we go?*

Fallon lunged up onto her feet and grabbed him in a sudden hug. *Thank you.*

Khan rocked back on his heels and set an arm around her, holding her close. *For what?*

Oh, I dunno . . . Fallon turned her face into the neck of his hood. *I'll think of something.*

Khan snorted and gently pushed her back. *Enough, let's get off this stage. I'm sweltering in this robe.*

Fallon followed Khan down the stairs at the back of the stage and stared at the design embroidered in heavy gold on the back of his robe. The design was the same one as his tattoo, only this time she could see what it was, a predatory raptor with a gold disk over its head. The wings were arched down as though soaring upward. *Where are we going? Where's Sobehk?*

Khan headed up the nearest aisle and the lift at the end. *You and I are going to the suite next to Sobehk's. I'm expecting a visit from a very upset young prince. Sobehk is waiting for us one level up.*

People stood to watch them pass, apparently trying to see Khan's carefully averted face.

Fallon focused on her feet as she followed him up the stairs rather than the people staring. *That reminds me, did you get them?*

The councilors? Khan's anger washed hot and heavy through the link. *No. One does not arrest an Ehnya'dhyt in public, never mind two. My men will take them in the halls quietly.*

Fallon stopped at Khan's side by a polished lift door. *Which one had the code?*

Khan hit the call button on the wall. *There was no way to tell with them standing that close together. I'll have to check them both personally as soon as they're collected.*

The lift door opened. *Ehnya'dhyt* Sehnby smiled from just within the lift doors. Against either side of the lift were two thoroughly human men in familiar uniforms, their bolt-rifles pointed directly at Khan's broad chest.

Fallon sucked in a sharp breath. *Moribund Company goons* . . . And neither she nor Khan had swords.

Ehnya'dhyt Sehnby dropped his chin. "Why don't you join me, *Ehnya'dhyt* Khansu?" His gaze focused on Fallon. "I wish to congratulate you on your new purchase."

Khan dropped her lead and lunged, snarling, into the lift, shoving the councilor against the back wall hard with his arm against the other man's throat.

Ehnya'dhyt Sehnby gasped as he stared at Khan. "You!" He grabbed hold of Khan's arms. "Impostor!" He snarled, snapping his long teeth in Khan's face.

Fallon lunged into the lift, snarling and lashing out at the guards with her booted feet.

Khan bared his teeth at Fallon. "Get the fuck away!"

Fallon felt the command slam through her collar. She jerked back out of the lift. "No!"

The door closed as the guards converged on Khan's struggling form.

"Khan!" She slammed her fist on the door. "Damn you!" She closed her eyes and reached, screaming through the collar's link. *Sobehk!*

Noise erupted around her.

Fallon turned to find armored guards and men in robes running at her. She didn't think, she dove under the seats and bolted on hands and knees. *Sobehk!*

An eternity of running under seats, dodging hands and hiding in shadows passed.

Isabeau! Sobehk's mental voice was furious and terrified, all at the same time. *Where are you?*

Sobehk? Fallon poked her head up from behind a seat. *Here!* She looked about. *I don't see you!*

I'm in front of one of the lifts. A trickle of relief threaded his voice.

Fallon's gaze was drawn to the glowing sapphire blue figure standing before a lift two doors away. His formal over-robe was gone, but it was Sobehk.

I'm coming! Lunging over the tops of seats, she dodged grabbing hands and shouting figures. She dove into the aisle and bolted to Sobehk's side, grabbing his robes with both hands.

Sobehk shoved her behind him and held up his hands. "I have her! It's all right! Was anyone hurt?"

The guards insisted that all she did was run. Even though she was supposed to be a dangerous Prime, no one was bitten or harmed in any way. Their mouths curved in derision. They were not impressed.

"You'd rather she'd lost control and attacked?" Sobehk bared his teeth at them. "Do you have any idea what she's capable of?"

The guards and a surprising number of the robed dignitaries backed up. Apparently more than a few had seen the ship's vid on the news broadcast. Apologies and compliments on her admirable control spilled from multiple throats.

Sobehk turned and hit the lift call button. "I'll get her back to her owner."

The guards and the rest of the crowd dispersed in a hurry.

The door opened. Fallon stood, releasing Sobehk's robes.

Sobehk pushed her into the lift. "Where's Khan?"

Khan . . . Fallon dropped to her knees as though struck. "They took him!" She turned and knotted her fingers into his robes. "They *took* him!" Sudden white-hot rage seared through her. She lunged back onto her feet, tugging on the front of his robes. "I have to get him back!"

"Isabeau!" Sobehk grabbed her upper arms, his blue eyes hot with anger. "*Who* took him?"

Fallon's lips curled back, and hate boiled in her snarling voice. "*Ehnya'dhyt* Sehnby and the Moribund Company."

"What?" Sobehk's face went slack. "*Ehnya'dhyt* Sehnby? Then it must have been him with the code to make you an assassin."

"Fuck that!" Fallon's claws dug into his robes. "I have to get Khan *back!*"

Sobehk shook his head. "Wait, this doesn't make any

sense! Why did they take *him,* and not you?"

"Because the arrogant idiot threw himself into the lift then ordered me out of it!" She released Sobehk so she could slam her foot against the lift wall. It made a very satisfactory bang. "I'm going to kick . . ." Bang! "His fucking . . ." Bang! "Ass!" Bang! "For doing something so *stupid!*" She kicked the wall twice, leaving a rather satisfying dent in the metal.

Sobehk paced. "I'll get his men on it."

"Good idea. You do that." Fallon paced the other way, thinking hard and fast. "You nail those fuckers to the wall while I go get him."

Sobehk jerked to a halt. "You *what?*"

Fallon stopped by the lift panel. "I couldn't get him before, because the lifts wouldn't open for me. I'm in one now. Now, I can go get him. I'll notify you as soon as I have him."

"Oh, Blood and Chaos, no you won't!" Sobehk's brows dipped and a growl rumbled. "You're not going anywhere without me!"

Fallon growled. "You are *not* getting hurt again trying to do something I can do better!"

The lift door opened behind Sobehk.

Sobehk snarled. "What the fuck can you do that I can't?"

Fallon lashed out and kicked him in the hip.

Sobehk flew backward out of the lift and landed on his back in a carpeted hallway. He gasped and sat up. "Isabeau!"

Fallon stuck her head out of the lift door. "If he's anywhere on this station, I can find him. You can't." She pulled her head back in and the door closed.

His fist thumped against the outside of the door. *Isabeau! Are you out of your mind?* Panic colored his thoughts.

Fallon moved to the lift panel. *Sobehk, I've been stealing people from the Moribund Company most of my life.* She pulled one of Khan's thin stiletto daggers from the seam of her boot. *I'll get him, but I need you to be ready to come get us once I get him out.*

Isabeau, this is insane! There was less panic in his mental voice and more anger.

No, it's not. Trust me. I know what I'm doing. She jammed the dagger into the panel's seam and peeled a corner of it back. *Go get his men and be ready to move fast. This won't take long.*

How much time do you need? His panic was definitely fading, and determination was replacing his temper burst with something much colder and far more vicious.

That depends on how far away he is. As soon as I have him, I'll contact you. She poked through the wires and microprocessors. The damned thing was in here somewhere; there was always one in a lift panel. *I have to concentrate. I'll contact you as soon as I know something.*

I'm going to beat you black and blue for this. He sighed. She could feel it.

Fallon smiled. *Absolutely.*

Annoyance mixed with a sharp burst of fear. *Don't you dare get killed!*

I am very good at not getting killed. There it was, down at the bottom in a smooth white coil.

Good. Pain slid across the link, sharp and hot, straight from the heart. *I love you.*

Fallon's smiled faded as her heart threatened to break. *I love you, too.* She had to take a deep breath to think around the knot of emotion he was generating. *But I can't think with you yapping in my head!*

His amusement washed through her, followed by terrific burst of cold hard fury. *I'll be waiting.* And then he was gone.

Her head came up. No . . . not gone completely. She

could touch him, but his thoughts were elsewhere. She nodded. It was time to make her call and get some work done.

Fallon pulled up the white communications coil and flipped the stiletto in her other palm. She unrolled a strand against the base of her wrist and stabbed the dagger through the fiber optic wire, direct linking to her biomechanics. She winced in pain then closed her eyes and accessed her personal communication's array.

"This is the Stationmaster . . . Hey, what channel are you on?" The voice was feminine and youthful.

Fallon licked her lips. "Is this Alice?"

"Yeah. Where did you get that name?"

Fallon released the burst of data Peter had given her a very long time ago.

"Peter has been fucking dead for the past century! Who the fuck do you think you are?"

Fallon released the second burst of data, the keys to her spectral code that would unlock the second message hidden in the first.

An electronic screech came over the line. "You bitch! You fucking virused me . . ."

"No, I didn't!" Fallon's fingers closed tight on the white wire crossing her palm. "I gave you the keys to the other code; the one inside the first!"

Silence.

The lift came to a sudden and jarring halt between floors.

Fallon grabbed onto the wall to keep from falling. The hair on the back of her neck lifted. She looked up at the four steel walls sealing her in. "Oh . . . shit." If this lift fell, there was absolutely no chance of survival. The station master would make sure of it.

More silence.

CHAPTER THIRTY-NINE

"Who the fuck are you?" The station master's feminine voice vibrated with anger, but she wasn't screaming.

Fallon's breath came out in a rush. She wasn't dead yet. "Alice, this is the Fallen Star from Never-land. And I have a major pirate problem."

"What's Peter's password?"

"First star on the right, and straight on 'til morning." Fallon had to close her eyes. Maker . . . she missed him.

"Oh, God . . . Did he . . . Did Peter give you . . . mine?"

"You're Alice. Your log-in is Wonderland. Password is . . ." Fallon had to take a deep breath. "Twinkle, twinkle, little bat; how I wonder what you're at."

"Oh, God . . ." Her voice shivered with nervous laughter. "He's alive. Peter's *alive*."

Fallon nodded, knowing that Alice could see it if she accessed the lift vid display. "I'm sorry to surprise you like this, but it's really important."

"What happened? I thought Peter, Never-land, was . . . destroyed?"

Fallon shivered with impatience, but she needed station master Alice's help if she was going to locate Khan. "Peter says he doesn't remember exactly what happened to shut him down. He was awakened about forty cycles ago, already hacked into and taken over by the Moribund Company."

"Moribund Company, huh? The salient ships are

bitching up a storm because that pack's been hacking and stealing ships."

Fallon frowned at the blank wall. "Salient ships? You mean the sentient ships?"

Alice snorted. "No. Most jump-capable ships are sentient to some degree. A salient ship is independently self-aware." A burst of static betrayed her irritation. "I don't believe the Moribund Company would hack stations, too! Oh, those . . . those . . . Assholes!" Another burst of static. "So why hasn't Peter contacted me?"

Fallon bit her lip. "He can't. The pirates have him blocked from directly contacting other stations or the sentient ships, and for a long time he had no idea who he was. Peter has been using the spectral code I gave you as an invisible firewall to hide behind for the past fifteen cycles while he pieced his memory back together. He found you and the others in a deeply hidden cache file. He doesn't know if the Moribund Company knows about the file, because he doesn't know what they hacked into when he was still offline." She swallowed. "Alice, you could be in danger."

Alice sighed. "Moribund Company has become something of a pest problem. God, I have to talk to Peter."

Fallon shook her head. "Dyson's Ring is monitored incoming and outgoing."

"Wait a minute, Peter is Dyson's Ring? I put data through there all the time. I thought it was a dead station, no sentience."

"It's Peter, but they'll never let you reach him. He's been trying for ages." Fallon nibbled on her bottom lip. "If you can find a way to incorporate the spectral code I gave you into your communications, you can contact Peter that way. It's completely invisible and undetectable to anyone who doesn't have the code keys."

"Who does have the codes keys?"

"Peter, me, probably one or two of Peter's lostlings . . ." Fallon looked up. "And one other person. He's on this station."

"On this station? Who?"

Fallon felt the anger and the hope rise around her heart, "His name is Khan, and the Moribund Company has him somewhere on this station. Alice, I need your help to find him!"

"Those sons of bitches . . . Shit, there are over eighty thousand bodies on this station. Do you have a way to identify him?"

Fallon grinned. "I have two, but they may have one of them blocked."

"Gimme what you got."

"One is the spectral coding. When it's active, it resonates with anyone else in possession of it. The other is my . . ." She winced. "My control collar."

"Your *control collar*? You're one of those . . . Skeldhi sex-slaves?"

Fallon hunched her shoulders then sighed. "Yes. I am. Khan is my . . . master, and I have to find him."

"Fallen Star, I have access to their coding. They don't know it, but I do. I can get that thing off you. You could let him go and you could be free. This is a big station; you could get lost in it really easy. I'll even help set up a new identity for you."

Fallon froze, shocked to the core. She could be free. She could be herself again. And alone again. She closed her eyes. She was tired of being alone.

"You could stay with me if you like. I could use the company, and you could help me get the word out to the rest of the stations about Moribund Company."

Fallon felt her heart slam in her chest. She could see

Peter again.

But she would never see Khan or Sobehk again. Pain stabbed sharply through her heart. "Alice, I'd like to. It sounds wonderful. But, I . . . can't."

"Yes, you can!"

"No, really, I can't. I . . ." Fallon closed her eyes. Maker, she was out of her mind! "Alice, I love him, and he loves me. I have to get him back."

"You . . . love him?" She sighed. "I understand. All right, we'll get you back your Khan. Where do we begin?"

Fallon looked up. "We begin by activating your code keys . . .

Alice released a burst of data. "Can you see him? Is he there?" Her voice sounded like any other excited kid with a brand-new toy.

Fallon frowned. "I think so." A very odd-looking figure sat on its haunches in the corner of the lift. It was round, had four legs that ended in tiny paw-like feet, a thick fluffy tail, small triangular ears at the very top of its very round head, and humongous slitted eyes of neon green, but it also had a smiling mouth that spread the full width of its head and it was striped — as though painted. It was obviously a fantasy figure rather than any kind of actual figure. "Is it a . . . feline?

"Yes!" She giggled. "Yes, he is!"

Fallon tilted her head from one side to the other. "Is he supposed to be that violet-purple color?"

"Yes! Yes, he is!" Alice laughed. "He's the Cheshire cat!"

Fallon's brows shot up. "Oh . . . okay." That was a cat? Alice apparently had quite an imagination, by way of felines.

"And you can see him?"

Fallon nodded. "Loud and clear. He's much too . . . bright to miss."

Alice giggled. "Good! Because I just sent him all over the station and no one can see him but you! Your spectral coding kicks ass!"

The Cheshire cat abruptly started bouncing up and down in circles, floating like a somewhat weighty balloon.

"I have a spy no one can see! Yes!" Alice released a very human whoop of joy.

The cat's head abruptly turned to face Fallon, disconcertingly separating from the bouncing cat's shoulders, and then the head started bouncing independently of the still turning and bouncing body.

Fallon's brows shot up. *Whoa . . . scary imagination.*

The lift started moving.

"Now that I've incorporated your coding, I think I know where your Khan is being kept."

Fallon's heart lurched. "You do? You found him?"

"Pretty sure. There are only two of you with that code, right?"

"Right."

"Then I found him. There's only one other spot that feels like you. I can get you through all the security doors, but it's still going to involve some climbing and crawling in places." She cleared her electronic throat. "I hope you don't mind the occasional . . . pipe?"

Fallon grinned. "I lived most of my life on an industrial station. Pipes are not going to be a problem."

"Good." Alice sighed. "Okay, all you have to do is follow the Cheshire cat. If you have a question, a smile is yes, and a frown is no."

Fallon's brows lifted. "A smile?"

The purple feline's mouth lifted into a huge, toothy, crescent grin. Abruptly the cat's mouth dropped into an equally huge frown.

Fallon blinked. There was no possible way that he could

have teeth in such an array of directions . . ."Oh . . . okay."
Definitely a cartoon figure.

The lift doors opened onto darkness.

"Okay, Fallen Star, on your way! I'm going to try to
reach Peter!"

Fallon looked directly at the Cheshire cat. "Thank you,
Alice."

The Cheshire cat stood up on his teeny purple back
paws, set a paw on his chest and bowed with a waggle of
his over-sized round head that made his ears flop and his
tongue loll.

"Thank *you*, Fallen Star."

Fallon smiled. "You can call me Isabeau; my name is Isabeau Fallon."

"Isabeau, how pretty! Now scoot! You've held up this
lift long enough. The repair crews are going nuts down
there."

The purple cat got up on his teeny back legs and proceeded to skip with rather high bounces into the dark,
glowing like a neon purple sign.

The pipe was big enough to walk upright in, though Sobehk would have had a hard time of it. It was also dark.
Fallon's night vision augmentations outlined everything in
bright green. Everything . . . except the purple cat. Her
spectral coding was reading the cat, not her eyesight, so
eye-popping purple he remained.

The Cheshire cat skipped over to the far right wall,
jumped up and shoved himself into a pipe opening that he
should *not* have been able to fit into. He squished, rather
like the balloon he strongly resembled and stuffed himself
in. He eased deeper, his striped tail flicking behind him.

Fallon grabbed the lip of the pipe and stuck her head in.
The purple glow was dead ahead. She eased her body into

the pipe then pulled herself forward, elbow over elbow.

She had followed the impossible purple cat through a number of dark, dusty hallways, fairly often relying on her night vision. There had been a bunch of ladders, more than a few unused and barely working lifts, and then the pipes, some big enough to walk in and some she had to crawl through. Unlike those back on Dyson's, none of the pipes had held water or other nasty liquids. They were dusty and not anything close to clean, but they appeared to have never been actually used.

Khan was going to explode when he saw the condition her leather suit had gotten into. She smiled. The thought was warming.

The Cheshire cat popped out of the far end of the narrow pipe with a hollow *fump*, very much like a balloon coming out of a tube.

Fallon eased her head out of the pipe. The steel plate floor was less than a foot below her. She looked up and blinked in astonishment. She was looking at the back end of a dull gray small cruiser. The Cheshire cat had brought her to a ship dock. Her eyes narrowed. If they had Khan on a ship, they were seriously stupid.

She stared at the flat black and ratty-looking Moribund Company courier craft and curled her lip. They were stupid.

Wrapped in a skin of sensor invisibility generated by her active spectral coding, she walked right through the blocky cruiser's alarm grid. Carefully, she crept around to the emergency access under the belly of the low-slung ship. The ship's sensors couldn't see her, but ordinary eyes saw her just fine.

She inserted a piece of wire 'borrowed' from the lift control into the wound on her wrist from talking to the station master and winced. She jammed the other end into the card-key panel. The wire cold-accessed her augmentation and allowed her programming to infiltrate and access the door's codes. The door opened in the semi-sentient ship without setting off the alarms.

Sucking on the wound in her wrist, she followed the bouncing purple cat down a passageway. She eased silently past the two guards yapping away in the ship's dining alcove then continued further into a door in the holding area.

Another rather painful cold access and the door slid open.

The room was small, gray and empty, except for a bar that stretched from the left wall to the right, and the scarred, unconscious man who gripped it with his arms spread as far apart as they would go, his knees buckled under him.

Khan.

He wore his leather pants and his boots, but nothing else. His robes were nowhere in sight. His creamy hair was still braided but matted with blood. Two nasty clotted bites gouged the shoulder on her right. His silver nipple rings gleamed bright against deep purple bruises all over his chest and stomach, but he was still in one piece.

That was the good news.

The bad news was that he was gripping the bar because the force-cuffs on his wrists were making him do it.

Fallon shook as she assessed what would have to be done to get him loose. She would have to hurt him. She didn't want to hurt him. Fallon fisted her hands. If he hadn't jumped into that damned lift in the first place . . . Anger washed the shakes from her hands.

She turned to the cat. "Is it possible to make some kind of distraction to get those two men out of this ship?"

The cat gave her a head-splitting grin, a nod, and a

jaunty wave. He spun in place and disappeared with a hollow pop.

"Was that . . . a purple . . . feline?"

Fallon turned sharply, her heart in her mouth. "Yes."

Khan's head was up and one eye was bruised closed. He groaned and got his feet under him. He pulled his head back behind the bar so he could stand. "Where's Sobehk?"

"Waiting for my call." She dug into the right side of her boot for his stiletto. "First, I have to get you out of here." She walked over to him and set her hands on the ball of his right shoulder, looking for the joint where his augmentations linked.

Khan snorted. "How? I'm wearing force-cuffs." He frowned. "How did you find me? And how did you get *in* here?"

"I break into ships, remember?" She located what she was looking for with her thumb. She turned to face him. "This is going to hurt. A lot."

He frowned. "What are you going to do?"

Fallon took a breath. "Did Sobehk ever tell you about the last time I got away from him?"

Khan frowned. "Yes."

"Did he tell you I was wearing force-cuffs at the time?"

His frown deepened. "Yes."

"Did he tell you I got one off?"

His brows lowered and his mouth tightened. "I thought he was exaggerating."

"He wasn't." Fallon snorted. "Can I assume that he told you what I did to do it?"

Khan winced. "Shit."

"I'll take that for a yes." Fallon raised the stiletto. "Khan, 'Syr, you can't make any noise."

Khan flinched back, but he wasn't going anywhere. "Isabeau, he bit me twice. He did that so the guards' beating

would hurt more. His venom is still active in my system."
He sucked in a breath. "I can't make any promises."

Fallon's hand tightened on the knife. "Khan, I have to
shut down your arm augmentations to free you." A fist
tightened around her heart. "There's no other way." She
looked away and had to blink to clear her eyes. "I'm sorry,
but it hurts, a lot."

"Do it. Do it fast."

Fallon nodded. "Fast. All right." She shook both her
hands to get her dexterity online. Her fingers tingled. She
set her hand on the ball of his shoulder and marked the
spot with her thumb. She set the point of the dagger where
she needed and jammed it in.

He gasped and threw his head back.

Fallon located the nerve bundle as fast as she could, feeling for the slight buzz of power. She stabbed deeper.

His arm dropped from the bar. Khan stared at his free
arm, his mouth opened as he panted. "Fuck . . ."

She pulled the dagger free.

Blood spilled.

She set her mouth on the wound and licked, hoping it
would slow the bleeding. With her free hand, she tugged
the cuff off and dropped it onto the deck. She turned to the
other shoulder, located and stabbed.

Khan jerked, choked and made a small, tight sound.

The sound nearly broke her. She bit down on her bottom
lip and tasted blood. She dug for the nerve.

"Oh . . . shit." Khan turned away, his eyes closed tight.
"Fuck, fuck, fuck . . ."

Fallon found it and stabbed into it.

His other arm dropped free and he fell back, landing
against the wall.

Fallon ducked under the bar and went to him. She
tugged the dagger free from his shoulder and set her

mouth on the bleeding wound. She tugged off the other cuff.

His hand came around to the back of her head, pressing her against him. He chuckled tiredly.

Fallon lifted her head and licked her lips. "What?"

He smiled sourly. "You were right. It hurt." His smile broadened. "A lot." He looked past her shoulder and nodded.

Fallon whirled around.

The Cheshire cat was back and he was bouncing, but he was not smiling.

Fallon wiped the dagger on her thigh. "I'm guessing it's time to go?"

The cat bounced higher and a grin appeared, but briefly.

Fallon jammed the dagger back into her boot and turned to Khan. "They're coming." She grabbed his limp arm and shook it hard.

Khan gasped, but his arm stiffened as it came online. "Son of a bitch!"

"Now, we have to go now." Fallon tugged him up onto his feet. "Let's go, let's go . . ."

Khan stumbled after her.

Fallon turned at the door. "I need you to activate your spectral coding to black pixie mode."

He blinked. "Huh?"

Fallon released a breath and rolled her eyes. "Just say 'black pixie.'"

His brows rose and he tilted his head. "Okay, black . . . pixie."

Fallon nodded. "Good, now you're invisible to their sensors." She grabbed his left hand. "Stay close!"

CHAPTER FORTY

The Cheshire cat moved out of the hold's door and to the right, making a great production of exaggerated sneaking with his front paws pressed back against the wall and his humongous round belly sticking out.

Khan smiled at Fallon, his fingers squeezing her shoulder.

Fallon led Khan through the ship and out the access door, closing it behind them. She darted across the dock, following the skipping purple cat.

The Cheshire cat froze in mid-skip. He floated, pretty much like a balloon, until he faced her, his expression clearly questioning.

Fallon's brows shot up. He probably wanted to know where she wanted to go next. She looked over at Khan.

Khan leaned back against a post and panted for breath.

Fallon winced with the pounding starting in her temples. He needed to be fed, which meant that he was more wounded than he seemed. There was no way he would be able to take the route she took to get here. She looked back at the cat. "Is there a parked glider anywhere nearby? A fast one?"

The cat gave her a head-splitting grin and started skipping away.

Fallon reached back and grabbed Khan's hand. "Come on!"

The battered glider was sitting against the wall under

the window of an office. Fallon frowned at it. That was the station master's idea of fast? Forget fast, she hoped it was in good enough condition to fly. She ducked down low and headed for it.

Khan followed, moving very stiffly, his mouth tight.

Up against the wall, Fallon eased over onto the glider's forward saddle, pulled out her piece of wire, jammed it into her wrist and set the end into the glider's ignition.

The turbines cranked and spun, the engines coming to life with a wild roar.

She looked at Khan and shouted over the maelstrom of wind and sound. "Get on! Get On!"

Khan threw his leg over the back saddle as the office door was flung open and an irate and large human came howling out.

"Shit!" Fallon kicked the glider into a flat, straight up lunge.

Khan shouted and grabbed onto her waist.

She stopped the glider's lunging rise only meters from the downward curving ceiling.

"Shit!" Khan gasped in her ear. "Don't get us killed!"

Fallon bared her teeth at him. "Shut up and let me drive!" She looked around. "Cheshire cat!"

The purple cat popped into being, lounging on her handlebars. It gave her a smile and a wave.

Fallon grinned at the cat then looked over at Khan. "Where do you want Sobehk to meet us?"

A klaxon went off somewhere in the dock.

The cat opened his mouth in clear worry and started pointing, clearly wanting them to pick a direction.

Fallon hissed. "Guess they figured out you're gone."

Khan grinned. "The Shinto gardens are close to the enclave; take us there."

Fallon nodded at the cat. "You heard him. I want the

shortest, fastest route out of here to the Shinto gardens."

The cat sprouted teeny-tiny wings and spun away.

Fallon set her feet on the pedals and gripped the glider's controls. She turned the glider sharply in midair and they were off.

The purple cat led them into a nearby shuttle tunnel marked with broad gold bands. A blazing grid of electricity marked the tunnel's far end.

Khan shouted in her ear. "We'll never get through the security grid!"

"Yes, we will!" She shouted back. "I have the keys to the kingdom!" They were upon the grid in two breaths. The grid dropped and they sped on.

"Mother Night! How did you do that?"

Fallon grinned and pushed the glider for more speed. "I have a guardian angel."

The cat swerved at breakneck speed into an upward tunnel painted with broad silver stripes, and then through another energy grid. Another swerve took them into a green-banded tunnel . . . and traffic.

Fallon's heart was in her mouth as she urged the glider up and over the two lanes of hovering traffic, bringing the small craft as close to the arched ceiling as she dared while following the purple cat.

They burst out of the tunnel and into station daylight over meters and meters of spreading forest.

Khan gasped and buried his face in her shoulder.

Fallon screamed for Sobehk with every ounce of mental volume she had.

Surprise and raw fury answered her. *Here!*

Fallon gasped in relief. *We're heading toward the Shinto gardens, but Khan doesn't have a robe, and it's full daylight!*

Shock and hope pulsed from Sobehk. *You have him?*

Fallon bared her teeth into the wind. *Of course I have him!* She felt a pulse in her collar. *Sobehk, that better be you!*

It is. Triumph and determination throbbed through the link. *I'm using the locater to find you.*

Something pinged against the glider's right wing, and then the left.

Fallon blinked. *What in fury . . .* She looked in her rear-view mirrors. Five flat black gliders were behind her, each carrying two riders in black uniforms. The passengers were pointing bolt-rifles. They needed cover, fast.

Alarm came from Sobehk. *Isabeau, what is it?*

We have five gliders on our tail. I don't think they're happy that I took Khan. Fallon glimpsed a path under the trees. She dove for it. The path was narrower than she had thought, and it had a lot of curves in it, but it was wide enough for the glider, and the shadows under the trees were a welcome coolness.

The Cheshire cat appeared just ahead.

The black gliders buzzed above the tree canopy.

Fallon smiled tightly. *Cowards.*

Worry pulsed from Sobehk. *Are they shooting at you?*

They were. Fallon urged the glider along the twisting paths the cat chose, dipping low to avoid branches. *I'm following a path under the trees; they're right over our heads.*

Keep heading the way you're headed. We're close. Anger and triumph shimmered from Sobehk. *When you come out stay low, very low.*

Fallon's brows shot up. *When we come out?*

Khan groaned. "Where's Sobehk?"

"He's on his way; he says he's close."

"Bloody Chaos, my back is on fire!" He hissed. "I'm sunburned all to Chaos and gone!"

Fallon snorted. "They bit you and beat you, and then I stabbed both your shoulders, and you're complaining about the sunburn?"

Khan snarled in her ear. "Just shut up and drive!"

Fallon grinned. Khan was in a pissy mood. *He must be*

feeling better.

Don't forget, stay low! Sobehk's sending throbbed with white-hot anger.

Fallon was too busy turning into a sharp and sudden curve to answer. The path opened wide, ending in brilliant and treeless sunlight. They burst out over a broad blue lake.

A lake echoing with the sound of roaring turbines from a dozen deep red gliders marked with black streaks roaring straight at her only two lengths higher.

Fallon dropped the glider as low as it would go. Water sprayed up from below, soaking them to the waist.

The red gliders roared directly over her head. *Mehdjay* officers in gleaming red armor wearing sculpted helmets with broad, dark sun-visors were mounted in pairs on the gliders. The passengers had bolt-rifles in their hands. Their white braids flew out behind them. They howled and engaged the black gliders at Fallon's back.

Rescue had arrived.

A red glider at the tail end with a lone rider swerved. He turned and dropped to fly at their side. *Get to shore.* Sobehk shoved the visor up on his helmet. *We need to get him under cove. His back is a mass of blisters.*

Fallon couldn't stop grinning. *Yes, 'Syr.*

Within the palatial suite's black and gold marble bedchamber, the silver-robed medic knelt among the gold sheets at Khan's side and smeared clear gel all over his back. His face was lined with maturity, but his blue eyes were bright with humor.

Khan hissed and gripped the black pillows. "Shit, shit, shit . . ."

The medic smiled briefly. "*Ehnya'dhyt* Khansu, I promise, the burning will pass within the hour."

Lounging in a black velvet chair he had pulled to the left side of the bed, Sobehk rolled his eyes and pressed his fingers to his temples. The blue and white sleeves of his robes spilled over the chair's arms.

Fallon, freshly showered and back in her red and black short robes, knelt at the edge of the bed on the deep black carpet at Sobehk's feet. The shower had done wonders for her body's aches, but not a damned thing for her splitting headache. Or her temper. Now that Khan was safely back, she was seriously pissed.

The medic finished spreading the gel and handed the white tube to his young assistant hovering at the foot of the bed.

The assistant bowed and slanted a quick glance at Fallon.

Fallon figured she was making the medic's assistant nervous with her scowling, but the throbbing in her head was making it really hard to give a shit.

The medic sighed. "*Ehnya'dhyt* Khansu, your sunburn will heal by tomorrow. However, your internal injuries will take more time. I suggest complete bed rest for two days before any exertions." His gaze flicked to Fallon. "Any exertions at all."

Khan groaned. "Great . . ." He sighed. "I thank you for your kind attention, *Sehnbay'syr*."

"It was my honor, *Ehnya'dhyt* Khansu." The regal medic rose from the enormous marble expanse of a bed, bowed, and left with his assistant at his heels carrying his medical kit.

Sobehk leaned back in the black velvet chair and tugged at his blue and white robes. "Oh, no sex for two days." He grinned. "I feel so bad for you."

Khan growled. "Pain in my ass."

Sobehk snorted. "You heard the master surgeon, not for

two days."

Khan groaned and thumped his fist among the pillows. "Pest."

Fallon narrowed her eyes at Khan. "I hope you get well soon so I can *kick your ass!*"

Khan lifted his head and glared at her. "What?"

Fallon bared her teeth at him. "What the fuck were you doing, throwing yourself into the lift like that? You stupid, egotistical *bastard!*"

Khan leaned up on his elbows, bared his teeth, and roared, "I did it to protect you!"

Fallon came up on her hands and knees. She was so pissed she replied with a feral feline scream before she could get the words out. "You could have *died!* Don't you *ever* do that again!"

Sobehk chuckled behind them. "Isabeau, you forgot the 'I'm better at fighting than you.'"

Isabeau growled. "I am better, I could have taken them!"

Khan growled. "What has that got to do with anything?"

Sobehk shook his head. "No, no, no, Khan. You're supposed to say, 'I'm the one that's supposed to protect you.'"

Khan curled his lip. "That's right, I *am* supposed to protect you!"

"What a load of crap!" Fallon snarled. "*I'm* better! *I* do the fighting!"

Khan's claws dug into the sheets. "I'm the master — you're the *rehkyt!* I'm responsible for *your* care!"

Sobehk grinned and nodded. "Now we're back on track!"

Khan shook his head. "What is this? A script?"

Sobehk smiled. "Something like that. You might as well memorize it. You're probably going to be using it a lot."

Fallon gripped the edge of the bed so she could get right up in Khan's face. "Hey! You, orange-eyed, white-haired, pain in my fucking ass! Listen to me when I'm bitching at you!"

Khan growled and focused on Fallon. "*Rehkyt . . .*"

"That's *upuaht rehkyt,* you arrogant bastard!" Fallon's head throbbed so viciously she could barely see through her watering eyes. "*I'm* the bodyguard! It's *my* responsibility to protect *your* skinny ass! So, fucking, there!"

Sobehk's brows shot up. "Uh oh, that's going to be a tough one to top, Khan."

Fallon abruptly dropped onto her belly. "Because I'm fucking right!" She closed her eyes to deal with the pain in her head and the ache in her heart. "I love you, and I could have lost you, you shit." Her breath hitched and she dropped her head. "Oh, bloody Fate . . . I almost lost you."

Khan's anger bled out of his expression and his growl disappeared. "You didn't lose me. You found me."

She gasped for breath and let the tears fall. "Fate . . . it hurts."

Sobehk shifted behind her. "Do you need to feed?"

Fallon shook her head as the tears slid down her cheeks. "No. He does." She whimpered softly. "My head is killing me."

Sobehk snorted. "Then get naked, get in the bed and feed him."

Fallon didn't bother to argue; her head hurt too much. She pulled off her robe, crawled over the edge and in among the sheets.

Khan shifted to one side and lifted an arm.

She rolled onto her back and scooted closer so he could sprawl partway on top of her. His skin was burning hot. His warm lips brushed her throat. She sighed.

Khan lifted up and smiled down at her. "I love you, too, you know." He brushed the hair from her cheek. "Thank you for rescuing me."

Fallon stuck out her bottom lip. "I shouldn't have *had* to rescue you."

Khan groaned and set his hot brow against hers. "Can we not be finished with this?"

Fallon winced. "Just bite me, damn you."

Khan set his mouth on her shoulder. His tongue swept her skin and then his long teeth pressed.

Fallon cradled his head and pressed into his teeth.

He bit, hard and deep.

Fallon gasped softly. The pain was fierce, but welcome.

He pulled his teeth free and his mouth covered the bite to suck at the wound. His hand moved up to cover her breast. His hand squeezed her breast with every swallow.

Fallon's headache receded and she moaned, clutching Khan to her. Heat coiled and tightened in her belly and moisture slicked her thighs.

Sobehk dropped his robes at the edge of the bed and slid in beside Fallon. His hand covered her hip then pushed her onto her side.

Khan moaned softly, rolling slightly onto his side. He did not stop drinking.

Sobehk pressed up behind Fallon. His cocks pressed rigidly hard and hot against her backside.

She moaned softly. "Oh shit, you're going to stick that big dick of yours up my ass."

Sobehk pressed a kiss to the back of her neck and slid his hand between her thighs to bend her knee, setting it on Khan's hip. "Yes, I am."

Demanding carnal hunger swamped Fallon, and it didn't matter that the larger cock was going up her ass, all that mattered was that she was about to be filled. She arched back toward him. His urgently hard primary cock pressed at the entrance of her anus. It was slick with gel. He must have greased it when she hadn't been watching.

"Open for me."

Fallon sucked in a breath and pushed. The broad cock-head spread her and invaded.

He groaned and his hand tightened on her hip. He surged deeper until his second cock reached the wet mouth of her cunt. He thrust and filled her.

Fallon moaned. His hot cocks filled her tight, right to the edge of pain, but he felt good. He felt right. She turned her head and Sobehk's mouth covered hers.

Sobehk's tongue swept against hers in a slow, drugging kiss, gently tasting and exploring. He slid out of her, and then rocked into her, out then in, in a slow, easy, comforting tempo.

Fallon moved against him in a gentle counter-rhythm that matched his kiss.

Sobehk's hand slid down her thigh, then between her body and Khan's to claim her clit. His fingers made leisurely inciting circles as his cocks filled and retreated, building a rich, decadent pleasure that mounted into a thick molten wave of increasing passion.

The soft sounds and musky perfume of shared pleasure rose from their bodies.

The base of Sobehk's cocks hardened and expanded, filling her and locking her tight. Tension and urgency crested. She moaned her need.

Khan's clawed fingers dug into her breast, drawing blood.

Fallon's breath stopped. Release took her in a hot wave of pleasure. She gasped into Sobehk's mouth.

A purr rumbled from Khan's throat.

Fallon's purr of contentment threaded with his.

Sobehk released her mouth to settle in closer. His lips brushed her throat and his hand rose to cover Khan's on her breast. His purr was so soft Fallon almost didn't hear it. "My two hearts," he whispered.

My two loves . . . She smiled and let sleep take her.

CHAPTER FORTY-ONE

"Khan, are you out of your mind?" Sobehk paced the broad arched black marble hallway, blocking Khan from going toward the suite's main doors. "We still don't know who has the other half of the damned code!" His blue and white robes whispered with his agitated strides. "You *cannot* let that boy in here!"

"We know that he is the target, so it's highly unlikely that he has it." Khan folded his arms. The black circlet around his brow and the black and gold thread of his long court robes gleamed under the hallway lights. He raised his brow. "Let me pass, *Dhe'syah*. He needs to know who has been trying to murder him."

Fallon leaned against the bedchamber's closed door. They had dressed her in Khan's signature black, scarlet, and gold, but this time she was in floor-length robes over pleated black trousers. Both of Khan's black-sheathed blades were in her red sash. It was the uniform of the court-level *upuaht*, the bodyguard *rehkyt* to a prince.

Sobehk groaned and moved to the side. "Don't get yourself killed."

Khan smiled. "Isabeau will keep that from happening." He moved toward the center of the broad formal hallway.

Fallon grinned, showing teeth. "I'll keep him in one piece, whether he likes it or not." She rolled away from the door and took her place one step behind Khan's right shoulder.

Khan nodded to the pair of scarlet armored, bolt-rifle

bearing *mehdja'dhyt*. The double doors opened.

The youthful councilor prince strode into the black hall, chin down and shoulders back. The lights gleamed on the rainbow-hued circlet on his brow. His pale gold hair flowed over the shoulders of his darker gold robes. He was clearly not pleased.

Ehnya'dhyt Dhuet, in his customary black and scarlet, shadowed his heels with a slight smile on his lips.

Khan glanced at Fallon. *Neither one has the code.*

Fallon released a soft breath. That was nice to know.

The young prince bowed gracefully. "*Ehnya'dhyt*, Prince Khansu."

Khan delivered a bow of equal grace to the young prince. "*Ehnya'dhyt*, Prince Aden." He turned and delivered another bow. "*Ehnya'dhyt* Dhuet. Welcome to my hall."

Prince Aden clasped his hands behind him and frowned up at Khan, apparently puzzled by something. "Prince Khansu, I would like to . . . speak with you, concerning a private matter?" His gaze flicked to Fallon.

"How fortunate, as I have much to discuss with you, Prince Aden." Khan turned to the left and held his hand out. "Councilors, if you would be so kind as to join me in my private chambers."

Khan's hospitality chamber was not particularly large — his dining room was much bigger — but it wasn't small by any means. The walls were pale gold with dark gold carpeting. A massive scarlet and gold carpet spread under the black glass table, framed by four tall black velvet chairs. A gold kaffa service occupied the center of the low glass table.

Compared to the opulence of the rest of the suite, the hospitality chamber was austere. Except that the chamber's back wall was commanded by an impressively broad window on space that held a gorgeous view of the local rainbow-hued nebula.

Fallon sighed as she stood behind Khan's wing-backed velvet chair. Of course he had to sit directly in front of the window, so she had to stand with her back to the loveliest view space had to offer.

The prince stared hungrily at the window's view from the facing chair on the left, but *Ehnya'dhyt* Dhuet, occupying the facing chair on the right, had no difficulty keeping eye contact with Khan.

Then Khan began to speak. He told them what he had learned of who was trying to murder the prince, and how, and some of what they had done to uncover and prevent it from happening.

The prince focused on Khan. "I knew it! I thought I recognized you!"

Khan nodded. "I'm impressed. It's very common for most to discount and ignore the lower-ranked."

The prince's mouth tightened. "I've had too many loyal servants save my life time and again. I would not discount the lower-ranked." He looked at Fallon and sighed. "So she was your *rehkyt* all along?"

Khan shrugged. "I am sorry for the deception, but it was the only way to discover who had programmed her to be a sleeper assassin."

The prince looked down. "I have ... suspected *Ehnya'dhyt* Sehnby on more than one occasion, but there was never any proof."

"I have suspected him for quite some time, which is, of course, why I shadowed him." *Ehnya'dhyt* Dhuet drew in a breath and released it. "I had originally come to ask why Sehnby had been taken into custody, but I find that I am quite pleased that you have done so."

Fallon stilled. She'd had no idea that Sehnby had been caught.

Khan glanced at Fallon. *He was collected only a few hours ago trying to leave the station. A certain purple feline made an appearance in my office and the necessary information suddenly appeared on my computational unit.* He frowned. *You never did tell me where that creature came from.*

Fallon smiled. *The Cheshire cat belongs to Alice, the station master. She hates the Moribund Company as much as I do.*

The station master? Khan stilled. *Of Port Destiny?*

The prince's violet eyes narrowed. "So, that code, the other half that makes Isabeau a sleeper assassin, is still missing?"

Khan nodded. "Yes, this is why I wished to speak with you. Sehnby did not have it on him or among his possessions. Would you happen to know who Sehnby was associating with? Someone he might not normally associate with?"

Ehnya'dhyt Dhuet leaned forward. "I believe I can be of help in this instance. There was a certain *sehn'dhyt*, a lower level medic, with whom he seemed to have an odd amount of contact."

The prince sat up straight. "That's right! I remember seeing this medic talking to Sehnby, right before the auction."

Khan frowned. "Do you have a name?"

Ehnya'dhyt Dhuet tilted his head. "I think it was something like . . . Mor?"

Fallon stilled then felt heat spark at the back of her skull. A memory came into in sharp focus; the memory of a data jack being removed from the back of her skull as she waked, dry-mouthed and groggy, right before she'd gone to see Sobehk.

No wonder she hadn't felt the delivery of the first half of the code. It hadn't happened until she was on the ship and the assassin was already dead. Mohr hadn't been anywhere near her until then.

Khan sighed. "I think I know where he can be found."

Fallon clenched her jaw. *The* Vortex. *Tah will know where he is.*

Khan glanced back at her. *Exactly.*

Prince Aden's violet gaze focused on Fallon. "I think it would be best to . . . retire him from duty. Permanently."

Khan folded his hands together within his flowing sleeves. "I think, my prince, you may be correct. The queen has a rather strict policy about those who choose to work with the Moribund Company."

The prince stared at Khan, his mouth open. "What?"

Ehnya'dhyt Dhuet leaned forward. "Moribund Company? Are you certain?"

Khan glanced away. "Sehnby . . . detained me within one of their ships until Isabeau found me and released me in a very daring rescue."

"A rescue . . ." The prince sat forward in his chair, staring hungrily at Fallon. "I envy you, Prince Khansu. I truly do. Your *rehkyt* is truly an impressive creature."

"Isabeau has many, many hidden talents, Prince Aden." Khan glanced at Fallon and smiled. "I am very pleased to have her."

Fallon felt embarrassed heat creeping into her cheeks. She pleased him . . .

Khan looked over at *Ehnya'dhyt* Dhuet. "My detainment on that ship should be sufficient evidence of Sehnby's . . . unsavory collaboration."

Prince Aden frowned. "Then Sehnby . . ."

Khan lowered his chin. "Yes, my prince. Sehnby engaged the Moribund Company's services to kill you."

Prince Aden lunged up from his chair, his hands clenched into fists. "I want him. I want to kill him myself." His growl rumbled low.

Khan lifted his chin, rose from his chair and glanced

away. "Then I must apologize because he is already on his way to the bowels."

The prince abruptly dropped his gaze and his growl disappeared. "Oh."

Ehnya'dhyt Dhuet rose from his chair and moved to the young prince's side. "If you like, I can bring up the files on the bowels and you can see for yourself exactly how much he will suffer?"

Prince Aden's head came up and he smiled. "Thank you, I think I'd like that."

Fallon's stomach clenched. *Bloodthirsty little thing, isn't he?*

He takes after his father. Khan sighed and smiled. *A very good friend of my father's.*

Fallon carefully blanked her thoughts. She really, really didn't want to know.

After a small amount of polite discourse, the two councilors left Khan's hospitality chamber and headed for the suite's main doors.

Prince Aden stopped in mid-step and turned around to face Khan. "Prince Khansu?"

Khan's brows shot up. "Prince Aden?"

"If . . ." Aden's gaze flicked to Fallon standing behind Khan's right shoulder. "If you should ever decide to . . . sell your rehkyt . . ."

Khan smiled. "You will be the first to be notified. I swear it on my honor."

Fallon pursed her lips. *Gee, thanks.*

Khan continued to smile. *You're welcome.*

Prince Aden grinned then turned on his heel and walked over to *Ehnya'dhyt* Dhuet. "Ha! I told you I'd get him to promise!" He stuck out his hand. "Pay up."

Ehnya'dhyt Dhuet rolled his eyes. "Can we continue this discussion *outside* Prince Khansu's suite?"

Prince Aden sighed impatiently. "You're just a sore

loser."

The guards opened the main doors.

Ehnya'dhyt Dhuet followed the prince out. "No, my prince, I am a polite loser."

Sobehk parked Khan's sleek black sportster shuttle alongside one of the heavily armored *Mehdjay* transports. He powered down the engines and the craft settled gently on the steel deck of the shadowed dock.

Directly across from them, the *Vortex* sat among its spill of landing lights. Four other intelligence transports and the full company of scarlet armored *mehdja'dhyt* intelligence officers were arrayed all around the grounded ship.

Alice, the station master, was more than pleased to help them arrest a member of the Moribund Company by locking the *Vortex's* release codes.

Vibrating with tension, Fallon popped the right back door and climbed out of the sportster.

Her soft-heeled over-the-knee boots didn't make a sound on the steel deck plates. She closed the door behind her and rolled her shoulders. Her black braid slipped over her shoulder and tumbled over her breast. The supple, gleaming leather suit was an incredibly perfect fit but a nightmare of engineering to get into. Khan had taken great delight in fastening the purely demonic number of crisscrossing straps and buckles that locked her into the suit from wrist to heel to throat.

Sobehk left the driver's seat and came around the front of the sportster. His overlapping black *Mahfeht* enforcer armor gleamed with midnight rainbow hues under the dock's uncertain lighting. Silver gleamed on the pommels of knives that had been tucked into sheaths down his arms and across his chest.

Khan stepped out of the front passenger seat in his scarlet and black *Mehdjay* robes of office. Beneath it he was as armored as Sobehk.

All three of them wore a pair of swords tucked in their scarlet sashes.

Fallon stared at the ship. A buzz of white lightning danced fiercely at the back of her mind. She knew what it was. She remembered it from before. But she had questions that needed answers before she could set it free.

Khan looked over at Fallon. "Isabeau, are you all right?"

Fallon averted her gaze. "I'm fine."

Khan stepped forward and headed for the ship. Sobehk fell into step at his left shoulder and Fallon fell into step at his right.

The *Vortex's Mahfeht* captain, in full black enforcer armor, stood waiting at the bottom of the ship's exit ramp, with *Sehnbay'syr* Tah in his customary silver robes on the captain's left and the ship's *Mahfeht* first officer on the right.

Khan stopped two sword-lengths from them and bowed. "Respected Captain." He nodded at the first officer and then *Sehnbay'syr* Tah. "My apologies for this inconvenience, but would you be so kind as to bring out *Sehn'dhyt A'syr* Mohr?"

Master surgeon Tah stiffened and looked over at the captain.

The captain shrugged and nodded.

Tah turned on his heel and went up the ramp and into the ship.

The captain frowned. "*Mehdjay'syr* Khan, if I may ask, what's going on?"

Khan smiled. "An inquest, Captain."

The captain's frown deepened. "You're arresting *A'syr* Mohr?"

"Arresting me?" *A'syr* Mohr appeared at the top of the ship's entrance ramp in full enforcer armor. His long pale hair had been pulled back into a snug braid. A pair of red-sheathed swords was tucked into his pale gray sash. He crossed his arms and his jaw clenched. "On what grounds, Lord Inquisitor?"

Khan lowered his chin but smiled. "You mistake me, *A'syr* Mohr. I have a question for you."

A'syr Mohr's brows lifted. "A question?"

"Yes." Khan's smile broadened. "Just one." He held out his hand. "If you would join us, I will ask, and then the *Vortex* will be free to leave."

A'syr Mohr relaxed his stance and unfolded his arms. He glanced at the scarlet armored guards all around then looked down at his captain and first officer.

The captain rolled his eyes. "Mohr, we've got a schedule to keep. Just get down here, answer his damned question, and let's go!"

A'syr Mohr scowled and came down the ramp, his boot heels thumping. He came around to stand next to the first officer, bowed, then squared his shoulders and pasted a smile on his lips though his eyes were narrowed and his jaw clenched. "I present myself for your question, *Mehdjay'syr.*"

Khan lifted his hand, glanced at the black band on his wrist. *He has the code. Be ready.*

Fallon drew in a soft breath and deliberately relaxed her muscles. She was ready. She was so very ready.

Khan dropped his hand and smiled. "Thank you, *A'syr* Mohr. You have answered my question." He smiled. "*A'syr* Mohr, you are under arrest for collaboration with the Moribund Company."

The captain jerked hard and the first officer gasped.

The guards from around the ship came running and

over a dozen live-steel blades were drawn from their scarlet sheaths.

A'syr Mohr's mouth opened in shock. "No!" He pulled his swords free lightning-fast and lunged straight for Khan.

Fallon lunged to intercept, diving under Mohr's blades, with both her blades out. She caught them on hers and held them.

Khan reached for her. "Isabeau!"

Sobehk grabbed Khan by the shoulder, pulling him back. "No! Let her go!"

Khan fell back with Sobehk.

Fallon's world closed down to herself, the blades of live-steel she'd engaged, and the man who had the answers to her questions. Rage seared the back of her mind, but she wasn't about to set it loose. Not yet, anyway.

She bared her teeth at Mohr. "Hi, there, remember me?"

CHAPTER FORTY-TWO

"Feral!" Mohr snarled, and the sour stink of ripe fear washed from his body.

"So you *do* remember me." Fallon grinned with her long teeth. "Care to answer a few of my questions, Mohr?"

He twisted to disengage his blades and stabbed in attack. "That's *A'syr* Mohr to you, *rehkyt!*"

Fallon turned his blades, avoiding him with disgusting ease. He obviously knew his weapons better, but he wasn't anywhere near as fast or as flexible as she was. She caught and trapped his blades again. "That's *upuaht rehkyt*, or haven't you been paying attention?"

"Bitch!" His blade danced down her blade and he slashed with the other.

She blocked, shifted around him and twisted her blades around his, trapped his blades again. She smiled. "I can be." She slid up his blades and nicked the bottom of his chin. "Who picked me to play assassin?"

He jerked back two steps, the back of his hand automatically wiping at his chin. It came back scarlet. His eyes widened. "You know?"

Fallon rolled her eyes. "Of course I know, you idiot, I'm a programmer. I know what's in my own head." She raised her brow. "Or did they leave that bit out?"

Mohr snarled and lunged, slashing. "You're no programmer."

Fallon blocked and closed, trapping his blades very close to his face. She grinned from a kiss away. "Wrong."

413

She whirled, dropped, and side-kicked him hard where his kidneys should be.

He gasped and was knocked two steps sideways.

Fallon lifted her blades and dropped her chin. "Ever hear of the Fallen Star?"

Mohr pressed a hand to his side, winced, and moved another step away. "Fallen Star, the ship-breaker, is a myth."

"Is that so?" Fallon smiled grimly. She'd bruised something. "Guess who found and then broke 'Syr Khan out of that Moribund Company ship?"

He stiffened, his eyes widening. "You?"

Fallon nodded hugely. "Yep. Me." She raised her swords and took a step toward him. "Who picked me to play assassin, Mohr?"

Mohr backed up a step and raised his swords. His eyes narrowed. "I don't know. I was told to watch for you by name."

Fallon inched closer. "How did you get my name?"

Mohr held his ground, swords up and plainly ready. "The cyborg gave it to me."

Fallon froze. "What?"

Mohr lunged into a slashing attack.

Fallon whirled under his blades and slammed a hard side kick into his stomach. "How? What did he say?"

Mohr gasped and fell back three steps. "The cyborg said it was waiting for you." He lunged at her, launching into a flurry of spinning kicks and slashes.

Fallon dropped under him then came up, diverting one blade and then the other. "Who sent him?" She slipped behind him and slashed the back of one knee joint. Blood threaded down the calf of his armor.

He gasped and staggered, but turned to face her, staying upright through his leg was clearly not working properly. "Who sent who?"

Fallon frowned. She nicked him in one the tendons. She'd been aiming for both. "Who sent Tusk? Who set him up to die?"

Mohr lifted his blades and stalked closer, favoring his nicked leg. "I have no idea who picked him, I was just told to watch for him."

Fallon's eyes narrowed and a smile curved her lips. This was what she was waiting to hear. She stayed where she was. She didn't even raise her blades. "Who told you to watch for him?"

Mohr stopped and frowned. "My contact."

Fallon eased one foot back and tensed to spring. "Name, please?"

Mohr's frown deepened. "Rudi"

Fallon smiled broadly. "Thank you." She let the banked rage take her in a white-hot rush. She lunged . . . and was swallowed by a white rushing storm.

The world slowed to a dreaming crawl. Mohr seemed to stand perfectly still, his blades up but frozen.

Fallon moved in on him, riding a burning white wave. Her blade slid across the back of one knee then she turned and took the back of the other.

He slumped slowly, achingly slowly. His chin lifted and his eyes went wide. It looked like an invitation.

Fallon had all the time in the world to simply reach out and caress his throat with first one blade then the other.

Pearls of bright scarlet spilled and flew outward in an elegant and slow arc all the way around his neck.

She turned away from the floating pearls, coming up on her toes, and she gently spun all the way around, and around, until the world just . . . slipped . . . away.

Someone was screaming very, very far away.

Fallon shifted sleepily. Her cheek was jammed against somebody's armored chest. She took a deep breath. Warm silk, sweat, rich musk . . . She sighed. Khan. She shifted and discovered that she was curled up tight and pinned against him. It was not a comfortable position to be in. His armor was pointy under all that silk. She groaned.

Her chin was lifted. "Isabeau?"

Fallon opened her eyes.

Khan's eyes were wide and his mouth tight. He abruptly relaxed and smiled. "It's passed. She's out of it."

"Damn. That was fast." Sobehk sounded relieved.

Fallon looked around and frowned. She was curled up on Khan's lap in the front passenger seat of the sportster. No wonder she was so cramped. Between his armor and the length of her folded legs, there wasn't a whole lot of room. She turned her head. Lights passed as the shuttle sped through a tunnel marked by broad gold bands.

Sobehk's hands held the steering wheel easily as he drove. He glanced at her briefly and smiled. "Hey, kitten, welcome back."

"Isabeau?" Khan encouraged her to turn back and look at him. "How do you feel?"

Fallon shifted. "Your armor is all hard and pointy."

Sobehk laughed. "She'll be just fine."

Fallon pushed to sit up so she could straighten her legs. "So, what happened?"

Khan shifted her so she could sit facing front, but he seemed disinclined to let her off his lap. "You killed Mohr."

Fallon frowned. The memory was fuzzy and very dream-like. "I think I remember doing it."

Sobehk snorted. "Oh, you definitely did it. You separated his head from his shoulders."

Fallon's mouth fell open. "I did not!"

Khan winced. "Yes, you very much did." He raised a

hand to his temples. "In fact, it made quite an indelible impression on my entire company of officers."

Sobehk snorted. "I seriously doubt you'll ever have another discipline problem in that company again."

Khan rolled his eyes. "At the very least."

Fallon frowned. "But I don't remember doing that at all."

Sobehk pursed his lips. "Probably because you were too deep in *rahyt* to remember."

Fallon did not like the sound of that. "Did I do anything else?"

Sobehk smiled. "Nope. Once you had a couple of swallows, you passed out and we left." He lifted his wrist, showing a deep bite and a livid bruise that had already faded to yellow and orange.

Fallon licked her lips. She could almost still taste him there.

"Out of curiosity, why the interrogation?" Sobehk frowned. "You already knew who set you up. I remember you saying his name, right before the cyborg's attack."

"I wanted to be absolutely sure." Fallon looked away. "Alice, the station master, has been in contact with Peter." She flinched. Peter wanted her back, but she didn't want to *go* back. "She'll get word to Peter, and Peter can . . . remove the problem."

Khan caught her chin and turned her to face him. "Why is this Rudi's removal so important?"

Fallon crossed her arms. "Tusk was my friend, and Peter's."

"Your friend?" Sobehk's brows shot up. "That insane cyborg that tried to kill you?"

"He wasn't always like that." Fallon stared out the window. "When I was little, Tusk was one of Peter's lostlings." The pain was old. She had lost her friend a very long time ago, but it still hurt. "His augmentations soured and it . . . did things to his mind. Peter had to . . . remove his memories of . . . Never-land, because he was too dangerous." Her fingers tightened on her arms. "And I had to help him do it."

Sobehk hissed. "Shit . . ."

Khan stroked her arm and her hair.

"Tusk was the one who opened the door when I first came to Never-land." Her heart clenched and it became hard to take a breath around the pain. "And I . . . killed him." She leaned against Khan's chest and closed her eyes.

Sobehk grimaced. "I'm sorry."

Khan swept his palm across her wet cheeks. "I'm sure your Peter will find a fitting end to this Rudi."

"Oh, I'm sure he will." Fallon sniffed and smiled tightly. "Peter is very handy with lift shafts."

They were in the lift rising from the parking deck when the headache hit Fallon right through the temples. She staggered and fell back against the lift wall panting. "Shit . . . My head . . ."

Khan sighed. "It would hit *now*."

Sobehk leaned over and scooped Fallon into his arms. "I'll take care of it as soon as we get in."

Fallon took a deep breath and smelled the rich aroma of Sobehk's skin. Her nipples tightened to hot urgent points under her suit. Her belly clenched violently, hot, wet, and hungry. She moaned and clutched at Sobehk's armor. It was seriously pointy against her side, but at that moment she didn't care.

Sobehk took a deep breath. "Oh yeah, there she goes." He smiled. "Rage fever."

Khan crossed his arms and stuck out his bottom lip. "Damn that medic."

Sobehk snorted. "You can have sex tomorrow."

Khan rolled his eyes and sneered. "Oh, that makes me feel so much better!"

The lift doors opened into the small side hall of Khan's monstrous suite.

Khan stepped out. "I'll file the reports and join you . . ."

"No . . . please." Fallon looked over at Khan, wincing under the throbbing in her head and desperate with a deep aching hunger. "I . . . need you."

Sobehk's brows shot up.

Khan sighed. "Screw the medic. Come on." He strode down the wide hall and headed for the bedchamber, jerking at his robes.

Sobehk followed grinning broadly. "You have internal injuries! That means I get to do the driving!"

Khan tossed an annoyed look over his shoulder. "Fine then, you drive."

Sobehk set Fallon onto the bed then turned and made haste to remove his armor.

Fallon grabbed for her crotch with both hands, but it only made the hunger worse.

Khan and Sobehk were out of their armor faster than Fallon had thought possible. Of course it was scattered all over the room when they'd finished removing all the pieces.

Mouthwateringly naked, the two of them climbed in among the gold silk blankets and scarlet pillows and attacked the buckles on her suit.

Sobehk glared at Khan. "Did you design this?"

Khan snorted. "Just keep unbuckling."

Fallon writhed under their hands. Heat coiled, clenched and tightened with demanding hunger. "Hurry! Please!"

Her boots and then finally the suit were tossed out of the bed and onto the floor.

Fallon reached up to grab Khan around the neck and pulled him down to kiss him. His moan tasted delicious. She raised her knees then wrapped her legs around his hips. She needed him in her body with violent urgency.

His knees spread under her, tipping her hips up to receive him. His primary cock nudged for entry.

Fallon released his mouth to gasp and arch. The bar piercing him was a delicious intrusion. His secondary cock pressed.

Khan gasped. "Sobehk."

Sobehk knelt behind him. "I'm right here."

Khan tilted his head to the side. "Deep and hard."

Sobehk closed his arms around Khan's chest, arms crossed, his hands splayed open over the black rings piercing Khan's nipples. Sobehk's mouth opened, revealing his long teeth. He sank them into Khan's shoulder and growled.

Khan's head came up and his eyes closed, his mouth open on a gasp. "Ah . . . yes!" He thrust and surged hard into Fallon's ass and cunt, raking her tender walls with the bars that pierced him.

Fallon bucked and cried out with the brutal pleasure of his possession.

Sobehk lifted Khan, and Fallon with him, Khan's knees spread over his thighs. He pulled his fangs from Khan's shoulder.

Khan fell forward over Fallon.

She arched up to take his mouth in an urgent and possessive kiss, her hips undulating under him, squeezing his hips with her thighs to fuck him.

Khan held still, balanced on his palms, letting her surge and retreat on his cocks. He moaned into her mouth.

Sobehk chuckled. "Somebody's hungry."

Khan rocked forward and shuddered. He pulled his

mouth away from hers and groaned then winced. "Fuck . . . you're big."

"Ah . . ." Sobehk's eyes closed and his head tilted back, his mouth open. "No, you're . . . tight!" He licked his lips and sighed. "Oh, it is so nice to be in here."

Khan groaned. "I'm glad you're enjoying yourself."

Sobehk grinned. "And you're not?" His hand closed on Khan's thighs. "Remember, I'm driving."

Khan growled. "Then drive, damn it! I have a nice tight cunt and ass here that needs attention."

Sobehk thrust.

Khan gasped and was driven forward into Fallon.

Fallon felt Khan's pierced cock strike something deep and delicious within her. She writhed to get more of it but couldn't quite reach it. "More!"

Sobehk smiled. "More?"

Khan turned his head and bared his teeth. "You heard her, more!"

Sobehk's claws dug into Khan's thighs. He thrust harder.

Fallon felt the echoing strike and bucked hard in reply.

Khan groaned. "Quit teasing and fuck, damn you!"

Sobehk growled. "I don't want to hurt you."

Khan choked out a laugh. "I like pain, remember?"

"You have injuries, remember?"

Khan sighed. "If it hurts that way I'll stop."

"You better."

"Open your damned link up and you'll know!"

Sensation bloomed within Fallon's mind. She could feel the delicious wet strength of her body holding Khan's, the tightness of Khan around Sobehk's cock, and the aching bliss of Sobehk within Khan's body. And she could feel her urgent, hungry need insinuating itself into their minds, stirring them with her violent appetite.

Sobehk growled and thrust, driving Khan forward into Fallon's wet, snug heat.

Aching, violent pleasure spilled across all three.

Sobehk gasped. "Oh . . . shit." And then he proceeded to fuck, hard and fast. Driven by her feral urgency, thought fled before the ravenous hunger of the body.

Moans and soft cries were punctuated by the sound of damp sweating flesh striking flesh. The rich, musky perfume of sweat and lust washed over them and intoxicated them. Echoes of dark, pain-edged pleasure washed in tides through their minds, stirring their passions to a maddening and mindless miasma of screaming urgency.

Sobehk's mouth opened on Khan's shoulder, and he sank his teeth in. The ripping pain of the bite seared through all of them.

Khan's shout threaded with Fallon's cry.

Climax surged with horrific speed and crested, the pressure mounting with murderous intent.

Sobehk's tongue swept across the burning wounds on Khan's shoulder. He moved his mouth closer to Khan's throat and sank his teeth in again.

Their breath stopped.

Release exploded, washing over them and drowning them in a hot wet tidal wave of violent and dark-edged pleasure.

They screamed.

CHAPTER FORTY-THREE

In the heart of Port Destiny Station's glittering night, the deep shadows of Khan's garden were fragrant with night-blooming flowers. Thousands of tiny lights glittered among the branches of every tree and bush, echoing the millions of lights that winked all around like stars.

Under three spreading oaks, Sobehk, his robes a pristine and opalescent white, knelt in the grass at Khan's feet, his head bowed.

Khan, arrayed in his formal court robes, set his hands on the kneeling man's shoulders.

Fallon stood at Khan's right shoulder in the long black and scarlet robes of her office as *upuaht rehkyt*, devoted bodyguard and body-slave to a prince. In her hands she held the meter-long, curved and deadly Moon Blade, the *dhe'syah*, the two-handed weapon of a prince's truest companion.

Behind Sobehk, *Ehnya'dhyt* Prince Aden and *Ehnya'dhyt* Dhuet stood as official witnesses to the small private ceremony.

A question was presented, Khan's voice solemn and etched with pain as he spoke the archaic words.

Tears were shed as Sobehk uttered the declaration of recognition.

Khan pressed a small blade to his wrist. Scarlet spilled. He offered his wounded wrist to Sobehk.

Sobehk pressed his lips to the cut then bit.

Khan gasped, his fingers clutching Sobehk's shoulder.

Sobehk swallowed once and pulled his mouth away. He delivered the traditional vow of service in a voice that trembled then broke.

Khan bid Sobehk to rise in a voice tight with emotion.

Sobehk came up on his feet, his head rising well above Khan's.

Fallon could barely see through her tears.

Khan turned and took the curved, two-handed weapon from her hands then held the weapon out to Sobehk across his palms. *"Dhe'syah."* My weapon.

Sobehk took it into his own hands. *"Deshryt."* My prince.

Fallon wiped her wet cheeks with her palm. *My loves.*

APPENDIX

The Language of the Skeldhi

Skeldhor Prime — Seht's home world

Skeldhi — the people of Skeldhor Prime, Imperium ship-speak bastardization of *skeldyht* / . . . of Skeldhor

-dhyt — (pl.) the people of . . .

Kwusehyr — a principal spaceport

dhe'syah — moon blade — a traditional weapon

rahyt — blood-rage

Tawrhyt — skeldhi ovulation cycle / implies 'season of sacred blood'

Titles:

- *mehnat* — royal (ornamental) collar

'Sey — lady mistress (pronounced: say)

'Syr — lord master (pronounced: seer)

'Syr'dhyt — generic lord master / . . . of an office

A'sey — respectable ma'am (non-royal)

A'syr — respectable sir (non-royal)

Atehf-mehnat — Queen's Consort / implies 'collared prince'

Atehf — prince consort

Deshryt — blood prince; direct relation to royal line / . . . of the blood

Dhe'syah — moon blade (weapon), also sworn vassal or liege man / implies "the lord's weapon"

Hedjhyt — crown princess

Kehpresh — war prince

Mehnat — royal (ornamental) collar

Pshent – Queen / implies 'Mother'
Sey'dhyt – generic lady mistress / . . . of an office
Syrdhyt – generic lord master / . . . of an office
Tahemryt – blood princess; direct relation to royal line / . . . of the blood

Law & Government
Maht – Law – Honor – Truth; the world order, justice, proper conduct

Ehnyad – The Council of Nine Elders
- *Ehnya'dhyt* – councilor / . . . of the council

Mahfeht – office of judicial enforcement and legal execution
- *Mahfeht'syr* – lord master executioner
- *Mahf'dhyt* – enforcer, also known as a hunter / . . . of judicial authority; legal executioner

Mehdjay – office of Intelligence and Security
- *Mehdjay'syr* – Lord-officer of Intelligence and Security
- *mehdja'dhyt* – Investigative Officer

Sehnbay – office of medicine / implies health
- *Sehnbay'syr* – master surgeon-engineer
- *sehn'dhyt* – medic / . . . of health

Uhra'eh – Office of the Military / implies "a group of fire-spitting serpents"
- *Uhra'eh'syr* – warlord / implies "Lord of the fire-spitting serpents"
- *uhra'dhyt* – a soldier / . . . of the fire-spitting serpents

Pets
deyjaht – skilled or trained rehkyt (m.) / implies 'educated male'
- *Nehkyx* – a punisher or trainer / implies 'whip'

- *Nehkyx'a'syr* — principal trainer

isfeht — outlaw; runaway rehkyt / implies disorderly, chaotic, insane

rekhyt — pet / implies 'captive bird'

seysaht — skilled or trained rehkyt (f.) / implies 'educated female'

seysehn — concubine / implies 'lotus flower'

shen — rehkyt obedience collar / implies 'to encircle'

teht — rehkyt in ovulation cycle / implies 'sacred blood'

upuaht — rehkyt guard / implies 'canine guardian'

YOU MAY ALSO ENJOY THE FOLLOWING FROM EXTASY BOOKS INC:

Lost Star
Morgan Hawke

Excerpt

"Look, you rusting pile of antique junk! I'm trying to save your ass here! Let me in!" Aubrey grabbed his throat, gasping for breath, and choked. The air on the freighter's sub-engineering deck was thick and foul with smoke from melted metal and fused wiring. "Morris! Are you listening to me?" He slammed his bruised fist against the control console, nearly knocking over the small light he'd rigged. Most of the lights had gone out in the first hit from the marauders. He didn't want to think about how close they had come to losing all life support, too.

"I hear you, tech engineer." The ship's tired and masculine mind-voice shimmered with a touch of annoyance across the wire jacked into the back of Aubrey's skull. "You do not have clearance for access. You are not the nav-pilot."

Aubrey fought to calm his beating heart, not that his heart was listening. "Morris, your nav-pilot is dead. He's dead with everyone else that was on your bridge. If you don't let me in, we'll be boarded, and you'll be torn apart for scrap!"

"I am already . . . scrap." Crushing depression and electronic interference colored the electronic mind-voice.

"I know you're old. Fate, damn you! But you're not dead yet!" Aubrey scrubbed a hand through what little hair he had left, nearly dislodging the jack in the back of his skull. Damned military-issue buzz-cut freaking itched. He leaned over the panel. "Morris, please! Let me in! There isn't anybody else with an array to talk to you and I'm not fucking ready to die yet!" His breath hitched. Fate, he hadn't even reached the legal age to drink yet. He closed his stinging eyes and took a deep breath. "And neither are the rest of the men on this ship. If you want to die, then fine, die! But let me save the ones who want to live first!"

Anger flickered deep in the ship's sentience.

Aubrey held his breath. Apparently, his comment about letting the crew die had pissed the ship off. That was good, very good. There was still a chance. If he could get access to the ship's controls, he could use the freighter's fully functional pulse cannons to clear a hole and try for a jump. If the ship didn't kill him with a power burst instead.

Information slammed into his skull to become sight, sound, taste, smell . . . and pain, hideous wrenching pain. Aubrey gasped and dropped to his knees. The ship was in agony. There were gaping holes all over the ship's hull. Wounds that bled air, water, and bodies . . . Bodies of people he knew.

Sheer stubborn will and deep terror forced him back up on his feet. He ignored the itch of tears streaking down his smoke-smeared face and threw every code he had into the ship's controls, grabbing for everything that still worked.

He found everybody still breathing and began opening doors, making safe passages for the crew to get deeper into the ship where he could do something about maintaining life support.

At the same time, he activated the pulse cannons and

aimed them at the corsair closing in to make contact against the starboard side. He knew that at this close range, he was going to damage the freighter more, but he could not afford to let the marauders board. They were only a small freighter with no military personnel capable of defending them, none still alive anyway. Once they got in, the game was over. They were utterly defenseless.

Aubrey smiled grimly and opened fire.

The pulse cannons burned a surgically precise hole right through the attacking ship's engineering core. The ship's sensors delivered a low casualty rating from the other ship, but all maneuver controls were offline.

The attacking ship veered off course diving right under them.

Aubrey shouted in triumph. "That's right, you stupid-assed shit-heels! The body manning these cannons actually knows what to fucking hit!" Abruptly, he lost clear sight of the second corsair. The ship's sensors were going out on the keel. They were in deep trouble if he didn't get them back in view.

Information trickled in from the remaining corsair. It was a sentience to sentience communication. It was meant to be hidden from the nav-pilot.

Aubrey smiled grimly. If he'd had a piloting array, he would have missed it, but he didn't. He had a programming array. His ability to interpret the ship's complete interior and exterior data was somewhat limited, nothing compared to the near physical connection a nav-pilot had. On the other hand, what he did have was one of the most complete mind-to-mind connections one could get with a ship.

And he'd been a very bad boy before the Agency had caught up with him.

He intercepted the communication without even trying. At the same time, he worked feverishly to reroute power to the sensors so he could see well enough to get a nice clean shot on the corsair dangerously close to his keel.

His personally doctored programs read the encrypted communications with pathetic ease. Those same programs were the reason he had been arrested and penal chipped, but they continued to prove useful every now and again.

The only reason the Agency hadn't fried his ass when they finally caught him, was because he'd been under-age, a minor, with no fatalities to his name. Instead, the Agency had offered him the chance to work off his sentence using his programming tech talents on whatever ship they posted him to.

It was that or a memory wipe.

He'd been grateful for the chance to keep all his hard-won codes and skills, and it had gotten him off-planet. As far as he was concerned, getting off that industrial waste of a planet had been worth being penal chipped.

The past two and a half Imperial standard years of being passed from ship to ship as a programming tech engineer hadn't been all that hard. The food sucked, but the work was simplistic compared to the programming stuff he'd done for sheer entertainment. The bulk of it was system updates. His mouth occasionally got him into trouble, but his rating as a minor had saved his ass from more than one disciplinary reaming. He smiled sourly. Thank the Fates for a scrawny graceless build that made him look years younger than he actually was.

He only had six more months to the end of his sentence — and his legal majority. Once he was free of the penal chip in the back of his skull, he had a nice long well-paying career ahead of him. He planned to get thoroughly drunk and thoroughly laid to celebrate his new life as a free man. If he lived that long. He sighed and focused on the coded communications being relayed.

The corsair was inquiring about damages.

Morris offered his external damage report and the fact that his nav-pilot was dead, without mentioning that they were still jump capable.

Aubrey grinned. Apparently, Morris wasn't ready to give up yet.

'Surrender. Will relocate sentience.'

He nodded. The other ship was trying to make some kind of a deal. That was pretty much expected. Obviously, they were after the ship's experienced sentience. There wasn't a damned thing on this old freighter that would interest marauders. They weren't carrying weapons.

'No survivors.'

No survivors? Aubrey sucked in a breath. But there were some seventy-odd people still breathing on this ship? He shot a line of data toward the other ship describing his survivors.

'Cut life support.'

What? Aubrey frowned. That had to have been a misinterpretation of the coded transmission. He inserted a message into the encrypted communication. Please repeat last transmission.

'No survivors. Disengage all life support.'

Aubrey gasped. Son of a fucking bitch! They wanted Morris to kill every living person on this ship? He ground his teeth. Fuck that shit! Out of sheer temper, he slammed a hijack code he'd made to catch small yachts for joyrides into the ship's connecting data stream. To get it past the preliminary firewalls, he added a doctored breaker-code and aimed the whole mess straight for their engineering console, bypassing their nav-pilot.

He'd been a very, very bad boy before the Agency nailed him.

Aubrey figured that the breaker-code wouldn't make it very far. The other craft was a corsair and far more sophisticated than the yachts the code was designed for, but he figured he'd at least cause enough trouble to make a limping escape.

The other ship's data poured into his skull. Suddenly his

vision of Morris and both corsairs was crystal clear. Aubrey gasped. Holy shit! He'd actually made connection.

A stream of bitching howled across the data stream.

Aubrey choked out a laugh. There was a very pissed off nav-pilot at the far end who had somehow found himself locked out of his own ship. Aubrey licked his dry lips and grabbed for control, telling the other ship to turn its ass around and make for jump. It was the only thing he could think of.

The ship fought his control. He wasn't giving it the right directives.

Grim humor colored Morris's sentience. "Like this boy . . ." Data streamed toward the other ship, bolstering Aubrey's commands.

The other ship turned away and their jump engines came online.

It was working? Aubrey rubbed sweat from his brow with his arm and checked his connection. It was solid. The other ship was taking his orders. Fate be damned, it was working! He threw back his head and shouted. "Take that you rat-bastards!" He hooted and punched the air, nearly knocking the cord from his skull jack. If there had been room to jump up and down, he would have done it.

Energy pulsed as folds of space unraveled and a third corsair wavered into local space nearly on their nose.

Every sensor on the ship burned white-hot, scoured by the energy backwash as space snapped back into place around the corsair catching Morris in the rebound.

Morris screamed in sensory overload.

Aubrey screamed with him. His array slammed all channels closed to protect the biological mind attached to it. The world receded to a pinprick of light at the very far end of a long black tunnel. He didn't even feel his chin smack hard on the engineering panel or his cheek hit the crash-littered deck plates.

ABOUT THE AUTHOR

Morgan Hawke

"For me, writing is more than a passion; it's an *obsession*. The stories crowd into my head. I write them down so I can get some peace. Where do I get my ideas? Rampant curiosity. I play the game of 'What If?' with everything I encounter. Everything I do and everything I see triggers a story to be told. I am a voracious reader of Romance, Science-Fiction, Fantasy, Horror, and Erotica, so naturally, my stories follow along the lines of what I like to read."

Morgan Hawke has lived in seven states of the US and spent two years in England. She has been an auto mechanic, a security guard, a waitress, a groom in a horse-stable, in the military, a copywriter, a magazine editor, a professional tarot reader, a belly-dancer and a stripper. Her personal area of expertise is the strange and unusual.

Ms. Hawke has been writing erotic fiction since 1998 and maintains a close and personal relationship with her computer and her cat.

CPSIA information can be obtained
at www.ICGtesting.com
Printed in the USA
LVHW011455281019
635545LV00001B/57

9 781487 426385